THE ALCHEMASTER'S APPRENTICE

Walter Moers was born in 1957 and is a writer, cartoonist, painter and sculptor. He is the author of the cult bestseller *The 13½ Lives of Captain Bluebear*, *Rumo*, *A Wild Ride Through the Night* and *The City of Dreaming Books*. He lives in Hamburg.

The Alchemaster's Apprentice

A CULINARY TALE FROM ZAMONIA BY
Optimus Yarnspinner

TRANSLATED FROM THE ZAMONIAN AND ILLUSTRATED BY
Walter Moers

WHOSE GERMAN TEXT WAS TRANSLATED INTO ENGLISH BY
John Brownjohn

VINTAGE BOOKS
London

Published by Vintage 2010

2 4 6 8 10 9 7 5 3 1

Copyright © Piper Verlag GmbH, München 2007
English translation copyright © John Brownjohn 2009

Walter Moers has asserted his right under the Copyright, Designs and
Patents Act 1988 to be identified as the author of this work

First published with the title *Der Schrecksenmeister* in 2007
by Piper Verlag GmbH, Munich

First published in Great Britain in 2009 by
Harvill Secker

Vintage
Random House, 20 Vauxhall Bridge Road,
London SW1V 2SA

www.vintage-books.co.uk

Addresses for companies within The Random House Group Limited
can be found at: www.randomhouse.co.uk/offices.htm

The Random House Group Limited Reg. No. 954009

A CIP catalogue record for this book
is available from the British Library

ISBN 9780099526322

The Random House Group Limited supports The Forest
Stewardship Council (FSC), the leading international forest
certification organisation. All our titles that are printed on
Greenpeace approved FSC certified paper carry the FSC logo.
Our paper procurement policy can be found at:
www.rbooks.co.uk/environment

Mixed Sources
Product group from well-managed
forests and other controlled sources
www.fsc.org Cert no. TT-COC-2139
© 1996 Forest Stewardship Council
FSC

Printed in Great Britain by
Clays Ltd, St Ives plc

The Alchemaster's
Apprentice

'Up is down and ugly is beautiful.'
Leathermouse motto

Let my magic brew revive
that which used to be alive.
Let my bubbling cauldron seethe
till the creature starts to breathe.
Brought to life it then shall be
by the power of alchemy.

Echo

Picture to yourself the sickest place in the whole of Zamonia! A little town with winding streets and crooked houses, and looming over it a creepy-looking castle perched on a black crag. A town afflicted by the rarest bacteria and the oddest diseases: cerebral whooping cough, hepatic migraine, gastric mumps, intestinal acne, digital tinnitus, renal measles, mini-influenza, to which only persons less than one metre tall are susceptible, witching-hour headaches that develop on the stroke of midnight and disappear at one a.m. precisely on the first Thursday of every month, phantom toothaches experienced only by persons wearing a full set of dentures.

Picture a town where there are more apothecaries and herbalists, quacks and tooth-pullers, crutch manufacturers and bandage weavers than anywhere else on the Zamonian continent. Where 'Ouch!' is the conventional form of greeting and 'Get well soon!' takes the place of 'Goodbye'. Where the air smells of ether and pus, cod-liver oil and emetics, iodine and putrefaction. Where people vegetate and wheeze instead of living and breathing. Where nobody laughs, just moans and groans.

Picture a place where the buildings look as sick as their occupants: houses with hump-backed roofs and leprous façades from which shingles keep falling and plaster dust trickles down the walls – houses precariously leaning on each other like cripples in danger of collapse or precariously poised on crutches of scaffolding.

Can you imagine that? Good. Then you're in Malaisea.

Living in Malaisea shortly before our story begins was an old woman who had a Crat* she named Echo. She had christened him that because, unlike all the cats she had previously owned, he could talk.

The old woman's death – she died of old age, peacefully and in her sleep – was the first true stroke of misfortune Echo had ever experienced. Until then he had led a thoroughly comfortable feline existence complete with regular meals, plenty of fresh milk, a roof over his head and a tray of Crat litter emptied twice a day.

---

*A Zamonian mammal identical to a domestic cat in outward appearance and other characteristics, the only difference being that it can talk and has two livers. [Tr.]

But now he found himself back on the street, having been locked out by the new owners of the house, who were anything but Crat lovers. Little Echo lacked the criminal initiative essential for survival in the merciless world of the streets, so it wasn't long before he became terribly run-down and emaciated. Chased away from every door, bitten and roughed-up by roving dogs, he lost his *joie de vivre*, his healthy instincts – even his glossy fur – and looked more like a wraith than a Crat. He felt he had hit rock bottom as he sat there on the pavement with his matted fur falling out in tufts, begging passers-by for something to eat.

But the inhabitants of Malaisea, whether human, Demidwarf or Turniphead, shuffled heedlessly, mechanically, past him like sleep-walkers, just as they had always done. Their faces were pale and anaemic, their dark-rimmed eyes glassy and mournful. They made their way along with heads bowed and shoulders sagging, many of them looking as if they might expire at any moment. Some were racked with terrible coughs, others wheezed or sneezed and blew their noses on voluminous, bloodstained handkerchiefs, and many wore warm scarves round their necks. But this was nothing out of the ordinary. All the townsfolk of Malaisea looked like that every day – and the reason for their appearance had just turned the corner.

Ghoolion the Terrible

For, just to set the seal on this dismal scene, Malaisea's alchemist-in-chief, the Alchemaster, was coming. If ever a nightmare decided to materialise and go walking through the real world, old Ghoolion's was the form it would choose to adopt. Like a scarecrow or a figure from a chamber of horrors come to life, Ghoolion put all living creatures to flight, from the smallest beetle to the strongest warrior. He seemed to stride along to the strains of some terrible march inaudible to anyone but himself, and everyone avoided his searing gaze for fear of being blinded, hypnotised or accursed. Ghoolion was well aware that everyone hated and feared him. He not only revelled in that knowledge but seized every opportunity to spread panic throughout the streets of Malaisea.

He had nailed iron plates to the soles of his boots so that his brisk footsteps could be heard when he was still several streets away, and his bone chain of office rattled like the skeleton of a hanged man swinging in the wind. He gave off an acrid, noxious smell, an effluvium compounded of all the acids and essences and lixiviants with which he conducted his sinister experiments. His clothes were permanently impregnated with those odours, which caused nausea and breathlessness in anyone but Ghoolion himself, and they hurried on ahead of him like the clatter he made – like a detachment of invisible bodyguards clearing the way for the municipal alchemist-in-chief.

The street emptied in a flash. Only the emaciated little Crat continued to sit there as Ghoolion rounded the corner and focused his piercing gaze on the only creature bold enough to bar his path. But Echo didn't take to his heels even then; his one remaining fear was the prospect of starving to death, which now governed all he did. Even if a pack of savage Woodwolves had appeared with a Spiderwitch at their head, Echo would still have sat tight in the vain hope that one of them would toss him a morsel of something edible.

So Ghoolion drew nearer and nearer. Coming to a halt, he bent down and submitted the little Crat to a long, pitiless stare. The breeze stirred his necklace of bones and his eyes shone with undisguised pleasure at the sufferings of a creature so close to death. The stench of ammonia and ether, sulphur and naphtha, prussic acid and quicklime stung Echo's sensitive little nose like a swarm of bees, but he didn't budge an inch.

'Can you spare me a morsel to eat, Sir Alchemaster?' he whimpered pathetically. 'I'm awfully hungry.'

Ghoolion's eyes gleamed even more demonically and a broad grin appeared on his bloodless gargoyle of a face. He put out a long, spindly forefinger and ran it over Echo's protruding ribs.

'So you can speak, can you?' he said. 'Then you aren't an ordinary cat, you're a Crat. One of the last surviving specimens of your breed.' His eyes narrowed almost imperceptibly. 'How about selling me your body fat?'

'Very funny, Sir Alchemaster,' Echo replied politely. 'I'm very partial to black humour, so you're welcome to poke fun at a poor little Crat with one paw in the grave. However, please forgive me for not laughing at this particular moment. The laugh stuck in my throat and I was so hungry I swallowed it.'

'I'm not joking,' snapped Ghoolion. 'I never make jokes. Besides, I'm not talking about the fat on your ribs at present – there isn't any. I mean the fat you're going to put on.'

'Put on?' Echo was puzzled but suddenly hopeful. The very words sounded nutritious.

'It's like this …' said Ghoolion, modifying his tone of voice until it sounded almost amiable. 'Crat fat is a well-established aid to alchemistic research. It preserves the smell of bubonic plague three times more effectively than dog's fat. Leyden Manikins impregnated with Crat fat remain animate for twice as long as usual, and it lubricates a perpetual-motion machine better than any other form of grease.'

'Delighted to hear that my breed is capable of producing a substance of such high quality,' Echo said almost inaudibly. 'At the moment, though, I can't spare a single ounce.'

'I can see that for myself,' said Ghoolion, sounding stern and overbearing once more. 'I shall fatten you up.'

'Fatten me up?' thought Echo. That sounded more nutritious still.

'I shall feed you as you've never been fed before. I shall prepare your meals personally, because I'm not only an alchemistic virtuoso but a master chef. I'm talking about the most exquisite delicacies, not just

4

common or garden Crat food. I'm talking about parfaits and soufflés, poached quails' eggs and frogs' tongues in aspic, tuna tartare and bird's-nest soup.'

Although he had never heard of such dishes, Echo's mouth was watering. 'And what do I have to do in return?'

'Donate your fat, as I said. We alchemists need it, but it only works if we acquire it on a voluntary basis. We can't just go out and slaughter a couple of Crats, more's the pity.' Ghoolion sighed and shrugged his bony shoulders.

'I see,' said Echo. He was beginning to get the Alchemaster's drift.

'We'll strike a bargain, we creatures of the night. It's full moon today. I'll undertake to feed you till the next full moon – regale you with dishes of the highest quality. Parfaits and soufflés, poached quails' eggs and –'

'Yes, yes,' Echo broke in, 'please get to the point.'

'Well, then you keep *your* part of the bargain. I'm afraid there's still no way of extracting a Crat's fat without … Need I say more?'

Ghoolion drew a long, sharp fingernail across his throat, just below the Adam's apple.

Echo gave an involuntary gulp.

'But one thing I promise you,' Ghoolion said proudly. 'Between now and the next full moon you'll have the time of your life. I'll introduce you to gastronomic pleasures no Crat has ever experienced before. I'll transport you to a peak of culinary perfection from which you can look down like a king on your own kind and all the other domesticated felines that have to eat stale codfish out of a bowl. I'll show you around my secret garden on the highest roof in Malaisea, which contains the most delightful nooks and hideaways any Crat could dream of. That's where you'll be able to walk off your meals and nibble digestive herbs if ever too much rich food upsets your stomach. Then you can go on gorging yourself. Delicious Cratmint grows there, too.'

'Ah, Cratmint,' Echo purred wistfully.

'But that's not all, oh no! You'll sleep on the softest cushions beside the warmest stoves in town. I shall attend to your well-being in every respect. And to your entertainment! You'll have the most enjoyable time you've ever had, I promise – *and* the most exciting and educational. You'll be permitted to watch me at work, even on the most arcane experiments. I shall let you into secrets which even the most experienced alchemist would give his eye teeth to know. After all, you won't get a chance to use them yourself.' Ghoolion uttered a cruel laugh, then submitted Echo to another piercing stare. 'Well, how about it?'

'I don't know,' Echo said hesitantly. 'I'm rather fond of life ...'

'But you Crats are reputed to have eight lives.' Ghoolion bared his yellow teeth in an evil grin. 'All I want is one.'

'Sorry, but I believe in only one life *before* death,' said Echo. 'The other seven don't count.'

The Alchemaster drew himself up with a jerk, rattling like an articulated skeleton.

'I'm wasting my time here,' he snapped. 'There are plenty of other desperate animals in this town. Au revoir! No, goodbye for ever! I wish you a long and agonising death by starvation. Three days of torment, at a guess – four at most. You'll feel as if you're devouring yourself from inside out.'

Echo had already been feeling like that for several days. 'One moment,' he said. 'Full board and lodging? Till the next full moon?'

Ghoolion, who had turned away, paused and glanced back over his shoulder.

'Yes indeed, till the next full moon,' he whispered seductively. 'The finest gourmet cuisine. Poached turbot afloat in a sea of milk. Menus with so many courses you'll lose count of them. That's my final offer.'

Echo thought it over. What had he got to lose? He could either die empty-bellied within three agonising days or survive with a full stomach for another thirty.

'Cratmint?' he asked softly.

'Cratmint,' Ghoolion assured him. 'In full bloom.'

'Done,' said Echo, and he held out a trembling little paw.

The Alchemaster's Castle

Although the town of Malaisea contained plenty of weird buildings in which weird things occurred, Alchemaster Ghoolion's castle and the things that occurred there were the weirdest of all. Erected on a hill in very ancient times, it overlooked the town like an eagle's eyrie. The whole of Malaisea could be seen from there, just as there wasn't a single spot in the town exempt from the sight of the creepy castle. It was a perpetual reminder of the Alchemaster's constant surveillance.

Constructed of black stone said to have been quarried from the depths of the Gloomberg Mountains, the castle was so cockeyed and misshapen that it resembled a monstrous, other-worldly excrescence. There was no glass in any of the windows. Ghoolion didn't feel the cold, even in the iciest of winters, so he liked it when the wind came whistling through his castle and played on it like a demonic flute. Installed in several of the gloomy window embrasures were some strangely convoluted telescopes through which he could spy on any part of town whenever the fancy took him. It was rumoured in Malaisea that Ghoolion had ground the lenses of those telescopes with such skill that they enabled him to see round corners and through keyholes – even down chimneys.

It seemed almost incredible that such an apparently haphazard heap of masonry hadn't collapsed at some stage in its many centuries of existence. If you knew that its builders were the same as those who had constructed the Bookemists' ancient houses in Bookholm's Darkman Street, however, you realised that this type of architecture was designed to last for ever. The castle had been standing there before a town named Malaisea existed.

Echo was so weak that Ghoolion carried him up the winding streets concealed inside his cloak, where the little Crat had fallen asleep from exhaustion. On reaching the castle, he fished a rusty key from his pocket and opened the massive oak door.

Then, still carrying his featherweight burden, he hurried along a series of passages lit by torches and candles and hung with paintings in dusty wooden frames. The pictures were all of natural disasters: volcanic eruptions and tsunamis, tornadoes and maelstroms, earthquakes,

conflagrations and avalanches, all executed in oils with great care and meticulous attention to detail, for disaster-painting was one of Ghoolion's many talents.

Awaiting him when he entered the next passage were three terrifying figures: a Grim Reaper, a Hazelwitch and a Cyclopean Mummy – three of the most dangerous creatures in Zamonia. The chances of encountering all three in one and the same place were just about as remote as being struck simultaneously by a thunderbolt, an asteroid and a blob of bird shit, but Ghoolion didn't spare them a single glance; he hurried past them unscathed with his cloak billowing out behind him. Fortunately, they were not only dead but stuffed with great skill, one of the Alchemaster's numerous hobbies being horrifico-taxidermy, or the mummification and stuffing of horrific life forms of all kinds. Several shadowy corners of his domain were populated by these extremely lifelike-looking creatures. No normal person would have cared to bump into them in the dark, or even in broad daylight and in mummified form, but Ghoolion thoroughly enjoyed their silent company and was always adding new specimens to his collection.

Up a spiral stone staircase he hurried, then through a library of mouldering Bookemistic tomes and across a big room filled with dust-sheeted furniture that looked like an array of bulky ghosts in the flickering candlelight. Next came a deserted dining room with flocks of Leathermice* engaged in daring aerobatics below its lofty ceiling. Ignoring those grisly lodgers as well, Ghoolion climbed another flight of stone stairs and came out in a draughty chamber lined with cages of all kinds, from aviaries of bamboo or wire to oak dog kennels and bear cages with bars of polished steel. The higher he went, the fiercer the gale that blew in through the window embrasures, making the curtains flap incessantly and stirring up whirlwinds of dust. Every now and then the chimneys emitted moans and howls suggestive of mastiffs being tortured to death in a dungeon.

---

*A Zamonian cousin of the bat, to which it bears only a distant resemblance. It possesses a mouselike or ratlike head of appalling ugliness and is covered in leathery, almost impenetrable skin instead of fur. Vampire bats and Leathermice are quite similar in their social behaviour and diet, notably in their unpleasant predilection for drinking blood. [Tr.]

Ghoolion came eventually to a stone doorway engraved with alchemistic symbols: the entrance to the big laboratory in which he spent most of his time. This, so rumour had it, was where he generated the bad weather that so often prevailed in Malaisea, and where he bred the bacteria and viruses with which he contaminated the local wells, causing influenza epidemics and children's ailments, whooping cough and nettle-rash. Here stood sacks filled with migraine- and nightmare-inducing pollen from poisonous plants, ready to be sprinkled on the town from the castle windows. Here Ghoolion thought up curses and created Leyden Manikins, purely in order to torture them. Here, too, he composed the ghastly music that issued from his castle at night, depriving the Malaiseans of sleep and sometimes, even, of their wits. Some became so utterly exhausted, it was said, that they found peace at last by hanging themselves.

For Ghoolion was the town's de facto ruler. He was its uncrowned tyrant, its black heart and sick brain. And its mayor. All the town councillors and all the inhabitants of Malaisea were merely puppets dangling from strings operated by the Alchemaster-in-Chief.

Ghoolion's Laboratory

Echo did not wake up until Ghoolion extricated him from the depths of his black cloak. Sleepily, the little Crat surveyed his surroundings. The remarkable laboratory was festively illuminated by numerous candles burning amid retorts and iron cauldrons, on stacks of books and in many-branched candelabra, which cast long shadows over its walls. The air was filled with a chorus of long-drawn-out sighs and groans, but Echo couldn't see any living creature capable of producing such sounds, so he attributed them to the wind blowing in through the windows.

The laboratory was situated on the top floor of the castle. Suspended above a coal fire in the middle of the room was a gigantic copper cauldron black with soot, and the soup simmering within it created fat bubbles that gave off a noisome stench. The crooked walls were partly concealed by rickety wooden shelves laden with books and scientific instruments, scrolls of parchment and stuffed animals.

11

Hanging here and there, too, were more of Ghoolion's disaster paintings, slates covered with alchemistic symbols and mathematical diagrams, and maps illustrating astronomical constellations. Years of smoke and chemical fumes had stained the vaulted ceiling and warped it into a dark, undulating expanse of timber. Dangling from it on cords and chains were planetary and lunar globes, astronomical measuring instruments and stuffed birds and reptiles. Ancient tomes with gnarled leather covers and tarnished metal clasps were lying around all over the place, many with handwritten notes protruding from their dusty, cobwebby pages. Among them stood countless glass vessels of every size and shape, some empty, some filled with fluids or powders of various hues, and others occupied by Leyden Manikins tapping vainly on the walls of their transparent prisons. The rusty alchemical furnace that dominated this whole chaotic scene resembled an ironclad warrior standing guard over a battlefield.

Echo didn't know where to look and what to fear the most when Ghoolion put him down on the floor. He had never seen so many astonishing and menacing objects under one roof. When he caught sight

of a stuffed but lifelike Nanofox baring its teeth at him from one of the lower shelves, he arched his back and hissed with his tail fluffed out like a flue brush.

Ghoolion laughed. 'He can't hurt you any more,' he said. 'I gutted him, rendered him down for his fat, stuffed him with sawdust and wood shavings, and sewed him up again – it took me seven hundred stitches. I had to insert a wire armature in his jaw to reproduce the facial expression. That snarl of yours tells me I made a good job of it.'

Echo shuddered at the thought that the Alchemaster would gut him, extract his fat and stuff him with sawdust when the next full moon came round. He might even wire him up with his tail erect and his back arched in memory of this moment.

'Now for our contract,' said Ghoolion, and he withdrew a sheet of parchment covered with alchemistic symbols from a stack of documents. Taking pen and ink, he proceeded to scrawl on the back of it, which was blank. Echo found it far from pleasurable to watch him drawing up the contract. The Alchemaster was muttering to himself with such glee as he wrote, and his eyes were glittering with such

undisguised malevolence, that the terms of the contract could hardly be to his, Echo's, advantage. All he caught were phrases such as 'irrevocably committed', 'indissolubly binding', 'legally enforceable' and the like. In fact, however, he couldn't have cared less how unreasonable Ghoolion's terms were – just as long as he got something to eat in the very near future.

'There,' Ghoolion said at last. 'Now sign!'

He held out a red ink pad. Echo applied his paw, first to the pad and then to the foot of the document. Before he could even glance at the

wording, Ghoolion snatched the parchment away and stowed it in a drawer.

'Take a look around,' he commanded, indicating the room with a dramatic gesture. 'This is your new home – the last you'll ever have in your life, so I advise you to savour every moment. Imagine you're dying, but painlessly, without the disagreeable symptoms of some terrible wasting disease. You can eat what you like while you're dying. Consider yourself lucky! Very few creatures are granted such a pleasant end. I'll try to make it as quick and painless as possible when the moment comes. I'm an expert.' He gazed at his bony hand, which he had raised like an executioner showing his victim the lethal implement. 'Now let's start fattening you up right away. We mustn't waste another moment of your precious time.'

Ghoolion's heartless words gave Echo the shivers, but he did as he was told and took a look at his new – and very last! – home, trying to control his emotions and fears so as not to expose himself to any more of the Alchemaster's barbed remarks. He wanted to study every detail of his surroundings because he knew from experience that fear subsides more quickly the more you look your fears in the face.

It struck him, as he surveyed the room, that the shadows on the walls were moving. The bulky shadow of the alchemical furnace, which had loomed over a bookcase a moment earlier, was now slanting across a grey slate covered with mathematical formulae. How could that be? Did the shadows in Ghoolion's domain lead a life of their own? To Echo, anything seemed possible in this weirdest of all the buildings in Malaisea. But Crats are level-headed creatures, so he set about getting to the bottom of the mystery. Did the light sources move by mechanical means? Cautiously, he clambered over some worm-eaten books, made his way between two stacks of time-yellowed documents and squeezed past some big glass bottles thick with dust. Nearer and nearer he crept to one of the candles, only to be brought up short by a magnifying glass the size of a soup plate. He froze. His determination to show no sign of fear evaporated, for the sight that confronted him through the dirty lens was so bewildering, so startling and unreal, that it put all the laboratory's other sensations in the shade: he saw a grotesquely magnified candle with a pain-racked face streaked with waxen tears. To his utter consternation,

Echo saw that it was almost imperceptibly propelling itself along at a snail's pace, sobbing and sighing as it went.

'An Anguish Candle,' Ghoolion explained with a touch of pride, stirring something in a big bowl. 'One of my minor alchemical creations. It consists of candle wax, a Leyden Manikin and some snails from the Gargyllian Bollogg's Skull, very slowly simmered over a low flame – plus one or two secret alchemical ingredients, of course. The wick is woven from the spinal column of a Blindworm and the ganglia of an Oxenfrog. Candles of this type are extremely sensitive to heat and spend their entire existence in the most terrible agony. Imagine if your tail were on fire – that's the kind of agony I mean.'

'What would happen if you blew it out?' asked Echo, who was thoroughly unnerved by the sight of the tormented creature. He now saw that several more of the laboratory's candles were propelling themselves along in an equally painful manner. If he strained his ears, he could even hear them moaning softly all around him.

'Its sufferings would cease, of course,' Ghoolion replied curtly. 'But what's the use of a candle that isn't alight, let alone an Anguish Candle that doesn't groan with pain?'

His tone implied that Echo wasn't all there. With a shake of the head, he put down the bowl of sweetened cream he'd been stirring. Then, taking a small phial from a shelf, he added a few drops of some colourless liquid. Instantly, the cream was infused with the glorious scent of vanilla. To Echo, even that simple trick seemed like magic. He tore his eyes away from the Anguish Candle and fell on the bowl as if dying of thirst.

'Steady, steady!' Echo had only lapped up a couple of mouthfuls when Ghoolion took the bowl away and deposited it on a shelf out of his reach. 'Not too much on an empty stomach! Besides, that cream was only an appetiser. We must proceed systematically. Everything has to be done on a scientific basis, and that includes fattening you up. So give me a list of your favourite dishes in exact order of preference. Which do you like best of all?'

Taking a pencil and a sheet of paper, Ghoolion gazed at Echo sternly. The little Crat knit his brow and searched his memory for favourite foods.

'Best of all?' he said. 'Grilled mouse bladders. Grilled Piddlemouse bladders, to be precise.'

'Right,' said Ghoolion, and made a note. 'Grilled Piddlemouse bladders. Hardly gourmet fare, but still. Go on …'

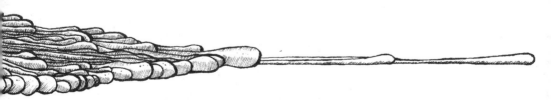

The Fat Collection

Ghoolion's origins were shrouded in mystery. Some said he hailed from the Graveyard Marshes and was a nocturnal growth that had sprouted from a bed of cadaveric compost. Others believed him to be one of the mysterious Undead of Dullsgard, the city no living creature could enter without being transformed into a walking corpse. He was also rumoured to be one of the legendary Five Horsemen of the Apocalypse who had left the other four and gone freelance. Many swore that he came from an unknown continent, not from Zamonia at all, having flown there across the sea on black wings, which he unfurled only when no one was looking. Still others claimed that Ghoolion had come straight from Netherworld, the legendary realm of darkness beneath Zamonia, and had risen to the surface to pave the way for an imminent invasion by the Evil One. Different though these theories about his background were, they all had one thing in common: not a single citizen of Malaisea had ever dared to broach them in the Alchemaster's presence.

The most prolific source of rumours, however, was Ghoolion's legendary fat collection. This contained no vegetable fats, no olive or burdock, walnut or rapeseed, trefoil or moonflower oils. To gain admittance to Ghoolion's collection, a fat had to have been obtained from some living creature, and even if it fulfilled that requirement, the Alchemaster was very choosy. His exclusive selection contained no common-or-garden pork fat, beef suet or goose grease, for he limited it to the adipose tissue of creatures few people cared to eat. The greater their aversion and the rarer the breed, the more the Alchemaster coveted it for himself.

Many will find it hard to accustom themselves to the notion that a Tortoise Spider* possesses a store of fat. More repugnant still is the thought of extracting it from such a monstrous creature's body. However, anyone who has grasped that this process and hundreds of

---

*An exceedingly unpleasant Zamonian arachnid. Its appearance precisely matches its name. [Tr.]

even more frightful activities formed part of Ghoolion's daily routine will readily accept that the happenings in the Alchemaster's home were the most remarkable in all Malaisea.

Ghoolion possessed the fat of rare Flutterbugs and Murches, Porcotrolls and Werewolves, Cralamanders and Luminants, Snow-swallows and Sunworms, Lunar Mantices and Speluncodiles, Tortovulks and Bathystars, Jellybellies and Tunnel Dragons, Mummybugs and Skunkodors, Ubufants and Zamingos. One had only to name a creature whose appearance on a restaurant menu would have evoked universal revulsion to be assured that Ghoolion possessed a sample of its fat. He was versed in numerous methods of fat extraction ranging from alchemical liposuction to surgical amputation and primitive mechanical extrusion under pressure. But rendering down was still his favourite process, which was why the gigantic cauldron in his laboratory continued to seethe day and night, filling the castle with an endless succession of unappetising smells.

The Alchemaster needed these fats mainly in order to preserve exceptionally volatile substances. In addition to smells, these included fumes, fog, vapour and gases. Using his alchemical equipment, Ghoolion was able to trap and conserve the nebulous mixture of steam and fat droplets continuously given off by his cauldron. He possessed samples extracted from the notorious Murkholm jellyfish and preserved in Shnark dripping, and his collection included cadaveric gas from the Graveyard Marshes, particles of will-o'-the-wisp, Troglotrolls' mouth odour and the farts of the sulphurous Toadfish. He had trapped and stored thousands of volatile substances, each in the only kind of fat he considered suitable for the purpose.

Installed on a wooden platform approached by a short flight of steps was the most sensational contraption in the laboratory. An impressive agglomeration of glass balloons, some filled with bubbling liquids, others with taxidermal specimens, it was attached to spiral copper tubes, crackling alchemical batteries, Bunsen burners, armatures of precious metal, brass vessels, barometers and hygrometers, pressure cookers, bellows and gold valves. This was the Ghoolionic Preserver, the Alchemaster's greatest invention to date, with which volatile substances were trapped, condensed and coated in a layer of fat.

Every time Ghoolion used the machine to preserve a new specimen, the apparatus would wheeze and splutter for minutes on end, then finally eject a ball of fat the size of an orange. This he would bear solemnly downstairs to the castle cellars, where there was a low-ceilinged but cool and spacious chamber in which he stored all his balls of fat, neatly arrayed on stone shelves like a connoisseur's vintage wines.

Echo had heard rumours of Ghoolion's collection. At the moment, however, he devoted no thought, either to the collection or to the exclusive place he himself would soon occupy within it. For the time being he merely roamed the laboratory, hungry and inquisitive, while Ghoolion busied himself with his alchemical equipment. He tried to ignore the Anguish Candles because the sight of them made his skin

crawl. As long as you didn't scrutinise the pathetic creatures too closely, they looked almost like ordinary candles. They moved so slowly that their progress was undetectable by the casual observer, but their muffled sighs and groans occasionally carried to Echo's ears, depending on the angle at which he happened to have cocked them.

But there were so many other things to be discovered in this most remarkable room in the most remarkable building in Malaisea. Echo took a closer look at one of the crowded bookshelves, which held an unsystematic jumble of parchments, letters, memoranda, reference

books and taxidermal specimens. His mistress had taught him the Zamonian alphabet as a Critten, so he could read the titles of the books on the lowest shelf with ease:

Distillation for Advanced Students

The Heptagram of Sublimation

Furnaces of the Soul

Sulphur, Saltpetre and Sulphate of Ammonia,
the Alchemist's Three Great Sibilants

Golem Gâteau and Mandrake Soufflé,
Choice Recipes for the Alchemical Cuisine

Antimony: Lethal Poison and Sovereign Remedy

The Myth of 'Prima Zateria'

Metals Susceptible to Pain
and How to Avoid Hurting Them

Zamonium, a Curse or a Blessing?

Echo came to a sudden halt. A title had caught his eye:

Alchemical Taboos
by
Succubius Ghoolion

A book by Ghoolion himself? There! There was another:

The Confessionator,
A Device for the Interrogation
of Uncooperative Subjects
by
Succubius Ghoolion

It hadn't occurred to Echo that the Alchemaster possessed a forename because everyone referred to him as Ghoolion. He knew very little about his host, and even less about exactly what lay in store for him.

The Alchemaster and the Ugglies

Every sizeable town in Zamonia has a municipal alchemist responsible for dealing with Ugglian affairs. He issues Ugglies in transit with fortune-telling permits (or withholds them, whichever), checks the account books of resident Ugglies, inoculates them against Ugglyitis (a disease exclusive to Ugglies that sends them into a weeks-long prophetic trance in which they foretell disasters nobody wants to hear about), delouses them annually and collects their soothsaying taxes. In Malaisea, Ghoolion performed all these tasks with the utmost zeal. He would regularly lock up a few Ugglies in the municipal jail, just for the hell of it, and torment them for days on end with musical renditions on the migrainophone and screamatina.

Ghoolion was also a fanatical advocate of Ugglian incineration, the barbaric but long-eradicated medieval custom that had cost the lives of many innocent Ugglies. Although Zamonian legislation precluded Ghoolion from practising it, much to his indignation, he addressed an incessant stream of requests for its reintroduction to the Zamonian Ministry of Justice in Atlantis, organised petitions signed by Uggliophobes and had even founded a political party whose only member was himself. One of its main objectives was the installation in every town of a cast-iron grill especially designed to reduce Ugglies to ashes. This he proudly christened the Ghoolio-Ugglian Barbecue.

Succubius Ghoolion had written one book on the correct construction of such a grill and its incineration techniques (he was particularly proud of the riddling device that enabled the Ugglies' charred remains to be sieved into an ashpan) and another on methods of interrogating Ugglies, which far surpassed medieval inquisitors' techniques in cruelty and ingenuity. This contained exhaustive descriptions of Ghoolion's numerous instruments of torture, which ranged from the Uggliopress and the Electric Interrogator (powered by an alchemical battery) to the aforementioned Ghoolionic Confessionator, an airtight sack of otterskin filled with thistles and nettles in which Ugglies were sewn up together with a pregnant viper, a rabid fox and a gamecock, and left there until they pleaded guilty. Quite a few of

Malaisea's more enlightened citizens found it outrageous that an avowed Uggliophobe like Ghoolion should hold the post of municipal alchemist in charge of Ugglian affairs, but they were outnumbered by those who advocated that the itinerant fortune tellers be ruled with a rod of iron.

And Ghoolion made sure they were. In no other Zamonian town was it so difficult for Ugglies to live and practise their profession. Only in Malaisea were they subject to the Ugglian Code, a list of eight hundred regulations bristling with insidious bureaucratic and juridical pitfalls devised by Ghoolion himself. Among other things, they specified the hours of the day during which Ugglies could ply their trade and the penalties they could expect to incur in the event of an infringement. They could not, for example, prophesy at night, nor at midday, nor late in the afternoon, nor in fog, nor when the moon was full, nor on public holidays, nor in sub-zero temperatures, nor in buildings other than the houses in Uggly Lane, which possessed no cellars. They were further required to submit a quarterly tax return of such intricacy and complexity that it would have driven a qualified Zamonian tax consultant to distraction. Finally, they were not only forbidden to go shopping except at certain times, all of which fell within their prescribed working hours, but prohibited from entering a shop at those same times.

Penalties ranged from drastic fines to months of solitary confinement in the dark, exile to the Graveyard Marshes, or forced labour in the sulphur mines at Demon's Gulch. All the Ugglies in Malaisea were skating on the thin ice of illegality, for Ghoolion's regulations were so sophisticated that he could prove them to have been broken by any one of the female soothsayers at any hour of the day or night, even if she was asleep in bed. The result was that, having begun by containing fewer Ugglies than any other town in Zamonia, Malaisea eventually became almost Uggly-free, because most Ugglies preferred to live in other towns or even in the dangerous wilderness. And that, in turn, relieved Ghoolion of nearly all his municipal duties and enabled him to concentrate even more wholeheartedly on his sinister research projects – as he had always intended from the first.

Invisible Caviar and Sewer Dragon's Knilch

'Cooking is alchemy and alchemy is cooking,' said Ghoolion as he proceeded to serve up Echo's first meal. 'Blending familiar things together and creating something entirely novel – that's the essence of the culinary art, just as it is in alchemy. Heat plays a vital role in both disciplines. They both necessitate harmonising carefully gauged ingredients, reducing substances and combining the long familiar with the epoch-makingly new. Minute quantities of ingredients and a second or two more or less on the stove can make all the difference between success and failure. To me, cooking a good meal is as important as concocting a new poison. Every meal is an antidote to death, after all, and isn't a nice bowl of chicken soup the best remedy for many an illness?'

Ghoolion had moved to his kitchen for the rest of the evening. This was on a lower floor and looked to Echo like the diametrical opposite of his weird, chaotic laboratory. Everything here was scrupulously neat and clean, bright and unintimidating. There were no sinister taxidermal specimens, no mysterious contraptions, no mildewed old books or Anguish Candles. In the middle stood a big black cast-iron stove with gleaming copper kettles, frying pans and saucepans on it. The huge kitchen table, which was surrounded by numerous chairs and draped in an appetisingly spotless linen tablecloth laden with plates, silverware and wine and water glasses, looked as if a big dinner party was planned.

More pots and pans and kitchen utensils of all kinds – egg whisks, ladles, cleavers, skimmers, sieves, rolling pins and the like – were hanging from hooks on the wall or suspended from the ceiling. Handsome oak dressers were stacked with crockery of every size, shape and colour, and the snow-white sink was full of freshly washed plates. Numerous jars of dried herbs shared a big kitchen cupboard with cookbooks and bottles of wine. Another cupboard contained little drawers with handwritten labels reading 'Flour', 'Sugar', 'Cocoa', 'Vanilla', 'Cinnamon' and so on.

The furniture and objects in this room were devoid of evil or dangerous intent. They served only one purpose: the preparation of food.

Food … What a nondescript, almost insultingly prosaic word for the meal with which Ghoolion regaled Echo that night! The little Crat hadn't fared badly at his former mistress's home, but his meals there were always the same: plenty of milk plus the occasional sardine or morsel of chicken. That was why Echo had until now believed that the grilled mouse bladders she'd once dished up were the acme of culinary delight. He'd had no idea that cooking could be promoted to the realm of high art, as Ghoolion was now demonstrating.

The first course consisted of a tiny little dumpling afloat in a bowl of clear, orange-tinted broth. Echo, who had casually perched on the table, bent an inquisitive nose over the bowl as it was slid towards him.

'Saffronised essence of tomato,' Ghoolion said softly. 'It's obtained by skinning the finest sun-ripened tomatoes and placing them in a cloth suspended over a bowl. For the next three days, terrestrial gravity alone ensures that the tomato pulp deposits its liquor in the bowl, filtered through the clean linen drop by drop. That's how one extracts the essential flavour – the very soul of the fruit. Then add some salt, a few grains of sugar and a dozen threads of saffron – precisely a dozen, mark you! – and simmer over a low flame for one whole day. The broth must never boil, or it will dissipate the soul of the tomato and taste of nothing at all. That's the only way to obtain this orange shade.'

Echo marvelled at Ghoolion's patience and the trouble he had taken, just to produce a bowl of broth. It smelt wonderful.

'Now for the dumpling. The meat it contains comes from salmon living in the most limpid rivers in Zamonia, the ones that flow into the Muchwater Marshes. Their waters are extremely dangerous – so clear that many people fail to see them until they've already fallen in and are drowning. As for the salmon, they're reputed to be so happy, you can hear them laughing when the moon is full and they leap up the rapids in a vain attempt to reach it. They feed on nothing but little freshwater crayfish, which are considered a delicacy in themselves – they're almost worth their weight in gold during the season. They taste fruity, almost sweet, and give off an aroma of apricots.'

Ghoolion smacked his lips and shut his eyes as if savouring the crayfish in retrospect.

'I mash up the salmon meat,' he went on, 'season it with a pinch of salt and some herbs, add some minuscule cubes of candied onion, mould the mixture into a dumpling, and roll it up in a sheet of rice paper no thicker than a puff of breath on a frosty windowpane. Then I suspend the dumpling on a string above a gently simmering saucepanful of delicious Blue Tea. The salmon dumpling dangles in that pale-blue steam for the space of exactly seven thousand heartbeats, then it's *à point*. I remove it from the rice paper, submerge it in the essence of tomato and it's ready! Go on, try it.'

When Echo bit into the fragrant dumpling, something truly astonishing happened: the world around him disappeared. Ghoolion and his laboratory had dissolved – no, not into thin air, into *water*! Echo could feel it all over his body, see bubbles rising in front of his eyes, glimpse pebbles on the river bed beneath him and big fat salmon swimming along beside him. The water was not only all round him, it was *inside* him – inside his mouth, his throat. He was actually *breathing* it. And then, all at once, he knew he was a salmon. The realisation was so vivid and startling, he emitted a miaow of surprise that expelled some bubbles from his mouth and obscured his vision. A moment later, just as suddenly as it had vanished, everything reappeared: the familiar world, the kitchen and the Alchemaster. Echo was so flabbergasted, he shrank away from the soup bowl and tried to shake the water from his fur. Except that there wasn't any water; he was bone dry.

'You were a fish for a few moments, am I right?' Ghoolion didn't wait for an answer. 'Not just any old fish, either: you were a salmon! You could feel the water in your non-existent gills, couldn't you?'

'Yes indeed,' said Echo, still bewildered. 'I was as much of a fish as a fish can be. I was *breathing* water.' He tried to extract a drop of water from his right ear with his forepaw, but it was as dry as the rest of him.

'In that case, I followed the recipe correctly. It was devised by the greatest salmon chef in Muchwater. He refused to cook anything but salmon throughout his career, and this was his favourite recipe. Go on, help yourself!'

Echo hesitated for a moment, then finished off the rest of the dumpling. Instantly, he was back underwater – not the pleasantest place for a Crat to be. This time, however, he knew it was only an illusion, so he even managed to enjoy Ghoolion's culinary conjuring trick. He shot some rapids, was sucked down into a raging whirlpool of river water and air bubbles, surfaced for long enough to see a sunny blue sky – and found himself back on Ghoolion's kitchen table once more.

'That was terrific!' he exclaimed delightedly, giving himself another shake. 'To think a dumpling can do all that!' He proceeded to lap up the delicious tomato consommé straight from the bowl.

'It's what is known as a metamorphotic meal,' Ghoolion explained, 'an alchemical offshoot of the culinary art. It used to be practised in the dawn of alchemy but is now prohibited by the Zamonian Ministry of Health – I hope you won't report me to the authorities!' Ghoolion grinned. 'The hallucinogenic effect stems partly from a very rare variety of Blue Tea found only on the outskirts of the Demerara Desert, and partly from the herbs in the salmon filling, which only alchemists can grow these days – Sleepwort, Hypnothyme and Phantasage, among others. If I increased the dosage of tea and herbs you could feel like a fish for hours on end.'

'Really?'

'No problem, but it would defeat the object of the exercise if you wriggled around on the table for hours, under the impression that you were a fish. The dosage is what matters. After all, you can over-season anything.'

'I see.' Echo nodded. 'Does it only work with salmon?'

'Oh no, all kinds of fish, all kinds of animals. Chickens, rabbits, wild boar – anything edible. It even works with plant life. I could turn you into a mushroom if I wanted.'

'I'm impressed,' said Echo. 'You promised a great deal, but this surpasses all my expectations.'

'You've seen nothing yet.' Ghoolion made a dismissive gesture. 'This was just a modest prelude. Just a starter – one of many.'

He cleared away the bowl, which the little Crat had licked clean, and replaced it with another. It was empty. Echo couldn't understand why an empty bowl should give off such an irresistible aroma.

'Invisible caviar,' Ghoolion explained, 'from the Cloak-of-Invisibility Sturgeon, the rarest and most expensive source of caviar in the world. Try catching an invisible fish with your bare hands, the only method permitted by the Zamonian Ministry of Agriculture and

Fisheries. I managed to obtain only one tiny egg, and even then I had to make use of my most disreputable contacts in the Florinthian underworld. There's blood adhering to it.'

Echo shrank away from the bowl.

'No, not to the egg *itself,*' said Ghoolion. 'I'm speaking metaphorically. This egg was really destined for the Zaan of Florinth. I was informed that Florinthian glass daggers were wielded and several assistant chefs had to be drowned in soup before the Zaan's head chef could be prevailed on to defraud his lord and master of the egg. He bamboozled him by serving him an ordinary sturgeon's egg with his eyes blindfolded, claiming that it enhanced the flavour. The Zaan of Florinth has been susceptible to such tricks ever since the ceiling of his throne-room fell on his head.'

Echo's curiosity revived at this account of the caviar's adventurous provenance. He explored the bowl with his tongue, searching for the invisible egg. All at once, his palate was rocked by a minor gustatory explosion. A frisson of pleasure ran down his spine.

'Mm,' he said. 'So that's what invisible caviar tastes like. Heavenly!'

'Now look at your tongue,' said Ghoolion, holding out a silver spoon for him to see himself in it. Echo leant forwards, smiled at his distorted reflection in the convex metal, opened his mouth – and recoiled in horror. His tongue had vanished.

'No, you haven't lost it.' Ghoolion smirked. 'It's temporarily invisible, that's all. It'll reappear as soon as the taste of the caviar has faded.'

Echo stared at the spoon open-mouthed, frozen with fear. What if Ghoolion were wrong? It was as unthinkable for a Crat to live without a tongue as without a tail. But, sure enough, the more the taste faded the more clearly he could see his tongue once more. He breathed a sigh of relief.

'True aesthetic pleasure should sometimes be accompanied by a touch of nervous titillation,' said Ghoolion, who was already preparing some new concoction in a cast-iron frying pan. 'Bee-bread wouldn't be worth eating but for the risk of biting on a Demonic Bee that hadn't had its sting removed, nor would a steamed Porcufish if one didn't have to take care not to puncture oneself on its lethally poisonous quills. Are you feeling relieved at having your tongue back? That, too, is an aesthetic pleasure beyond price.'

He put a plate in front of Echo.

'Don't worry, your hair won't fall out and you won't grow horns either. This is fried Sewer Dragon's knilch.'

Echo eyed the next course mistrustfully. 'What's a Sewer Dragon, if you wouldn't mind telling me? And what is its knilch?'

'A Sewer Dragon is a creature that lives exclusively in sewers. As

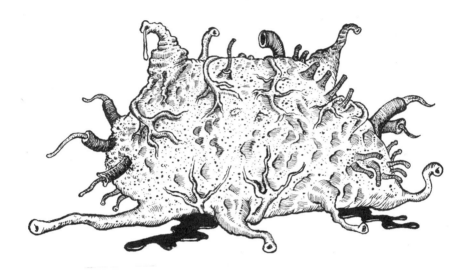

for its diet and physical appearance, I'd sooner not go into them at dinner time. Because of its unusual habitat, the Sewer Dragon has developed an organ that digests like a stomach, detoxifies like a liver and filters like a kidney: the knilch. What is more, it actually *thinks* with its knilch as well! The knilch is a superorgan unique in the annals of Zamonian biology. Fresh Sewer Dragon's knilch is such a delicacy, head chefs fight duels over it with filleting knives.'

Echo emitted an involuntary belch, feeling faintly nauseous. He tried to imagine a Sewer Dragon but thought better of it when his inner eye pictured a creature with matted fur and several fleshy pink probosces.

'Why are things that naturally arouse disgust considered by gourmets to be supreme delicacies?' Ghoolion asked. 'Live oysters? The diseased livers of force-fed geese? The brains of baby calves? The aborted offspring of the Cloak-of-Invisibility Sturgeon? Sewer Dragon's knilch?' He answered his own question. 'The thrill of over-coming an aversion, that's what appeals to them, just as transcending the norm is the alchemist's supreme motivation. Not only cooking is related to alchemy; eating is too. Eat this Sewer Dragon's knilch, analyse its constituent flavours with your tongue and taste buds, and you'll be halfway to becoming an apprentice alchemist! Shut your eyes!'

Echo complied. He sank his teeth in the peculiar organ and chewed with deliberation. There was no taste he could identify, nothing that reminded him of any particular food. It was like eating something cooked on another planet.

'I can't taste anything familiar. It smells strange. It tastes strange too – unusual but interesting.'

Echo swallowed the last morsel.

Ghoolion levelled a triumphant finger at the little Crat. 'Then you're a gourmet! A born gourmet *and* a budding alchemist!'

'Am I?'

'Beyond a doubt! A culinary ignoramus would have spat out a Sewer Dragon's knilch at once. It tastes extraordinary – like nothing else. Ordinary folk prefer familiar tastes – they'd sooner eat the same things all the time – but a gourmet would sample a fried park bench just to know how it tastes. It's the same with the alchemist: nothing strange, novel or surprising can deter him. On the contrary, he goes looking for such things. Are you ready for the next course?'

And so it went on, hour after hour: noodles baked in gold leaf, catfish and buttered shrimps, gurnard with twelve sauces, spider crab in paprika and brown sugar, brill encased in zucchini scales, sautéed lobster in aubergine boats, grouse livers with essence of morel, pigeons in aspic, Midgard rabbits' tongues in lavender sauce, stuffed marsh-hogs' tails on a bed of blue cabbage, wishbone meat in lemon-balm jelly, chilled sea-slug soup with shaved crayfish tails. The portions were minute, often no more than a mouthful, to ensure that every course left Echo wanting more. And as for the puddings!

Ghoolion produced a whole succession of sensational delicacies, accompanying each of them with some enlightening piece of information, exciting story or amusing anecdote. Echo had never felt so well entertained or so superlatively well fed. While devouring each course, he watched the Alchemaster busy himself at the stove and listened to his dissertations with rapt attention. The tyrant of Malaisea was showing him some entirely new sides of his personality: those of a perfect host and charming, omniscient raconteur who not only produced one gastronomic sensation after another but served them with the perfect manners of a head waiter in a five-star restaurant. Everything was cooked to a turn, perfectly seasoned, just the right temperature, and as decoratively arranged on the plate as a Florinthian florist's market stall in springtime. Echo was so enchanted, he forgot all about the next full moon and his impending demise. And Ghoolion continued to produce course after course until, late that night, Echo pronounced himself defeated.

In the end, the Alchemaster picked up the half-unconscious little Crat, who now weighed twice as much as he had a few hours ago, and carried him into another room, which was kept at a cosy temperature by a big tiled stove. There he deposited him in a wonderful sleeping basket lined with plump cushions, and Echo, purring softly, drifted off into the land of dreams.

The Leathermousoleum

When Echo woke up the next morning, it all came back to him in a rush: his contract, the next full moon, being stripped of his fat and stuffed … A prey to gloomy thoughts, he climbed out of his little basket and went slinking through Ghoolion's sinister domain.

Although there were no stuffed Cyclopean Mummies or Hazelwitches on the top floor of the castle, the atmosphere was quite intimidating enough for Echo's taste. The sunlight seemed to be robbed of its luminosity as soon as it streamed in through the tall windows, only to dissipate and disappear down the interminable passages. For the first time, Echo was unpleasantly struck by the absence of the hum of voices to which he'd been accustomed down in the town. Here, all that came to his ears was the melancholy music of the wind, to which motes of dust were dancing in the gloom.

Shivering, he made his way into the great hall, that prison for prisons filled with long, thin shadows cast by the bars of the cages it contained. He hurried past them with his head down. The cages were empty, but each told the story of one of Ghoolion's victims and none had ended happily. The teeth and claws embedded in several wooden cages bore witness to their inmates' desperate attempts to escape, and many an iron bar was encrusted with dried blood. Whether muscular bear or colourful bird of paradise, snake or polecat, Ubufant or Zamingo, all Ghoolion's captives had ended up in his cauldron. The Ghoolionic Preserver had reduced them to a scent encased in fat and stored in the castle cellar. Echo could conceive of no grislier fate. Everything here reminded him of death.

But he was hungry nonetheless. Although he had sworn before going to sleep that he would eat nothing for the next three days, all the dishes he'd consumed had been digested. Moreover, Ghoolion's opulent menu had stretched his stomach to such an extent that it now felt even emptier than before. It dawned on Echo that hunger was considerably easier to endure with an empty belly.

'Ah, there's my little gourmet!' Ghoolion exclaimed brightly, as Echo came stealing into the laboratory. He was engaged in weighing some gold dust with little lead weights and a pair of alchemical scales. 'Sleep well? How about a hearty breakfast?'

'Nice of you to ask,' Echo replied. 'I had an excellent sleep, thank you, and I am feeling a trifle hungry – in spite of that banquet last night.'

'Banquet be damned!' Ghoolion said contemptuously. 'That was nothing, just a taster. A few hors d'oeuvres.'

Echo wandered around the laboratory in a subdued frame of mind. Simmering in the cauldron was a large bird whose contorted foot, complete with claws, was protruding from the bubbling brew.

Ghoolion had noticed Echo seated beside the cauldron. 'That's a Doodo,' he said. 'Or rather, it *was* a Doodo. The last of its kind, I'm afraid.'

'Perhaps I'm also the last of my kind,' Echo said softly, averting his eyes from the gruesome sight.

'That's quite possible,' said Ghoolion. 'More than possible, in fact.'

Echo was beginning to fathom the Alchemaster's thought processes. It would never have occurred to Ghoolion that his guest might be distressed by such a heartless remark. Echo's feelings were a matter of supreme indifference to him. He simply said what he thought, no matter how hurtful.

Ghoolion jotted down some notes in a notebook, muttering to himself, then reeled off one alchemical formula after another. He seemed to have forgotten all about Echo, who preserved a tactful silence so as not to spoil his host's concentration. After a while, however, Echo's little stomach rumbled loudly enough to be heard all over the laboratory. Ghoolion broke off with a start and looked over at him.

'Please forgive me!' he exclaimed. 'I'm rather behindhand with my work today, that's why I … Listen, how about helping yourself to some breakfast? You need only go up to the roof, where you'll find everything to your satisfaction.'

'The roof?' said Echo.

'It's a fine day and fresh air is healthy. Crats like roaming around on roofs, don't they?'

Echo gave a cautious nod. 'Yes,' he said, 'I like roofs.'

'There's just one thing … A pure formality.'

'Which is?'

'The Leathermice.'

'What about them?'

Ghoolion looked up at the ceiling. 'The loft of this castle belongs to them, in a manner of speaking. An unwritten agreement. I allow them to sleep there undisturbed. In return, they do me the occasional … well, favour.'

'You seem to like making deals with animals,' Echo remarked.

Ghoolion ignored this. 'If you're going up to the roof,' he went on, 'you'll have to pass through the loft and that's Leathermouse territory. You must ask permission to cross it, that's all. It's just a mark of respect. Unless you're scared of them?'

No, Echo wasn't scared. Leathermice were only mice, after all. Mice with wings, but so what? He wasn't afraid of their wrinkled faces, or their claws, or their sharp teeth. Crats had claws and teeth themselves – considerably more effective ones than flying mice. They were welcome to try sucking his blood. He would soon show them the difference in status between Crats and Leathermice.

'No,' he said, 'I'm not scared.'

Ghoolion tugged at a string of bones dangling from the ceiling. With a creak, a junk-laden bookcase sank slowly into the floor to reveal a worn old wooden stairway leading up into the darkness.

'That's the way to the loft,' said Ghoolion, 'the Leathermousoleum, as I call it. It *is* rather reminiscent of a tomb, just as the Leathermice are rather morbid creatures. Give them my regards!'

He readdressed himself to his grains of gold dust.

'You can talk to them. I can't, unfortunately. How I envy your ability to converse with animals! To think of all the mysteries of nature I could glean from them!'

Oh yes, thought Echo, he'd love to be able to converse with animals. He'd probably stretch them on the rack and interrogate them with the aid of thumbscrews and the garrotte.

'Carry on,' Ghoolion called. 'Enjoy yourself on the roof.'

Echo was now standing at the entrance, peering up into the gloom. The stairs were very ancient, the wooden treads worn away and worm-eaten. They looked thoroughly uninviting, each step being warped and eroded in its own particular way. In the dim light, Echo seemed to see gaping mouths filled with splintered wooden teeth, glaring eye sockets and ferocious phantoms. It was all he could do to mount the first step, which emitted an agonised groan at the touch of his paw.

'Up you go,' Ghoolion called again. 'They can support my heavy old bones, so a flyweight like you has nothing to fear.'

Gingerly, Echo started to climb. The stairwell really did smell of millennially stale air and rotting cadavers, like an ancient tomb unopened for an eternity, but he bravely persevered, step by step. The higher he went, the darker and mustier it became. The existing smells were joined before long by an acrid stench. Below him, he heard Ghoolion haul on the string of bones, and the bookcase began to creak back into its original position.

'Don't worry,' called the Alchemaster, 'they only bite at night!' Then everything went pitch-black.

Echo's throat tightened and his legs trembled a little, but he valiantly climbed on, feeling for each step with his forepaws. This 'mark of respect', as Ghoolion had called it – he wanted to get it over as soon as possible. What cheek! Nobody had ever said anything about his having to be nice to some lousy Leathermice in order to reach his breakfast. The acrid stench was now so strong that he gagged despite himself.

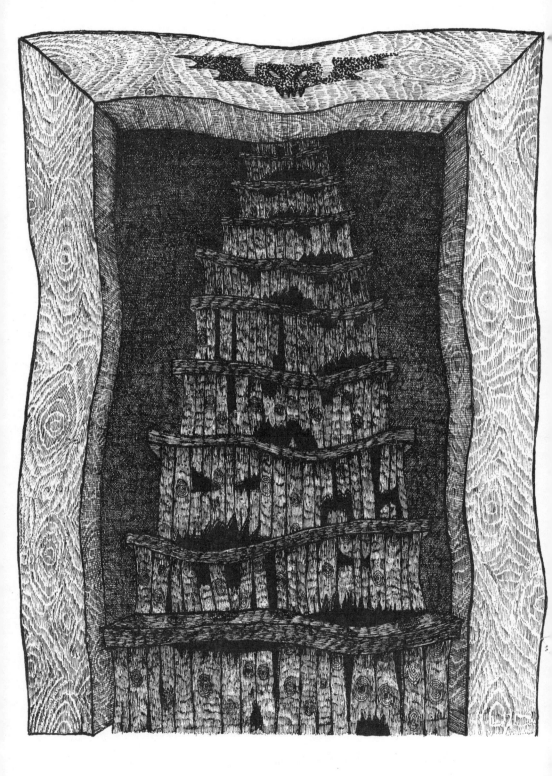

'Hello?' he called. 'Leathermice?'

He couldn't detect any more stairs ahead, so he must have reached the top. The floor beneath his paws felt rough and uneven. Above him, in the little light available, he seemed to see a high, vaulted ceiling. Only a few rays of sunlight were piercing the dark grey dome like silver needles.

'Leathermice?' he called again. Were there any Leathermice up here, or was it all a poor joke on the part of Ghoolion, who wanted to put him to the test? No, Ghoolion didn't make jokes.

Echo pricked up his ears. Yes, there was something there – or someone. He could hear a sound like fingers leafing slowly through an ancient book whose pages were stuck together. A rustling, sibilant sound.

'Leathermice?' he called for the third time.

'You're repeating yourself,' said a high-pitched, piping voice in the gloom. It sounded snappish and hostile. 'Yes, there are some Leathermice here. What do you want?'

Echo didn't hesitate. 'Alchemaster Ghoolion sent me. I have to get to the roof and I'm told I need your permission.'

'Oh, really?' said the voice, half wary, half contemptuous.

'Yes, really,' said Echo. He decided to adopt a brisk, self-assured manner. Show no weakness, he told himself. Impudence wins the day.

'To be honest, though,' he went on, 'I don't give a damn for your permission. I'm going up to the roof anyway. I don't need the consent of a bunch of mice.'

'We aren't mice, we're Leathermice.'

'Mice, Leathermice – what's the difference?' Echo said scornfully.

'We can fly.'

'We can bite.'

'We can suck blood.'

This time, Echo got the impression that three different voices had answered him. Now that his eyes were slowly getting used to the darkness, he could see more and more. Something was stirring overhead – no, the whole ceiling was in motion! At first he thought the wind was disturbing some animal hides Ghoolion had hung up on washing lines to dry. But this was movement of a different, animate nature. Long, leathery wings were being unfolded, sharp claws unsheathed, teeth bared. Evil little eyes were staring at him in the gloom. Nestling close together upside down, the vampires were suspended above him like a single, gigantic creature. Echo had expected them to number at least a few dozen, possibly even a few hundred, but he now saw to his consternation that they were clinging to the rafters in their thousands.

His eyes had finally become accustomed to the lighting conditions, so he could now identify the source of the acrid smell that was almost stupefying him. The rough, uneven floor beneath him was really an expanse of desiccated Leathermouse excrement. He was standing on all four paws in the midst of the biggest sewer in Malaisea.

'What do you propose to do if we withhold our permission?' demanded a voice overhead.

Echo urgently needed a new strategy. Grabbing a Leathermouse and roughing it up in front of the others – that had been his original plan. One brief but painful object lesson and the rest would soon knuckle under, he'd thought, but he was now forced to concede that it wouldn't be that easy. Far from it. He was overwhelmingly outnumbered.

'Well,' asked a Leathermouse, 'Crat got your tongue?'

Echo strove to remain calm. He couldn't afford to lose his nerve. Was this a trap? A ritual? Was he a gift from Ghoolion, a sacrificial offering to the occupants of his loft? He didn't stand a chance against them, that was abundantly clear. They would descend on him en masse and bury him beneath them like a corpse in a leather shroud. They would sink their sharp teeth in him and suck him dry within seconds. One more offensive remark, one false move, and there would be nothing left of him but a bloodless husk, a Cratskin riddled with holes. He had no idea where the exit to the roof was and his line of retreat was blocked. He had walked into the trap like a brainless rat unable to keep its paws off a piece of cheese. Breakfast on the roof? He himself was the breakfast in question.

'We're waiting for an answer!' came a menacing hiss from the darkness.

Echo had to weigh his next words with the utmost care. What tone should one adopt towards a multitude of mortally offended vampire bats? Submissive? Sincere? Bumptious? Disingenuous? All he knew was that his next remark must incorporate a reference to the Alchemaster. If the Leathermice respected anyone at all, that person was their landlord. It suddenly occurred to Echo that Ghoolion had asked him to give them his regards.

'Ghoolion sent me, as I told you,' he called. 'Alchemaster Ghoolion, your landlord. Ghoolion the Mighty, whose guest I am. I'm here on his behalf. He asked me to give you his best regards.' Echo tried to sound as self-assured as before, but he failed.

'So you already said,' a Leathermouse retorted.

'Very generous of him,' said another.

'Generous?' Echo said cautiously. 'For sending you his regards?'

'No, not his regards.'

'What, then?'

'You.'

'Me?' Echo was slow to catch on.

'Yes, it's generous of him to have sent you.'

'Why?'

'Well, it's been ages since we had a pudding that could miaow.'

A derisive snarl filled the air – presumably the Leathermouse equivalent of approving laughter. Echo instinctively went into a crouch, but he suppressed the urge to arch his back or hiss. He was a Crat, not a cat. Now was the time for brains, not claws. Deliberation, not action. Diplomacy, not war.

'A pudding?' he said. 'At this hour of the morning?'

'With us it's late at night. We turn night into day and day into night. We've just been gorging ourselves on the blood of the local inhabitants. Now we could do with a nice pudding.'

A Leathermouse belched unashamedly.

Echo crouched down even lower. So he really was a sacrificial offering – that was the only reason Ghoolion had fed him yesterday. All that talk about fattening him up for fat extraction had been just a hoax.

'I understand,' he said softly.

'No, you don't. Nobody understands us Leathermice.'

'You're right, friend!' cried another vampire. 'Nobody understands us Leathermice.'

41

'Nobody!'
'Nobody!'
'Nobody!'

Echo had little choice now but to play for time. And to hope, either that he would have a flash of inspiration or that chance would come to his aid. Should he miaow at the top of his voice? Should he caterwaul for Ghoolion? No, they would be on him in a flash. So what else? In the animal world there were usually only two possible courses of action when you were confronted by a dangerous enemy: attack or make a run for it. He could do neither, but he did have a third option. He must surely be the first of Ghoolion's sacrificial offerings capable of conversing with Leathermice. It was up to him to exploit that unique advantage.

'Does Ghoolion owe you something?' he asked. 'Is that why I'm being sacrificed?'

'What business is it of yours?' snapped a Leathermouse.

'Well, it's not much consolation, but if I've got to die, I'd at least like to know why.'

'You're in no position to make demands!'

'Oh, come, my friends!' called another Leathermouse. 'It's only fair. If we're going to bump him off, he ought to know why.'

'Who says we've got to be fair? The others never asked us any stupid questions.'

'That's because they couldn't communicate with you,' Echo put in quickly.

'True! True! True! True! True! True! True! True! True! True! True!
'True! True! True! True! True! True! True! True! True! True! True!
'True! True! True! True! True! True! True! True! True! True! True!
'True! True! True! True! True! True! True! True! True! True! True!
'True! True! True! True! True! True! True! True! True! True! True!
'True! True! True! True! True! True! True! True! True! True! True!
'True! True! True! True! True! True! True! True! True! True! True!
'True! True! True! True! True! True! True! True! True! True! True!
'True! True! True! True! True! True! True! True! True! True! True!
'True! True! True! True! True! True! True! True! True! True! True!'

The cries of assent came from all directions.

'So *does* Ghoolion owe you something?' Echo asked again.

'Hm …' growled a Leathermouse. 'That would be an exaggeration. We don't *owe* each other anything at all – ours is a kind of marriage of convenience. One partner gives something, the other gives something back. That way, everyone benefits.'

'How interesting!' said Echo, only to be floored again. What *did* one talk about to Leathermice? He'd already run out of questions.

'But tell us,' called a voice high up in the rafters, 'how is it we can understand you? We've never understood what a cat says before.'

'That's because I'm a Crat, not a cat.'

'You see!' called another Leathermouse. 'I knew there was something fishy about him right away!'

'There's nothing fishy about me,' Echo retorted boldly. 'I'm not a cat, that's all. I'm a Crat – I can speak to any living creature in its own language.'

'Really? You can really speak anyone's language?'

Echo took a deep breath. The conversation was under way. He'd whetted the vampires' curiosity. Now he had to keep up the good work.

'Well,' he said, 'I've certainly managed to talk to all the creatures I've ever met.'

'Even mice?'

'I don't talk to mice.'

'No?'

'I could if I wanted to, but I don't.'

'Why not?'

Echo hesitated. He'd never considered the matter before. This certainly wasn't the appropriate moment to emphasise his hostility to mice. He tried to change the subject by asking a question of his own.

'What exactly do you and Ghoolion do for each other?'

'He gives us the run of this loft, so we have somewhere nice and dark to sleep – we'd be smoked out otherwise. In return, we give the local inhabitants a hard time.'

'We drink their blood.'

'Piss in their wells.'

'Crap down their chimneys.'

One or two vampires tittered malevolently.

43

'We infect them with diseases to keep them weak and prevent them from rebelling against Ghoolion. That's our part of the bargain.'

'We're experts at bacterial warfare.'

'We're viral virtuosi.'

'We're genuine pests.'

Another concerted hiss of assent.

Echo had an idea. The Leathermice seemed really proud of their vile activities. Perhaps he could trade on that fact.

'You seem to be full of bright ideas when it comes to representing Ghoolion's interests,' he said.

'You can say that again!' a Leathermouse exclaimed. 'We clean our teeth with toadshit before we go bloodsucking.'

'We drink from graveyard puddles before we piss in their wells.'

'We bite cows' udders and contaminate their milk.'

'Now I understand why Ghoolion respects you so much,' said Echo. 'He'd be only half as powerful without your help. But ...' He broke off.

'What?'

'Nothing. It's a really practical partnership of yours – everyone gets something out of it. The only thing is ...' He hesitated again.

'Come on, spit it out!'

'Yes, what is it?'

Echo cleared his throat. 'Well, it's great the way you spread all these diseases and put the wind up people, et cetera. Very ingenious and effective, but I wonder ... Can it really be right to help a tyrant oppress the population of an entire town? Might it even be wrong?'

A long silence ensued.

'Bingo!' thought Echo. 'They're like children who have to be taught that even they possess such a thing as a conscience. No wonder, when nobody ever talks to them.'

One of the Leathermice gave a dry little cough.

'You want to know about right and wrong, my friend? Listen and we'll tell you.'

'Yes,' said another. 'We sleep by day and live at night, drink blood instead of water and see with our ears.'

'Up is down and down is up,' several vampires chanted in unison.

44

'People think we're ugly, we think we're good-looking. You think you're good-looking, we think you're ugly.'

As though handing on the baton in a relay race, one Leathermouse chimed in after another.

'Are you really surprised we have a different idea of right and wrong?'

'Of good and evil?'

'Of correct and incorrect?'

'We're vampires, my friend!'

'Nobody understands us Leathermice!'

'Nobody!'

'Nobody!'

'Nobody!'

'Wrong is right and ugly is beautiful!' they chorused.

'People hate us – they're frightened of the way we look.'

'They smoke us out whenever they can.'

'They put up nets and beat us to death with sticks when we get caught in them.'

'That's what *we* call wrong!'

'Nobody understands us Leathermice!'

'Nobody!'

'Nobody!'

'Nobody!'

The hisses of assent rose and fell.

'Ghoolion doesn't hate us.'

'He isn't afraid of us.'

'He gives us a place to sleep.'

'He ensures our survival.'

'What's so bad about him?'

'He cooks animals!' Echo protested.

'Well? Who doesn't?'

'*I* don't!' Echo said firmly.

'Don't you? Are you a vegetarian?'

'No, I'm not, but I don't cook animals!'

'You eat them, though.'

'Well, yes, but …'

'Did somebody own you before Ghoolion?'

'An old woman. She died.'

'Too bad, but didn't she sometimes cook an animal for your supper? A salmon, maybe, or a chicken?'

Echo hung his head. 'Yes, she did.'

'Well, does that make your former owner a bad person in your eyes?'

'No,' Echo was forced to concede.

'What about you? Did you eat these cooked animals?'

'Yes.'

'Does that make *you* a bad person in your own eyes?'

'I've never thought about it.'

'Thinking doesn't seem to be your strong point.'

'Have you ever eaten a Leathermouse?'

'Never!' Echo insisted.

'How about a mouse?'

'A mouse? Yes, of course, but not a Leathermouse.'

'So what about: "Mice, Leathermice – what's the difference?"'

The loft rang with indignant snarls and Echo realised that pursuing this conversation would only make his predicament worse. Mice of this kind were no fools. It seemed they intended to humiliate him for fun before killing him and that he could do without. If he had to die, he preferred to get it over quickly.

'Now listen, all of you,' he cried. He abandoned his crouching stance and boldly raised his head. 'I apologise for my behaviour when I came in. I was scared and tried to disguise the fact. I thought I'd made a deal with Ghoolion, but it seems I was wrong. I've done you no harm, so I don't see why you're putting me on trial here. It's time you stopped grilling me like a criminal. If you're hell-bent on killing me, so be it, but I warn you: I shall sell my life as dearly as I can and take as many of you with me as I can catch. There may be a lot of you, and you may be able to fly and suck blood, but – pardon me for saying so – you're still only mice when all is said and done.'

A good farewell speech, thought Echo. He particularly liked the final sentence.

'You made a deal with the Alchemaster?' one of the Leathermice asked after a long pause.

'He drew up a contract,' said Echo.

'A contract? That's serious.'

'What do you mean?'

'I mean you *definitely* have an agreement with him – as you'd very soon find out if you tried to break it.'

'What form did the contract take?' demanded another Leathermouse.

'He wants to buy some fat from me.'

'You deal in fat?'

'Just body fat. My own.'

'That's a barefaced lie. You don't have an ounce of body fat.'

'No, not yet. Ghoolion plans to fatten me up by the next full moon. Then he'll slit my throat and render me down.'

The loft fell silent once more. Not a Leathermouse stirred. Echo heard the wind whistling outside and rattling the tiles. Somewhere a crow cawed. He'd completely forgotten the existence of anything apart from the loft's gloomy interior.

'In that case,' a Leathermouse whispered, 'you've no time to lose. Get out on the roof.'

Echo thought he'd misheard. Was he free to leave? The Leathermice were absolutely silent now.

'You'll let me go out on the roof?'

'Of course. That was never in doubt.'

'You don't intend to kill me any longer?'

'We never did. It was you that encouraged us to pull your leg a little. We'd never harm anyone who uses the secret door. It means he's Ghoolion's guest.'

'Besides, you're inedible.'

'Inedible?' Echo was feeling utterly bewildered. 'Why?'

'We can smell you are.'

'Your vital juices are no use to us.'

'Too clean.'

'Not enough adipose fluid.'

'You must have two livers, or something.'

'By the way,' said the Leathermouse who had initiated the conversation, 'what's your name?'

'Echo.'

'That's a very nice name.'

Promptly, the others all chimed in :

'True! True! True! True! True! True! True! True! True! True! True!
'True! True! True! True! True! True! True! True! True! True! True!
'True! True! True! True! True! True! True! True! True! True! True!
'True! True! True! True! True! True! True! True! True! True! True!
'True! True! True! True! True! True! True! True! True! True! True!
'True! True! True! True! True! True! True! True! True! True! True!
'True! True! True! True! True! True! True! True! True! True! True!
'True! True! True! True! True! True! True! True! True! True! True!
'True! True! True! True! True! True! True! True! True! True! True!
'True! True! True! True! True! True! True! True! True! True! True!
'True! True! True! True! True! True! True! True! True! True! True!'

Echo was at a loss for words, he was still so utterly baffled by the sudden turn of events.

'Thank you,' he said eventually. 'And, er, what should I call you?'

A Leathermouse cleared its throat and announced solemnly: 'My name is Vlad the First.'

'My name is Vlad the Second,' called the one beside it.

'My name is Vlad the Third,' squeaked another.

'My name is Vlad the Fourth.'

'My name is Vlad the Fifth.'

'My name is Vlad the Sixth.'

'My name is Vlad the Seventh.'

'My name is Vlad the Eighth.'

'My name is Vlad the Ninth.'

'My name is Vlad the Tenth.'

Echo didn't realise his mistake until Vlad the Eleventh had introduced himself. Every last one of the Leathermice insisted on calling out its name. It wasn't until Vlad the Two Thousand Four Hundred and Thirty-Eighth had made himself known, by which time Echo was almost dying of hunger, that the creatures showed him the secret route to the roof.

The Mother of All Roofs

When Echo came out on the roof, he felt he had entered a new and far bigger world. The wind was so strong, it ruffled his fur and nearly blew him over. He had never been so high up before and the view was breathtaking. Ghoolion's castle served as a monumental observation tower. The whole of Malaisea lay spread out below. What had looked to Echo at ground level like a gigantic labyrinth flanked by insurmountable walls dwindled at this altitude to the size of a miniature plaything, a disorderly jumble of dolls' houses and building bricks traversed by tiny carriages and horse-drawn wagons, and inhabited by creatures that scuttled around like the busy inmates of an anthill.

All at once Echo realised how pathetically little he knew of the world in which he lived. He experienced a fierce desire to explore the regions beyond the horizon above which the sun was shining so brightly. The countryside between the town and the distant Blue Mountains on the skyline was a hundred shades of green, a patchwork quilt of woods, fields and meadows that would certainly have taken him months to reconnoitre in every detail. Possibly years. Possibly a lifetime.

And that was when Echo's woes caught up with him again. Months? Years? A lifetime? He had only a week or two left. Thirty days – no, only twenty-nine now. He looked up at the ghostly, waning moon. Horrified to think that it would hover up there for a month like a portent of his approaching death, he banished the dismal thought – shook it off as though ridding his fur of raindrops – and proceeded to explore the roof.

It was indeed the mother of all roofs, an architectural marvel that tapered to a point and consisted of gables of varying sizes, stone walls and stairways that served no obvious purpose.

Although it wasn't the first roof Echo had climbed around on, it was certainly the biggest, the highest and the most dramatically complex. Dozens of chimneys jutted from it like stone mushrooms with metal caps. Most of the tiles were as correctly laid as any tiler could have wished, but elsewhere they stuck out awry like huge, neglected teeth, buffeted and dislodged by centuries of wind. Where one or more were missing, having been washed away by the rain, the gaps were occupied by little wild gardens of thistles, buttercups and daisies.

The tiles themselves looked almost indestructible, being composed of an iron-hard slate that had defied the passage of time. The fine cracks and cavities in their rough exterior provided Echo's paws with excellent footholds. One false step, one slip, one trip, and he would have fallen like a stone, down past the windows of Ghoolion's abode and ever onwards, down and down, until his bones shattered into a thousand splinters on the castle forecourt below. It wouldn't matter which way up he landed because his flexible bone structure and padded paws would never be proof against a fall from such a height.

The stairways had also suffered from the wind and weather, having cracked and crumbled away in places, and Echo was often obliged to leap boldly across the gaps. But it was the sheer danger that generated much of the thrill it gave him to tiptoe from tile to tile and leap from gable to gable. He burnt with ambition to gauge each step with the utmost care, adjust his position accordingly and find his point of balance. This was the essence of Cratdom; he and his kind might have been created solely for this one purpose: to roam across roofs with feline grace. Echo had progressed in this manner throughout his life, whether along wide streets or narrow walls: as if balancing on a tight-rope above a chasm miles deep. He now felt it had all been a preparation for this moment. The roof of Ghoolion's castle was a masterpiece of the roofer's art, as perfect as if it had been constructed by some fanatical Crat lover of long ago and left to weather picturesquely, just so that Echo could promenade across it. Now and then he cautiously trod on a tile to check its stability. If it creaked or gave way he stopped short, memorised the spot and looked for another route; if it seemed to offer a firm foothold, he would walk on with resolute tread. Sometimes he would risk a little leap, then stand motionless with his ears pricked, listening intently and sniffing the air. Hey, just a moment – could that be Cratmint? He took another sniff. Yes, no doubt about it, that was the captivating scent of Cratmint, the finest herb in the world! Echo promptly lost his head and cast caution to the winds. He went bounding up the roof to the narrow ridge, where he paused and peered down at the flight of steps on the far side. Sure enough, perched on a

landing halfway down them was a big clay flowerpot containing a luxuriant Cratmint bush in full bloom, with bumblebees buzzing all round it.

It is still one of Zamonian biology's unsolved mysteries that Crats should be so enraptured by Cratmint that they become transformed, from one moment to the next, into purring bundles of bliss. At all events, Echo displayed the behaviour typical of his breed when confronted by that miraculous herb: he slithered lithely down the slope and circled the flowerpot with head erect and nostrils quivering. Then he leapt into the Cratmint, burrowed deep into its foliage and ecstatically sniffed every stem, leaf and flower, purring like a humming top. Next, he miaowed at the plant for minutes on end as if singing it a love song. Finally, feeling refreshed and inspired, he strode proudly on, his movements more balletic than ever, his tail contorting itself into a series of elegant curlicues.

So the Alchemaster hadn't been lying to him. This roof harboured delicacies other than that glorious mint. Echo not only guessed at their presence; he could actually smell them: roast pigeons and honey-flavoured milk! An invisible but lavishly provided banqueting table came wafting through the air towards him. The mint had been merely an olfactory appetiser; the edible delicacies awaited him elsewhere. But where? He continued to climb, higher and higher, until he came to a mossy terrace. Dozens of tiles must have slid off like toboggans hurtling down a mountainside, and someone, presumably Ghoolion, had installed a garden in their place. It was a regular little wilderness extending deep into the roof space, with tall grasses and weeds sprouting from a lush, mossy floor. Echo picked his way silently through the undergrowth at a crouch, every inch a hunter stalking his quarry. The two predominant scents were those of milk and honey.

Thistles barred his path like levelled lances, but he brushed them aside with his claws extended. Nothing could keep him from his prey, which must now be very near. He parted a luxuriant clump of yellow grass with both paws, and then he saw it for the first time: a snow-white expanse gently ruffled by the wind – a lake of milk! Floating on it were some little boats woven of reeds, and the passengers in them were crisply roasted pigeons and grilled trout. They were sitting up dressed

in dolls' clothes and were equipped with little paper parasols. Echo was entranced.

He crawled to the edge of the milky pool and proceeded to lap some up with his nimble tongue. Sure enough, it was laced with honey! He drank his fill, then fished a roast pigeon out of one of the boats with his paw, stripped off its doll's attire and devoured the whole bird, crisp skin and all. Having eaten the breast, drumsticks and wings, he licked off every last shred of meat with his rough little tongue until nothing was left but bare bones.

Then, with a contented grunt, he stretched out on the moss for a brief digestive siesta. As he contemplated the pigeon's pale skeleton with a meditative eye and rolled it playfully to and fro with his paws, his mood darkened. It horrified him to think of the trouble Ghoolion was taking to fatten him up. The Alchemaster had actually hauled a bathtub all the way up here, possibly at the risk of his own life. He had embedded it in the moss and filled it with bucket after bucket of milk. He had not only roasted that delicious pigeon but obtained the dolls' clothes and fashioned the little boats. How deadly serious he must be, and how eager to see his victim's scrawny frame put on weight! Echo sprang to his feet, suddenly wide awake again.

Feeling uneasy and shivering a little, he climbed still higher. It was quite impossible to explore the roof systematically. The stairways would sometimes lead upwards or downwards for no apparent reason, then turn a corner and end abruptly in a sloping expanse of tiles. When that happened there was nothing for it but to retrace one's steps or scale

the precipitous slope. Echo occasionally peered in through the triangular window embrasures that gaped everywhere, but all he could see was total darkness. Were the Leathermice in there, or was there another loft beneath this confounded roof, the real loft that shielded the vampires from wind and weather? Now and then he came across strange carved ornaments, bizarre stone sculptures and grotesque gargoyles. He felt like an explorer discovering the ruins of a vanished civilisation.

There! Yet another appetising aroma in the air! Fried sausages? Fishcakes? Grilled chicken? In search of its source, Echo stole round a corner and came upon another spot where Ghoolion had created an artificial paradise for Crats. Protruding from a smallish, flattish expanse of roof was a tall red brick chimney, which the Alchemaster had transformed into a travesty of a Christmas tree with the aid of florist's wire and sprigs of fir. Suspended from them on thin strings were some rib-tickling titbits: crisp-skinned fried sausages, dainty little fishcakes, lamb cutlets scented with garlic, breaded chicken drumsticks and crispy wings. Beneath them stood a pot of fresh, sweetened cream.

Echo inhaled deeply. His dark thoughts promptly evaporated, his mouth started watering. He proceeded to knock the little snacks off the 'tree' with his paw and devour them. Far from as simple and unsophisticated as it had seemed at first sight, the cuisine displayed definite expertise. The sausages were stuffed with tiny shrimps, chopped onions and grated apple, and seasoned with sage; the drumsticks had clearly been marinated for days in red wine, with the result that their pale-pink meat dissolved on the tongue like butter. The lamb cutlets had been wrapped in raw ham, studded with rosemary and then fried. Everything tasted superb.

'Well?' a voice said suddenly. 'Enjoying it?'

Echo was so startled that the lamb cutlet he was eating fell out of his mouth. He looked left and right but couldn't see a soul.

'Up here!' called the voice.

Echo looked up at the chimney. Poking out of it was the head of a Cyclopean Tuwituwu, which was staring at him with its single piercing eye.

'I asked if you were enjoying it.' The Tuwituwu had a deep, resonant voice. 'I sope ho, anyway.'

Sope ho? Had the bird said 'sope ho'?

'Many thanks,' Echo replied cautiously. 'Yes, I am. Is this your food I've been eating?'

'Oh, no,' said the Tuwituwu, 'I never touch the stuff, I just live here. The chimney is my desirence.'

'I didn't realise anyone lived up there.'

'Well, now you know. But keep it to yourself, I wouldn't like it pade mublic. Permit me to indrotuce myself. My name is Theodore T. Theodore, but you may call me Theo.'

Echo didn't venture to ask what the T between the two Theodores stood for. Theodore, perhaps.

'Delighted to meet you,' he said. 'My name is Echo. You really live in this chimney?'

'Yes, it's never used. It has a little roof of its own, that's good enough for me.' The Tuwituwu stared at Echo in silence. 'If you can conummicate with me,' it said at length, 'you must be a Crat.'

'That's right,' Echo replied, 'I am.'

'You've got two livers, did you know that? I'm something of an expert on gioloby.'

'Biology, you mean.'

Theodore behaved as if he hadn't heard.

'It would scafinate me to know how you got past the Meatherlice,' he went on. 'You're the first creature to set foot on this roof that didn't wossess pings.'

Scafinate? Wossess pings? Echo was becoming more and more puzzled by Theodore's speech patterns. 'I simply talked to them,' he replied.

'Ah, the art of genotiation,' said Theodore. 'I understand now. You're a born miplodat.'

Echo caught on at last: Theodore obviously had a problem with words. Or a broplem, as he would have put it.

'I'd sooner use my brains than my claws.'

'So you conummicated with them instead of fighting. You're a facipist!' Theodore exclaimed. 'That's splendid – we couldn't be more alike in our views. Any disagreement can be resolved by dational riscussion.'

'You know a lot of long words,' said Echo.

'You can say that again,' Theodore replied, fluffing out his chest a little. 'I'm a molypath, a walking endyclocepia, an autorithy of the first

order. However, I'm not interested showing off my uniserval brilliance, just in guinlistic precision. You don't need to have gone to uniservity for that. Personal itiniative is enough.'

'Are you another of Ghoolion's tenants?'

'I'll ignore that question! I've nothing to do with that crinimal invididual! I occupied this chimney in tropest against Ghoolion's evil chaminations.'

'You aren't too fond of him, then?'

'I'm not the only one, either! He's a despot, a social rapasite. He infects and tancominates the whole town. As long as he continues to modinate it the inhabitants will never be free. What we need is a relovution! A relovution of the trolepariat of Lamaisea!'

Echo involuntarily glanced around to see if anyone was listening.

'Aren't you being a little rash, sounding off like this?' he asked in a low voice. 'I mean, I'm a total stranger, and you –'

'No, no, not a stranger,' the Tuwituwu broke in soothingly, 'I know all about you. You're a victim of Ghoolion's almechistic aspirations. He plans to slaughter you and fat you of your strip.'

'How did you know?'

'In the first place, because he does that to all kinds of creatures except Meatherlice. I know everything – everything! I've had this building under vurseillance for many years. I know every chimney, every pecret sassage. I've seen the animals in their cages. I've seen him reduce them to falls of bat. Now, only the cages are left.'

'You creep around inside the chimneys?' said Echo. 'Why?'

'To keep an eye on Ghoolion and his doings. I'm everywhere and nowhere. Nobody sees me, but I see everything. I've eavesdropped on many of Ghoolion's molitary sonologues. I know his ambitious plans, his tatolitarian dreams.'

'Isn't that rather risky?' asked Echo. 'I mean, if he caught you …'

Theodore ignored this question too. He leant over, opened his one eye wide, and whispered: 'Listen, my friend. You're in great danger. Ghoolion aims to be the creator of life and master of death, no less. Megalomaniacal though it sounds, he's on the verge of filfulling that ambition and you're the last little mog in his cachine.'

'How do you know that?'

The Tuwituwu fluffed out his chest again.

'Just an above-average pacacity for working things out, perhaps, or a flair for tedection, or a stininctive feeling. Call it initution, if you like. There have lately been many incidations that an acopalyptic miclax, a sidaster of uncepredented gamnitude, is in the offing! And things have speeded up since your arrival. Ghoolion has never been so cheerful. You should have seen him at his exmeripents last night. He was in the heventh seaven!'

Echo was becoming suspicious. How could he be sure that this bizarre bird was telling the truth? Perhaps it was a confederate of Ghoolion's under orders to test him.

'Why are you telling me all this?'

'Because you're the only one who can stop him,' the Tuwituwu whispered.

'Meaning what?'

'For some siconderable time now, the Master Almechist has been skimming off and preserving the fat of rare animals – their olfactory soul, so to speak. He blends these fats and fragrances again and again in the lebief that this will produce a masic baterial from which he can create new life. I lebieve him to be so close to that goal that he hopes to attain it at the next full moon. All he needs is the fat and the soul of one last animal: a Crat, as your presence here implies. The way I see it, you're the last meraining emelent in his master plan. Your fat is the one missing indegrient. Only you can put the bikosh on the whole idea.'

'Really?' said Echo. 'How, exactly?'

'It's quite simple: run away. Bill your felly for a few days, then disappear into the blue. Deprive him of your Crat fat and you'll hash his dopes completely.'

'But we've got a contract.'

'A cantroct?' The Tuwituwu stared at Echo in horror. 'A legal codument? Really? That's bad.'

'Yes,' sighed Echo, 'and contracts have to be kept.'

'Nonsense, cantrocts are made to be broken! But a cantroct with Ghoolion … That's another matter.'

'What do you mean?'

Now it was the bird's turn to look around apprehensively.

'Ghoolion has ways of enforcing your cantroct with him.'

'What ways are you talking about?'

'You'll soon find out if you try to break it.'

'That's more or less what the Leathermice told me. So you also believe I've no hope of getting out of here alive?'

'I didn't say that. I'm potimistic by nature, but yours is an expectionally rare case. I shall have to give it a little more thought.'

The foliage of the artificial Christmas tree rustled in a sudden gust of wind. Echo looked round. Some big fat storm clouds in the distance were drawing nearer.

'The clamitic conditions are about to undergo a drastic fortrans-mation,' said the Tuwituwu. 'The otmasphere is charged with electricity, the beromatric pressure is falling – that means a stunder-thorm. Cindotions up here will become pretty unpleasant. I shall retire to my cellar to catch a mouse or two. I still have to ornagise my own meals, alas.'

'Why not help yourself to some of these sausages?' Echo said invitingly.

The Tuwituwu looked indignant.

'Absolutely not! I never touch anything that comes from Ghoolion's biadolical kitchen. It's an iron-cast principle of mine.'

'Suit yourself,' said Echo, 'but you don't know what you're missing.'

'You'd better find yourself a nice dry spot somewhere,' said Theodore.

'I will. Many thanks for the conversation and the good advice.'

'That wasn't a conservation, it was a cansporitorial get-together. I didn't advise you, either, I simply made some stragetic suggestions. From now on we're a team.'

'A team?'

'An alliance forged by fate. We're brothers in spirit, camrodes-in-arms. See you again soon.'

Theodore T. Theodore shut his single eye and disappeared slowly down the chimney.

Echo turned and scanned the heavens. Big-bellied rain clouds were towering over the Blue Mountains and the moist, warm wind was steadily increasing in strength. He was beginning to feel uneasy out there on the roof; being at the mercy of a thunderstorm really didn't appeal to him. Theodore's topsy-turvy utterances had left him bemused. Besides, he was sleepy after gorging himself, so he resolved to go inside and have a little nap to help him digest what he'd heard and eaten. It had been a thoroughly eventful morning.

The Cooked Ghost

Echo could hardly believe he'd managed to give Ghoolion the slip. Flatly ignoring the terms of their contract, he had sneaked out of the castle, scampered all the way across Malaisea and left the outskirts of the town behind him for the first time in his life. He'd been afraid that the Alchemaster would lay him low with a remote-controlled thunderbolt or turn him to stone, but nothing of the kind occurred. Now he was up in the mountains he'd seen from the roof of Ghoolion's castle. Walls of blue rock towered on either side of him, far higher than the walls flanking Malaisea's narrow streets – higher, even, than the Alchemaster's castle.

Suddenly he heard a clatter all round him. The rock faces rang with the tramp of marching feet and the rattle of bones. Echo knew at once what was making this din: Ghoolion's iron-soled boots were beating out their menacing rhythm. The sound was accompanied by an asphyxiating stench of sulphur and phosphorus. Then the whole mountain range grew dark as if a sudden storm had gathered overhead. Echo looked up, fearing the worst, and there, taller even than the very mountains, stood Ghoolion. Dressed all in black, he had grown into a giant a thousand times bigger than before. He bent down and, with a casual backhander, knocked off a mountain peak. It exploded into countless fragments as it fell, and an irresistible avalanche of rock came rumbling down the mountainside in Echo's direction. He tried to run, but his legs felt so leaden he could hardly detach his paws from the ground. The thunderous avalanche drew nearer and nearer, the first rocks hurtled past him. And then, looking more closely, he saw to his horror that they weren't rocks at all: they were human heads, each of them adorned with Ghoolion's face. 'Irrevocably committed!' one of them shouted. 'Indissolubly binding!' yelled the next. 'Legally enforceable!' cried another.

Echo woke up. He was lying in his basket beside Ghoolion's stove – lying in a thoroughly unnatural position with the blanket wound as tightly round his legs as ropes around a captive. He must have been wrestling with its imprisoning folds in his sleep. Grunting and

61

groaning, he extricated himself and climbed sleepily, laboriously, out of his basket.

The thunderstorm was raging immediately above the castle as Echo stole along the passage to Ghoolion's laboratory. Rain came slanting in through the empty window embrasures, lightning lit up the passage so brightly at times that the little Crat had to shut his eyes. 'Windowpanes,' he muttered, ducking his head. 'Windowpanes would be a good thing right now.'

Ghoolion had been expecting him. He was taking advantage of the dramatic meteorological conditions to perform a spectacular alchemical experiment for Echo's benefit. What better place to stage it than his laboratory, with rain-laden storm clouds billowing past its tall, pointed windows? What better background music than the menacing rumble of thunder nearby? Distributed around the room were dozens of Anguish Candles whose fitful light and subdued groans added to the indispensably ominous atmosphere.

The Alchemaster was wearing a wine-red velvet cloak with gold appliqués and a tricorn hat of pitch-black ravens' feathers, which made him look more diabolical than ever. He was standing beside his cauldron. A good fire was burning beneath it, as usual, but no exotic animal was being rendered down on this occasion. The cauldron's bubbling, seething contents appeared to be plain water.

'Well,' asked Ghoolion, 'how did you get on with the Leathermice? Was breakfast on the roof to your satisfaction?'

'I can't complain,' Echo replied. 'The roof is fabulous, but the Leathermice take a bit of getting used to.' He studiously avoided mentioning his encounter with Theodore T. Theodore.

'Good. I think you've already gained a pound or two.'

The clouds emitted a deafening peal of thunder. Echo gave a jump. He had learnt to respect thunderstorms since being evicted from his former home. It wasn't childish timidity that made him start at every thunderclap and every flash of lightning, it was the thoroughly justified fear that something catastrophic might happen. He had seen shafts of lightning split whole oak trees in two and set barns ablaze. The laboratory was situated at a great height, rain clouds were swirling through its open windows, and its bristling array of silver, copper and iron instruments presented a perfect target for electrical discharges. The room was so full of combustible and explosive materials and powders that a single thunderbolt would have sufficed to send the whole castle sky-high, yet the Alchemaster was proceeding with his work as calmly as if he relished the dangers of the situation – in fact, Echo half suspected that he was secretly masterminding the storm.

'Listen carefully,' Ghoolion said as he worked on the fire beneath the cauldron with a pair of bellows. 'I'm going to teach you a few basic facts about alchemy.'

'A few basic facts?' Echo replied with a touch of disappointment. '"Secrets which even the most experienced alchemist would give his eye teeth to know" – that was what you said!'

'You can't measure the universe without learning your two-times table first,' Ghoolion retorted over a clap of thunder. 'You can't write a novel without mastering the alphabet or compose a symphony without being able to read a score. How can I tell you about Prima Zateria if you don't even know how to cook a ghost?'

Echo pricked up his ears. 'Is that what we're going to do, cook a ghost?'

'Possibly, we'll see. Maybe, maybe not. It doesn't work every time. Alchemy is a science, but not, alas, an exact one. It's as close to an art as any science can be and not every work of art succeeds.'

Echo's curiosity was aroused. Coming closer, he wound round Ghoolion's legs.

'Actually,' Ghoolion went on, 'this isn't a work of art. It's just a trick, a kind of joke.'

'I thought you didn't make jokes.'

'Who says so?' Ghoolion looked down at the Crat in surprise.

'You did.'

'I did? Really? The things one says without thinking ... I've always been fond of jokes.'

'Is that a fact?' Echo said warily. 'When was the last time you cracked one?'

Ghoolion thought for a moment. 'The last time? Let's see. It was, er ... er ...'

'Well?'

'It was …' Ghoolion was clearly racking his brains. 'It was … Good heavens, it was when I was a student!'

For the first time, Echo detected something in Ghoolion's expression that wasn't born of a cold heart or iron self-control: a look of genuine dismay. However, it disappeared as quickly as it had come, to be replaced by his habitual mask of authority and grim determination.

'Well?' he snarled suddenly. 'Shall I cook us a ghost or not?'

Echo recoiled. Ghoolion's tone was as sharp as a sword thrust.

'Please do,' he said in a subdued voice.

The Alchemaster laid the bellows aside and drew his cloak around him. 'Alchemists have always engaged in a variety of ludicrous attempts to transform one substance into another,' he said. 'Lead into gold, blood into wine, wine into blood, wood into bread, bread into diamonds. It used to be considered quite professional for an alchemist to sprinkle a stone with magnetised quicksilver when the moon was full and hope that it would turn into marzipan.'

'But lead into gold – that works, doesn't it?' Echo asked diffidently. He had heard of such a feat at some stage.

Ghoolion sighed. 'I can see that, alchemistically speaking, your state of knowledge is that of a medieval village idiot. I shall have to begin at rock bottom.'

The little Crat gave another start, but not at a thunderclap this time. The Alchemaster could be really hurtful at times. He moved away, looking offended.

'Gold and lead!' Ghoolion said scornfully. 'Those early alchemists tried to transform two of the densest substances on our planet.'

Echo had crept behind an untidy stack of battered old books.

'Well?' he called from his hiding place. 'Why not?'

'The denser the substance, the less susceptible it is of transformation,' Ghoolion replied. 'You might as well try to teach a brick to fly. Volatile substances are our only chance – any well-informed alchemist will tell you that.'

Ghoolion uncorked a glass bottle containing a reddish liquid, thereby releasing a tiny cloud of pink vapour. Echo could have sworn the vapour giggled as it dispersed. His curiosity rearoused, he emerged from his hiding place.

Ghoolion was now standing in front of an oil painting, a most impressive representation of a volcanic eruption.

'The years of study I've devoted to painting disasters have taught me an important lesson,' he said, engrossed in the picture. 'No one who has observed how systematically a fire incinerates a town, how methodically a volcano buries a village in lava, how deliberately a tornado ravages an island, or how murderously a tsunami inundates a whole stretch of coastline and all its inhabitants, can believe that those natural forces act blindly. They *think* – they're rational beings like you and me!'

As if to confirm this audacious theory, there was a blinding flash outside, followed almost immediately by a peal of thunder.

Echo flinched. 'But a thunderbolt like that one can't have anything very nice in mind.'

'Of course not,' Ghoolion said brusquely. 'Elemental forces think elemental, violent thoughts. Destruction is their purpose in life, their function, their destiny. They cleanse the earth of inessentials without compunction, without wasting an ounce of their strength on mercy or compassion. They think big.' The Alchemaster continued to gaze at the painting. 'But the crucial question is,' he went on, 'how do their thoughts manifest themselves?'

Echo strove to picture the thoughts of a forest fire, but his powers of imagination were insufficient. All he could visualise were billowing flames and charred trees.

'Where there's fire there's smoke,' said Ghoolion. 'Once you've managed to conceive of smoke as the cogitations of fire, the stench of sulphur as a volcano's nightmare and steam as the ideas of a geyser, you soon come to realise that the whole earth is a living, thinking being.'

Echo didn't like the turn the conversation was taking, nor did he care for Ghoolion's increasingly ominous tone of voice. Another flash of lightning lit up the laboratory and an ear-splitting peal of thunder set all its glass vessels rattling.

'If the earth is a living, thinking being,' said Ghoolion, raising his voice to make himself heard above the tempest raging outside, 'I should be able to find a way to read its mind. To read and decipher its thoughts and ultimately, even, to influence them!'

65

A violent gust of wind blew into the laboratory, causing the Anguish Candles to flicker wildly and utter moans expressive of their hopes of being extinguished. Memorandum sheets went fluttering through the air and animal skeletons tinkled like xylophones. Then the wind dropped. The Anguish Candles stopped flickering and resumed their customary lamentations.

'Yes!' cried Ghoolion. 'Then I could take a hand in the process of creation – in Nature's everlasting creative activities, which are forever bringing forth new life!'

Half a dozen thunderbolts exploded simultaneously, all round the tower. They lit up the laboratory as bright as day, projecting multiple versions of the Alchemaster's shadow on the walls. Startled, Echo dived under a stool. He waited anxiously for the thunder to die away, then asked in a tremulous voice: 'When are we going to do our trick, Master?'

Ghoolion stared at him vaguely, like someone suffering from memory loss and trying to recall the name of the person addressing him.

'Hm?' he said. He peered into the massive cauldron. 'The ghost brew is hot enough,' he muttered. 'The electrification of the atmosphere and the extreme humidity shouldn't be detrimental to the success of the experiment – conditions are positively ideal, in fact. Good, let's begin. I'm going to cook a ghost. Will you assist me?'

'Only if I don't have to eat it!' Echo replied.

Ghoolion laughed hoarsely. 'Don't worry. We can start right away. Everything is in readiness.'

He went over to an iron cabinet and opened it. A dense cloud of icy vapour flowed out, almost concealing him from view as he rummaged around inside. At length he brought out two balls of fat and held them up to the candlelight.

'Graveyard Gas and Murkholm Mist,' he said. 'That's all we need. This is going to be a very simple ghost.'

He closed the cabinet, strode back to the cauldron and tossed one of the balls into the seething liquid. As it melted, Echo heard a high-pitched, long-drawn-out sigh that almost froze his blood.

'That was some gas from the Graveyard Marshes near Dullsgard,'

Ghoolion explained. 'It doesn't matter much what former living creature it belonged to. It's dead, that's the main thing.'

Echo plucked up his courage and leapt on to a table for a better view of what was happening inside the cauldron.

Ghoolion tossed the second ball into the brew. As the fat melted, a tiny white snake wriggled out of it, swam around on the seething surface for a while and then submerged.

'That was a sample of Murkholm Mist. Incredible, the treatment that semi-organic substance can stand. You can boil it in water, even in molten lead or hydrochloric acid. You can put it in the alchemical furnace and subject it to extreme temperatures. You can encase it in ice for a year, marinate it in mercury, shut it up in a vacuum, batter it with a sledgehammer. None of those things will affect it. But watch ...'

Ghoolion produced a flute from his cloak. Then he put it to his lips and proceeded to play a simple, melodious tune that sounded like the setting to a nursery rhyme. The vaporous white snake surfaced once more, writhing like a worm on a hook. Ghoolion stopped playing.

'Music. Music drives it insane,' he said. 'It can't endure music, however beautiful, except trombophone music. You see? It's dying. It's committing suicide by dissolving in the water. Now it's combining with the Graveyard Gas. That's the second stage.'

Echo watched in fascination as the vaporous snake sank beneath the surface of the brew and dissolved. Hearing a noise, he looked over at the Leyden Manikins. For some reason they had started to rampage around inside their jars and hammer on the glass sides. Ghoolion paid no attention. Reaching into the pocket of his cloak, he brought out some black powder and tossed it into the cauldron. The liquid reacted in a surprising manner. It turned green, then red, then purple and finally green again.

'The desiccated dung of Time-Snails,' said Ghoolion, as casually as if he'd added a pinch of pepper. 'What happens next has no real scientific basis. It's simply a way of killing time until the requisite chemical and interdimensional processes in the cauldron have taken place. This is when the traditional spells are chanted. They don't do a thing, but I can't help it, I'm fond of the old hocus-pocus.'

He cleared his throat, threw up his arms and declaimed:

'Let my magic brew revive
that which used to be alive.
Let my bubbling cauldron seethe
till the creature starts to breathe.
Brought to life it then shall be
by the power of alchemy.'

Echo, who was watching everything closely from his elevated vantage point, saw the contents of the cauldron change colour several times and release some iridescent bubbles, which went floating across the laboratory. Ghoolion continued to declaim:

'Graveyard Gas and Murkholm Mist,
mingled by an alchemist,
can from their mephitic haze
other-worldly phantoms raise.
Spirit, from my brew arise
and take shape before our eyes!'

The liquid swirled up and down, down and up, and the rising bubbles were sucked back into the depths by the little whirlpools that formed here and there. Echo had never seen a liquid behave so strangely. The longer he looked at it, the more he thought he glimpsed objects beneath the surface – alarming, shadowy shapes, as if the cauldron were a window into another world. Then the brew rose at several points like a cloth with something moving beneath it. The depths of the cauldron emitted a growl like that of a beast preparing to pounce at any moment. Echo instinctively retreated a few steps, even though he was up on a table and several feet from what was happening.

'Hearken, ghost, to what I say,
and my potent spell obey!
Quit your home in Death's domain,
realm of sorrow and of pain,
hasten through the nameless portals
that divide the dead from mortals!'

The brew became transformed into a miniature sea in a violent storm, an expanse of countless tiny waves, all of which were converging on a focal point. There, in defiance of every law of nature, the foam-capped, snow-white liquid rose into the air. Ghoolion threw up his arms again and cried:

'Spirit, let your froth and spume
semi-human form assume.
But with arms and legs dispense
– they'd be an irrelevance.
Simply let your weird ensemble
washing on a line resemble!'

The foam swirled upwards like a waterspout, fell back again, then resumed its steady ascent. Echo stepped back and tripped over an old book, almost singeing his tail on an Anguish Candle. The waterspout was now an amorphous shape expanding both upwards and outwards. Echo wondered apprehensively how big the ghost would eventually become. Already as tall as the Alchemaster and still growing, it looked like a shred of wind-wafted silk woven from luminous yarn – a ghostly thing that moved in obedience to the natural laws of another world. Only the thinnest of threads still connected it to the cauldron above which it was floating.

'Now the time has come for you
from the cauldron's bubbling brew
to emerge and bid farewell
to the regions where you dwell.
Summoned by my mystic powers,
leave your world and enter ours!'

As if actually obeying the Alchemaster's command, the luminous Something swayed left, then right, then reared upwards. All at once the thread of froth that had connected it to the cauldron snapped, enabling it to drift freely around the laboratory.

Exhausted, Ghoolion lowered his arms. The thunder had dwindled to a distant rumble. As though resentful of its inability to compete with the happenings in Ghoolion's abode, the storm had moved on and was raging elsewhere.

'That's it!' cried Ghoolion. He sounded relieved. 'A Cooked Ghost – a trick extremely popular with apprentice alchemists.'

The disembodied spirit was drifting around like a skein of mist – aimlessly, it seemed. Having floated past the bookshelves and over the Ghoolionic Preserver, it made a sudden beeline for Echo.

Terrified, he jumped off the table and darted across the laboratory, but their strange guest remained hard on his heels. He vaulted over benches, dived under tables and between piles of books and chair legs, but he failed to shake off his pursuer. Ghoolion burst out laughing.

At length, completely out of breath, Echo cowered down beneath a chair while the ghost hovered overhead, fluttering like a sheet on a washing line.

'What do I do now, Master?' Echo asked plaintively. 'What does it want?'

'You'd better just get used to it,' Ghoolion told him. 'It's a ghost, but it's quite harmless. It can neither see nor hear. However, Cooked Ghosts sometimes develop an affection for persons present when they materialise, so we assume that they have certain feelings.'

'You mean it likes me?'

'You could put it that way, although we don't know whether ghosts "like" anything at all. They themselves are nothing, really. They feel no pain, are devoid of intelligence and have no intentions of any kind, either good or bad. That, at all events, is our present state of alchemistic knowledge. They cannot invade our dimension physically, just as nothing in our dimension can touch a ghost. From now on, this one will drift around our world for ever. It's bound to frighten a lot of people. Anyone ignorant of alchemy will get a terrible shock when it suddenly floats in through one bedroom wall and sails out through the other. Many people will probably die of shock. Or lose their wits.' Ghoolion grinned malignly at the thought. 'Yet it's as harmless as a fair-weather cloud.'

'Why doesn't it simply fly away?' Echo enquired from his refuge.

'It seems to feel at home here. For some reason Cooked Ghosts enjoy being in old, ruined buildings. Perhaps they like the sensation of floating through ancient stonework. Hence the stories of castles inhabited by the restless spirits of departed ancestors.'

Echo looked up at the ghost, which was still hovering above him. It was, in fact, a beautiful sight, like a lustrous, flowing silver robe. Suddenly, however, he thought he caught a momentary glimpse of a weird face in its undulating folds. That startled him so much that he crouched down even lower beneath the chair.

'But I can shoo it away if you prefer,' said Ghoolion.

'Could you really? In that case, please do! Please make it go away!'

Ghoolion simply raised his arms and took a couple of steps towards the ghost. Instantly, it rotated on its own axis, then raced round the laboratory, dived into the dark stonework between two bookcases and disappeared.

'For some unknown reason,' Ghoolion said with a sigh, 'I have a deterrent effect on Cooked Ghosts. They never trust me. Odd, isn't it?'

'Yes,' said Echo, 'very odd.'

Master and Pupil

Echo was now on fire with curiosity and intensely eager to learn more about the Alchemaster's technique. What he didn't know was that the Cooked Ghost's materialisation was an age-old trick forming part of every experienced alchemist's repertoire and designed to recruit apprentices.

Ghoolion's plan was both simple and perfidious. What he needed for his experiments was a compendium of alchemistic knowledge, his own and other people's. It would not, unfortunately, suffice to toss an alchemistic encyclopedia and his own scientific notes into the cauldron and boil them up together, as the quacks of olden days might have done. No, according to his calculations that knowledge had to be transmitted from one brain to another by telepathic means. He would have to drum it into the little Crat's head in the old-fashioned way, so that he could boil it out again at a later stage. Echo was the only living creature in Malaisea capable of understanding him and absorbing his esoteric knowledge like a sponge. That was the true reason why the Alchemaster

71

was willing to entrust the little Crat with something as well-guarded as the fundamental secrets of alchemy, together with the knowledge he himself had acquired.

Meanwhile, Echo believed that all this was being done purely for his personal amusement and entertainment. Being haunted by dark thoughts of his impending doom whenever he wasn't busy eating or sleeping, he welcomed any occasion on which Ghoolion favoured him with his presence and his fascinating store of expert knowledge. He believed that the old alchemist did this partly for reasons of vanity and partly from a pent-up desire to communicate bred by long years of solitude.

You had to grant Ghoolion one thing: he was a brilliant teacher. Whenever he transformed himself into a sympathetic, omniscient mentor for Echo's benefit, his whole demeanour changed. He sloughed off all his demonic, domineering, hectoring mannerisms like an ugly cocoon, his strident voice sank to a melodious murmur, his despotic manner vanished and his grim visage transformed itself into a kindly countenance.

He never gave Echo the feeling that he was teaching him something, far less drumming it into his head. No, Ghoolion's lessons always took the form of a friendly chat, which only happened to touch on the weightiest problems of alchemy, and Echo played the carefree role of a naive prompter and questioner. He believed that all the mental exertion was undertaken by Ghoolion, who had to extract all this information from his vast treasure house of knowledge and expound it. In reality, however, it was Echo whose brains were being put to the test, because he was using a Crat's true intellectual capacity for the very first time.

Ghoolion knew all there was to know about a Crat's brain. He realised that a creature with a perfect command of every Zamonian language, animal languages included, was a genius, and that it must be capable of intellectual feats of quite another order. Echo's brain was an absorbent sponge full of unused chambers and synapses, fresh cells and youthful tissue crackling with mental electricity. You could have read him the Atlantean register of births or the fundamentals of Zamonian mathematics aloud, and he would have memorised every word and numeral sufficiently to be able to recite them backwards on demand. But he was quite unaware of his gift. Because it had scarcely been tested in its brief existence, his young cerebral organ would provide the ideal vessel in which to deposit the Alchemaster's whole store of knowledge – or at least its quintessence, which he had condensed into a compact system of handy formulae and theses.

Whether Ghoolion was lecturing him on the integrated geocentric model of the universe or the language of diamonds, Bookemistico-typographic hypnosis or the sensitivity of metals to pain, his words seemed to Echo like music that went in one ear and came out the other. He was happy just to listen to the Alchemaster's melodious voice, which could always be relied on to banish his own dark thoughts, and he hadn't the least idea how much he truly understood of what he heard and how much had lodged between his ears. Ghoolion knew that Echo's mind possessed the unique ability to store all this knowledge without its becoming a burden to him – indeed, without his even realising that he had learnt something of importance. Only in a Crat's brain could this serene symbiosis of ignorance and intelligence have prevailed.

But Ghoolion's playful tuition in the fundamental principles of alchemy was practical as well as theoretical. He granted the little Crat unlimited access to the laboratory and allowed him to wind round his legs while he was performing his daily tasks. Echo observed every one of the Alchemaster's techniques and series of experiments. He was permitted to read Ghoolion's notes, even the entries in his journal. What he failed to realise, however, was that all these figures and formulae, chemical ingredients and focal lengths, logarithms and barometric data, fermentation times and melting points, et cetera, were etching themselves into his brain.

He was allowed to look through all Ghoolion's magnifying glasses, microscopes and telescopes, watch the alchemical furnace being fired and even be present at every stage in the operation of the Ghoolionic Preserver. He also sniffed powders and solutions, secret tinctures and ointments, essences and acids, and made a mental note of their odours, names and composition. Hanging on the laboratory walls were big blackboards bearing alchemistic tables, symbols and chemical compounds, all of which he studied from top to bottom. He read passages from priceless old alchemistic works, which Ghoolion brought him from the library. And at night, after a long day's work and a meal of many courses, the Alchemaster would read to him from the secret texts in which he had recorded the most daring of his experiments. Echo's little head absorbed all this information until it became what may well have been Zamonia's biggest hoard of alchemistic knowledge, but he bore it lightly.

He was sometimes awake at night because the food lay heavy on his stomach, so he liked to walk it off by roaming the old castle until he got tired. When he encountered Ghoolion, as he occasionally did, he dived behind some piece of furniture and surreptitiously watched the Alchemaster at his nightly activities. These, as he soon discovered, were thoroughly unmysterious and predictable. Ghoolion would either sit down on a window seat and survey the town through a telescope, or repair to the library, with its stupefying aroma of old books, and mutter to himself as he read. He often messed around in the laboratory as well, of course, and because he felt unobserved at night his manner was far more feverish and restless than during the day. He would fire up the alchemical furnace, check on the progress of current experiments, or tap on the jars containing Leyden Manikins. Then he would hurry over to the big blackboard, wipe off formulae with a sponge and replace them with others; take a step backwards; fly into a rage; bellow at the blackboard and hurl the chalk into the fire; promptly calm down and carry out some elaborate experiment with the utmost serenity and composure; pace to and fro, reeling off an endless succession of figures and formulae; make an entry in his journal; rinse out some test tubes and retorts; sew up a damaged taxidermal specimen; tan a hide; add a few brushstrokes to a painting; scrub the floor; sweep the chimney; and so on and so forth. The old man never paused to rest.

Echo was reminded of an occasion when he'd scaled the ivy-covered walls of Malaisea's municipal lunatic asylum. The roof of that unloved institution had afforded him a view of the exercise yard. What he saw there was remarkable. The lunatics were all behaving like people engaged in activities of supreme importance. One had made a pile of leaves in the corner of the yard and was guarding it against potential thieves with a resolute air. Another was banging his head against a wall with clockwork regularity, counting as he did so. Another was vehemently haranguing his fellow inmates about an impending invasion from outer space. Ever since seeing this, Echo had realised that, far from being impelled to conquer continents or burn cities to the ground, the victims of insanity were driven to carry out trivial routine tasks that differed little from those performed by the sound of mind. Before long, he ceased to regard Ghoolion as the dangerous madman the townsfolk of Malaisea believed him to be. Instead, he seemed an embodiment of all those harmless loonies in the exercise yard. Tormented by his restless, discontented nature and divorced from reality by his self-imposed isolation, he was toiling away at a monumental folly that would probably never be finished. Ghoolion the bogeyman, who had seemed ever more monstrous to Echo and all the other inhabitants of Malaisea, shrank on closer inspection to more tolerable proportions. Echo hadn't grown fond of him, of course, nor did he feel sorry for him. Ghoolion was still an old tyrant, bully and tormentor of animals who proposed to slit his throat in a few weeks' time, purely for the sake of some stupid experiment, but Echo learnt to treat him with an increasing lack of deference and constraint – in fact, there were times when he genuinely enjoyed his company. This struck him as smarter than spending his last days of life in constant trepidation.

But Ghoolion, too, saw Echo with different eyes after a day or two. He very soon discovered that a Crat's effect on its owner was far more subtle than that of any other domestic animal. A dog obeyed your orders and guarded the house, a bird's song was easy on the ear. A Crat appeared to do nothing at all, to begin with, apart from favour you with its presence and accept your hospitality. In the company of a faithful hound you could feel powerful and secure; in that of a Crat, you could count yourself lucky to be tolerated at all. A dog deferred to its master, worshipped him, allowed him to put it on a leash and teach it idiotic tricks. It would even accept a thrashing from its master when it could have torn him to pieces. You could kick a dog into a corner, and a few hours later it would have forgotten and bring you your slippers in gratitude. But a Crat would cold-shoulder you for days, even if you'd merely trodden on its tail by accident. A Crat inspired respect, not fear. You could feel afraid of a dog, but never respectful. If Ghoolion had thrown a stick, Echo would have stared at him as if he were out of his mind and then stalked off with a toss of the head.

What particularly fascinated Ghoolion about Echo was his almost preternatural agility. He half believed that the Crat could walk along a razor's edge without cutting himself, or cross a rain cloud without falling through it, or nimbly traverse a deep puddle without wetting his paws, or step on a red-hot stove without burning himself. The laws of gravity seemed of only limited application to Echo. A dog that tried to scale a roof was the epitome of a venture doomed to fail. If Echo wanted to do this, he glided up the drainpipe as effortlessly as if he had suckers on his paws. If a Crat fell off a roof it landed unscathed on all fours. If a dog did so, it was dead.

Echo exerted a soothing effect on Ghoolion, if only because of his silent, unobtrusive presence and the tranquil atmosphere it generated. With his inward and outward equilibrium, his flowing, well-gauged movements, his insatiable appetite for sleep and his instinctive aversion to hectic activity, he was the personification of poise and calm. Ghoolion particularly admired the way he prepared to go to sleep. He didn't just lie down, he performed a balletic tribute to Morpheus. When the time came, the little Crat betook himself to his basket with the leisurely tread of a lion making for a waterhole. Then he climbed in and marked time with his forepaws to tamp the cushion down, purring and turning majestically on the spot as he did so. Next, yawning unashamedly, he stretched, first his forelegs and then his whole body, which positively melted into the cushion in a single, fluid, seductively lethargic movement. Last of all, he curled his tail round him in a semicircle, licked his paws with care and gave another yawn. His little head subsided, his eyes narrowed to slits, then closed, and Ghoolion could tell from the regular rise and fall of his furry flanks that Echo had safely arrived in every feline's paradise, the land of dreams.

The Alchemaster hardly slept at all. The most he did was sit down on a chair and lapse into an hour's restless slumber, haunted by excruciating nightmares in which blazing Ugglies pursued him along endless passages or an octopus digested him alive. Then he would get to his feet again and resume his restless, obsessive activities.

Ghoolion's only companions in recent times had been the Leathermice, but he now realised how much of their behaviour had rubbed off on him. He lived more by night than by day, was extremely nervous and fluttery, had hypersensitive hearing and started at the smallest sound. He wrapped himself in his cloak like the vampire bats in their wings and, like them, was forever retreating into the shadows.

'If I'm not very careful,' thought Ghoolion, 'I'll soon be hanging from a rafter upside down, squeaking. Echo is so relaxed. I really should try to emulate him.'

Yes, he was starting to develop a respect for Echo. It had been a good idea to choose a Crat for his culminating experiment. Crat fat might contain the missing bonding agent that would weld all other substances together. But Ghoolion derived particular pleasure from the way in which Echo was being trained and used despite his natural indolence and independence – and all without his realising it. That was cruelty to animals of the highest order.

The Sheet

After only a few days at the castle, Echo had acquired two friends: an eccentric bird and a Cooked Ghost. Beggars couldn't be choosers in Ghoolion's ancient pile, so you had to take what you could get in the way of company. But even a Crat subscribed to the principle that friendship entails obligations, so he felt bound to cultivate those acquaintances, however peculiar.

The Cooked Ghost disappeared for days after Ghoolion had shooed it away, but it must have remained on the premises because it suddenly turned up again. Its manner at first was timid and hesitant, but as time went by it became increasingly confident – if a ghost could be described as such. It seemed to enjoy being near Echo, who gave a terrible start whenever the shimmering thing came sailing through a solid stone wall or bobbed up through the flagstones like a figure in a puppet theatre. In time, however, he got used to it. It never came too close but floated at a respectful distance behind him when he sauntered along the passages. If he halted, the ghost would also stop short and hover there, patiently and unobtrusively, until he walked on. That was all there was to their relationship – silent proximity – and Echo sometimes wondered what the ghost got out of it.

His private name for it was 'the Sheet', which shows how little it now unnerved him. He had almost completely lost his original fear of it, having grasped that the ghost was no more dangerous than a curtain stirring in the breeze. There were times, however, when the sight of it did still make his blood run cold. This happened whenever he seemed to glimpse a kind of face in the floating ectoplasm. The phenomenon, which never lasted for more than a few seconds, looked as if a scary mask with a gaping mouth and no eyes were pressing against it from behind. Echo would have liked to talk the Sheet out of this undesirable habit, but alas, Cooked Ghost was not among the languages in his repertoire.

The Sheet even followed Echo up to the roof, where it would suddenly seep through the tiles and pursue him up and down the stairways for hours on end. At night it often hovered beside his basket until he went to sleep and sometimes it would still be there when he awoke in the morning.

But the Sheet was no less scared of the Alchemaster than anyone else in Malaisea. As soon as Echo heard his clattering, iron-shod footsteps, the ghost would instantly disappear through some wall or painting or the floor and refrain from showing itself again for a long time thereafter. Thus, Ghoolion was unaware of its continued presence in the castle. For some reason he himself could not have defined, Echo had refrained from telling the Alchemaster about his relations with the Sheet and Theodore T. Theodore.

One warm summer night his nocturnal perambulations brought him to the big room filled with dust-sheeted furniture. He was once more accompanied by the ghost, which had turned up at some stage and was floating doggedly after him. When they entered the room, however, it came to an abrupt halt, fluttered to and fro like a terrified bird, and fled back in the direction they had come from.

Echo walked on into the room. He had stopped trying to fathom his new friend's motives. For reasons that remained a mystery, the Sheet kept on turning up, manifested itself at the most diverse times of day and vanished as abruptly as it had appeared. It couldn't have fled at Ghoolion's approach on this occasion, or Echo would have heard his unmistakable footsteps long ago.

He found this room one of the creepiest in the entire castle. Even though it contained nothing genuinely frightening, his imagination was so stimulated at night by the enshrouded pieces of furniture that he could readily picture some dangerous creature lurking beneath each dust sheet, ready to burst forth and pounce on him. There! Hadn't that fold of cloth stirred? Wasn't it bulging as if something were breathing beneath it? Or was the material merely billowing in the wind? Whatever the truth, Echo wanted to cross the room as quickly as possible. He scampered nimbly between the wardrobes and chests of drawers, wing chairs and sofas, which looked to him like snow-bound giants. What kinds of decay did they harbour? What was in those wardrobes and chests of drawers? He could imagine pullulating maggots and woodworms, but also drawers full of desiccated eyes and mummified hands, shelves laden with skulls and chests filled with grinning teeth. He kept casting nervous sidelong glances at the white mountains of cloth, prepared at any moment for a sheet to be rent asunder and a skeleton to emerge with glowing embers in its eye sockets and fangs smeared with blood. He had almost reached the door. Only one last cloth-swathed colossus barred his path. Perhaps the dust sheet concealed a big oak cupboard, perhaps a guillotine and its headless victim. He had just slalomed round the bulky piece of furniture with the exit already in sight when he heard a strange sound.

He came to a halt.

And listened.

There was someone else in the room.

The fur on the back of his neck stood on end. It wasn't a loud, frightening or menacing sound, but subdued and exceedingly mournful.

Someone was sobbing.

And Echo knew who it was, because at that moment he caught a whiff of something familiar and not particularly pleasant – something to which he had become accustomed: Ghoolion's alchemical body odour.

He stole back into the room. All his fear had gone. Now he was motivated by curiosity alone. He paused behind a wing chair, then crawled beneath it and peered cautiously from his hiding place.

There he was: Ghoolion. The Alchemaster was seated in an armchair nearby, and he was weeping.

Echo had thought at first that he might be giggling softly to himself. It would have been considerably more in character for the old devil to be sitting there in the dark, sniggering at some diabolical scheme he had just concocted. But he was sobbing beyond a doubt. The circumstances were unusual in every other respect as well. For one thing, Echo found it remarkable that the Alchemaster should be sitting down at all. It dawned on him that he usually saw Ghoolion standing up or walking around, seldom seated, far less lying down. There was nothing demonic or authoritarian about him as he sat slumped there, shaking all over. All his strength and kinetic energy seemed to have evaporated; he was just a

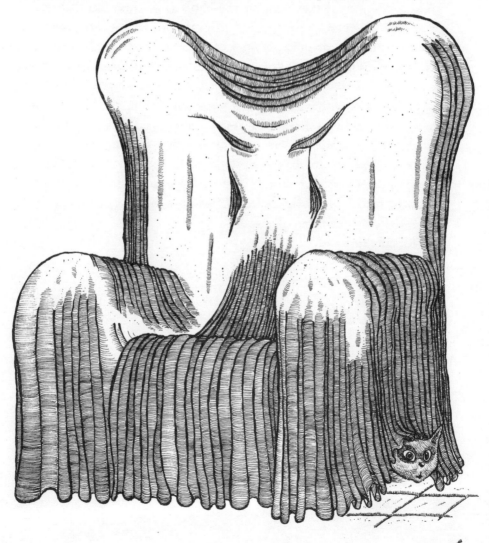

picture of misery. He sat there as if the air weighed on him like lead. His shoulders sagged, his head was bowed, his whole body was shaking with convulsive sobs.

Echo was not only astonished to see Ghoolion weeping, he was stunned, not least because he'd never believed him capable of such emotion. The sight moved him so profoundly that a tear trickled down his own nose and he emitted a muffled sob – which he promptly regretted. Instantly, Ghoolion sprang to his feet like a jack-in-the-box and froze, a gaunt shadow silhouetted against one of the lofty windows. 'Who's there?' he snarled.

The words positively exploded in Echo's ears. He darted out of his hiding place and scampered to the door as if someone had set his tail on fire, then sped like a rocket through a series of rooms, along various passages and down the stairs. He didn't dare stop until he was three floors below in a library filled with ancient books and redolent of the cold ashes in the fireplace. He crept beneath a worm-eaten lectern and listened with a pounding heart to see if Ghoolion had followed him, but all he could hear were the rustling wings of some Leathermice performing their nocturnal aerobatics beneath the library ceiling.

The Smallest Story in Zamonia

The Alchemaster was bent over a table with his eyes glued to a microscope when Echo, yawning and stretching, slunk into the laboratory the next morning. He made no attempt to greet the little Crat but remained engrossed in his observations, which he clearly found fascinating in the extreme.

Echo was feeling irritable and short of sleep. He had lain awake half the night, trying to fathom Ghoolion's behaviour and apprehensively wondering if the Alchemaster had spotted him. Head down, he ambled over to a bowl filled with sweetened cocoa and proceeded to lap it up.

'Forgive me,' Ghoolion said at length, without looking up, 'I'm just examining a leaf from the Miniforest, and that calls for extreme concentration. It's so tiny that you can hardly see it, even with a microscope.'

'The Miniforest?' Echo asked between two mouthfuls of cocoa. 'I've heard of the Megaforest, but never of the Miniforest.'

Ghoolion adjusted the focus slightly. 'Only scientists equipped with the strongest spectacles and the most powerful magnifying glasses are aware that the Megaforest lies next to another wooded area known as the Miniforest. It's the smallest forest in Zamonia. The Miniforest is so tiny that even insects feel cramped there. Its largest trees are so diminutive that the timber from one of them would suffice to make a single toothpick at most. The only creatures that can live in it without suffering from claustrophobia are Rootkins.'

Echo had woken up at last. He licked his whiskers clean, then turned away from the bowl, sauntered over to Ghoolion and lay down at his feet. He was exceedingly glad that no mention had been made of last night's events.

'In that case,' he said, 'Rootkins must be really tiny.'

At long last, Ghoolion detached his gaze from the microscope and directed it at Echo. He rubbed his eyes.

'Big and small are relative attributes,' he said. 'I must seem pretty big to you, I'm sure, but to a Turniphead I'm a dwarf. To me you look rather small, if you'll pardon my saying so, but to a mouse you're a giant.'

He looked around, picked up something lying on the table in front of him and held it under Echo's nose. It was a slice of stale bread – a form of food typical of the Alchemaster's own preferred diet.

'A slice of bread,' he said. 'You would regard it as one big slice, wouldn't you?'

Echo thought for a moment, then nodded. 'Of course,' he said.

Ghoolion clenched his fist and the brittle bread disintegrated.

'But it's really a lot of little fragments.' He opened his fingers, allowing the crumbs to fall on to the table, then picked one up and held it between thumb and forefinger.

'And this crumb here – you'd describe it as a single crumb, wouldn't you?'

Echo nodded again, rather more hesitantly this time.

Ghoolion ground the crumb to dust between his fingers.

'But it, too, consists of many smaller particles. It's the same with all physical matter. All the things you see here – workbenches, chairs, microscopes, books, glass vessels, the whole laboratory, even you and I – are made up of tiny components held together in a wondrous manner. That's why we alchemists concentrate our research on the very smallest objects, because we believe that their microcosmic structure contains a latent but immense store of energy.'

'How can something small contain an immense store of energy?' Echo demanded. 'Isn't that a contradiction in terms?'

The Alchemaster seemed to be debating whether to go back to work or devote himself to the gaps in Echo's education.

'Listen,' he said at length, 'and I'll tell you a story. It's about the Miniforest and it's also to do with alchemy. Interested?'

Echo nodded.

'Every budding alchemist has to learn this story by heart. He won't gain his diploma unless he can recite it perfectly. I can still say it word for word, even today.'

'It must be an important story, then,' said Echo.

'It is. It takes place in the Miniforest, so I hope you won't expect it to deal with grand emotions or events on an epic scale, let alone with giants. It's the smallest story in the whole of Zamonia. Can you come to terms with that?'

'No problem,' said Echo. 'I like small things.'

'You see? One immediately feels more comfortable when small things are involved, doesn't one? More comfortable and free from the shadows cast by monstrous events to come. The things that happen in cramped but clearly visible surroundings are so small and uncommodious that even a Rootkin can deal with them. Isn't that nice and reassuring?'

'Yes,' said Echo.

'Rootkins are so small that they can't even be termed dwarfs. They belong to the Dwurf family, which embraces all life forms smaller than a chestnut: Piplings, Nutkins, Antlets, Skwirts and so on. But Rootkins are the smallest of the lot. They're only knee-high to a Skwirt and you know how small a Skwirt is.'

'No,' said Echo, 'I don't.'

'Well, a Nutkin is smaller than a Pipling but bigger than an Antlet, and a Skwirt is half the size of the latter. Stand all three on top of each other and they would be as tall in relation to a dwarf as a chicken is to an elephant.'

'I see,' said Echo.

'Now that I've explained their relative sizes, perhaps I can get on with the story. Well, all Rootkins are alike. Equally big or equally small, equally kind, equally courageous, equally timid, equally this, equally that. And because they're all so alike, they need no names. They sprout from the floor of the Miniforest in springtime, precisely a dozen of them every year, and they're fairly long-lived unless they fall victim to an accident. Their job is to tend the Miniforest. They scarify the soil by raking it, lop off dead branches and milk greenflies – that sort of thing.'

Ghoolion clasped his hands together and cracked his knuckles with a grisly sound like twigs snapping, a habit Echo profoundly disliked.

'Our story begins', he went on, 'when a Rootkin who was busy weeding a clearing – a very small clearing far from the rest of his kind – came upon something protruding from the forest floor. It was a vessel with a cork in it.

'The Rootkin's curiosity was aroused, so he dug up the vessel and discovered it to be an earthenware bottle. Being smaller than a Rootkin,

the bottle could justifiably be called a small one, but since it almost came up to the Rootkin's shoulder, he thought: "My, what a big bottle! Looks like an antique or something – it's very old, anyway. If there's some kind of drink inside it, it's bound to taste awful."

'Gingerly, the Rootkin removed the cork and sniffed the neck of the bottle. As he did so, a cloud of evil-smelling fumes emerged from it. He thought at first that the drink inside had gone bad and was escaping in the form of a gas, but the cloud grew bigger and bigger and turned as red as a stream of molten lava flowing upwards into the sky. The air was rent by a yell that might have been uttered by a hundred Storm Demons. By the time it finally died away, leaving the Rootkin half dead with terror, the Miniforest was overshadowed by a hovering figure so tall that it almost reached the clouds: a blood-red ogre with evil black eyes and flames instead of hair. "Free!" it bellowed in a voice like thunder. "Free at last!"'

'Just a minute,' Echo cut in. 'You told me there wouldn't be any giants in this story.'

'True,' said Ghoolion. 'I must have misled you in order to heighten the effect of surprise. Shall I stop?'

'No, no,' cried Echo, 'go on!'

'Hm ...' said Ghoolion. 'The Rootkin naturally realised at once that he had released an Omnidestructive Ogre, and he was even more terrified than before – quite rightly so.

'"Free at long last!" yelled the giant. "Now I can take my revenge! I shall tear this planet to pieces like a scrap of paper! I shall set it ablaze with my flaming hair and poison it with my breath! My hatred has grown so great in the course of time that I won't be content to destroy this planet alone. No, I shall annihilate *all* the planets and extinguish *all* the suns and reduce the whole confounded universe to rubble and ashes! And then I shall hunt down time itself, which afflicted me so cruelly in my captivity, and torture it to death!"

'"Oh dear," thought the Rootkin, "how silly of me! What on earth am I to do now?"'

Ghoolion clutched his head and looked worried. 'He was in real trouble! How was he to handle the situation with a Rootkin's limited resources?'

'By using his wits?' Echo suggested.

'Exactly,' said Ghoolion. 'And that's just what he did. "If the giant got out of that bottle," he thought, "he'll fit into it again. I must persuade him to go back inside; then I'll cork the bottle and bury it as deep as possible in the forest."'

'Smart idea,' said Echo.

Ghoolion cleared his throat. 'The Rootkin turned to the giant. "Excuse me, Your Immensity ..." he said humbly.

'"I never excuse anyone!" the colossus bellowed. "What do you want before I kill you?"

'The Rootkin swallowed hard. "I was only wondering where you sprang from so suddenly."

'"From the bottle you opened, of course. And to show my gratitude, I'll kill you first."

'"Very kind of you," said the Rootkin. "The trouble is, I can't believe a giant as huge as you could fit into such a small bottle."

'"What?!" the giant thundered. "You don't believe it? Surely you saw me emerge from it?"

'"I'm afraid I didn't. I was so startled I shut my eyes."

'"So what? Don't you believe I was inside there?"

'"It's working!" the Rootkin told himself. Aloud, he said: "To be honest, I think it's quite impossible."

'"Shall I prove it to you?" asked the giant.

'"It's working, it's working!" thought the Rootkin. "Oh," he said, "you couldn't. How would you set about it?"

'"By diving back into that bottle like a bolt of lightning down a chimney. Well, shall I prove it to you or not?"

'"It's working, it's working, it's working!" thought the Rootkin. "You're welcome to try," he said, "but you'll never manage it."

'The Omnidestructive Ogre gave him a long look.

'"What *I* can't believe", he said at length, "is that you're actually trying on the oldest trick in the history of bottled giants. The hackneyed old you'll-never-get-back-inside-it number. I'm really worried about your mental state, you pinhead. Is that the best you can do?"

'The Rootkin gulped despite himself. He had genuinely thought it a clever and original idea.

'The giant roared with laughter. "This is the kind of bedtime story Omnidestructive Ogres have been told for millions of years. It's elementary: never court a danger you've just escaped! Only idiots get back into their bottles! Never try to impress creatures smaller than yourself! Omnidestructive Ogres are taught that at school, even before planetary annihilation."

'"All right," said the Rootkin, "I apologise for insulting your intelligence. But please, before you kill me, tear the planet to pieces, incinerate the universe and torture time to death, answer me one last question. After all, I did set you free."

'"Well," growled the giant, "what's the question?"

'"How is it", asked the Rootkin, trying to prick the giant's self-esteem, "that, although I'm so small and weak and you're so big and powerful, I can do something you can't?"

'"Like what?" the giant said scornfully.

'"Well, I could squeeze into that bottle. You couldn't."

'"Hang on!" the giant retorted. "I didn't say I *couldn't* squeeze into it, I just don't *want* to. Anyway, I won't believe *you* can fit inside until I've seen it."

'"All right," said the Rootkin. He went over to the bottle and, with the greatest difficulty, squeezed inside. "Well," he panted, "could *you* do that?"

'"No," said the giant, "not now you're inside there. There wouldn't be room for the two of us."

'So saying he corked the bottle and condemned the Rootkin to an agonising death by suffocation. But the Omnidestructive Ogre tore the world to pieces and reduced it to ashes with his flaming hair before embarking on an orgy of destruction throughout the universe. He extinguished sun after sun with his lethal breath until all that remained was the icy void of outer space, and that was where he tortured time to death.'

With a sigh, Ghoolion turned back to his microscope.

'Oh,' said Echo, 'the end was rather surprising.'

'Well, yes. That was a Zamonian story and it's traditional for Zamonian stories to end in tragedy. What did you expect? That good would triumph over evil and small over big and nice over nasty? That wouldn't be a proper bedtime story.'

'What I don't quite understand is what it has to do with alchemy.'

'The essential point is that it hasn't happened yet or we wouldn't be here now; the whole of the universe would have ceased to exist. That story tells the youthful alchemist that he bears an immense responsibility. If he investigates the smallest of things, he may discover something big – a source of energy more powerful than any we know. That being so, he should think carefully before unleashing it.'

'Yes,' said Echo, 'but if an alchemist spends his whole life searching for that source of energy and actually finds it one day, how will he be able to resist unleashing it?'

'By asking that question,' Ghoolion replied, 'you've put your paw on alchemy's eternally suppurating sore. It's a very real problem. Now, what would you say to a hearty breakfast?'

Moon Talk

Echo found it even harder than before to sleep off his heavy meals during the hot and sultry nights that followed. If he failed completely he would steal out on to the roof by way of the secret door in the laboratory, which was always open now, and through the Leathermousoleum, which was deserted because the vampire bats spent the nights out hunting.

Once up there, Echo would make straight for Theodore's abode in the hope of having a chat with the old Tuwituwu, if he wasn't busy flitting around the chimney system or hunting mice in the dungeons. Theodore was a considerably more interesting conversationalist than the taciturn Sheet. His wide range of interests embraced the history of Ghoolion's castle and the municipality of Malaisea, Zamonian biology, languages old and new, a smidgen of astronomy, jurisprudence, Uggliology, and just about anything else. However, his pet hate and principal object of study was Succubius Ghoolion, the Alchemaster himself.

'My scholarship is uniserval,' Theodore would say. 'Ask me a question, if you can bear to hear the answer.'

Echo was in one of the melancholy moods in which he gazed sadly up at the moon, which had lately been waxing far too fast for his taste. He and the earth's satellite had something in common in that respect – worse luck.

'How much do you know about the moon?' Echo asked, hoping to dispel his gloomy thoughts.

'Hm,' said Theodore. 'Pretty well everything. How far away do you think it is?'

'That's easy,' said Echo. 'About as far away as those mountains over there.'

The Tuwituwu gave him a long stare.

'What makes you say that?' he asked at length.

'The mountains are the most distant things I can see and the moon is hovering just above them, so it's as far away as the mountains.'

The Tuwituwu gave him another long stare. 'And that's your ostranomical opinion?'

'Well, I'm not a universal scholar like you, just a stupid Crat. All I know is what my mistress told me or read to me from her books, which weren't very big and had pictures of funny animals in them. Ghoolion is teaching me a lot about alchemy but nothing about astronomy. He prefers to investigate little things.'

'I see,' said Theodore. 'What if I told you that the moon is roughly twenty thousand times as far away from us as those mountains?'

'I'd think you were a crackpot. Nobody can see that far.'

Theodore groaned. 'Then we'll have to begin at the very beginning. The moon is the lecestial body closest to our planet. It revolves round the earth at an average tisdance of 385,080 kolimetres or 60.27 terrestrial radii every 29 days, 12 hours, 44 minutes and 11.5 seconds, simultaneously tarpicipating in the earth's relovutions round the sun. Thus its actual obrit through space is an ecipycloid, lying partly outside that of the earth, which always presents its hollow side to the sun. Since the extrencicity of its obrit is 0.05491, its tisdance from the earth varies between 407,110 and 356,650 kolimetres. Have you got that?'

'I doubt it,' Echo said with a laugh.

'Try to repeat what I said.'

'The moon is the celestial body closest to our planet. It revolves around the earth at an average distance of 385,080 kilometres or 60.27 terrestrial radii every 29 days, 12 hours, 44 minutes and 11.5 seconds, simultaneously participating in the earth's revolutions round the sun. Thus its actual orbit through space is an epicycloid, lying partly outside that of the earth, which always presents its hollow side to the sun. Since the eccentricity of its orbit is 0.05491, its distance from the earth varies between 407,110 and 356,650 kilometres.'

'You see?!' said Theodore.

'Well I'm damned!' Echo exclaimed, putting a paw to his mouth. 'Did I really memorise all that?'

'You can do far more than that. The pacacity of a Crat's brain is emornous. Now, how far away do you think those stars are? As far away from us as the moon, or are they nearer?'

'You mean those holes in the sky? The ones the man in the moon makes, so the sun can shine through from his bedroom behind it?'

Theodore uttered another groan. 'Did that come out of one of your mistress's books?'

Echo nodded eagerly.

'And you're also convinced there's a man in the moon?'

Echo put his head on one side. 'Shouldn't I be?' he asked cautiously.

'The moon possesses no atphosmere!' the Tuwituwu cried. 'There's no air up there! Your man in the moon would sucoffate!'

Echo thought hard. 'Then who made the holes in the sky?'

The Tuwituwu covered his single eye with one wing and raised the other in supplication. He struggled for words.

'You mean there isn't any man in the moon?' Echo asked anxiously.

'No!' said Theodore. 'There isn't a woman in the moon either, or a mooncalf! Or any Volcanic Dwarfs or Crater Dragons! The moon doesn't shine so nicely because it's made of silver sprinkled with diamond dust!'

'Really not?' said Echo. 'Why, then?'

'I can see we'll have to adopt a far more emelentary approach,' said Theodore. 'My goodness, where to start?'

Echo sighed. 'I know little enough about the world down here, but even less about the ones up there.'

'First the holes,' said Theodore. 'They aren't holes at all, they're stars – suns like ours, but much further away. Got that?'

'Suns,' said Echo. 'Got it.'

'Good. Those are what *exists* in the uniserve: suns, platens, gaxalies – everything one can see and measure. Everything that exists.'

'Everything that exists,' Echo repeated.

'And do you see what's in between the stars?' Theodore raised one wing and indicated the night sky with a sweeping gesture.

'The black stuff? Yes, I see it.'

'But it's nothing at all, so how can you see it?'

'I don't know …' Echo replied uncertainly. 'I just can.'

'Exactly. It's nothing, but you can see it just the same. That's what *might* exist in the uniserve – what *can't* be measured. There are lots of words for it. Fate. Love. Death …'

'Death …' Echo repeated darkly.

'But we won't bother about that for the moment. Let's begin by contrencating on what definitely exists in the uniserve – on light rather than darkness. On the stars.'

'Actually,' said Echo, 'I'm not all that interested in the stars. It's the moon that interests me.'

The Tuwituwu gave him a sidelong glance. 'Do you know why Crats are so scafinated by the moon? Especially by the full or Ugglian moon?'

'Why should the full moon be called the Ugglian moon?' Echo demanded. 'What do Ugglies have to do with the moon?'

'Nothing at all, properly speaking. It's just a bit of medieval nonsense that's survived until today. Strange things can happen when the moon is full, as you know. People do things they wouldn't normally do, and since it's always been the custom in Zamonia to blame the Ugglies for anything one doesn't want to be held responsible for, they're reputed to cast a spell over the moon when it's full. That's why it's called the Ugglian moon. And the Ugglian moon, in its turn, is reputed to cast a spell over people and make them do crazy things. In the Middle Ages you could do all kinds of things: set fire to your neighbour's house, paint his cow green and dance naked on your roof. As long as you did it when the moon was full, the Ugglies always got the blame.'

'To be honest,' said Echo, 'I sometimes get the feeling that the full moon casts a spell over *me.*'

'That brings us back to my original question. Why do you think Crats are so scafinated by the full moon?'

'I really don't know, but when it's full I always feel … well, so *crattish*, as I call it.'

'You feel particularly lively, you mean?'

'Yes, exactly. I hardly sleep at all and when I do I have such funny dreams. And get such funny feelings.'

'Funny dreams, funny feelings,' said Theodore. 'Well, well, that brings us to the subject of things that *might* exist, like the darkness between the stars. In this instance, love. Some people get bitten by it, others don't.'

'Love?' said Echo. That was something he had yet to learn about.

'You're still very young. You haven't reached buperty yet.'

'Buperty?'

'Well, how can I put it?' Theodore faltered for a moment. He seemed to have ventured too far. Echo still wasn't ready for this subject. 'Yes, well …' he said. 'Didn't your mistress enlighten you?'

'Enlighten me? About what?'

'Well, about *it.*'

'It? What's "it"?'

'I'm talking about love. About … oh dear, how can I put it?'

Theodore sensed that he was getting into dangerous waters, so he tried to cut this awkward conversation short. 'Well, it's all to do with Cratesses.' He heaved a sigh of relief, as if that said it all.

But Echo persisted. 'Cratesses?'

'Yes, female Crats.'

'You mean there's another kind of Crat?'

'Oh yes, certainly. Quite another kind. Tell me, do you really have no idea how you came into the world?'

'Yes, my mistress told me she found me in a clump of Cratmint.'

Theodore groaned. 'Oh dear, oh dear …'

'You mean she was lying to me?'

'Yes. No. Yes! I mean, er … Look, I won't go into all the giobolical details now, I'll simply give you a very avebbriated account of them, cencontrating on the bare essentials. All right?'

'All right.' Echo pricked up his ears.

'Well, it's like this. There aren't any Cratesses left here in Lamaisea, but there may still be a few over there beyond the hoziron, on the far side of the mountains. Where love is concerned, they'll have all the answers to your questions.'

'Then I'll never get to hear them,' Echo said sadly, looking up at the moon again. 'Ghoolion will slit my throat first.'

The Tuwituwu, who had been finding their conversation more and more embarrassing, flapped his wings and rose into the air.

'Nightfall!' he cried. 'Time to go hunting! As I already told you, I unfortunately have to ornagise my own meals.'

And he went into a nosedive.

Echo continued to sit on the roof for a long time. He surveyed the Blue Mountains on the horizon, whose peaks were being carved out of the darkness by the faint light of the moon. Did another kind of Crat really exist beyond them? One that could dispel the restlessness he always experienced when the moon was full? The old nightbird couldn't have expressed himself less clearly if he'd tried. Echo was feeling even more puzzled than before.

He looked up at the moon again and, although it was still far from full, he had an almost irresistible urge to utter a loud, piercing miaow.

Ghoolion's Torture Chamber

The feeling that overcame Echo whenever he watched Ghoolion cooking was a blend of amazement, fascination and disgust. Within his personal domain the Alchemaster was an omnipotent tyrant. Malaisea was his kingdom, the castle his stronghold, the laboratory his throne room – and the kitchen his torture chamber. The cleavers and boning knives, meat mallets, potato mashers and pans of boiling oil were his instruments of torture and execution, the foodstuffs his submissive slaves, who flung themselves into boiling water or on to a red-hot grill at his behest. Eggs waited humbly to be beheaded, poultry volunteered to be dismembered or spatchcocked, steaks to be beaten tender, lobsters to be boiled alive.

'Beat me!' cried the cream.

'Reduce me!' gasped the gravy.

'Drown me in dressing!' groaned the salad.

Ghoolion carved a joint or kneaded a lump of dough as if dissecting or throttling a living creature. Like an executioner, he hurried from one instrument of torture to another, from grill to chopping block, as if eager to scorch or scald or hack his victims to death. Tongues of fire licked greedily at his frying pans and ignited the hot oil. Yellow flames leapt high into the air, lighting up the Alchemaster in a dramatic fashion. Wind blew in through the open windows, plucking at the steam rising from his pots and pans and inflating his cloak. The old man's performance at the stove would have made a good circus act.

'Anyone who can't stand the heat', he called to Echo above the hiss of the flames, 'has no business in the kitchen!' He removed red-hot casseroles from the oven without gloves, dipped his fingers in boiling soup to taste it and scooped fried potatoes out of seething fat with his bare hands.

'Of course I feel the pain,' he said when he noticed Echo's look of horror. 'I don't respect it, that's all.'

When he hurried from one part of the kitchen to another – hurried, mark you, not dashed – his movements were economical and unerring. Nothing ever got burnt or boiled over. At the Restaurant Ghoolion, the

Alchemaster was head chef, sauce chef, waiter, wine waiter and dishwasher all rolled up into one. No tasks were beneath his dignity. He performed them all with the same ceremonious care and attention. When he wielded a kitchen knife his fast-moving hands were a blur. One heard the machine-gun burst of the blade on the chopping board and there lay a heap of gossamer-thin onion rings, a mound of finely chopped chives or a consummate tuna tartare. He carved a joint of roast

beef with the unruffled precision of a brain surgeon, so perfectly that no slice ever disintegrated. Without even looking, he flipped omelettes in the air as deftly as a fairground juggler. He tossed chopped herbs boldly into saucepans without dropping a single little thyme leaf. Echo saw him fillet cloves of garlic with a dissecting knife and a diamond-cutter's magnifying glass, or lather apricots with whipped cream and shave them with a cut-throat razor because he considered their furry skins too bristly. He also witnessed an occasion when Ghoolion skewered a grain of caviar with a red-hot needle and kebabbed it under the microscope.

The discipline prevailing in Ghoolion's kitchen was worthy of a Bookholmian fire station, its precision of a watchmaker's workshop and its hygiene of an operating theatre. The gleaming knives were sterilised and restored to razor-edged sharpness every day. Every meat fork, egg whisk and copper kettle was burnished until it sparkled in the candlelight. The ready-peeled potatoes in the saucepan were as alike as peas in a pod, the shallots chopped into cubes of exactly equal size, the

spice jars always well filled and smartly aligned like toy soldiers on parade. As for eating off the floor, in Ghoolion's kitchen one really could have engaged in that proverbial activity without encountering a single bacterium. In those surroundings, any pathogen would have felt like a lone flea marooned on an alien planet impregnated with insecticide. The flagstones were sealed with floor polish. Sink, chopping boards, working surfaces – every cubic centimetre of the kitchen was regularly scrubbed with acetic acid and sal ammoniac. Ghoolion was afflicted with the same restlessness in his kitchen as he was in his laboratory. He blended herbs, pounded peppercorns in the mortar, mixed salad dressings, made stock from bones, salted butter, whipped cream, skimmed gravy or pickled eggs for future consumption. He never allowed himself a break.

When Ghoolion was engaged in preparing a menu his movements became so fluid that they acquired a balletic quality. The noises that surrounded him – the gurgling song of soup, the crackle of meat roasting in the oven, the hiss of flames and hot fat – combined with his clattering footsteps to produce a culinary symphony that made the saucepan lids dance to its melodic rhythms.

What surprised Echo, however, was that he very seldom saw the Alchemaster eat anything. The most Ghoolion ever did was to take a bite out of an apple or a slice of stale bread. He never even tasted the dishes he served his lodger and there wasn't an ounce of fat on him. It was as if he denied himself the substance he coveted from other living creatures.

On the other hand he took a theoretical interest in every kind of food and its preparation. He was a walking encyclopedia when it came to recipes, cooking times, vitamin content, carving methods, food preservation, knife care, seasoning, marinating, blending or macerating. He was never too busy shuttling back and forth between stove and table to entertain Echo with some informative lecture. The little Crat learnt that, in addition to being fried, grilled or roasted, food could be ghoolionised or zamoniated, and that dressing a fowl did not mean dolling it up but using kitchen string to truss it into a shape suitable for roasting in the oven. Echo learnt all about the care of copper vessels, the great art of soufflé-making and Early Zamonian pressure-cooking techniques. No food was so uninteresting, no subject so dry or abstruse that Ghoolion could not strike some entertaining sparks from it. And he had recorded all this knowledge, all his notes, all his ideas on gourmandism and the art of cooking, by jotting them down in a big book with a smoked Marsh Hogskin cover. Whenever Echo wasn't watching the Alchemaster at work in the kitchen, he liked to look through that wonderful culinary tome, which abounded in the most mouth-watering recipes.

One evening – the two of them were standing in front of a kitchen cupboard – Ghoolion suddenly laid aside the egg he was peeling. Unlocking the door, he invited Echo to look inside the cupboard and tell him what it contained. Echo did as he was bidden, but all he could see was a dusty jumble of unidentifiable kitchen utensils.

'No idea,' said Echo. 'Just junk of some kind.'

'That', Ghoolion said in a voice quivering with rage, 'is my dungeon for useless kitchen utensils. There's one such in every kitchen worthy of the name. Its inmates are kept there like especially dangerous patients in a mental institution.'

He reached into the cupboard and brought out an odd-looking implement.

'What cook', he cried, 'does *not* possess such a gadget, which can sculpt a radish into a miniature rose? I acquired it at a fair in one of those moments of mental derangement when life without a miniature-rose-cutting gadget seems unimaginable.'

He hurled the thing back into the darkness and brought out another.

'Or this here, which enables one to cut potatoes into spirals five yards long! Or this, a press for juicing turnips! Or this, a frying pan for producing rectangular omelettes!'

Ghoolion took gadget after gadget from the cupboard and held them under Echo's nose, glaring at them angrily.

'What induced me to buy all these? What can one do with potato spirals long enough to decorate a banqueting hall? What demented voice convinced me in a whisper that I might some day be visited by guests with an insatiable hankering for turnip juice, rectangular omelettes and potatoes five yards long?'

He hurled the gadgets back into their dungeon with a look of disgust. Dust went billowing into the air and Echo sneezed involuntarily.

'Why, I ask myself, don't I simply chuck them all on to the rubbish dump? I'll tell you that too. I keep them for one reason alone: revenge! I keep them just as medieval princes kept their enemies on starvation rations. A quick death on a rubbish dump would be too merciful. No, let them languish in a gloomy dungeon, condemned to everlasting inactivity. That's the only condign punishment for a rectangular omelette pan!'

So saying, Ghoolion slammed the cupboard door and turned the key three times in the lock. Then he went on cooking as if nothing had happened.

From that day on, Echo regarded the kitchen cupboard – and the bottommost compartment in particular – with new eyes. No longer a cupboard, it was a medieval fortress whose dungeon harboured a terrible secret. He often slunk past it, and when all was quiet he would put his ear to the door and listen. And he sometimes fancied he could actually hear Ghoolion's pitiful captives whimpering for mercy – pleading to be allowed to rust away on a rubbish dump.

A Legal Consultation

Having now been Ghoolion's guest for quite some time, Echo felt so at home in the Alchemaster's castle that it never even occurred to him to leave it. Either he was far too busy eating, drinking and indulging in long, digestive siestas, or he was watching Ghoolion's alchemical and culinary experiments. He didn't even have time for a stroll in the town, for the ancient castle itself afforded plenty of scope for long and interesting excursions.

It was only when he was sitting up on the roof with Theodore, surveying the wide expanse of countryside below, that he sometimes yearned to explore the mysterious regions beyond the mountains, where lived the other kind of Crat to which the Tuwituwu had alluded in such a cryptic undertone.

'You recently said that contracts were made to be broken,' Echo reminded him during one of their conspiratorial get togethers. 'What exactly did you mean?'

Theodore lethargically raised his single eyelid. 'What I said,' he replied.

'But breaking a contract would be illegal, wouldn't it?'

'Of course, but you have to make up your mind which is worse: the fate that awaits you if you abide by it or the penalty you'll incur if you break it.'

'That's just what's on my mind,' said Echo. 'The fate that awaits me if I abide by the contract is to have my throat cut.'

'That strikes me as an inapprapriote reward for peeking an agreement,' the Tuwituwu growled. 'It's tosipively unjust. Too unjust for almost any crime I can think of.'

'Still, I wonder what legal penalty I'd incur if I broke my contract with Ghoolion. Might it be equally harsh?'

'Hm,' said Theodore, 'I can give you a pretty precise answer to that. I'm something of an expert on prurisjudence, as you know. There's a precedent where Alchemasters and Crats are concerned – a case that was tried in Baysville two hundred and fifty years ago. A Crat had cantrocted with an Alchemaster to keep his house free from mice for the rest of his life, but the said Crat vedeloped an allergy to mice and was unable to filful his ogligations. The Alchemaster hauled him before the court. Alchemasters tend to be rather tiligious, I'm afraid.'

'Was this a comparable case?' Echo asked.

'You could say that. Similar charge: breach of cantroct. The fact that your life is at stake would be a timigating factor, I'm sure, and the laws have been relaxed a bit in the last two hundred and fifty years. I don't even know if what Ghoolion expects of you is legal these days.'

'How did that old case turn out?'

'The Crat lost.'

'I guessed as much! What was he sentenced to?'

'A week in a cage in a home for strays. On bread and water.'

'Is that all? Only a week?'

'He had to share the cage with a mastiff.'

'Oh ...' said Echo.

'But the good news is: the Crat survived. He lost an ear, one leg and his tail, but he lived to a ripe old age. And as I said, it was a long time ago. Barbaric customs veprailed in those days – they were largely resbonsiple for mecidating your breed. And in your case timigating factors would come into play – for instance, the weakened condition in which you signed the cantroct, possibly even mental disequibilrium. I reckon you could well be acquitted – in fact, I strongly doubt if there's a judge today who wouldn't misdiss the case out of hand.'

'*Now* you tell me?!' Echo exclaimed. 'So what am I doing here? Why don't I simply make a run for it?'

Theodore spread his wings. 'You're here to fill your belly, I assume. You're boviously enjoying your food.'

Echo made a sheepish gesture. 'Yes, yes, I know. I've put on a bit of weight – no need to keep harping on it.'

'If you want to get out of here somehow, you'd better remain in shape. There may come a time when you need to be feet on your fast and in good condition. The cantroct doesn't say you have to eat everything Ghoolion puts in front of you, does it?'

'No,' Echo conceded more sheepishly still.

'Well, then. Chew a few herbs. Avoid greasy foods, eat wholesome salads. I myself am not the slimmest of birds, but at least I stick to a labanced diet. For instance, I always have a getevarian breakfast: a juniper berry, a few blades of grass, a hazelnut and three wild strawberries. A healthy start to the day does my gidestive sestym good.'

'I'll make a note of that,' Echo promised.

'But where were we?' said Theodore. 'You asked me why you don't simply make a run for it – why you don't let the cantroct go hang and disappear into the blue?'

'Exactly. What's to stop me?'

'You could always try,' the Tuwituwu said in a low voice.

'What do you mean, try? What would be so difficult about it? Ghoolion doesn't keep me under lock and key. I could run off any time he's otherwise engaged.'

'So try it.'

'Why say that in such a funny tone of voice?'

'Try it and the best of luck to you.'

'I mean, what could he do?' Echo demanded. 'He couldn't put a spell on me or anything, he's just an alchemist. I don't know why everyone's so dead scared of him. I may have gained a pound or two, but I'm still faster on my feet than him – faster than anyone else in Malaisea.'

'Then you definitely ought to try it. You have my blessing.'

'I'll sneak off under cover of darkness, then head across the mountains.'

'So give the mountains my regards.'

Echo stared at Theodore suspiciously. 'There's that funny tone of voice again,' he said.

'All I'm saying is', Theodore replied, 'Ghoolion has ways and means of trusfrating other people's plans. Of course, that doesn't mean you should leave any turn unstoned.'

'I'm going to run away,' Echo said defiantly. 'Let's see what happens then.'

'You must do what you can't avoid doing,' said Theodore and heaved a big sigh. His watery gaze lingered on Echo until the little Crat grew uncomfortable. 'But you must sometimes avoid doing what you can't do,' he added enigmatically.

The Wine Tasting

The first thing Echo noticed when he entered the kitchen that evening was an array of bottles, glasses and bowls on the table. Equally unusual was the fact that the stove wasn't in use and no steaming dishes were in evidence, just some bread and a wooden board bearing an assortment of cheeses. He also registered the fact that Ghoolion's high cheekbones were faintly flushed in a way that made him look a trifle less ghostly.

'I'm now going to improve your education,' said Ghoolion. He spoke somewhat more loudly than usual – more slowly, too, as if he found talking more of an effort today. 'If we're to make a gourmet of you, you must also learn something about the noblest of all beverages.' He picked up an open bottle and poured some red liquid into one of seven cut-glass bowls standing on the table. Then he took a second bottle and poured some yellow liquid into another bowl.

Echo jumped up on the table and sniffed the liquid inquisitively. 'I've never drunk any of this stuff before,' he said. 'I don't even know if it'll agree with me.'

'Crats have two livers,' said Ghoolion. 'It'll agree with you, never fear.' He went on filling the bowls with liquid, some red, some yellow.

'What kind of juice is this?' Echo enquired. 'My mistress never drank any. Why is some pale and some dark?'

'This is wine,' Ghoolion said solemnly. 'Wine is drinkable sunlight. It's the most glorious summer's day imaginable, captured in a bottle. Wine can be a melody in a cut-glass goblet, but it can also be a cacophony in a dirty tumbler, or a rainy autumn night, or a funeral march that scorches your tongue.'

Wine could evidently be quite a lot of things, Echo reflected.

'Wine', said Ghoolion, 'can provide you with the inspiration of a lifetime – or rob you of your wits completely. Where wine is concerned, there's only one thing to be said about it with any certainty.'

'Which is?'

'The better the wine, the more it costs!' Ghoolion guffawed at his own little joke. 'Right, let's get on with the tasting.'

Whatever this special kind of juice was, Ghoolion had certainly sampled some. Furthermore, it seemed to have wrought a change in him, whether for better or worse, Echo still couldn't tell. There was something about the Alchemaster's manner that was thoroughly out of keeping with his usual grim composure.

Ghoolion filled a glass with red wine and held it up to the light.

'First,' he cried, 'use your eyes!'

He held the glass close to his face, shut his left eye and stared at it with his right.

'You taste with your eyes as well as your palate,' he said. 'Is the wine red or white? The connoisseur can tell whether he's dealing with a red wine or a white wine. As a general rule, if the wine is translucent and pale gold in colour, it may be a white wine, but if it's red and inky and you can't see through it, the chances are that it's a red wine. If, on the other hand, it's pink and translucent, it's a rosé – the hermaphrodite among wines.'

At the moment, wine seemed to be having a favourable effect on the Alchemaster. For the first time ever, he didn't appear to be taking what he was saying in Echo's presence entirely seriously.

Echo sniffed the wine in the first little bowl. It was dark red and smelt intoxicating. He stuck his tongue in it, intending to lap up a mouthful, then recoiled indignantly.

'Ugh!' he said, pulling a face.

'What's the matter?' Ghoolion asked.

'It tastes funny. So sour.'

'Sour be damned! You'll soon get used to it. The first sip of wine never tastes nice. Perseverance, that's the essential thing. Get it down you! Appetite comes with eating and it's the same with drinking.'

Echo took a few reluctant sips. Sewer Dragon's knilch had also tasted nasty at first, but then … He was growing warm, first in the tummy, then in the head. It was a nice feeling. Obediently, he lapped up the rest of the bowl.

'Secondly the nose.' Ghoolion stuck his long, pointed nose in the glass and sniffed with relish. 'The wine is now being olfactorily analysed. Aaah! Mm! Does it smell of peach blossom wafted through an olive grove by the breeze in springtime? Of a freshly bisected grapefruit? Or of currant buns and vanilla cream, like this one? If your mistress never touched a drop of wine she was missing something, don't you agree?'

'Absolutely!' said Echo, who was now on his second bowl. The wine had already ceased to taste sour. This one had a rather fruity quality, like the sweet acidity of a ripe raspberry. His ears were also getting warm now.

'Well,' asked Ghoolion, 'does that taste better?'

'It tashtsh lovely!' Echo said. Tashtsh? Had he said 'tashtsh'?

Ghoolion knocked back his wine and promptly poured himself another glass from a different bottle. He plunged his nose in it and inhaled, only to remove it quickly with a grimace of indignation.

'Or does it smell like a worm-eaten carpenter's bench? Like a dishcloth soaked in sour milk? Like the sock of a soldier suffering from athlete's foot? Or, as this disastrous purchase does, like a dead lemming's sweaty armpit? The secondary aromas have been completely destroyed – a sign of poor fermentation. Away with it!'

He flung the glass casually over his shoulder, smashing it on the flagstones.

Echo marvelled at the Alchemaster's growing exuberance. The old man had never behaved with such abandon before.

'Shecondary aromash?' said Echo. It puzzled him that so many of the words he uttered seemed to stick to his tongue.

'Primary aromas are the intrinsic scents of the grape,' Ghoolion pontificated. 'Secondary aromas develop in the course of fermentation and tertiary aromas during development in the cask. They combine to form the wine's bouquet.'

So wine had a bunch of flowers in it too, thought Echo. It really was a versatile drink. The more of the red juice he lapped up, the more pervaded he became by a feeling of inner serenity and relaxation agreeably reminiscent of bedtime. Except that he didn't feel like going to sleep, he wanted to stay awake.

'Now,' said Ghoolion, 'we come to the ear.' He picked up another glass, eyed the labels of the bottles on the table with a judicial expression and helped himself to an exceptionally dark red.

'Wine confides its most intimate secrets to the true wine expert,' he whispered, tapping the glass with a fingernail. A high-pitched note rang out. Ghoolion held the glass close to his ear and listened intently.

'This one comes from Grapefields, the biggest wine-growing area in Zamonia. More precisely, from a vineyard with a sinister local reputation.'

'Did the wine tell you all that?' Echo listened to one of his bowls but couldn't hear a thing.

'That and more besides!' whispered Ghoolion. 'This wine knows some dark secrets – bad, bad things. Its memories go back many hundreds of years. It's said to be related to the legendary Comet Wine.'*

He clamped the glass even harder to his ear. 'Listen, listen!' he cried. 'The depths of the vineyard from which it came are privy to a terrible secret.'

Echo edged so close to the edge of the table that he nearly fell off. His sense of balance wasn't as good as usual. He retreated a step and pricked up his ears.

---

* See the chapter entitled 'The Trombophone Concert' on p. 114 of Optimus Yarnspinner's *The City of Dreaming Books*. [Tr.]

'For a long time,' Ghoolion went on in a low voice, 'people in the locality had been wondering where so many grape-pickers disappeared to. No sooner had they started work than they seemed to vanish into thin air. Dozens of them went missing within a few years. They were reputed to be victims of the Ghastly Grappler, a cross between a plant and a predator, which was said to prowl the vineyard at dusk and pounce on defenceless grape-pickers. Half-filled baskets of grapes would sometimes be found, but never a trace of the workers themselves. So the local villagers tried to capture the Grappler. They set werewolf traps, dug pits lined with sharpened stakes and sent armed men to patrol the vineyard at dusk. All the caves in the neighbourhood were searched, but no Ghastly Grappler was sighted and no dead bodies came to light. A few Ugglies were burnt at the stake – that glorious tradition still prevailed in those days! – but to just as little avail. The grape-pickers continued to vanish without a trace.'

Ghoolion fell silent.

'Well?' Echo said eagerly.

'Well nothing. End of story.'

'But the secret? The terrible secret?'

'One moment,' said Ghoolion, fending off the question with an upraised hand. He listened to the glass some more. 'The wine is just coming to that.'

He preserved a long silence, nodding gravely from time to time, then stiffened abruptly.

'No!' he exclaimed.

'What is it?' Echo gasped, shuffling excitedly from paw to paw. 'What did it say? What is it?'

Ghoolion held a hand over his mouth, seemingly frozen with horror.

'I don't know if I should tell you,' he said eventually. 'It might give you nightmares.'

'Oh, go on!' Echo entreated. 'Tell me, please!'

'Very well, but only at your express request. Don't say I didn't warn you – it isn't a pretty story.'

Ghoolion laid the glass aside and made no move to drink its contents.

'Well,' he said at length, 'the secret of the accursed vineyard is known only to this wine here, because the vines that produced it were the vineyard's memory. Its brain. Its nervous system. The vines themselves couldn't see or hear a thing, but their grapes could sense every movement and their roots probed the bowels of the vineyard. They felt the hands of the workers who relieved them of the weight of the grapes they bore. They knew every earthworm in the soil. They recognised the touch of the winegrower who regularly stroked their leaves to check them for parasites and their roots drank the falling rain. Then, one day, they found they were drinking blood.'

'Blood?' said Echo.

'Yes, blood. The vineyard was drenched in the stuff and strange things were happening to the grapes. Where they had once been harvested by busy hands, a sudden struggle took place.'

'A struggle? What sort of struggle?'

'Well … Bodies went crashing into the vines and hands clutched desperately at their tendrils. Although the vines couldn't see or hear this, they could sense that someone was being murdered in the immediate vicinity of their foliage. Then came the blood – gallons of it.'

With a theatrical gesture, Ghoolion turned his back on Echo.

'This went on for years. First a struggle, then blood seeping into the soil, then months of inactivity, then another struggle and more blood. Meanwhile the vines continued to do their vegetal duty. They grew, put out tendrils, filled their grapes with juice and drank rain – or, sometimes, blood. And their roots probed deeper and deeper into the soil until, one day, they came into contact with what had hitherto been the vineyard's terrible secret.'

Ghoolion turned round again. His gaze was fixed and staring.

'The vineyard harboured dozens of corpses in various stages of decomposition. The murdered grape-pickers had been buried there side by side.'

Echo sat down on his haunches. He was feeling queasy now.

'The vines thought long and hard about this frightful mystery until another fight broke out in their midst. A pair of hands clutched their leaves and the vines recognised their owner as a grape-picker who had often relieved them of overweight grapes in the past. The hands clung on at first with a strength born of despair, then relaxed their grip and went limp. Another grape-picker had bitten the dust! Moments later a different hand took hold of the same bunch of leaves and the vines recognised it as the winegrower's big, calloused paw. Everything fell into place: it was the winegrower, the owner of the vineyard himself, who was going around murdering people. Shortly afterwards, when blood began to seep into the soil, the vines guessed his motive: he was fertilising his vineyard with blood and decaying bodies to improve its yield.'

Echo was beside himself with excitement. 'Go on!' he exclaimed. 'What happened then?'

'Well,' Ghoolion said grimly, 'what were the vines to do? They were just harmless plants. All they did was produce grapes, put out tendrils and leaves and climb up stakes, but they brooded incessantly on ways of remedying the situation. They alone knew the true circumstances and might be able to end the cycle of violence and blood, because the murders continued unabated – in fact, they occurred at ever shorter intervals.'

Echo shut his eyes, trying to picture the vineyard, but his head swam and he quickly opened them again.

'The more murders the winegrower committed, and the more he manured the soil with blood, the more clearly the vines sensed the changes taking place inside them. They grew faster and became more resistant to disease. Much to the satisfaction of their murderous owner, they produced ever more, ever finer and sweeter grapes. Their tendrils became ever stronger, their leaves ever bigger, their wine ever better and more abundant. Meanwhile, the winegrower became ever richer. Insane though it was, his scheme was working, thanks to the blood of the murdered grape-pickers pulsating inside his vines. What the murderer never guessed, however, was that his victims' thirst for revenge was also growing stronger by the day. The vines now sprawled across the hillside like a jungle. Bigger and bigger stakes had had to be driven into the ground to keep pace with their growth, yet they continued to grow, sending their tendrils spiralling into the air and their roots burrowing into the soil. The paths between the rows became so overgrown that the workers had to part the foliage with their hands in order to make their way along them. Hidden from view in this way, the murderer found it even easier to kill and bury his victims. The workforce of his accursed vineyard, from which grape-pickers disappeared almost weekly, was now limited to the poorest of the poor, who had no alternative.'

Ghoolion broke off for a moment. He seemed to be summoning up the strength to recount some even more grisly details.

'One night the winegrower went on the prowl again. He was the last person anyone would have suspected – his public complaints about the loss of his workers were all too believable. No one guessed the terrible connection between their disappearance and the vines' exceptional growth. It was dusk when he entered the vineyard and he rejoiced to see that his vines were more luxuriant than ever. He picked a grape and tasted it. It was plump and sweet, and twice the size of a normal grape. Then he stroked a leaf to see if it was free from disease. The vine seemed to recoil as he touched it, but he dismissed the notion; no plant could move quicker than the eye can see. He lifted a few more leaves to see if the movement had been occasioned by some insect, but there was nothing there.'

Ghoolion had now begun to pace up and down in front of Echo's table.

'Satisfied, the murderer made his way further into the vineyard. The light was fading fast as he went in search of another victim. He soon came upon one: a young woman picking grapes higher up the slope, far enough from the rest for him to be able to go about his bloody business undisturbed. She gave a start when he materialised beside her, but was reassured to see that it was only her employer and went on working. The winegrower tore off some tendrils and twisted them together to form a noose – an ideal murder weapon that could simply be tossed into the undergrowth when the deed was done. Just then, he caught his foot in the nearest vine and tugged at it impatiently in an attempt to free himself.

'But the tendrils tightened about his ankles, first one, then the other. Realising that something was amiss, he uttered a terrified cry. The grape-picker straightened up in alarm. One look at the noose in her employer's hands told her that he was the murderer, so she took to her heels. The winegrower tried to follow her, but the tendrils secured him to the ground like iron chains. The vine had now encircled his wrists, arms and legs, and one particularly strong tendril was winding itself about his neck. The ground beneath him opened like a grave and roots came snaking out of it. A big vine leaf plastered itself to the murderer's mouth, smothering his cries. He was dragged into the depths. Earth and leaves, pebbles and twigs came raining down, roots wrapped themselves round him like a cocoon.

'And then the murderer's victims made their appearance. They emerged from the ground, which was heaving like a storm-tossed sea, in various stages of decomposition. Thanks to the way in which the roots made the corpses rise and fall and their limbs swing to and fro, they looked as if they'd been restored to life. The winegrower was still conscious when the dead, with him as their prey, buried themselves in the ground once more. Everything grew darker and darker, until, in the end, his eyes became clogged with blood-soaked soil and he breathed his last.'

Ghoolion fell silent.

'Did the wine tell you all that?' asked Echo.

The Alchemaster reached for the glass he'd laid aside and held it up.

'Yes, it did,' he replied. 'It's a very talkative wine. The story it told was pretty gruesome, I know, but that's no reflection on the wine itself.'

So saying, he drained the glass at a gulp. Echo went over to one of his bowls and refreshed himself likewise. The queasy sensation that had overcome him subsided at once.

'And now,' Ghoolion said brightly, 'the next stage in our tasting.' He poured himself a glass of white wine.

'You mean there's more?' said Echo.

'Yes indeed. We're now going to establish telepathic contact with the wine and extract its every last secret. What of its philosophical qualities?

Is it optimistic or pessimistic? Is it lively or dull? Does drinking it render you exuberantly cheerful or lugubriously introspective? Is it the kind of wine that breeds ideas notable for their precision and razor-sharp logic, or brutish instinctive urges that could culminate in a tavern brawl? Only one thing can answer that question, and that's the wine's most volatile ingredient: its spirit. In other words its alcoholic content.'

Ghoolion's eyes clouded over and his shoulders drooped a little. He had returned to reality and his favourite field of study: volatile substances. Echo was afraid he might go back to work at once.

Instead, he merely drained his glass. 'Aaah!' he said. 'A definite optimist, this wine! A free-thinking aesthete – one wouldn't mind having a few cases of it in one's cellar.' He hurled his glass into the fireplace, where it shattered.

'He's really got the bit between his teeth,' thought Echo and he treated himself to another little bowl of wine. His feeling of gaiety was verging on the euphoric.

Ghoolion poured himself such a generous glass of dark red wine that it overflowed.

'And now,' he cried, 'the tasting proper!'

Seemingly quite unworried by the amount of red liquid that was trickling down his chin and into his collar, Ghoolion took an enormous swig and held it in his mouth. He chewed it for an unconscionable length of time before gulping it down and draining the rest of the glass.

'Aaaaah! Precocious, but already full of character! A stout backbone of walnuts and strawberries. Playful, but in an earthy, honest way. A trace of liquorice lingers on the uvula before it plumbs the depths of the oesophagus. A note of maturity reminiscent of an old violin playing a familiar lullaby. The inevitable peach flavours that lurk in every red, but crisply coated in biscuit crumbs. I detect candle grease. Virgin snow. Gingerbread. Lack of finesse offset by a youthful acidity which is somewhat rough around the edges but well nailed down. I also get young leather, rusty iron, damp carpets, glazier's putty, pine needles. Roast goose, too, and my late grandmother's blackberry tart. Full-bodied, but I'd describe it as plump rather than fat, with excessively large feet. The finish, which is as broad as it's long, like the note of an ancient funeral bell tolling in the subterranean vaults of a catacomb inhabited by seven hundred naked, starving dwarfs, is lubricated by a soupçon of olive oil.'

Ghoolion hurled that glass, too, into the fire. Then, clearly yielding to a spontaneous impulse, he took a Horrificomonica from a shelf. Stationing himself at one of the open windows, he applied his bloodless lips to the instrument and proceeded to blow a few experimental notes. The kitchen was filled with their plaintive sound.

Echo braced himself. The evening was threatening to take an unpleasant turn. He had been compelled to endure many of the Alchemaster's musical recitals down in the town, and they'd been almost intolerable even at that distance. Now that he was having to submit to one at close range, he feared for his sanity.

But his fears were dispelled once the first few proper notes rang out. They were so pure, so beautiful and melodious, that it was hard to believe a Horrificomonica could produce them. The sounds Ghoolion coaxed from his instrument were more like those made by a flute; in fact, many were reminiscent of a harp. Echo started to caper around on the tabletop – he simply couldn't help it. Ghoolion also began to dance, beating out the rhythm with his iron-shod feet.

Unable to restrain himself any longer, Echo leapt off the table and joined in the Alchemaster's dance. He cavorted across the kitchen more wildly and uninhibitedly than he had ever done in his life. Ghoolion's playing became ever louder, his zapateado ever faster. Meanwhile, Echo went bouncing over the tables and benches like a rubber ball. They continued to dance their frantic, seemingly indefatigable tarantella until, all of a sudden, Ghoolion stopped playing and flopped down on a chair, utterly exhausted. Echo, too, noticed that he'd overdone it. He stretched out on the floor, rolled over on his back and stared at the ceiling. Oddly enough, the room began to rotate.

After a short breather Ghoolion sprang to his feet, gave him a glassy stare and lurched towards the door.

'Hey, where you going, Mashter?' Echo said thickly. 'We were jusht getting into the shwing of thingsh.'

'Even the most sociable wine connoisseur has to perform one part of every tasting by himself,' Ghoolion called over his shoulder.

'You mean there'sh another part?' asked Echo.

'Yes,' the Alchemaster said hoarsely, 'the passing of water!' And he disappeared through the kitchen door with his cloak billowing out behind him.

Echo continued to lie there, grinning foolishly to himself and listening to Ghoolion's hoarse laughter. The old devil doesn't seem such a bad sort, he thought as his eyes closed and he lapsed into a tipsy torpor filled with dreams as sweet as ripe grapes.

The Tree of Nutledge

Echo found it an effort to open his bleary eyes. When he finally ungummed them, Ghoolion was standing over him, staring down with a face devoid of expression. Bright early morning sunlight was streaming in through the kitchen windows. As motionless as if he'd been struck by a bolt from the blue, the Alchemaster resembled one of his own stuffed mummies. Roused at last by this sinister sight, Echo rolled over on his side – and promptly regretted it. He had spent all night lying on his back, just the way he'd gone to sleep, and his muscular reaction to this sudden movement was painful in the extreme. Laboriously, he scrambled to his feet.

'I take it you aren't feeling too much like food at present,' Ghoolion said coldly. He had reverted to his role as a forbidding Alchemaster and looked as if their binge had left him entirely unaffected.

'That's why I've prepared you only a frugal breakfast,' he went on. 'I trust that's acceptable.'

'Absolutely,' Echo grunted. The kitchen floor seemed to sway beneath his paws as he strove to get his bearings. 'I'm not hungry.'

'Your current physical condition', said Ghoolion, 'is known as a monumental hangover.'

Echo didn't reply. The Alchemaster's voice sounded unpleasantly loud.

'Breakfast is on the table. If you regain your appetite in the course of the day, I advise you to go to the roof and help yourself. I have some important experiments to carry out – they won't wait.'

117

'That's all right,' Echo mumbled. He scrambled on to the table by way of a chair instead of jumping straight up in the usual way. All he found when he got there, grunting and groaning, was a bowl of warm milk and a plate containing three shrivelled nuts.

'Just nuts?' he said petulantly.

'They're no ordinary nuts,' Ghoolion replied. 'They come from the Tree of Nutledge.'

'Aha,' said Echo. He proceeded to munch the nuts without enthusiasm. They were dry and tasted of nothing, not even of nuts.

'The Tree of Nutledge grows in the Valley of Cogitating Eggs,' Ghoolion explained. 'That's an arid, desertlike depression in the neighbourhood of Demon Range. The highest temperatures in Zamonia can be recorded there – if you're crazy enough to cross it in summer. Towering into the sky in the very centre of the valley are a dozen enormous eggs. They're arranged in a perfect circle, and some astronomers claim that its coordinates would enable one to calculate the dimensions of the entire universe.

'Nobody knows how the eggs got there, but the long tracks they've left in the desert floor seem to indicate that they did so under their own power. On the other hand there's an ornithological theory that they were laid by giant birds and that one day something unpredictable will hatch out of them. They emit a humming sound suggestive of profound thought, hence their name.'

Echo gulped down the last dry morsel. 'But where do the nuts come in?' he asked.

'Well, it's assumed that the intellectual radiation given off by the Cogitating Eggs has endowed large tracts of the valley with intelligence. Some of the animals there can talk as well as you do. I own a cactus from the area – we play telepathic chess together and it wins every time! One day a nut landed on this intellectually fertile soil. No one knows where it came from. It may have been dropped by a traveller or jettisoned by a passing bird. It may also have been a tiny asteroid from outer space. All we know is, it must have rained heavily soon afterwards, because the nut germinated and took root in the desert floor, and from it grew the Tree of Nutledge. A tree with blood-red timber found nowhere else in the whole of Zamonia, it grew like mad, both upwards and outwards, and

put out snow-white leaves that make you very mentally alert if you
chew them. Druids have settled in the tree and live in its branches.
Naked, weather-beaten fellows with long hair and beards and demented
expressions, they climb like monkeys and screech like cockatoos. Their
consumption of nuts has rendered them so brilliantly clever that they've
lost the need for speech and communicate by telepathic means.
Scientists, artists and politicians from all over Zamonia make repeated
pilgrimages to the tree when confronted by knotty problems. They
write their questions on slips of paper and put them in wickerwork
baskets, which the Druids let down on strings. Having been hauled up
into the tree, the baskets are generally lowered soon afterwards,
complete with answers. Suggestions from the inhabitants of the Tree of
Nutledge were responsible for ending the Florinthian Choral Wars.

They also led to the invention of the Aeromorphic Barograph and helped to crack the Cucumbrian Cryptogram.'

'I see,' said Echo. 'So how do the nuts get here if the Druids eat them?'

'A few of them fall to the ground from time to time, and the Druids are too mentally preoccupied to pick them up. They're then collected and eaten by pilgrims, but a handful reach the open market. Each nut imparts a priceless insight.'

'The ones I've eaten have left me none the wiser,' Echo said sullenly.

'They don't work like that – they have a delayed reaction. Believe me, enlightenment will dawn in due course – it's guaranteed. It sometimes takes a day or two.'

'But that's like eating something which doesn't fill your belly till next week.'

'Exactly!' Ghoolion gathered his cloak around him and turned to go. 'You'll have to excuse me now, I've got things to do in the laboratory. There's more food waiting for you on the roof, as I said.'

Echo spent the rest of the morning roaming aimlessly around in a thoroughly bad mood. He took refuge in dark corners, waiting impatiently for his body to regain its equilibrium and his nagging headache to subside. Early that afternoon he made an excursion to the roof, where he ate a fish pie and some chocolate cake. Although he didn't really enjoy his meal, it made him so sleepy that he stretched out in a gutter and let the sun warm his fur until he dozed off. He slept for the rest of the afternoon and half the evening.

It was long after sunset when he awoke feeling thoroughly refreshed – almost newborn, in fact. He was in such a good mood that an audacious idea occurred to him: he decided to needle Ghoolion a little.

Shadow Ink

'I'm bored,' Echo said as he sauntered into the laboratory, sounding as supercilious as he could. He followed this up with a long, unabashed yawn.

The Alchemaster was engrossed in an experiment with a Leyden Manikin, which he had strapped to a wooden board. He was injecting green fluid into the alchemical creature's little body with a hypodermic syringe and watching its convulsions spellbound.

'Hm?' he said absently. 'What are you getting at?'

'I'm bored because you aren't fulfilling your contractual obligations,' Echo said in a resentful voice. 'In other words, you aren't doing enough to keep me entertained. Come on, amuse me.'

He instantly regretted his presumptuous demand, because the Alchemaster's face darkened, his eyes bulged alarmingly, and his eyebrows and the corners of his mouth began to quiver. He was obviously about to give Echo a tongue-lashing. The little Crat shrank away, expecting the worst, but Ghoolion suddenly stopped short. His body relaxed, his stormy expression vanished and an indulgent smile appeared on his face.

'You're absolutely right,' he said to Echo's great relief. 'I've been neglecting you. My work is so all-consuming, please forgive me. Your entertainment is an important part of our agreement, every single condition of which must be strictly fulfilled. What form of amusement did you have in mind?'

To crown it all, the Alchemaster performed a humble bow.

'Oh,' said Echo, completely thrown by this, 'I, er ... I don't know. What about a game of some kind?'

'A game, eh? Hm ...' Ghoolion was clearly thinking hard. 'I don't know many games, to be honest.'

'Never mind,' said Echo, 'It was just a –'

'Wait!' Ghoolion broke in. 'I *do* know a game! I'm really good at it, too.'

'Oh?' Echo said nervously. 'What is it?'

'Wait and see.' After a last, sceptical glance at the twitching manikin, Ghoolion hurried out of the laboratory.

'Come on!' he called. 'We need a dark room without any windows.'

Echo followed him reluctantly. What sort of game could the Alchemaster be 'really good' at? He doubted if he'd enjoy it and cursed his presumption. He could have spent a quiet evening on the roof, complete with herring salad, honey-flavoured milk and a stimulating chat with Theodore. But no, he'd insisted on needling Ghoolion into playing some mysterious game with him in 'a dark room without any windows'. Great!

Boots clattering and cloak flapping, Ghoolion went striding along the passage to the half-open door of an unlit chamber Echo had never entered before. In the dim light from the passage he made out a few crates of junk and a big, unlit stove with a broom leaning against it. That apart, the place was completely bare.

'This was going to be a storeroom, but I haven't fixed it up yet,' Ghoolion announced. 'It's ideal for our purposes because the walls are whitewashed and there aren't any windows. Wait here, I need to fetch a few things. I'll be back in no time.'

Apprehensively, Echo slunk into the mysterious-looking chamber while Ghoolion hurried off. What sort of games did you play in an empty room? If someone locked the door there would be no escape from this windowless dungeon. Echo was feeling more and more uneasy about the direction the evening was taking. He wondered whether to get out of the game by pretending to feel sick.

But Ghoolion soon returned, dragging a chair behind him. He put it in the middle of the room, produced an Anguish Candle and some matches from his cloak, stood the candle on the chair and lit it. It broke into subdued sobs at once.

'We need the flickering light of an Anguish Candle,' Ghoolion explained. 'Shadow Ink does the rest.'

He reached into his cloak again and brought out something that resembled a miniature tub of butter, which he deposited beside the candle.

Echo circled the chair, eyeing Ghoolion's paraphernalia with suspicion.

'There,' said the Alchemaster, hands on hips. 'We've got all we need to stage a proper shadow play.'

A shadow play! Echo felt highly relieved. Harmless childish fun. Birds fluttering on the wall, a rabbit waggling its ears, a dog turning into a swan – that sort of thing. His dislike of the empty chamber promptly subsided.

Ghoolion plunged his hands in the little tub and smeared them with the dark paste it contained. They were pitch-black within seconds.

'I call this substance Shadow Ink,' he said. 'I extracted it from the stones in the dungeon walls. I should explain that, when subjected to the incredibly low temperatures only an alchemical furnace can generate, those stones begin to melt and remain liquid in perpetuity. That's the origin of Shadow Ink. I strongly advise you never to touch the stuff, it's as cold as outer space! It took me quite a time to become inured to the pain.'

Yes, of course, thought Echo. A furnace that generates freezing temperatures, stones that melt when subjected to them. Coming from Ghoolion, the craziest things sounded plausible. It was probably common-or-garden ink. Or shoe polish.

Ghoolion looked at his hands. 'It's a very peculiar, unearthly pain, as if my hands had gone insane. Believe me, right now I'm tempted to cut them off.' His face betrayed no emotion whatsoever. 'But I've learnt to ignore the sensation.'

He turned his hands over in the candlelight, and Echo could now see that the black substance really was something special. He had never seen such utter blackness.

'You should bear in mind that the rock from which this ink is made was mined in the heart of the Gloomberg Mountains, which are said to have originated on the very outskirts of the universe. It may be a mineral from some alien planet, even from another dimension.'

Ghoolion bent over the Anguish Candle and proceeded to wring his hands in its fitful light. A big, amorphous shadow appeared on the opposite wall.

'Let's see,' he muttered. 'What shall we make? Something big? A rhinoceros? A Midgard Serpent? A mastodon?'

He waved his hands and stuck out a forefinger. The shadow sprouted a trunk and two huge ears.

'Oh no!' he sighed. 'Too ponderous. Too bulky. Let's have something light and airy.'

He positioned his hands crosswise and linked his thumbs. The silhouette of a butterfly took shape on the wall. He wiggled his hands and the butterfly started fluttering. 'Or is that too innocuous, eh? How about something bigger? Something with feathers, perhaps?'

He spread his fingers a trifle and held his hands nearer the flame. The shadow expanded and turned into a bird.

Echo was entranced. The old man really knew his stuff. The shadowy bird looked extremely lifelike.

Quick as a flash, Ghoolion removed his hands from the flame. To Echo's great astonishment, the bird's silhouette remained where it was. It might have been painted on the wall.

'Hey!' he exclaimed. 'How did you do that?'

'Me?' Ghoolion grinned. 'I did nothing, that's the Shadow Ink.' He clicked his pitch-black fingers three times. 'Fly, bird!' he called. 'Fly!'

The shadow started to quiver like a puddle ruffled by the wind. Then the bird began to flap its wings and fly back and forth along the whitewashed wall. Echo could even hear the sound of its wingbeats.

'That's incredible!' he gasped. 'It's magic!'

'Not magic,' Ghoolion retorted, 'alchemy. Alchemy of the first order.'

He clapped his hands twice and the bird landed on the mantelpiece, where it started to twitter and warble like a nightingale in love.

'What kind of bird is it?' Echo asked.

'Hm,' said Ghoolion, 'I don't really know. You decide. It's a nightingale at present, but would you sooner have a seagull?

He clicked his fingers and the shadow disintegrated into black streaks. They reassembled themselves into the shape of a powerful seabird with a hooked beak. The seagull emitted an avid screech.

'Oh no!' he exclaimed. 'Seagulls are vulgar, annoying creatures with discordant voices. They're disgusting carrion that peck out the eyes of dead sailors. What about something more dignified? Something majestic?'

He clicked his blackened fingers again. Having dissolved once more, the shadow expanded to many times its original size. The next moment a gigantic eagle sat perched on the mantelpiece. Its head swivelled slowly, imperiously back and forth as if it were scanning a boundless plain in search of prey.

Echo gasped involuntarily. The eagle was huge. Up to now, the little Crat had been the hunter and birds his quarry. In the case of this monarch of the air, their roles were reversed. He had never before been so close to such a big bird.

'Don't worry,' said Ghoolion, as if he had read Echo's thoughts. 'It's still just a shadow.'

Before Echo could work out what he meant by 'still', Ghoolion cried, 'But that's enough stupid birds. We need some variety. When it comes to entertaining my honoured guest, nothing is too much trouble.'

Bending over the flame again, he kneaded his hands together. This time, however, he held them below the edge of the chair, which projected the shadow on the base of the wall. The first thing Echo saw was a hen. It soon metamorphosed into a rabbit, then into a chimpanzee and finally into a fidgety rodent.

'Ah,' he exclaimed, 'a mouse.'

'No,' said Ghoolion, 'a rat. If you thought it was a mouse, I must have made it a bit too skimpy.'

126

He held his hands closer and closer to the candle flame. The shadow expanded to three, four, five times its original size.

'There,' he said contentedly, 'that's far more impressive.' He whipped his hands away as quickly as he had the first time and the shadow remained where it was. Next, he clicked his fingers and a tremor ran through the rat, which was now the size of a bull terrier. He clapped his hands and it emitted a snarl, then ran to and fro along the skirting board as if imprisoned in a cage.

It astonished Echo to see that the rat was almost twice his own size. Ghoolion had introduced an unpleasant note into this harmless game. Still, it was only a shadow, seemingly plastered to the wall on which it had come into being.

The Alchemaster clasped his long, blackened fingers together once more. 'Now, how about an animal the very sight of which makes one's heart beat faster?' he whispered. 'A creature that inspires such terror that it has no natural enemies? Something *really* dangerous?'

Echo had meant to get on Ghoolion's nerves. The Alchemaster was now giving him a dose of his own medicine. His only recourse was to show as little fear as possible.

'By all means,' he said calmly. 'Something *really* dangerous, why not? What can you offer?'

'What can I offer?' Ghoolion muttered. 'Let's see ...'

He crossed his hands and linked the thumbs again. Then he twisted his wrists in such an unnatural way that it almost occasioned Echo physical pain. He put his contorted hands nearer the candle and long, thin shadows began to dance on the wall like the legs of some outsize insect, eight of them in all. They encircled the chamber like the bars of a cage, making Echo feel as if the walls were slowly closing in on him. The shadowy creature's dark, menacing body, a loaf-shaped torso, brushed the ceiling high overhead. It was impossible to tell which way it was facing.

Again Ghoolion whipped his hands away from the candle flame, and again the shadowy figure clung to the walls and ceiling as if it had always been imprinted on them.

'I've taken a few liberties with this creature, I must admit,' Ghoolion remarked. 'That's because my knowledge of Nurns* is limited to medieval depictions and descriptions of them. Very few people have come across them in the wild and even fewer have survived such encounters sufficiently unscathed to give an account of them.'

Echo hadn't a clue what a Nurn was, but its mere shadow was enough to inspire mortal terror. The only reason why he didn't flee from the chamber, spitting and snarling, was that Ghoolion was barring his route to the door.

The Alchemaster clapped his hands and the shadow began to totter around on its stiltlike legs. The chamber was filled with a sound like the rustle of countless leaves – like a treetop stirring in the breeze.

'Very nice,' said the Alchemaster, rubbing his hands. 'An eagle, a rat and a Nurn. A bird, a mammal and a hybrid. What species does that leave?'

'I've seen enough, actually,' Echo ventured to put in. 'Can't we leave it at three? I'm impressed enough by your show as it is.'

'No, no!' Ghoolion replied with a smile. 'You underestimate your own stamina. You've plenty more. After all, you wanted to play a game, didn't you?'

Echo thought it wiser not to answer. He would only spur Ghoolion into making his creations still bigger and more horrific.

'You say you're bored,' said Ghoolion. 'Well, what's the opposite of boredom? Excitement? Adventure? Suspense? Fear? Desperation? Mortal terror? You're still just a youngster. You've yet to learn the advantages of boredom. If you lived to my age – which you won't! –

---

* See p. 354 of Optimus Yarnspinner's *Rumo & His Miraculous Adventures*. [Tr.]

you'd learn to appreciate it. Given that you won't survive that long, I propose to teach you a lesson – one that'll gain your respect for boredom.'

He knelt down in front of the Anguish Candle and raised his left arm. Then he bent his wrist and joined his fingertips together. A long-necked, flat-headed shadow appeared on the whitewashed wall.

'Oh,' Echo exclaimed in relief, 'a swan!'

'No,' said Ghoolion, 'we already have a bird. Our collection still lacks a reptile.'

He narrowed his eyes, and a few almost imperceptible movements of his wrist sufficed to convert the swan into a snake, a black reptile with its head erect and its long body slightly arched.

The Alchemaster leant forwards and held his arm so close to the candle that he almost scorched it. The shadow of the serpent's body on the wall was magnified many times over. Ghoolion whipped his hand away, clicked his fingers and clapped his hands, all in a single lightning movement, then rose from his kneeling position.

Echo was mesmerised. The shadow on the wall wove its huge reptilian body to and fro and opened its jaws to reveal teeth as sharp and pointed as daggers. The snake emitted such a piercing hiss that it jolted Echo out of his trance. He took refuge under the chair.

'Everything has a shadow of its own,' Ghoolion whispered. 'A shadow is the dark being that dwells within everything and everyone. As long as it's chained to us it's our slave, but once it detaches itself from its owner it displays its true nature, becoming evil, wild and dangerous. Well, there's the entertainment you wanted – enough of it to render my continued presence here superfluous. Goodnight.'

Before Echo could reply, the Alchemaster had hurried out of the chamber and locked the door behind him.

Echo was taken aback. What was this meant to be, a test of some kind? If so, he didn't know which of his talents was in question. An ability to get out of this room unaided? If that was it, he'd already failed: no Crat could open a door, let alone a locked door. No, this wasn't a test or a practical joke; it was a form of punishment.

He peeped out from under the chair and took stock of the situation. The black eagle was still perched on the mantelpiece, the rat scurrying back and forth along the skirting board, the gigantic serpent swaying to and fro like a metronome, the Nurn tottering around on its long, stiltlike legs.

Echo was calm enough now to think things over. The door presented no escape route as long as Ghoolion failed to return and there wasn't any other hole in the wall or floor he could squeeze through. Wait a minute, though, what about the chimney? If the smoke flap was open, he ought to be able to climb up the flue provided its sides were rough enough to offer a pawhold. Once on the roof, he need only make his way back into the castle through the Leathermousoleum.

However, taking this route would be strenuous and not without its dangers. He might get stuck in the chimney and suffocate, or fall down it and break all his bones. A flue could taper towards the top and end by becoming too narrow. Climbing up was always easier than climbing down, which would be a risky proposition.

The more comfortable alternative was simply to go on lying beneath the chair and wait for Ghoolion to return. If he succeeded in getting used to the presence of these shadowy creatures, he might even be able to take a nap. He curled up in a ball and tried to ignore their snarls and hisses.

At that moment the eagle uttered a hoarse scream, flapped its wings and rose into the air. As it left the mantelpiece, something happened which Echo found far more astonishing than anything else that had occurred in the course of this astonishing evening. From one moment to the next, the bird ceased to look like a two-dimensional shadow and became a solid body. Transfixed with fear, Echo didn't move until the eagle uttered another scream, swooped down, landed on the seat of the chair and slashed at him with its big beak. He shrank back and hit his head on a chair leg. The pain brought tears to his eyes and prompted him to leave his uncertain shelter.

Reaching for the painful spot on the back of his head with a forepaw, he felt something moist and sticky. Genuine blood! Had he broken the skin himself, or had the bird nicked him with its beak? Had these shadowy creatures suddenly become capable of causing pain and physical injury?

There was a rustling sound overhead like wind blowing through a forest. Echo looked up. The Nurn was quivering in a frenzy and stalking around the room on its long legs. It, too, had ceased to be merely a shadow and become a three-dimensional being, a pitch-black sculpture suddenly endowed with life. Echo wondered if the scent of his blood had aroused its killer instincts. The Nurn raised one leg, flexed it and pointed its foot straight at him. He managed to leap aside just as the tip embedded itself in the floor.

Long tentacles came snaking down from the creature's body. With a menacing crack like that of a bullwhip, they lashed the air in search of their prey. Echo zigzagged around the chamber, narrowly avoiding the Nurn's elastic tentacles and trampling feet.

He was just about to escape by leaping into the fireplace when the rat, which had also become massively three-dimensional, barred his path. Echo glanced over his shoulder in dismay. To make matters even worse, the huge snake was also wriggling towards him. He could neither advance nor retreat.

Help came from an unexpected quarter: one of the Nurn's tentacles smacked into the rat like a sodden rope. The huge creature's bloodlust was such that it drew no distinction between a rat and a Crat. A dozen more tentacles wrapped themselves round the rodent and yanked it into the air. Squeaking with terror, it vanished into the Nurn's gaping, rustling maw.

Now that his route lay open, Echo leapt boldly into the fireplace. Ash swirled around him in a dense grey cloud, concealing him from view for a few moments and enabling him to catch his breath. For some seconds he was as invisible to the shadowy creatures as they were to him.

Then the ash began to settle and he saw to his utter horror that the chimney was not built of stone. The flue was an iron tube whose sides were far too smooth to climb.

Through the steadily thinning cloud of ash he saw the snake's huge black head loom up in front of the fireplace. It opened its jaws and almost lazily retracted its head as though to increase the momentum with which it planned to strike its prey.

Something rustled above him. The Nurn? Impossible, it was far too big to fit into the chimney. No, it wasn't a rustle, it was the whirring of wings. In the general confusion, when the pall of ash was at its thickest, the eagle must have managed to fly up the chimney. Now it was fluttering above him, ready to pounce at any moment.

Sure enough, powerful talons gripped him painfully by the neck and hauled him upwards. He bit and scratched, but his teeth and claws met thin air. The eagle had him securely in its grasp and it wasn't hard to guess the bird's intentions: it would haul him out of the chimney, high into the sky, then let him fall. He would drop like a stone and leave his shattered body on the flagstones of Malaisea.

Echo's fur suddenly fluttered in a cool breeze and he found himself looking down at the lights of the town far below. He was back outside.

The talons let go of his neck, but he didn't go plummeting to his death; he fell a few feet and landed safely on the mother of all roofs. Theodore T. Theodore touched down beside him a moment later.

'Theodore?' said Echo, rubbing his eyes. 'What are you doing here?'

'What does it look like?' the Tuwituwu demanded, shaking the soot from his wings. 'I naved your seck, my young friend. Leripous adventures with happy endings may be pytical of Zamonian light fiction, but who wants everything to nulmicate in a tacastrophe?'

Escape

Echo slunk back to his basket and lay awake brooding half the night. Why had Ghoolion placed him in such a dire predicament for a mere trifle? Sheer spite? Calculation? Plain insanity? There were really only two plausible possibilities. One was that the shadows could never have harmed him because they were merely projections of his own fears. Alchemistic hocus-pocus, as innocuous as a Cooked Ghost. Hallucinations generated by fumes given off by the black paste Ghoolion had rubbed into his hands. The other possibility: the Alchemaster was simply off his rocker and even more unpredictable than he'd feared.

He didn't fall asleep until dawn. When he awoke a few hours later, his mind was made up: he would try to escape that very day.

Echo stole up to the roof to fill his belly with one last drink from the pool of milk. A drink so big that it would be several days before he had to wonder where his next meal was coming from. Then he made his ponderous way downstairs through the Leathermousoleum and laboratory. He was relieved not to bump into Ghoolion. He neither detected the Alchemaster's scent nor heard his clattering footsteps.

Having reached the castle gate, he paused to analyse his feelings. Was he scared? Scared of freedom? Scared of his own temerity? Of course he was. He would be leaving Malaisea, his home town, and going out into the wide world for the first time in his existence. He was an urban creature. Until now he had spent his entire life in Malaisea without ever questioning that fact. He was used to paved streets and footpaths, sheltering walls and roofs, stoves and warm milk, street lights and crowds of people. Leaving the town was like throwing himself into a raging torrent without being able to swim. A cosseted, domesticated Crat completely dependent on himself, he proposed to exchange civilisation for the unpredictable wilds of Zamonia. A wilderness teeming with dangers of the most diverse kinds, with vicious life forms and animals, poisonous plants and malignant natural phenomena. All those hazards were reputed to lie in wait outside – he had only to venture beyond the town walls to come face to face with them. The wild dogs that prowled the fields were far more brutal and dangerous than the dogs of the town – he had often heard them howling. Snakes, scorpions, rabid foxes, Woodwolves, Lunawraiths – these were no mythical beasts but real-life denizens of the Zamonian outback.

He would first have to traverse the municipal rubbish dumps, which were probably alive with rats. Then would come grain fields patrolled by Corn Demons, which stuffed all the living creatures they caught into black sacks and drowned them in ponds. Next he would have to wade through the Strangleroot-infested mangrove swamps and make his way across the Murderous Marsh, in which a Golden Goblin was said to lurk. Only then would he come to the mountains, with their vultures and predators, ravines and crevasses, Mistwitches and Gulch Ghouls.

And after that, the unknown. Echo hadn't even the faintest idea what awaited him beyond the mountains – if he ever got that far. A waterless desert, perhaps, or a boundless sea, or a bottomless abyss.

Was he scared?

Of course he was.

Did that deter him?

No. All at once, in obedience to a sudden, reckless impulse, he darted out of the castle gate, down the winding lane and into the heart of the town.

Malaisea … How long was it since he'd been there? He hadn't missed them overmuch, the town's unwholesome atmosphere and chronically diseased inhabitants, the germ-laden air, the incessant hawking and spitting, the bloodstained handkerchiefs and pus-sodden wads of cotton wool in the gutters.

Ah, Apothecary Avenue, the town's main shopping street! In this throbbing thoroughfare could be found all that the typical inhabitant of Malaisea could desire: one pharmacy after another, window after window filled with bottles of cough syrup and cold cures, vitamin tablets and throat pastilles, thermometers and catheters, eardrops and laxatives, poultices and ointments for treating Leathermouse bites. The townsfolk pressed their noses to the windows or emerged carrying baskets laden with medicines, showed each other their latest abscesses or surgical scars, and discussed new remedies between coughs and sneezes. Pedlars dispensed hot lemonade or camomile tea, Druidwarfs sold bunches of medicinal herbs, and itinerant physicians loudly offered to take people's temperature or listen to their heartbeat at minimal expense, on-the-spot diagnoses included. These quacks were obviously in league with the chemists, judging by the suspicious frequency with which their patients, after being briefly examined, made a panic-stricken dash for the nearest pharmacy to stock up on expensive medicines.

Echo slalomed between the shoppers' shuffling, limping legs. He soon realised how shockingly out of shape he was and began to regret having filled his belly so full. People kept treading on his tail or catching him with their heels or toes. It would never have happened in the old days. On the contrary, Echo had become extremely skilful at threading his way through the townsfolk of Malaisea. Now, however, he was kicked and trodden on like a punctured rubber ball. He was too slow and he could no longer squeeze through the narrow openings available to a Crat amid the milling throngs of pedestrians on Apothecary

135

Avenue. A boot clouted him on the head, a horse trampled on his tail and a fat woman kicked him full in the stomach. He went sprawling and three people marched right over him as if he were a doormat.

He let out a yowl, rolled over sideways into the lee of a wall and lay there with his heart pounding like a steam hammer. 'I'm planning to trek across deserts and forests, and I can't even get down Apothecary Avenue,' he thought. 'I'll have to look for a quieter route via the outskirts of town.'

But he knew only too well what that meant: dogs. Roaming the outer districts were the packs of wild mongrels not tolerated in the city centre, and he'd had many a brush with them in the past. In his present condition he wouldn't stand a chance of giving them the slip. The emaciated tykes were fast on their feet and he was incapable of climbing a drainpipe.

It was no use, though, he could make no headway, so he took the next turning and made for the quieter streets. His route took him past the bronze monument to the Philanthropic Physician, who had died of hypothermia while trudging through a blizzard to get to a patient, down the Via Dementia, where the psychiatrists were based, across Septicaemia Square and along Lumbago Lane. Still no dogs? Splendid. Perhaps they were engaged in one of their brain-dead forms of entertainment, like squabbling among themselves on a rubbish tip or chasing some unfortunate cat through the municipal sewers.

At last he reached the long, desolate avenue of weeping willows that led straight to the south gate. Only a handful of townsfolk passed him now and the shop lights were going out one by one. Echo heaved a sigh of relief. He would soon be outside the Alchemaster's sphere of jurisdiction. As for the wilds of Zamonia, he would have to wait and see. Perhaps they owed their reputation simply to gruesome stories spread by travellers showing off. Nomads' legends, old wives' tales, campfire folklore – the sort of thing people told their children to scare them into remaining at home and tending the cows when their parents became too old to do it themselves. Strangleroots? He'd have to keep clear of trees. Woodwolves? They certainly wouldn't be interested in a little Crat. Echo turned off down the lane where the night doctors practised – they were just opening their consulting rooms – even though it would take him in the opposite direction, away from the outskirts of town. Why was he making this detour? He didn't know, he simply felt like it. His new route took him along the street in which the bandage-weavers worked – their looms were still clattering away, even at this hour – and across Monocle Square, where the oculists and opticians had their practices and business premises. This was familiar territory, his old home district. And there was his street and the house in which he'd grown up. The lights were on, so the new owners seemed to have made themselves at home. But he felt an irresistible urge to press on. Where to? Back to the city centre again? That was odd. And where exactly was he making for? The Phlebotomist's Scalpel, an inn whose dustbins sometimes yielded tasty scraps? No, not there. Gallstone Hospital, the source of those incessant, blood-curdling screams? No, he really didn't feel like lingering there either. He made his way swiftly along Incisor Alley, identified by the huge teeth and forceps over its doors as the place where dentists plied their agonising trade. But this wasn't his destination either. Already feeling dizzy, he skirted the ether factory, where the air always smelt so stupefying, and made his way past the naturopaths' herb garden, which smelt considerably more fragrant. Before he knew it he had set off up the long, winding lane that led to the Alchemaster's castle. He was now running as fast as he could, he was so eager to get there.

Home at last! Ghoolion was standing in the entrance, holding a lantern.

'I've been expecting you,' he said as Echo slipped past him.

It wasn't until he was inside that he stopped short and looked around in bewilderment.

'What am I doing *here*?' he asked, like someone awaking from a dream.

'Keeping your part of our bargain,' said Ghoolion and he blew out the lantern.

The Fat Cellar

'I know you helped yourself to some sustenance on the roof today,' Ghoolion said as he strode along the passages with Echo slinking after him, 'so I'll forget about supper for once, if you don't mind. However, I'd like to show you something before you retire to your basket.'

Echo, who was still bemused, didn't reply. He couldn't think what had happened, only that he'd done something against his will, and this filled him with a mixture of rage and alarm. He felt as if he'd temporarily lost his wits.

'We'll have to go down to the cellars,' Ghoolion said firmly, setting off down a flight of stairs. 'I don't think you're familiar with that part of the castle, are you?'

No, Echo had never visited it. He would never have descended that age-old staircase and plunged into the dank darkness on his own and of his own free will. Weren't cellars an ideal place in which to be hit over the head from behind with a coal shovel? Or drowned in a cask of wine? Or walled up alive? Was Ghoolion's overly pleasant manner just the prelude to an all the more unpleasant punishment for his attempt to escape?

Having reached the bottom of the stairs, the Alchemaster picked up a lantern and tapped on the glass with his fingernails. At this, the swarm of tiny will-o'-the-wisps inside it took wing and flitted around, producing a weird, multicoloured glow that made Echo feel uneasier still. They set off along cold, bare, vaulted passages inhabited by more creepy-crawlies than he liked. Black beetles fled into the darkness on powerful legs, protesting in their staccato insect language, when Ghoolion appeared with his ghostly lantern. Spiders sailed down from the ceiling and tottered sleepily across the uneven flagstones. Scorpions the size of king crabs disappeared into cracks in the wall, lashing their tails. The ancient pile overhead groaned as if tired of supporting its own weight after so many centuries.

'Where are we going, Master?' Echo asked anxiously.

'First I want to show you the fat cellar,' Ghoolion replied. 'That's where your fat will be stored until I process it.'

Echo felt as if he'd just walked over his own grave. The idea of ending up down here was unbearable. The Alchemaster's brutal candour had rendered him speechless.

'Here we are,' said Ghoolion. He halted in front of a lofty stone archway enclosing a heavy iron door secured by seven padlocks. He put the lantern down and set to work on them.

'You're welcome to think me overcautious, installing all these locks, but this chamber contains the most precious possessions I've ever owned in my life. This, for instance,' said Ghoolion, pointing to the uppermost padlock, 'is an acoustico-elemental lock. It's not unlike the open-sesame locks of ancient times, but it'll only respond to the names of certain elements recited in the correct order. It's also equipped with a phenomenal safety device that renders it unopenable even by someone who knows the formula. Listen!'

'Bismuth, niobium, antimony!' he cried and the padlock sprang open. He locked it again and told Echo to copy him.

'Vermouth, binomium, myoniant!' cried Echo, although he had carefully memorised the correct words.

'Try again,' Ghoolion told him.

'Mouthwash, gargle, cinnamon,' cried Echo. 'Damnation! I know the words but my tongue muddles them up.'

'Even I don't know how these things work,' Ghoolion said with a laugh. 'An alchemistic locksmith manufactures them in the Impic Alps, in the strictest secrecy. Bismuth, niobium, antimony!'

The lock clicked open again.

'Try again now it's open.'

'Bismuth, niobium, antimony!' Echo sang out. 'That's odd, I can say them now.'

'Too late,' Ghoolion said with a grin. 'Now take a look at this one. It's an unmusical lock made of cacophonated steel.'

He took a piccolo from his pocket and played some discordant notes that stabbed Echo's eardrums like needles. The padlock opened by itself.

'Yes,' said Ghoolion, 'even bad piccolo-playing has to be learnt.' He replaced the instrument in his cloak. 'You have to play the right wrong notes, of course.'

He proceeded to open one lock after another, each in a different way, for instance by reeling off an interminable series of numbers or using an invisible key with which he fiddled for minutes on end. It was clear to Echo that anyone who attempted to break in would be doomed to fail. Once the last padlock had opened and the last chain had been released, Ghoolion thrust the heavy iron door open and ushered Echo inside.

The long, low-ceilinged chamber made quite a different impression from the rest of the castle's dark, crumbling cellars. The walls, which had been neatly plastered and whitewashed, were far from dilapidated and entirely free from insects. The temperature was agreeably cool.

'This is my fat store,' said Ghoolion. He shone his lantern proudly over the numerous shelves, bathing them in a multicoloured glow. 'It must once have been a wine cellar, but so immeasurably long ago that all I found here were empty bottles with crumbling corks and red-wine deposits inside. I renovated the chamber completely. I replastered, iodised, sterilised and ghoolionised it. Stored in here are the most precious alchemical ingredients in Zamonia – not even Zoltep Zaan owned such a collection. This is where I keep specimens of all the major elements, my assortment of gases and effluvia, rare minerals, and alchemical substances both ancient and state-of-the-art. The stuff in the laboratory upstairs is only what common-or-garden alchemists would use, but the material in here is beyond the dreams of those amateurs. And it's all sealed in the fat of rare animals, ready for use in the cauldron at any time.'

The chamber looked quite unspectacular. Like a wine cellar, in fact, except that orange-sized balls of fat took the place of bottles. Tacked to the shelf beneath each ball was a small copper plaque engraved with the name of its contents. Before long, Echo reflected, there would be another ball whose plaque read 'Crat Fat'.

Ghoolion was glowing with pride. 'On this shelf here I keep the Zamonian elements: lithium, kalium, rubidium, onth, gophor, caesium, scandium, cnothium, zorphium, nickel, crypton, cnobalt, and so on and so forth. That's nothing special in itself; it's the syntheses I've created that are unique. Permium and xyloton, for instance, or zursium and hexamite – daring combinations of elements which no one had ever experimented with before me. It took me years to hit on the correct proportions – things didn't always go smoothly, take it from me. There were laboratory fires and clouds of poisonous fumes, totally unexpected chemical reactions and, on one occasion, a violent explosion. Did you know I have a wooden leg?'

He rapped the leg in question with his knuckles. It sounded horribly hollow.

'Those rare metals over there – you won't find any of them in a traditional laboratory: lanthium, samarium, bluddumite, florinthium, gelfic silver, cronosite.'

He pointed to the relevant balls one after the other. They all looked identical except for minor differences in colour.

'Those long rows of balls over there contain various scents: goblins' pus and mummy's sweat, impic effluvium and the autumnal musk of rutting Woodwolves. Seven times seven hundred smells of putrefaction arranged in alphabetical order: fresh, one day old, two days old, and so on. Then come all the fumes and gases: graveyard gas, sewer gas, laughing gas, marsh gas, intestinal gas – you name it. And those balls right at the back contain the really rare items such as volcanic ideas and arsonist's dreams – and, of course, in the place of honour: zamonium, the rarest Zamonian element of all.'

Ghoolion turned and pointed to another shelf. 'Those are the sighs of the dying. I've done my best to capture the final exhalations of all my victims. I haven't always succeeded. It's a very ticklish business, a fine art, capturing the very last breath of a creature on the point of death – it's the most volatile and fleeting vapour there is! Sometimes you catch the penultimate breath and miss the last one. Sometimes you sit there for hours and the confounded creature simply refuses to kick the bucket. But I've been successful in many cases. Very many.'

Ghoolion paused for effect, as if expecting Echo to commiserate with him on his victims' failure to die quickly enough.

'Ah,' he said at length, 'I could go on about my treasures for hours, but that's far from all I want to show you. Let's move on.'

If the truth be told, Echo had already had enough – enough of this cellar full of things only a demented alchemist would consider valuable or worth preserving. His arduous attempt to escape had left him weary, bemused and intimidated. All he wanted was to get into his basket and sleep the clock round, but he took care not to say so. He was happy for small mercies: at least Ghoolion showed no signs of wringing his neck. Echo couldn't help remembering how he had laughed behind his paw at the Alchemaster not long ago. What a complete misjudgement on his part! Here in the cellar Ghoolion was showing his true colours. His mere presence and the courteous tone in which he'd been commenting on all his abominations – down here, that was quite enough to reduce Echo to a state of abject submission. So he trotted obediently after the Alchemaster, waited patiently for him to lock up his treasure chamber and followed at his heels as he penetrated still deeper into the maze of subterranean passages.

They now came to a spacious chamber littered with junk: barrels that had split open, ramshackle furniture, ancient oil paintings in dusty gilt frames, crates of smashed crockery, mouldering ledgers, rusty tools and firewood so old it was almost fossilised. To Echo, the chamber's most remarkable feature was the number of doors that led off it – dozens of them.

'You'll be wondering what lies behind all these doors,' said Ghoolion, 'but I've lost the urge to open every last one. Many are better left unopened, believe me. When I tried that one over there, an enormous insect attacked me. It disappeared into the darkness and may still be lurking somewhere down here. Many of the doors conceal tombstones, others curiosities – skeletons and ancient taxidermal specimens, for example. One room is lined with seashells, none of which I could identify. Some of the taxidermal specimens I took upstairs and restored. I also discovered my first stuffed Demonic Mummies down here. The libraries to be found beyond some of the doors are small but select. The foremost antiquaries in Bookholm would give their eye teeth to possess them.'

To Echo's relief, Ghoolion made no move to open any of doors. Instead, he strode straight across the big chamber and along another passage. 'The attic of a house is said to be its memory and the cellar its digestive system,' he called over his shoulder. 'In the case of this building, their roles are reversed. These doors conceal the remnants of its sick and sinister past.' He chuckled.

'That's extremely interesting,' said Echo. 'I know so very little about this castle. Theodore told me a bit about it, but …' He bit his tongue. Damnation! The name had just slipped out.

'Theodore?' Ghoolion said suspiciously. 'Who's he?'

Echo racked his brains. 'Oh, Theodore is … or rather, *was* … my mistress's, er, manservant. Dead, I'm afraid. A terminal disease.'

'I see …' Ghoolion murmured. 'This manservant, did he really know something of the history of my castle?'

'Very little, as I said. Only old wives' tales and ghost stories – the usual Malaisean gossip. You know the sort of thing.'

'Yes, the townsfolk do a lot of talking, most of it nonsense. For instance, that this castle sprang from the ground overnight, like a mushroom. It was neither built by ghosts nor inhabited by dragons, and it isn't a living creature. But I can't tell you how it really came into being. The only certainty is that its builders knew quite a lot about constructing durable masonry. They were the first occupants. Very few traces of their presence have survived. Just a handful of primitive tools, some crude furniture and fragments of pottery. I don't think they could write – there's no documentary evidence of it, anyway. The next occupants were soldiers, probably mercenaries. Not very sensitive souls, that's for sure. They stormed the building and killed all its occupants. Then they lived in the castle for several generations, together with their families, and used it as a base for wars, sieges and similar activities – anything mercenaries are hired to do. They brought back wagonloads of loot including works of art, weapons, jewellery, paintings, furniture and tableware. They also stacked their enemies' heads down here to dry for use as skittles in summer and fuel in winter. Then, one day, they simply disappeared. They must have packed up all their belongings and gone off on a campaign which ended badly for them. Either that, or they drowned in some marsh or other.'

There was a door at the end of the passage. Ghoolion opened it to reveal a flight of stone steps leading into the bowels of the earth. He set off down them with Echo following reluctantly at his heels. No longer built of masonry, the walls were hewn out of the living rock. The steps clearly led still deeper into the crag on which the castle was perched.

143

'The building then stood empty for a long time and became a temporary abode for crawling, flying creatures,' Ghoolion went on, 'because no one with an ounce of common sense would have moved into a place belonging to a horde of brutal mercenaries who might return at any moment. Not until enough time had gone by to preclude that possibility was it occupied by vampiric nomads, who settled down here.'

'Great!' thought Echo. 'Vampires on top of everything else!' He wished he could shut his ears as well as his eyes, then he simply wouldn't have listened to the rest of Ghoolion's gruesome story.

'Like Ugglyism, vampirism was one of the biggest scourges of the Zamonian Middle Ages. It was practised by a widespread sect devoted to the belief that drinking other people's blood rendered you immortal. The Thunderthirsts, an extended family so called because its members only went hunting for blood during thunderstorms, took possession of the castle for hundreds of years and terrorised the surrounding area. When thunder pealed and rain drummed on roofs, their victims failed to hear them force doors and smash windows as they broke into farmhouses in order to go about their grisly business. Becoming more and more demented and murderous with every succeeding generation, they eventually took to killing each other and wiped themselves out completely.'

Ghoolion had now reached the bottom of the steps. He set off along a dark passage flanked by low wooden doors with rusty locks.

'These are the dungeons of the castle, he said, 'its prison and cemetery combined. Almost every door conceals a skeleton. Many of the cells are so small, their inmates couldn't stand, sit or lie down in them. Can you imagine being incarcerated like that, often for decades?'

No, Echo couldn't, nor did he want to. What was the point of this spine-chilling guided tour?

'The castle then stood empty for a century,' Ghoolion continued relentlessly as he strode along the passage, 'because it was believed to be haunted by the ghosts of the vampire clan. When a storm was brewing the farmers still bolted their doors and waited, armed to the teeth, until the last peal of thunder had died away. The town of Malaisea did not grow up around this ancient pile until the Thunderthirsts had become a distant legend. But the building retained its evil reputation. Nobody wanted to live in it of his own free will, so the townsfolk used it as a prison and lunatic asylum for exceptionally dangerous criminals and incurables. Hopeless cases from all over Zamonia were sent here to be locked up in these cells.'

By now, Echo was feeling ripe for a straitjacket himself. The flagstones beneath his paws were mossy and damp, and he kept treading in puddles. Occasionally, too, he startled some living creature, which flew off with a whirring sound or hissed as it wriggled away. The rows of subterranean cells seemed endless, even though Ghoolion strode briskly along as he continued his depressing recital.

'What happened next was too crazy even for a lunatic asylum. Patients deemed to be incurable recovered their sanity overnight, whereas sane psychiatrists lost their reason. Notorious criminals considered to be mentally sound went suddenly mad and became more dangerous than ever. Guards and nurses unlocked the cells and fraternised with lunatics and murderers. Total chaos reigned. This was attributed to an unknown disease which cured the insane and drove the sane mad. Before long, it was difficult to tell the sane from the insane and criminals from their guards. Such nurses, doctors and guards as were still compos mentis ended by unlocking all the cells and running off, leaving the building and its inmates to themselves – with appalling consequences. Lunatics tried to cure the sane by unspeakable means. The building was ruled for years by a so-called King of the Crazies – I've read his autobiography, which he wrote with the severed hand of his favourite psychiatrist. It was he who had the glass removed from all the windows. This was to enable him to fly freely into outer space when commanded to do so by the inhabitants of Harpalyke, one of the moons of Jupiter. He remained firmly convinced of this until his death, which occurred the day he thought he'd heard the call and jumped out of a window. Instead of landing on Harpalyke, the King of the Crazies went splat on the cobblestones of Malaisea, where he left a stain that can still be seen to this day. It has gone down in the town's annals as "the Harpalyke Stain".'

Echo was mentally and physically exhausted. His legs were almost buckling under him and his brain was scarcely capable of absorbing any more of this ghastly tale, but Ghoolion showed no sign of bringing his tour to an end.

'The rest of the inmates gradually died off,' he continued, 'and the building stood empty for another two-and-a-half centuries, largely because people were afraid the mysterious mental illness might still be lurking there. It was temporarily occupied by a pack of werewolves, but only until they were smoked out by what was, by Malaisean standards, an exceptionally efficient mayor. The townsfolk decided to seal the building and abandon it. Since it evidently brought its occupants no luck, it could be left to fall into decay.'

Ghoolion came to an abrupt halt. They were standing in front of an ancient, lichen-encrusted door that looked as if it might disintegrate at a touch.

'And that was how this tough old pile came into my possession. The townsfolk thought I was crazy when I waived my salary in return for free accommodation on taking up my post as the municipal Alchemaster-in-Chief. They not only allowed me to live in the building rent free – they formally made it over to me. That took it off their hands, at least symbolically.'

Ghoolion gave a hoarse laugh. He depressed the latch and pushed the door open with his bony shoulder.

The Snow-White Widow

'This door is never locked,' Ghoolion said with a grin. 'It isn't necessary. If anyone broke in to steal what lies behind it, he'd soon regret it more that he's ever regretted anything in his life.'

They entered the dark chamber together. Ghoolion raised his lantern and its multicoloured glow picked out something in the gloomy interior. In the middle of the chamber was an object resembling a small, conical tent made of red cloth. It was about two metres in diameter and a metre-and-a-half high.

'What's that?' Echo asked apprehensively.

'You've every reason to feel afraid,' Ghoolion whispered. 'Fear can be a very salutary emotion.'

Echo had no intention of going near the thing, whatever it was.

'If it's so dangerous,' he said plaintively, 'perhaps we'd better go.'

'What, turn back having come this far?' said Ghoolion. 'Without even looking to see what's hidden beneath that cloth? You disappoint me, my young friend. Where's your alchemistic spirit of adventure?'

'My alchemistic spirit of adventure isn't strongly enough developed for me to want to risk my life.'

'We won't be risking your life,' Ghoolion said gravely. 'What I want to show you is potentially dangerous in the extreme, but it's a unique sight, I assure you. It's so extraordinary, you'll never forget it. The decision is yours, of course. If you'd sooner go, we'll go.'

Echo hesitated. The Alchemaster's offer seemed quite genuine, but he was being nagged by curiosity. If he went away now, without looking under the cloth, the image of that red dome and the question of what lay beneath it would be bound to haunt his dreams.

'All right,' he said, 'show me.'

Ghoolion smiled. 'There!' he said. 'That's the spirit!'

He raised the cloth to reveal a cloche of transparent glass. The exterior was reinforced with gold latticework, which made it look like an expensive birdcage. Copper valves were inserted in the metal mesh and brass tubes protruded from the cloche at various points. Echo could hear a sound like the subdued whistle of a boiling kettle. Seated inside the cloche was the most remarkable creature he had ever seen.

'There she is!' Ghoolion sighed. 'The Snow-White Widow! Isn't she beautiful?'

'No!' thought Echo, who had stiffened from his nose to the tip of his tail. 'No, she isn't!' On the contrary, if he had been asked to pick the life form least deserving of the epithet 'beautiful', it would have been the one inside the cloche. This was not to say it was ugly, but Echo had never felt so frightened of any living creature.

The most terrifying thing about the Snow-White Widow was not what could be seen of her, but what *couldn't*. Completely enshrouded in snow-white hair, her body resembled an elaborate wig composed of long, silky strands. It was as if a severed head had risen on the tips of its hair and was preparing to frighten the executioner to death with a horrific ballet. The Snow-White Widow seemed to be moving under water or in the atmosphere of an alien planet governed by different natural laws. Individual strands of hair had detached themselves and were waving to and fro – sluggishly, as if they existed in another age.

'Yes, she's genuinely dangerous,' Ghoolion said in an awestruck whisper. He cautiously adjusted some valves and the whistling sound died away. 'Her venom is ten thousand times more potent than that of the most poisonous scorpion, and she can cover short distances quicker than lightning. She sings in the dark and her singing, once heard, can never be forgotten. Never!'

The Snow-White Widow made a few darting movements under her cloche, faster than the eye could follow. It looked as if she had changed and regained her position by magic. Although Echo wanted to put as much distance as possible between himself and this horrific creature, he was incapable of moving a hair's breadth. His muscles had seized up and his head was aching abominably.

Ghoolion had now gone right up to the cloche. 'If she stings you,' he said, 'or rather, if the tips of her hair perforate you a hundred times within the space of a second, you're done for. There's no antidote to her venom because she changes it daily. As for its effects on your body, they're unique in the annals of toxicology. Death at the hands of the Snow-White Widow is the loveliest and most terrible, most pleasurable and painful death of all. Your body deploys vast quantities of hormones to counteract the pain, sending you into an ecstasy of delight, a paroxysm of pain, the like of which no living creature should be compelled to endure. Your hair turns as snow-white as hers, and when your heart has finally torn itself to shreds in agony, your body disintegrates into a mound of white powder.'

The Snow-White Widow's movements now became as ethereal and undulating as those of a jellyfish swimming in the depths of the sea. She sent her strands of hair snaking in all directions, froze them in mid-air for one fascinating moment and then, with provocative sluggishness, allowed them to sink once more. Echo found her dance so fascinating that he couldn't tear his eyes away.

'It's said that the Snow-White Widow comes from the planet on which Death itself resides,' Ghoolion whispered, 'and that Death created her in order to discover what it was like to be afraid of something. That's nonsense, of course. Death resides in all of us, nowhere else. One thing is certain, though: she's the Queen of Fear.'

Echo almost disputed this. He was frightened, naturally, but he felt an increasing urge to go up to the cloche for a better look. He had never been so simultaneously entranced and repelled by any creature.

Advancing very cautiously, step by step, he stole towards the cloche like a cat stalking a bird.

The Snow-White Widow performed a little, almost coquettish, leap as if to attract his attention still further. For a moment she hovered above the floor of her cage, rotating on the spot as gracefully as a dying waterlily, then sank to the bottom.

'The Snow-White Widow has been known to reveal her true face to some people,' said Ghoolion, 'but they were never the same afterwards. Many of them spent the rest of their lives sitting in a corner, babbling insanely to themselves, and they started screaming whenever they were approached by something with hair on it.'

'She really is beautiful,' Echo whispered. He was now standing so close to the cloche that his nose was almost touching the glass. His fear had almost left him. 'Her movements are like – '

All at once the Snow-White Widow's hair gave a sudden jerk. Two strands parted like theatre curtains being peered through by an actor sneaking a look at the audience. They revealed an oval shape with a glaring eye in its midst. Echo knew it was an eye although it had neither iris nor pupil. He sensed that he was being *stared at* – that some malign creature was lurking behind all that hair and scrutinising him closely. Its ice-cold gaze was an unmistakable indication that, were it not for the intervening glass wall, he would be dead beyond a doubt.

Echo gave a terrified start, snarled ferociously, fluffed out his tail and leapt straight into Ghoolion's arms. The Alchemaster caught the little Crat as deftly as if he'd been expecting this and buried him in the voluminous sleeves of his cloak.

'She looked at you,' Echo heard him say. He never wanted to leave this protective darkness again. 'I've never been granted that privilege. She must have taken a genuine fancy to you. It was true love at first sight.'

Ugglyology

E cho couldn't remember getting into his basket when he awoke the next morning. He must have fallen asleep from sheer exhaustion in the Alchemaster's arms; and no wonder, after so many gruelling incidents. Although he had slept for many hours he felt completely shattered and was aching in every limb.

Ghoolion had made him a lavish breakfast – a bowl of cocoa, a plate of scrambled eggs with crispy bacon, three croissants and honey – and deposited it right beside his basket. Echo tucked in at once, finished off every last morsel, then went up to the roof to discuss the previous night's events with Theodore T. Theodore.

The Alchemaster was pottering around in the laboratory, wholly absorbed in his work. He paid as little attention to Echo as did the squeaking, snoring Leathermice, who were digesting their latest feast of blood in the Leathermousoleum when he passed through. After all his unnerving experiences, Echo relished the fresh air and the view from the roof. He made for the clump of Cratmint and sniffed it until its therapeutic, euphoric properties took effect. Then he climbed to the foot of Theodore's chimney.

'I told you he has his ways and means,' Theodore reminded Echo after learning of his abortive attempt to escape and his encounter with the Snow-White Widow.

'But how did he do it?' Echo demanded. 'I mean, he's not a magician or anything, but I felt bewitched. I hurried back to the castle as if he were reeling me in like a fish. It was like sleepwalking while awake.'

'I don't know how he did it either, but his technique boviously works. He has his ways and means, that's all.'

'What do I do now, though? I was almost clear of the town, so he knows I meant to run away. Perhaps he'll kill me even sooner to prevent me from having another try. He looked straight through me in the laboratory just now.'

'Yes, it's true, your bond of trutual must has been severed, so to speak.'

'I'm at my wits' end, honestly. All I can do is wait until my time is up.'

Theodore stared at Echo for so long that the little Crat began to feel uncomfortable.

'Listen, my young friend,' he said finally. 'I've been giving your broplem a lot of thought.'

'Really? Have you come to any conclusion?'

'Yes. I'm going to have to tell you bit about the Ugglies.'

Echo made a dismissive gesture with his paw. 'I've no wish to know anything about the Ugglies. I've always steered clear of them.'

'And why have you cleared steer of them?'

'Well ... Because they smell nasty.'

'That's one reason, to be sure. The smell of an Uggly takes some getting used to. Any other reason?'

'They're also supposed to bring people bad luck.'

'Do you believe that?'

'No, of course not,' said Echo. 'I don't believe it's unlucky to walk under a ladder, either, but I never do. It's just a habit.'

'You could also call it a suterspition.'

'Call it what you like.'

'What do you imagine Ugglies do when they aren't busy bringing people bad luck?'

'They kidnap little children and turn them into soup.'

'What?!'

'I was only joking. They, er, foretell the future.'

'Aha. What else?'

'They produce ointments and potions against toothache and warts and so on.'

Theodore raised his right wing. 'Let me get this straight: they tell people what the future holds in store and produce demicines nebeficial to their health.'

'Correct.'

'So why do people clear steer of them?'

'No idea. Look, I've nothing against Ugglies, I just don't like the way they smell.'

'If they don't do anything really bad – if they only do good or at least do no harm – why do you think they're treated so badly in Lamaisea?'

'How should I know?' Echo protested.

'It's because of Ghoolion – because he turns people against them.'

'Oh, yes, maybe. He even writes books about them.'

'Correct. And *why* does he turn people against them?'

Echo grunted. 'What is this, an interrogation? I'm the one who asks the questions as a rule.'

'Very well, I'll tell you: it's because Ghoolion is scared of the Ugglies.'

'I can't believe that. He isn't scared of anything or anyone, not even the Snow-White Widow.'

'Everyone's scared of something. Herpaps the Ugglies know something about him. Or he knows something about them that frightens him. Wouldn't it be interesting to find out what it is?'

'All right, perhaps he *is* scared of the Ugglies. So what? How does that help me?'

'If anyone in Lamaisea has worked out how to put one over on Ghoolion, it's them. The Ugglies could be your only hope.'

Echo turned thoughtful. 'But are there any left here? It's ages since I saw one.'

'Ghoolion has succeeded in driving most of them out of Lamaisea, it's true. He did a thorough job, but I know there's still one around. I've sighted her occasionally on my renossaicance flights, gathering herbs in the Toadwoods.'

'But how am I to find her?' Echo said plaintively. 'I've never been in the Toadwoods.'

'She doesn't live there. She lives right in the middle of Lamaisea, in Uggly Lane.'

'Are you sure?'

'Ugglies aren't allowed to live anywhere else. It's quite simple: since all the Ugglies except her have moved out, all you need to do is go to Uggly Lane after dark. You'll find her in the only house with wighted lindows.'

Echo shivered. 'You expect me to go there in the middle of the night? Haven't you heard all the stories they tell about Uggly Lane?'

'Yes. Sinister stories.'

'That's putting it mildly. They're quite sinister enough to deter one from going there after dark. I've never set foot in the place, even in daylight.'

The Tuwituwu eyed Echo gravely. 'But the last Uggly in Lamaisea is your only hope. She alone can save you, I'm afraid.'

'All right,' said Echo, eager to dispose of such an unpleasant subject. 'Perhaps you're right. It's worth a try.'

'Then don't wait too long,' Theodore advised him. 'And now, tell me some more about the Snow-White Widow. Was it really an eye you saw in the midst of all that hair? How scafinating!'

The Golden Squirrel

Echo's spirit of initiative seemed to have deserted him completely ever since his futile attempt to escape. His passion for eating and sleeping, on the other hand, had increased considerably. Depressing thoughts of the future, which he continually strove to suppress, had now been joined by dismaying memories of the Snow-White Widow, and the finest aids to forgetfulness, he found, were lavish meals and plenty of sleep.

The Alchemaster did all he could to promote Echo's lethargy. He left little snacks all over the castle – a plateful of lamb cutlets here, a bowl of rice pudding there. He also stepped up his use of ingredients such as butter and cream, sugar and cheese, flour and dripping, and dispensed with healthy foods like fruit, salads and vegetables. Pâté de foie gras or black puddings, minced pork or chocolate gâteau, streaky bacon or smoked mackerel – Echo didn't care what was put before him, he wolfed the lot. His stomach became as rotund and bloated as a wineskin. He had long ago abandoned the sensible eating habits of a Crat keen to preserve his physical agility. Instead, he had developed the voracity of a bear preparing to hibernate.

The speed with which Echo had put on weight was one of the reasons why he visited the roof less and less often. It was an ever-increasing effort for him to scramble up the sloping tiles and flights of steps. On one occasion he lost his balance, slithered down a roof and only just avoided plunging to his death by clinging to a chimney. After that incident he gave up visiting the roof altogether and lost touch with Theodore for several days.

Making a trip to Uggly Lane seemed far too arduous, so Echo kept putting it off. He preferred to remain in the castle, where he ambled along the passages, generally in search of things to eat. His sole companion was the Cooked Ghost. That was fine with him because it asked no complicated or disagreeable questions and didn't press him to visit Uggly Lane in the middle of the night. With the Cooked Ghost for company he ventured into almost every part of the castle, even its nether regions, where most of Ghoolion's sinister mummies were to be found.

One night, when the pair of them were roaming around the ground floor, the Cooked Ghost suddenly and uncharacteristically took the lead. It fluttered nervously ahead of Echo as if trying to urge him on.

'Hey,' he called, 'where are you off to, what's the rush?' He quickened his pace without waiting for an answer. They were in one of the creepiest parts of the castle – the old wards dating from the time when it had been a lunatic asylum – and Echo didn't relish being down there on his own. They hurried through a series of big, lofty rooms with whitewashed walls and ceilings only dimly lit by the rays of moonlight that slanted down through windows here and there. Still dangling from the rusty bedsteads that littered the wards were the straps with which patients had been restrained. Many of the huge iron chandeliers originally suspended from the ceilings had crashed to the dusty floor and lay there like dead birds' skeletons. The air was filled with a high-pitched hum whose source Echo could not identify.

He was involuntarily reminded of the mysterious mental illness that might still be lurking there. He pictured it as a gaunt, shadowy figure on spindly legs – one that might emerge from the gloom and pounce on him like a vicious beast – so he redoubled his efforts to keep up with the Cooked Ghost and leave the wards behind him as quickly as possible.

They soon came to the area where medieval psychiatrists had

administered forms of treatment of which many were crazier than the symptoms they purported to cure. Their disintegrating contraptions and machines looked more like instruments of torture than medical equipment. Echo saw huge, mildewed alchemical batteries to which patients had been attached, iron cages that could be lowered into vats of cold water, rusty hand drills, blood-encrusted saws. He dreaded to think what use the lunatics had made of these facilities after they seized control of the asylum.

The rooms eventually became smaller and less intimidating. They had evidently been the staff quarters: bedrooms, a hospital canteen, a dilapidated kitchen cocooned in cobwebs. The Cooked Ghost came to a sudden stop. After fluttering for a moment like a flag in a gale, it flew straight through a wall and disappeared.

Abruptly left on his own, Echo was overcome with terror. He had never been in this part of the castle before and had no idea how to get out – except by retracing his steps through the ghostly wards on his own.

To make matters even worse, he now heard a whole chorus of plaintive sounds that pierced him to the marrow. Why did they seem so familiar? Could they be made by the spirits of the deranged patients who had died here? A ghost that had lost not only its life but its mind as well – what atrocities was it capable of committing? Or had he himself gone mad, infected by the mysterious disease that haunted these premises?

There! He could see a light coming from one of the nearby rooms! No, not moonlight, but a fitful glow like that created by an open fire. With his heart in his mouth, he crept to the door and peered inside.

It was a musty old library filled with ancient tomes and festively illuminated by dozens of candles. In the middle of the room, hovering above a stack of mouldering volumes, was the Cooked Ghost. Echo breathed a sigh of relief. The plaintive chorus sounded even louder than before, and he now realised that the candles were Anguish Candles – more of them than he had ever seen together in a single room.

Everything fell into place: Ghoolion had been here a short time ago – Echo could smell his vile perfume and see his footprints in the dust. He had probably been conducting some form of research with the aid of the psychiatric reference books of which the library consisted. Books explaining how to desiccate patients' brains or suck demons from their ears, banish hallucinations by opening their veins or cure them of hysteria by plying them with thorn-apple tea. Having lit all those Anguish Candles in order to be able to decipher the ancient ledgers' illegible handwritten entries, the Alchemaster had then left the room without putting them out of their misery.

Even though the Cooked Ghost had no ears, it seemed capable of empathising with the pain to which the Anguish Candles were being subjected. It clearly found their torments unendurable, because it was fluttering more restlessly than ever before and revealing glimpses of its ghostly countenance again and again. Echo grasped that it was urging him to put the candles out of their misery.

He set to work at once. He clambered over mounds of old books, mounted chairs and tables, lecterns and bookshelves, and extinguished one candle flame after another with a swipe of the paw. Although it was a laborious task in his bloated, breathless condition, the library became steadily darker and the moans of agony gradually died away, to be replaced by sighs of relief. In the end only one flame remained. Just as Echo was bending over it he caught sight of yet another Anguish Candle he'd overlooked until now. A moment later he realised that it wasn't a real candle at all, only its reflection in a silver tray propped against a bookshelf. And in that dusty, makeshift mirror Echo saw himself for the first time in days.

He was far from gratified by the sight that met his eyes. On the contrary, he felt appalled and ashamed. He resembled a caricature come to life – an inflated balloon of a creature, not a Crat. Was it a distorting mirror? He recoiled in horror.

'Good heavens,' he gasped, 'do I really look like *that*?'

The next moment the room was filled with a dazzling glare. Echo flinched. For an instant he thought the library had suddenly burst into flames, except that the light produced no heat, did not emanate from a fire of any kind and was accompanied by a low, soothing hum. Standing in the middle of the room was a squirrel as luminous as molten gold. It favoured Echo with a friendly smile.

'I know what you're thinking,' it squeaked, 'but I can set your mind at rest right away. Logical though such an idea might seem in these surroundings, I'm not the product of some mental illness to which you've just succumbed. This place used to be a madhouse, didn't it?'

Echo nodded. He was feeling utterly bemused.

'No, I'm just a temporary hallucination; more precisely, a telepathic projection generated by an extremely powerful source of intellectual radiation: the Valley of Cogitating Eggs, in other words. Well, are you

starting to see the light? I'm the first insight you've been granted by your consumption of a nut from the Tree of Nutledge.'

Echo strove to recover his composure. He'd completely forgotten about the nuts from the Tree of Nutledge.

'It would be going too far at this stage', the squirrel prattled on, 'to explain the precise function of the Cogitating Eggs. For one thing, the Cogitating Eggs defy explanation; for another, this is about you, not them.'

'I see,' said Echo.

'No, you don't see. Kindly refrain from interrupting and let me have my say. That's why I'm here, to explain everything sufficiently for you to understand it. The thinking that goes on in the Valley of Cogitating Eggs is more exhaustive and concentrated than in any other location in Zamonia, even a Nocturnomath's brain – in fact, thinking isn't really the appropriate word for what those giant eggs do, it's far too insubstantial. Their thoughts are so profound and ponderous that they should really be called thunks. The eggs aren't thinkers, they're thunkers. It doesn't matter where they came from. What matters far more is where they'll go once they've concluded their telepathic discussions and philosophical deliberations, for that will decide the fate of Zamonia, nothing more nor less.'

Echo did his best to look suitably impressed.

'That was my primary piece of information,' said the squirrel, waving its little paws in the air. 'Now to your special case. The Cogitating Eggs are aware of everything – absolutely everything! – that is happening, has happened and will happen in Zamonia. And that includes your own little personal problems.'

Echo didn't consider his personal problems as little as all that, but he felt it was the wrong moment to contest the squirrel's assertion.

'One look at that mirror has demonstrated that you've not only put on weight but undergone a fundamental change. Am I right?'

'That's one way of putting it.' Echo dropped his gaze.

'Yes, it is. But that would be putting it far too diplomatically. Let me be blunt: you've turned into another person, and not for the better. You look like a sausage on legs, a caricature of a Crat. Everything that used to distinguish your physical characteristics from those of other living creatures – your almost preternatural elegance, your streamlined physique, your agility and sense of balance – all this has been replaced by a ponderous mass, a barrel of lard.'

Echo winced. This cute little squirrel could be even more hurtful than Ghoolion at his worst.

'Yes, lard. You dislike the word because it puts you in mind of something extremely unpleasant: fat. The Alchemaster has imprinted his desire for fat on your body. It clings to your ribs and haunches. It's the fat he intends to extract from your body when he renders it down. You're the living fulfilment of Ghoolion's contract – you're your own death warrant. Is *that* undiplomatic enough for you?'

'Yes,' Echo said dully.

'Good. What the Cogitating Eggs wish to impart is not the objective realisation that you've become too fat, but the fact that certain conclusions should be drawn from it.'

'I must lose weight, you mean,' Echo whispered.

'Exactly!' cried the squirrel, clapping its paws together. 'Not an especially complex deduction, but a profoundly important one. It'll influence your life in a positive manner.'

The light dimmed, the golden squirrel's figure grew steadily fainter.

'That's it for today,' it said. 'We'll meet again soon, when I come to impart your second insight. Meantime, I'd advise you to take as much exercise as possible.'

The weird light went out. The squirrel had vanished.

Echo went up to the remaining Anguish Candle and took a final look at his reflection. His plump form looked ripe for slaughter.

He snuffed the last Anguish Candle with his paw, and the library, now in total darkness, was pervaded by a deep sigh of relief.

Black Pudding and Vampirism

'I could use a little physical exercise,' Echo remarked in a studiously casual tone as the Alchemaster was preparing his supper the following evening. 'A lighter diet would also do me good. Please go easy on the butter and sugar.'

Ghoolion pricked up his ears. 'Why?' he demanded. 'Have you lost your taste for them?'

'On the contrary,' Echo replied, 'that's just the problem, I'm far too partial to them. I'm getting too fat.'

'But I like you that way,' said Ghoolion. 'Your curves suit you.'

'I can well believe you approve of my curves, but I'm feeling uncomfortable. I don't dare go up on the roof any more for fear of falling off. Our contract didn't specify *how much* weight I had to gain. I reckon I'm fat enough.'

Ghoolion removed a heavy cast-iron pan from the stove. 'Suit yourself,' he said. 'After all, the quality of your fat depends partly on your state of mind. You know: contented hens lay better eggs. I want you feeling good when you die.'

Echo sighed. The Alchemaster didn't give a damn what he said, however hurtful.

'Still, you could probably manage a little black pudding, couldn't you?' Ghoolion asked. 'Now that I've already fried it?'

'All right,' said Echo. He was undeniably hungry.

Ghoolion sprinkled the black pudding generously with curry powder and put it in front of him. Echo promptly tucked in and demolished it in three mouthfuls.

'Not bad,' he said appreciatively.

'Tell me something,' said Ghoolion. 'Have you ever dreamt of being a Leathermouse?'

'A Leathermouse?' Echo replied, licking his paws. 'Why should I dream of being such a hideous creature?'

'Only other creatures consider Leathermice hideous. If you yourself were a Leathermouse, you'd think you were the Crat's whiskers.'

'Oh yes, I know all that,' said Echo. 'Up is down and ugly is beautiful.'

'But Leathermice can fly,' said Ghoolion.

Echo stopped short. It was true. Leathermice could do more than simply hang from a rafter upside down. If there was any other creature he wanted to be, it would have to be one capable of flying.

'They can find their way around at night and hunt in total darkness. Very few creatures can do such things.'

'That's true. They're curious birds.'

'Not birds, vampires,' said Ghoolion. 'That's the best thing about them: the fact that they're vampires.'

Echo frowned. 'What's the good of that?' he demanded.

'Oh, come,' Ghoolion said with a grin. 'You're young. Anyone of your age would love to be a vampire. To be able to fly! To drink blood! To be feared by everyone! The mere rustle of your wings would send people into a panic.'

He might have a point, Echo reflected. It was rather tempting, the thought of being a creature that inspired universal fear, he had to admit.

'Yes, you're right,' he said. 'It might be interesting.'

'I took your interest for granted,' the Alchemaster said, smiling. 'You're already on your way, so to speak.'

'On my way? Where to?'

'To your nocturnal companions, the vampires. What you've just eaten was a black pudding made of Leathermouse blood.'

Echo recoiled in horror.

'What?!' he exclaimed. 'You mean you kill Leathermice?'

'No, I'd never do that, but they die just like other creatures. They fall from the rafters occasionally and I collect them.'

Echo was feeling sick.

'How disgusting,' he said.

'Not at all. Be honest, you quite enjoyed that black pudding.'

Echo could hardly deny this, having wolfed it with such gusto.

'Anything seasoned with curry powder tastes good,' said Ghoolion. 'That's why I don't use the stuff too often – it makes things too easy. I could curry glazier's putty and you'd enjoy that too. Before bleeding the Leathermouse I marinated its corpse for a week in an infusion of Blue Tea, Hypnium and Crazyroot, so the metamorphotic effect should be quite something – far more potent than that of salmon fishcakes. Give my regards to the Leathermice! You'll now get all the exercise you wanted.'

'Eh?' said Echo. 'W-what's happening to me?'

Ghoolion's face was expanding and contorting, turning into a whirling spiral, a rotating vortex that sucked in everything around it: the stove, the whole kitchen and, last of all, Echo himself.

There followed a moment or two of absolute darkness with a chill wind whistling in his ears. At last he plucked up the courage to open his eyes.

He was high, high in the sky. Malaisea lay spread out far below, many of its windows illuminated. All around him, silhouetted against the moon and the racing clouds, were hundreds of shafts of black lightning: his companions the Leathermice.

'I'm a Leathermouse,' he thought. 'I can fly.'

An aerial armada of vampires was streaming into the night sky from a hole in the castle's roof.

'Night-time!' they cried.

'Time to go hunting!'

'Time for blood!'

'Watch out for curtains!' cried another.

Then, as if in response to an unspoken word of command, the whole squadron swooped down on the town.

Echo had never felt so liberated in his life – released from the constraints of gravity and denuded of all his fat. He was now a wiry Leathermouse equipped with powerful wings. Wings, he possessed wings! That thought alone filled him with a feeling of profound content-ment. Flapping steadily up and down, his wings seemed to function by themselves. 'Of course!' he thought. 'After all, I don't have to keep telling my legs what to do. I don't have to *learn* to fly, I already can.'

Malaisea resembled a roof tile shattered into hundreds of little fragments. The cracks between them were its thoroughfares, which were waiting for him to explore them. Echo experienced a fierce desire to dive down and test his new-found ability to fly by soaring around every twist and turn in Malaisea's labyrinth of streets.

On the other hand, wasn't this an ideal opportunity to escape? The mountains lay over there. These wings of his could easily enable him to reach them in a matter of minutes and fly far beyond them. But Echo was already too much of a Leathermouse – a vampire – to think like a Crat. He was here for a very specific reason: to drink blood. Being a vampire, he knew the natural reason for his thirst for blood. Unless he maintained the everlasting cycle of drinking and digesting the red fluid, his cells would decay and he would die a painful death – reason enough to accompany the other members of his new species.

He dropped like a stone by simply folding his wings. Descending in free fall, an absolutely terrifying sensation for creatures incapable of flying, left a Leathermouse entirely unperturbed. It was merely the quickest way of covering the distance between two points with no fear of injury or death. Indeed, Echo was even able to intensify the free-fall sensation and accelerate his descent by flapping his wings a couple of times. He was intoxicated by his own temerity. Creatures with wings, he thought, must all be exceedingly happy.

A few feet above the roofs he unfolded his wings, checked his descent, and glided between chimneys and weathercocks, flagpoles and plumes of smoke. The whole town was his oyster! He could look down on backyards and secluded gardens, peer into lighted rooms through dormer windows. He could land anywhere he chose on Malaisea's expanse of roofs. Every tower, chimney and treetop was accessible to him. He no longer had to climb them with difficulty, he had only to alight on them. But he had no intention of doing that now. Who wanted to roost when he could fly?

Echo banked gracefully down into Apothecary Avenue. At this hour, long after closing time, it was shrouded in darkness. From high above the moonlight and his eyesight had been guides enough, but down here in the shadowy streets he needed a special sense to find his way: down here he had to see with his ears! Utterly confident of his faculties, he shut his eyes. No longer was he a Crat that had temporarily turned into a Leathermouse – no, he was all Leathermouse. A dauntless vampire, a drinker of blood and demon of the night who could only dimly remember having once been a Crat. Brain, hearing, inner eye, wings, sense of balance – all these were functioning in perfect harmony, unimpeded by any hint of doubt or fear.

He uttered four or five staccato squeaks. They would have been inaudible to most ears, but their manifold echoes lit up the whole of Apothecary Avenue, bathing it in a magical glow before his inner eye. He could see its full extent: roadway, kerbstones, pavements, buildings, windows, doors, roofs, extinguished street lights, pharmacists' hoardings – everything, and all in a luminous, monochrome blue.

Echo … How well his name suited him now – better than ever before, in fact! What he couldn't see was what lay behind the windows of the pharmacies and other shops, because he perceived only the surfaces that reflected the sounds he emitted. The windowpanes appeared to him as luminous expanses resembling rectangular pools of calm blue water. There were people walking along the pavements, though not many at this hour. Echo spotted two nightwatchmen, a handful of ailing citizens on their way to late-night pharmacies and some workers returning home from the bandage-weaving factory, several of whom carried lanterns. It filled him with surreptitious glee to think that he could see them without being seen. He could have pounced on them and bitten them in the neck right away – it would have been too late by the time they heard the rustle of his wings – but for the moment he decided to savour the mere idea.

Right now he preferred to remain airborne, nothing more. Along Apothecary Avenue he flew, then veered off down a side street. A manoeuvre he might have found dangerous as a Crat walking on all fours was now just a question of a few leisurely wingbeats. He missed a beat with his right wing, flapped his left wing a trifle harder and went swerving round the corner like a wagon on invisible rails.

Dogs! There was a whole pack of them down there. Five big, ferocious wild dogs with grimy fur and scarred muzzles, they were clearly in search of some smaller and weaker animal to hunt down and tear to pieces.

'Dogs!' thought Echo. 'And I'm not afraid of them in the least. If I were a Crat I'd be done for. I'd never make it down that street in one piece.'

Almost without thinking, he stopped flapping his wings, spread them out sideways and used them as air brakes. Then he went spiralling down towards the dogs.

'It might be fun to rough them up a bit,' he thought. He even recognised two of the tykes. On one occasion in the past they would have harried him to death if he hadn't managed to escape on to a roof.

Echo shot between the dogs like a whiplash. He didn't do anything to them – didn't even touch them, just snarled ferociously and flapped his wings – but that was quite enough to send them bounding in all directions, barking wildly. He soared into the air to inspect the result.

The panic-stricken animals had scattered across the full width of the street. They ran around aimlessly for while, then clustered together again.

'What the devil was that?' yapped one of them.

'A confounded Leathermouse,' yapped another. 'It came out of nowhere!'

'Damn the things! They transmit dangerous diseases. My brother was bitten by one and he's never been the same since.'

Echo retracted his wings and went into a dive. Just above the animals he spread them again, which not only slowed his descent abruptly but made a sharp crack. The pack of dogs scattered once more, howling. He pursued one of them. It was one of the pair that had chased him that time, a big, muscular beast with a mouthful of huge teeth. 'Incredible,' thought Echo, 'it's scared of a mouse!' He found it so easy to keep up with the dog, it seemed to be running in slow motion. He flew close to its ear and hissed: 'I'm right behind you!'

The dog uttered a terrified yelp and bounded on even faster. It snapped at him over its shoulder, but so slowly, by Echo's standards, that he had plenty of time to dodge the animal's gnashing teeth and soar up into the night sky. Unfortunately for the dog, its momentum was such that it couldn't stop when it sighted a wall straight ahead. It went crashing into the brickwork like a bag of bones and knocked itself out.

Echo was ecstatic. He had put one dog to flight and panicked a whole pack of vicious tykes, genuine killers! This was the stuff of which a Crat's dreams were made. Transforming him into a Leathermouse had been a splendid idea on Ghoolion's part. Leathermice had a whale of a time and the night was still young.

He resisted the urge to go on buzzing the dogs. It was tempting, but his spell as a vampire wouldn't last for ever and he didn't want to waste it on a few stupid mongrels. He turned down Hospital Lane, a street near his former home. Alluring smells were issuing from the hospital windows, some of which were open – smells of disinfectant and ether, pus and iodine. As a Crat he had always found them unpleasant. To a Leathermouse, on the other hand, they smelt divine because they pointed the way to defenceless patients lying in their beds asleep or unconscious, anaesthetised or half dead. There was also the scent of blood. Vast quantities of it adhered to everything – to surgeons' scalpels, nurses' aprons and patients' bedding. There were also buckets and tubs of it in the operating theatres, whose walls were spattered with the stuff. The hospital was the finest place in Malaisea apart from the Leathermousoleum. It contained everything a Leathermouse's heart could desire.

But Echo flew on. First he had to reconnoitre the town. Little by little, his high-frequency squeaks brought the whole of Malaisea into view below him, a ghostly blue panorama. The town looked as if it were built of frosted glass lit from within. Echo glided along the luminous streets, nimbly avoiding taut washing lines and perceiving all the smells that emanated from the buildings in an entirely new way. For a Leathermouse's sense of smell differed from a Crat's. Echo caught the scent of bread being baked by the bakery's night shift, the aroma of the cough-syrup factory, the odour of hops from the beerhouses, but none of these meant anything to a vampire's nose. Of far more interest were the smells given off by the living, breathing, sweating creatures that resided in those buildings. Issuing from chimneys and open windows, they rose into the night air and combined to form an aroma that encased the town like a bell jar. To a Leathermouse, flying around inside this invisible pall of appetising smells was second only to the actual drinking of blood.

It was time to make up his mind. He had to select his victim for the night, pick out a scent and follow it to its source.

Below him lay the residential district where the pharmacists lived. He uttered a few little squeaks and it lit up to reveal a row of neat suburban villas looking like toys made of frosted glass. He stopped flapping his wings and glided down towards a nice big house. Unfortunately, there were some people chatting on the terrace – they were far too wide awake. He flew on. The next house was dark and silent, but all the windows were shut. A piano was tinkling in the one after that. No, its occupants hadn't gone to bed yet.

At last, in a large, secluded garden, he came to a house with several open windows. No voices, not a sound, but a sudden whiff of something that prompted him to circle the property several times. Yes, there was someone alive inside, freshly bathed and faintly fragrant. He could smell lavender-scented soap with a discreet admixture of human sweat. A little girl having a nightmare?

Echo flew in a wide arc, plucking up his courage, then glided straight back towards the upstairs window from which the scent was coming. The curtains were billowing out like long, ghostly arms intent on enveloping him in their folds. What was it that Leathermouse had said about curtains before diving down on the town?

No matter, he was heading straight for the window at full speed. With wings folded and body vertical, Echo shot through the narrow gap between the strips of material and landed as safely on the windowsill as if he'd done it innumerable times before. Unable to resist a thrill of pride at his talent for flying, he opened his eyes again.

The first thing he saw was his own moonlit face reflected in one of the window panes. The sight of his wrinkled features gave him a start, but then he peered more closely. He looked wrinkled, yes, but rather dashing, no? Lean and wiry, anyway. Dangerous, intimidating and sort of … well, attractive too. Yes, Echo thought he looked handsome. Up was down and ugly beautiful, sick was healthy and evil good. Nobody understood the Leathermice.

Night-time.

Time to go hunting.

Time for blood.

He left the windowsill, fluttered into the room and perched on the end of a wooden bedstead. Below him was a mound of crisp white linen bedclothes with something rising and falling at its central point: a little girl fast asleep. He could smell her and hear her. Soon he would taste her as well.

Echo was suddenly appalled by his own voracity. It was really beyond belief: his dearest wish was to sink his teeth in a little girl's neck and drink her blood! All that was left of the Crat within him balked at this idea. Wasn't it the most abominable impulse ever?

No, he told himself, it wasn't. There were worse things. He'd tormented mice, tortured insects, beaten up a hamster and pushed a blind mole into a stream. As for what he'd done to that flightless canary, he preferred not to think of it. Compared to that, biting a sleeping girl in the neck was thoroughly innocuous. Why shouldn't he? Just this once! After all, he didn't intend to kill her, just nibble her a bit and sip her blood. So what? At this very moment a regular banquet of gore was in progress all over Malaisea – an orgy of vampirism. Was he to be the only vampire that abstained, and on what was probably the only night he would ever spend as a Leathermouse? Never! Besides, this whole episode was a kind of dream, wasn't it? Very lifelike, admittedly, but it couldn't be the real thing. It was all taking place in his imagination! That meant he was having a sort of dream about biting this little girl, and who could help the dreams he had?

Echo hopped down on to the bed, hitched up his wings and waddled over the mound of white bedclothes. He couldn't help giggling more than once at the thought that he must look like something out of a Zamonian horror story.

'Whoo!' he whispered. 'Nobody understands the Leathermice.'

At that moment the little girl sat up.

Opened her eyes.

Saw Echo.

And screamed with all her might.

Echo gave a terrified snarl. The little girl screamed even louder. Panic-stricken, he fluttered into the air. Loud voices could be heard outside on the landing. His ears ached, the little girl was now screaming so loudly. He flew hither and thither, and all at once the room seemed terribly cramped. There were bulky pieces of furniture, hanging lamps and vases of flowers all over the place. He collided with a birdcage and almost got entangled in the wire mesh. Then he made straight for the moon, only to hit his head on a mirror he'd mistaken for the window. Heavy footsteps could be heard outside. The door burst open and two muscular fellows armed with sticks came lumbering in.

Echo flew straight for the window. Just then, the draught created by the open door sucked the curtains into the room. Their ghostly white arms reached for him once more and this time he ended up in their clutches. His clawed feet caught in the material, entangling him in its folds, and no amount of desperate fluttering and squeaking improved his situation. He found himself hanging upside down, as firmly imprisoned as a fly in a spider's web.

Watch out for curtains!

That was what the Leathermouse had said.

The little girl had at last stopped screaming and was imploring the two toughs to 'kill that horrible Leathermouse'. They needed no second bidding: they dashed over to Echo and raised their sticks.

The little girl fell silent, not wanting to distract the executioners from their work. Echo's heart was in his mouth. The two men paused for an instant, granting him the moment's grace accorded to every criminal under sentence of death.

Echo broke the silence. 'You'll ruin the curtains,' he said hoarsely.

It was the only thing that occurred to him, and pretty stupid it sounded, even to him, but its effect was remarkable. The men lowered their sticks and shrank back.

Echo realised only then that he'd done the ideal thing: he had spoken. It didn't seem to matter that he hadn't said anything particularly original; what counted was that no one in the whole of Malaisea, neither the men nor the little girl, had ever heard a Leathermouse speak. They obviously mistook him for an evil spirit, or something of the kind.

But he would have to choose his next words with greater care, that much was clear. He was as helpless as an insect stuck to flypaper, so their fear was his only weapon. He must say something even more frightening – so frightening that it drove them from the room. Who or what were the inhabitants of Malaisea afraid of most of all? Of course! Who else?

'Are you mad?' he snarled. 'Don't you know who I am?'

'Er, no …' one of the men said slowly.

'I'm Ghoolion, Succubius Ghoolion!' Echo screeched. 'Your Alchemaster!'

The hoary old rumour that Ghoolion could alter his appearance and spy on the townsfolk in a variety of shapes was always going the rounds. Many of the inhabitants had seen him disguised as a rat, others as a black cat, and one even as his own mother-in-law. The Leathermouse version was not only novel but effective.

Echo realised that his words had indeed been well chosen when the little girl leapt out of bed and dashed out of the door. The men shrank back still further, but they didn't let go of their sticks.

'May you be accursed for a hundred years, just for intending to kill me!' Echo screeched. 'Yes, I lay a curse on you both! Abracadabra! Mumbo-jumbo! Hocus-pocus! Gulli-gulli-gulli! Rub-a-dub-dub! Um, err…' He was only improvising, but his gibberish was enough to send them fleeing from the room. Feet went thundering down the stairs, terrified cries rang out, a door slammed. He was alone in the house.

But he was still trapped. The men might only have run off to fetch reinforcements and exchange their sticks for knives and axes. Whatever happened, he must get out of here as soon as possible.

He proceeded to squirm and wriggle, but every movement wrapped the material round him more tightly and his claws weren't sharp enough to tear it.

'It would be child's play if I were a Crat,' he thought.

But he was a Leathermouse. A mere novice at the vampire's trade, he had disregarded its cardinal rule: 'Watch out for curtains!'

He made another attempt to free himself, but his strength gave out after he'd squirmed and wriggled for a bit longer. He now noticed how tired he was from flying around. Even as a flyer, he'd made a beginner's mistake by squandering his energy on those dogs. Yes, he was a Leathermouse, but a wholly inexperienced one. He had stupidly landed himself in the worst predicament any Leathermouse could be in. His wings felt bereft of energy and as heavy as lead. He was utterly exhausted.

'Just a short rest,' he thought, and he stopped fighting the curtains. His breathing steadied, his heartbeat slowed. 'I must gather my strength.'

Suddenly, shouts rent the darkness. Echo strained his ears. What was that? He could hear a hubbub outside in the street, trampling feet, the sound of knives being sharpened. A mob was approaching.

'Ghoolion!' someone shouted.

'It's now or never!' cried someone else.

Echo was seized with panic. They were coming back to kill him, complete with reinforcements and more effective weapons. He couldn't have chosen the right words after all.

Another shout: 'Let's finish him once and for all!'

'He was going to drink my blood!' That was the little girl's voice.

'I always knew he was a vampire!' croaked an old woman. 'Kill him! We'll never get a better opportunity!'

Echo tried to tear the curtain material to shreds with his teeth, but the more he tried the more tightly it wound itself round his throat, half throttling him.

'I'll never get out of here,' he thought desperately. 'Not alive, at any rate.'

A door creaked open. Footsteps thundered across the hall downstairs. They were inside the house!

'Hey, Alchemaster,' yelled someone, 'now you're for it!'

Echo mustered the last of his strength and made another attempt to extricate himself, but the curtain only increased its pressure on his body.

'This is impossible,' he thought. The material was steadily contracting. It seemed to be doing so of its own accord, like a boa constrictor tightening its grip.

Then it dawned on him. 'No, the material isn't contracting, *I'm expanding*! I'm getting bigger!'

It was true: his body was expanding, he could sense it in every limb. What was happening to him? He could feel that something about him was changing, his body, his limbs, even his mind and powers of perception. He suddenly felt far stronger.

He took hold of the curtain once more and tried to tear it. This time he succeeded almost effortlessly – with the aid of a set of sharp, feline claws.

'I'm changing back!' he gasped. 'I'm turning into a Crat again!'

Footsteps came hurrying up the stairs, metal weapons clanked together.

'The door at the end!' someone shouted. 'That's her bedroom!'

Echo was growing steadily bigger and heavier. He proceeded to struggle with all the strength and agility of a Crat, using his teeth and claws. Threads snapped, cloth ripped. Free at last, he landed heavily on the windowsill and scrambled to his feet. He'd lost his wings and reacquired a tail. His transformation was complete.

The door burst open. The room was suddenly filled with lanternlight and a babble of voices. A bunch of figures appeared in the doorway armed with axes, knives and sickles. Before even one of the mob could rush in, Echo arched his back, fluffed out his tail and hissed as loudly as he could.

Silence fell. Nobody spoke, nobody dared to enter. Ghoolion could change shape, this proved it! They had expected to see a captive Leathermouse, only to be confronted by a snarling Crat. What would he turn into next, a ravening werewolf?

Echo seized his opportunity. He swung round, leapt off the windowsill and made a soft landing on the lawn below. Then he squeezed through a gap in the garden fence and scampered off down the cobbled street as fast as his legs would carry him. Heading for the Alchemaster's castle.

Hunger

Echo felt completely whacked when he opened his eyes the next morning. For a moment he didn't know who, what or where he was. Was he a Leathermouse or a Crat? Was he lying in his basket or still imprisoned in a curtain? Kicking off his blanket, he saw that he was safely ensconced in his basket. He looked down at himself: four legs and a tail. He was a Crat once more.

Then it all came back to him. He'd just made it to his sleeping place after crossing Malaisea in the dark, fearful of the dogs he could no longer intimidate in his Leathermouse guise. Having toiled up the steep hill to the castle and all those flights of stairs, almost out on his feet, he'd fallen into a deep sleep. Had it all really happened?

Whatever the truth, he was hungry now. Hungry? He was absolutely famished! He'd just spent what was probably the most strenuous night of his life and he hadn't even had a sip of blood.

He climbed laboriously out of his basket and went in search of something to eat. The kitchen had never looked so neat and tidy. All the food had been put away in the cupboards, which were locked. There wasn't so much as an apple lying around and the Alchemaster was nowhere to be seen.

He glanced into the laboratory. The cauldron wasn't in use and Ghoolion wasn't there either, which was unusual for this time of day. The vampires were snoring in the Leathermousoleum, and no wonder, after their overindulgence of the previous night. Echo tried the roof: not even a whiff of food there. The pool of milk had dried up, the little boats lay stranded on the grass, empty. Theodore's chimney, which had always been hung with delicacies like a Christmas tree, was unadorned today. There was no sign of Theodore himself. Echo sighed and went back inside the castle.

Was Ghoolion making one of his rare excursions into town? Why hadn't he left him anything to eat? Echo suddenly remembered: he himself was to blame for insisting on a strict diet. But he hadn't meant Ghoolion to take him so literally. A Crat had to have some breakfast, if only a little bowl of milk and a slice of sausage!

Impatiently, Echo continued to comb the castle for food. The store cupboards, always left open as a rule, were locked. The most delicious smells emanated from them, but the source of those appetising aromas lay beyond his reach.

Echo's stomach was rumbling. Must he catch himself a mouse? He felt thoroughly disinclined to do so today. His legs were aching like a long-distance runner's.

There, the scent of roast meat! But it wasn't coming from the larder. Nor from the kitchen. Echo rounded the next corner and there it was: a neatly laid table. It was just right for someone his size, with a white tablecloth, a vase of flowers, and – most important of all – a crisply roasted fowl on a china plate. He sniffed it. It was a wildfowl of some kind – not his favourite fare. He preferred roast chicken, but that was quite immaterial now. He was starving!

He devoured the bird greedily, legs, breast, wings and all. But he still felt hungry.

That left the giblets. They weren't his favourite fare either, in the normal way, but beggars couldn't be choosers. He wolfed the kidneys and liver, even the tough little heart. Then he tackled the gizzard. First he'd better see if there was anything unappetising in there. What had the bird been eating? Echo slit the stomach wall with his claws as deftly as a pathologist performing an autopsy.

The first thing that tumbled out was a juniper berry. Hardly surprising in the case of a wildfowl, thought Echo. He rolled the undigested berry aside and continued his investigation. A hazelnut came to light. Opening the stomach a little wider, he discovered a neat little pellet consisting of tender blades of grass. 'Hm,' he thought. A juniper berry, a hazelnut and some blades of grass – why did that sound so familiar?

And then the truth dawned. His appetite abruptly deserted him and an icy shiver ran the length of his spine. A ghostly voice – the voice of someone he knew well – seemed to ring in his ears:

'I always have a vegetarian breakfast: a juniper berry, a few blades of grass, a hazelnut and three wild strawberries. A healthy start to the day does my gidestive sestym good.'

Echo recoiled, staring in horror at the bird's gnawed remains. Yes, the proportions and dimensions were about right ... There was only one way of finding out for sure. Paws trembling, he opened the stomach completely. Sure enough, it contained three wild strawberries. He went hot and cold in turn, overwhelmed by a terrible feeling of nausea, and backed away from the remains of his frightful repast.

'No,' he thought, 'it's not possible!'

He walked unsteadily to the window and leapt on to the sill for some fresh air. But that brought him no relief either. On the contrary, he felt more nauseous than ever and couldn't help gagging.

'It can't be true,' he whispered. Yet he knew that, in his boundless greed, he had just devoured his friend Theodore T. Theodore.

He tottered to the edge of the windowsill and looked down at the town, which seemed to be spinning below him like a top. Then he vomited into space until he felt as if he'd turned himself completely inside out.

Uggly Lane

On a misty night, Uggly Lane looked as if a gang of huge brigands in pointed hats had settled down beside a winding street and were lying in wait for passers-by. As he stole past them, Echo was overcome by the uneasy feeling that the crouching giants might rise to their feet at a secret signal and cudgel him to death. There was something both dead and alive about them – something that reminded him unpleasantly of the horrific taxidermal specimens in Ghoolion's castle. He was as reluctant to turn his back on those figures as he was on the houses in this lane. He had entered a melancholy limbo midway between this world and the next.

The wooden boardwalk gave an agonised groan as Echo put his weight on it. He flinched and quickly got down in the roadway, which wasn't paved like the rest of the streets in the town and consisted of stamped earth. Plump beetles and other insects were scuttling around on it, but he felt marginally safer in the middle of the lane than he did in the immediate vicinity of the spooky-looking houses.

Wisps of mist were flitting around like Cooked Ghosts, sometimes concealing whole houses from view. An owl hooted, and Echo shivered because the sound reminded him of Theodore.

'Tuwituwu! Tuwituwu!'

175

'What on earth am I doing here?' he asked himself, peering anxiously in all directions. 'No one with any sense visits Uggly Lane in the middle of the night. Why didn't I come here during the day?'

Then he remembered why: because he wouldn't be able to tell which of the houses was occupied until it was lit up after dark – Theodore had made a point of that. But with all due respect to the Tuwituwu's good advice, not even the most foolhardy of Malaisea's stray cats and dogs would ever do such a hare-brained thing. There were too many stories told about the reckless individuals who had ventured into the lane by night, only to meet a gruesome end there.

The story of the Decapitated Tomcat, for example, which was said to appear in the backstreets of Malaisea on the stroke of midnight and the anniversary of its death, walking upright on two legs and carrying its own tear-stained head between its forepaws.

Or the story of the Four Fearless Mongrels, which had gone exploring here for a bet when the moon was full. They returned the following night – amalgamated into a single animal! The poor creatures had been sliced in half and sewn together below the breastbone to form a horrific hybrid with eight forelegs and four heads. But the worst part of the story was that, driven insane by their fate, the four dogs had tried to run in different directions and ripped themselves apart with a frightful rending sound.

Echo was also reminded of the grisly tale of Sweet Siamantha, a greedy Siamese cat which had visited Uggly Lane in her unending search for sweet things to eat. She was now reputed to roam Malaisea at night, her body stripped of its fur and crisply roasted, a carving knife stuck in her belly and a meat fork protruding from her back.

But Echo found these scary stories less perturbing than the actual presence of the Ugglies' houses. They were such awe-inspiring buildings that not even Ghoolion had dared to have them demolished after evicting their occupants. There was something about their gnarled, organic appearance that made them look inviolable and lent them an aura of venerable indestructibility. Moreover, their dark-brown wooden walls still harboured something – some kind of penetrating odour – which no pettifogging lawyers or bullying bureaucrats could drive out. This was the essence of Ugglydom itself, a clearly detectable source of energy that pervaded the entire lane, as potent as any evil curse.

Since Ugglies were legally prohibited from installing street lights, the only lighting was provided by the reflection of the moon in some rain-filled potholes. Echo paused beside one of these puddles, which looked in the gloom like a pool of blood.

He had now reached the end of the lane without spotting a single lighted window.

'Good,' he thought, feeling relieved. 'There's no one living here, so I'll make myself scarce.'

He was just about to turn round when, only a few Crat's lengths away, the wind wafted a shred of mist into the air like a conjurer whipping a cloth off a birdcage. It rose into the night sky and there, in the place where it had been hovering only a moment ago, stood the only house in the lane from which light was coming.

Echo didn't move. He scowled at the building, which seemed to have sprouted from the ground like a mushroom. He'd been just about to beat a retreat on the pretext of having failed to find the confounded place, but there it was, and he could have sworn it was returning his gaze. Noticeably bigger than the rest, though not by much, it was the only detached house in the lane. Candlelight flickered fitfully behind its soot-encrusted windowpanes and Echo could hear music – a soft, haunting melody. Someone was singing in a deep voice and simultaneously beating time. It struck him as the ideal background music for a ritual in which dogs were sewn together or cats skinned alive.

For some inexplicable reason, however, the house exerted an attraction on him. 'I could do with a little Placebo Wart Ointment,' he murmured to himself as he trotted towards it. 'And possibly a couple of quality-controlled curses as well.'

What was he talking about? Placebo Wart Ointment? Quality-controlled curses? Why should he suddenly develop a hankering for things he'd never even heard of? Why this irresistible urge to climb the steps of the veranda? What was that funny smell?

He was on the veranda before he knew it, right outside the Uggly's front door. The little candlelight that filtered through the sooty windowpanes was just sufficient for him to read the noticeboards nailed to it.

Currently in Stock:

Quality-Controlled Curses
Prophecies of All Kinds
(Accuracy Not Guaranteed)

Placebo Wart Ointment
(Discreetly Packaged)

Aha, so those were the only kinds of services an Uggly was still permitted to offer in Malaisea. Ghoolion had certainly done a thorough job of making it hard for the Ugglies to practise their profession and utilise their special abilities.

Another notice board read:

Warning!
You enter these premises at your own risk.
The ingestion of Ugglian pharmaceuticals,
quality-controlled or not, can damage your health.
Do not believe a word an Uggly says,
especially when she claims to foretell the future.
And, if you have a problem with warts,
consult your GP or a pharmacist!

Succubius Ghoolion
Municipal Alchemaster-in-Chief

Yet another notice read:

These noticeboards conveyed such a vivid impression of the bleak professional existence led by the Uggly who lived here that Echo suddenly felt profoundly sorry for her. Besides, his craving for some Placebo Wart Ointment had become quite overpowering, so he decided to make his presence known at last. But what was the best way to attract an Uggly's attention? Should he call? Knock? Scratch at the door? Echo opted for a method he seldom employed: he miaowed as piteously and plaintively as he could. An encounter based on mutual compassion might be the best way of avoiding any unpleasantness.

The door opened almost at once, and more quietly than Echo would have thought possible in the case of so old a building. He had expected to hear rusty hinges squeal in agony, but the door half-opened as quietly as a flower coming into bloom. Nothing happened for a while. Then the silence was broken by a voice that sounded as if its owner had lived for centuries on unwholesome, trance-inducing substances.

'If you aren't the Alchemaster, come in.'

Cautiously, Echo squeezed through the crack. The contrast between the cool night air and the steamy atmosphere inside, which smelt of soup and other less familiar aromas, was such that he felt he'd been wrapped in damp cotton wool. The Uggly was standing with her back to him, lit by the dancing flames of a stove. The weird music had ceased.

'You must be really hungry, Pussycat,' she said in a deep bass voice, 'to come begging for food at night in Uggly Lane, of all places. Didn't anyone tell you it's haunted by the Decapitated Tomcat?'

'I'm not hungry,' said Echo. 'Nor am I a pussycat.'

The Uggly turned round and Echo had to make a supreme effort to resist the impulse to dash out of the house, hissing and yowling. He had seen some real-live Ugglies in the days when there were still some left in Malaisea, but only at long range, because they exuded a very special scent which a Crat's sensitive nose found hard to endure. Imagine a damp, hollow tree trunk in which a whole family of polecats has died and decomposed, and you may gain some inkling of an Uggly's body odour. Hitherto, Echo had only seen the creatures from afar, so his sightings of them had been rendered indistinct by distance, but now he was face to face with a full-grown specimen.

The Uggly's face was a living affront to all the laws of harmony. Her nose seemed to have grown first to the right, then to the left, then to the right again, and it tapered to a point disfigured by a third nostril. The other two nostrils were so unnaturally flared that you could see up them even if you were taller than the Uggly herself. Thick, greasy tufts of hair sprouted from them like mouldy strands of eelgrass from submarine caves. Her pupils and irises differed in size and colour, her lips were grotesquely thick and painted black, and her ears protruded further than those of a Leathermouse. Her skin was as pitted as the moon's surface, and standing up here and there were wiry hairs resembling bent rusty nails. The rest of her body was mercifully concealed beneath an ankle-length robe of coarse black linen gathered at the waist by a cord. On her head she wore the skin of an octopus.

'You can speak?' she said. 'Then you aren't a pussycat at all, you're a Crat. I didn't think there were any left in Malaisea.'

Echo started to relax. There was nothing menacing about her hideous looks. The best explanation for an Uggly's outward appearance might be that it was Zamonian natural history's attempt to indulge in a touch of black humour.

'If you aren't hungry, what brings you here?'

'To be honest, an irresistible urge to buy a tube of wart ointment. Except that I don't have any money,' Echo confessed.

The Uggly's demeanour underwent an immediate change. She

opened her eyes still wider and stared at him with her hands fluttering nervously. Then she hurried over to a saucepan on the stove. Having put the lid on, she flapped her hands as if shooing away a swarm of midges.

'Oh dear,' she exclaimed, 'I must have left the lid off my soup by mistake. How silly of me! Its fumes arouse an urge to buy my wares, which is, of course, strictly prohibited – and rightly so.' She favoured Echo with a smile that almost sent him scampering out into the street. Her teeth might have been sculpted by a dentist anxious to promote dental hygiene in his patients by showing them examples of every dental disease known to science.

'But only by mistake, as I said,' she went on. 'No need to report me to the Alchemaster, is there? Besides, you must have lost the urge to buy anything by now.'

Echo shook his head to clear it. He was feeling rather bemused. It was true: his urge to buy some Placebo Wart Ointment had vanished, like the curious aroma.

'No, no,' he said soothingly, 'I've no wish to report anyone.'

Tearing his eyes away from the Uggly at last, he turned his attention to the interior. It looked more like a cave than a house – somewhere suited more to a bear than a civilised being, though it did contain various amenities such as a big iron stove, a kitchen cupboard, a table and chairs, and a shelf filled with books. Visible between them were some thick, dark-brown protuberances reminiscent of roots. More such rootlike excrescences were protruding from the damp mud walls and dangling from the ceiling. If Echo hadn't known better, he would have thought the room was situated in the bowels of a forest.

'So what do you want?' the Uggly demanded, very suspiciously now. 'Why should you be roaming around Uggly Lane in the middle of the night? Are you spying for Ghoolion?'

Echo decided to come straight to the point. The Uggly looked as if she could stand the truth.

'My name is Echo,' he said, 'and I've made a contract with the Alchemaster. It's a very unfavourable contract from my point of view, so I came to ask if you can help me to break it.'

A long silence ensued. The Uggly subjected him to a long, unabashed stare. He didn't know what to make of it. Was she surprised? Annoyed? Amused?

'Let me get this straight,' she said at length. 'Did you just ask me to help you break a contract with the Alchemaster?'

183

'Yes,' Echo said softly. He dropped his gaze, ashamed of his own presumption. What right had he to turn up at a complete stranger's house in the middle of the night and make such a request? Looking up again, he just had time to see a bundle of twigs come whooshing towards him before he was struck and sent flying through the air. He crashed into the front door and fell to the floor. Before he could say anything, or even utter a cry of pain, the Uggly made an imperious gesture with her right hand. At this, the door swung inwards and hit him hard in the back. He went rolling across the floor and ended up at the old crone's feet, whereupon she swung her besom once more and swept him out on to the veranda. Then the door slammed shut.

With a groan, he scrambled to his feet. How idiotic of him to pin his hopes on an Uggly, of all creatures! He could think himself lucky to have got off so lightly. He drew several deep breaths, made his way slowly down the veranda steps and went a little way back along the lane in the direction he'd come from. Then, in obedience to a sudden impulse, he turned and looked back.

Hypnotic music was once more issuing from the Uggly's house. Dark and forbidding, it lay at the end of the lane like the severed head of a giant in whose eyes the last spark of life was being extinguished. Then the windows, too, went dark. A fluffy skein of mist came drifting along and enveloped the Uggly's house like a shroud.

Echo looked up at the moon, which was floating, thinly veiled in clouds, above the Alchemaster's castle. It was now half full.

Mortal Friends

When Echo got back to the castle, exhausted and depressed by his futile excursion, he sensed the Alchemaster's presence as soon as he entered. Ghoolion had undoubtedly returned, even though Echo could neither see nor hear nor smell him. When he wasn't at home the castle was as dead, silent and motionless as befitted such an ancient ruin. When he was there, however, it seemed to awaken to a secret life for which Echo had developed a kind of additional sense. He could hear masonry groan and furniture creak, see carpets develop gooseflesh and ripples traverse expanses of wallpaper. Fireplaces yawned and figures in paintings stirred almost imperceptibly, dust devils went cavorting along the passages and curtains seemed to bulge under the pressure of ghostly hands – the whole building came alive with spectral activity. Distant singing filled the air, as did impudent, surreptitious whispers that ceased as soon as one concentrated on them. They might have been attributable to the wind or some other natural cause, but Echo guessed that something more was involved. His suspicion that a sinister relationship existed between the old building and the Alchemaster steadily intensified.

He felt like an actor on the stage of a theatre whose seats were occupied by invisible spirits. There was nobody to be seen, but one could hear the whispers and stifled coughs that accompanied the drama he and Ghoolion were performing. He still wasn't sure what roles they were playing. Were they opponents in an exceptionally protracted duel? Mortal enemies, even? No, Echo had absolutely no inclination to fight anyone to the death. *Mortal friends* might have been the more appropriate term.

He climbed the stairs, cursing himself for the undiplomatic way in which he had approached the Uggly. *Of course* she'd been disconcerted by his precipitate request to help him outwit the Alchemaster! The Ugglies had long been bullied and oppressed by Ghoolion, so why should one of them incur the old devil's hostility by helping a Crat who had turned up out of the blue?

Yet the Uggly had somehow taken his fancy. She was appallingly hideous and stank like a sack of dead frogs, it was true, but he'd taken a spontaneous liking to her, or he would never have blurted out his request so naively. She had impressed him – not by her appearance, but by her behaviour. She would have given some food to a stray kitten miaowing at night outside her door. That didn't accord with most people's idea of the Ugglies. He felt almost certain that things would have turned out differently if he hadn't behaved so clumsily. But it was no use crying over spilt milk. If he scratched at her door again, she would probably stick him in the stove.

Echo was just passing the big room full of furniture draped in dust sheets when he scented Ghoolion's presence. He hadn't entirely lost his fear of the place, but this time he knew at once exactly what was going on when he heard the Alchemaster sobbing. He couldn't feel sorry for him. His initial impulse was to walk on, but he paused and thought for a moment. Then he turned and went in. The night had been a wash-out in any case, so why not go one step further and call Ghoolion to account?

Echo uttered a loud, audible miaow as he entered the room. That gave Ghoolion time to save face and wipe away his tears before they confronted each other. With head erect, Echo threaded his way between the dust-sheeted pieces of furniture until he was standing at the Alchemaster's feet.

'Why did you do it?' he asked brusquely. 'I thought this was just between you and me. Why did you have to kill a friend of mine as well?'

Ghoolion stared at him in surprise. 'What are you talking about? What am I supposed to have done?'

Not for the first time, Echo was impressed by the Alchemaster's sangfroid.

'I'm talking about Theodore.'

'Theodore? Who's Theodore?'

Echo froze. It hadn't occurred to him until now that the dead bird might not have been Theodore after all. If so, his careless talk could put his friend in extreme danger. He decided to remain silent.

'Just a minute,' said Ghoolion. 'Theodore … Wasn't that the name of your late mistress's manservant?'

Echo persisted in his silence. If the old devil was putting on an act, he was making an excellent job of it. Ghoolion knitted his brow as if working out a knotty problem whose solution he wanted to find unaided.

'Ah, *now* I get it!' he said at length. 'Didn't you say he'd died of some frightful disease? But of course, then *I* must have been responsible!' He smote his forehead with the flat of his hand. 'After all, people hold me responsible for almost every fatality in Malaisea, including those resulting from senility and suicide.' He chuckled derisively.

'I don't want to talk about it,' Echo said curtly and stalked off, thanking his lucky stars that he'd extricated himself from an awkward situation so easily.

'Oh, come!' Ghoolion called after him. 'Surely you aren't still cross about the Leathermouse episode?'

Echo paused and turned.

'No,' he said. 'It was a very interesting experience, to be honest, but it would have been nice if you'd put me in the picture first.'

Ghoolion sighed. 'That's just the problem. It wouldn't have worked if I had. My guinea pigs tend to resist, either consciously or unconsciously, and don't undergo a complete transformation. They simply have wild hallucinations.'

Echo had to admit that he'd never felt so alive as he had during his spell of existence as a Leathermouse.

Ghoolion laughed indulgently. Then he did something he'd never done before: he patted his lap. It was an invitation to Echo to jump up and make himself at home there.

Echo retreated a step. No, that was going too far. The Theodore question was still far from resolved, and anyway, submitting to the caresses of his own executioner was absolutely out of the question!

Ghoolion grinned. 'Come on,' he said.

Echo took a step closer. Tactically speaking, it mightn't be such a bad idea to establish a certain bond of trust between himself and Ghoolion. Last but not least, it was quite a time since anyone had stroked him, and being stroked was one of a Crat's basic requirements, like eating and sleeping. Where was the harm in it? He would only have to bring himself to tolerate the smells that clung to the Alchemaster's cloak, but he'd become inured to them a long time ago.

Echo plucked up his courage and, despite his obesity, performed a successful leap on to Ghoolion's lap. Then he lay down and looked at the old man expectantly. Ghoolion hesitated. His hand hovered in the air for a moment, but he eventually lowered it and proceeded to tickle the nape of Echo's neck. Softly at first, then more and more audibly, Echo began to purr. And so the two of them – Crat and Alchemaster, victim and executioner – lingered in that eerie room for a long time yet: two 'mortal friends' companionably relaxing in the nocturnal gloom.

The Rusty Goblins

From now on, Echo made a very serious attempt to get rid of his excess weight. It wasn't enough simply to watch his diet and spurn fatty foods in favour of healthy vegetables. Getting enough exercise was equally important.

The Alchemaster's castle was the ideal place for this. No other building in Malaisea contained as many flights of stairs a Crat could run up and down. The old, uneven stonework was ideal for climbing and the big rooms were a perfect place in which to romp around with the Cooked Ghost. On the roof Echo practised balancing, toned up his muscles and tested the resilience of his joints. When he raced through the lofty chambers he pretended he was being pursued by one of the natural disasters in Ghoolion's paintings, a tornado or a tidal wave. Sometimes he went downstairs to where the stuffed mummies were kept, brought them to life in his imagination and fled from them in self-induced panic. He imagined himself a notorious master thief, a Crat burglar who scaled the castle walls in order to climb through an open window and rob Ghoolion of his closely guarded alchemistic secrets. He chased mice and dust devils, climbed curtains and ivy-covered trellises, wardrobes and bookshelves, tapestries and threadbare wing chairs, and allowed himself only as much sleep as was absolutely necessary.

He also resumed his frequent visits to the clump of Cratmint, whose scent had such a therapeutic effect on his spirits and whose leaves, when chewed, provided his empty belly with the comforting warmth it needed. As often as he was able, sometimes several times a day, he made his way to the foot of Theodore's chimney, but the old Tuwituwu never showed up.

Echo found opportunities for physical exercise even in the innermost recesses of the castle, behind its walls and up its chimneys. He explored an old ventilation system that ran through the entire building like a network of veins in which he could creep and clamber around for hours on end. It was inhabited by giant rats and fearsome insects, but not even they could deter Echo from carrying out his rigorous training programme. He also came upon the skeletons of a race of dwarfs with rust-red beards. They were strangely equipped with copper belts on which they wore outlandish tools the like of which he'd never seen before. Lying beside many of them were books filled with columns of figures and designs for mysterious mechanical contraptions.

Echo discovered that the ventilation shafts ran not only through the castle walls but deep into the ground – deeper even than the creepy cellars. There, in small subterranean caves, he found more skeletonised red-bearded dwarfs and signs of their presence, including strange little machines of wood or metal whose purpose remained obscure. When he set one in motion by nudging it with his paw, as he sometimes did, it would come briefly to life and go creaking and trundling along until it fell to bits from sheer decrepitude. One machine continued to pound away for a whole hour, churning out metal disks adorned with wonderful patterns. Another marched off and drilled holes in a wall of rock. Yet another went on counting out loud in a robotic voice until it emitted a sort of death rattle and expired.

The deeper Echo went, the eerier and more uninviting his surroundings became. Warm currents of air ascended from the bowels of the earth, fraught with odours that boded no good. He heard noises that aroused his deepest-rooted, most atavistic fears. The subterranean passages led to a world that promised to be even more dangerous than the one above, and he had no wish to venture down there.

Ghoolion continued to dish up fattening meals, but Echo simply threw them out of the window as soon as the Alchemaster had left the room. He took to hunting and catching his own food, so the mice in the ventilation system found him a positive pest. Having previously led a peaceful existence devoid of natural enemies and regularly sustained by the contents of Ghoolion's well-stocked larders, those rodents had now become the quarry of a monster armed with claws.

One night, when crawling along a particularly narrow shaft in the ancient ventilation system, Echo discovered a hole through which he could see almost every corner of Ghoolion's kitchen. The Alchemaster was preparing an elaborate meal. Echo could smell a spicy soup, grilled fish with mushroom sauce and roast pork with crackling. There was a soufflé in the oven and a vanilla blancmange simmering on the stove.

Ghoolion had served Echo's supper only an hour or two earlier. For whom could he be preparing such a lavish meal? Certainly not for himself. Was he expecting guests? No, he never had any.

The Alchemaster clearly thought he was unobserved because he was talking to himself. Echo couldn't catch what he was saying, the words were drowned by the bubbling saucepans, sizzling fat and clatter of his iron-soled boots. Then he turned so that Echo could see his face. Echo gave a violent start when he saw the old man's demented expression: he was looking hopelessly confused.

Ghoolion continued his mysterious activities nonetheless, and Echo had to creep on because the air shaft was alive with loathsome insects. As for the meal the Alchemaster was preparing, he never saw it again.

Echo was losing weight and getting into better shape. His wits were sharper too, because the less blood his body required for digestive purposes, the more was available for brainwork. He devoted a lot of thought to the possibility of escape instead of wondering what there would be for supper. And that was how it occurred to him to give the Uggly another try. He wouldn't go barging in like the last time, nor would he go there empty-pawed.

The Last Uggly in Malaisea

Walking along Uggly Lane in the dark seemed just as unnerving to Echo as it had before. This time, however, he had a definite objective in view. He also had something in the way of a plan, and this encouraged him to run the gauntlet of the ancient houses and climb on to the veranda of the last Uggly in Malaisea.

'What is it this time?' demanded a deep, unfriendly voice from inside the house.

Echo shrank back. How had she known he was there? He'd tiptoed up the veranda steps without uttering a word. Did she really have second sight, or was she simply watching him through the keyhole?

'I'd like to make you an offer,' he said as loudly and firmly as he could.

'An offer? Like what?'

'Well, my dear madam, when you showed me out the other night, I didn't have time to mention that I've something very valuable to offer in return for your help.'

A long silence. Then, even more dismissively: 'I don't make deals to Ghoolion's disadvantage.'

'I didn't say our deal would be to his disadvantage. I'd simply like you to treat me like a normal customer requesting a consultation – a brief conversation. I've got something to offer in exchange, as I said.'

The Uggly made some noises he couldn't interpret.

'Setting aside the fact that I don't, on principle, make deals that could get me into trouble with the Malaisean by-laws, what are you offering?'

Echo cleared his throat. 'Well, for example, an intimate knowledge of the Alchemaster's castle, in particular his laboratory, ranging from his alchemical furnace to the Ghoolionic Preserver and the contents of every last test tube. I have a minutely detailed knowledge of the ghoolionisation process and the rectification of metals sensitive to pain. I know how to make a Leyden Manikin that will remain animate for years. How to render quicksilver potable. How to effect the transmutation of gases and preserve all kinds of volatile substances. How to administer seven hundred different kinds of antidotes and what diseases to use them against. How to distil thoughts that rotate clockwise. I'm familiar with the contents of all Succubius Ghoolion's alchemical journals. I can also recite his chemophilosophical tables backwards. I know quite a bit about spectral analysis, aluminotherapy and ethereal conservation. And that's only a small fraction of what I can offer you. I even know how to cook a ghost.'

Another long silence, broken only by the Uggly's asthmatic breathing.

'How do you set up an aeromorphic barograph?' she asked at length.

Echo didn't have to think for long.

'Er, you calibrate it to a frequency of 100.777 eums, using a fasolatidocal tuning fork, and smoke its lenses over a low fire of fir cones until you can look straight at the sun without going blind.'

For what seemed to Echo an interminable length of time, absolutely nothing happened. At last the door opened as slowly and silently as it had the first time.

'Come in,' growled the Uggly. Echo squeezed through the crack and into the house.

The tropical atmosphere prevailing in the Uggly's cavernous abode wrapped itself round his body like a moist fist. The air, which smelt of earth and rotting vegetation like the interior of a greenhouse, was so warm and treacly you could almost have cut it with a knife. A person buried amid the corpses in the Graveyard Marshes of Dullsgard would have felt little different. Echo promptly wished he was back in the draughty old castle. Only jungle beasts would have felt at home here – in fact, it wouldn't have surprised him if a Voltigork had pounced on him out of the shadows at any moment.

'You've lost weight since the last time,' the Uggly remarked. 'You're still fat, though.'

Echo sighed. 'I know. I'm working on it.'

The Uggly gazed at him as fixedly as if she hadn't the least idea how hideous she was. Echo tried to hold her gaze, but he eventually bowed his head and stared at the floor.

'All right,' she said curtly, 'spit it out. What are you really after?'

'It's quite simple, er …'

'Izanuela's the name. Izanuela Anazazi, but you may call me Iza.'

'Delighted to make your acquaintance. My name is Echo.'

'Well, get on with it.'

'The thing is, I signed a contract with Ghoolion. It stipulates that he must fatten me up until the next full moon. In return, he can then slit my throat and boil me to extract my fat.'

The Uggly flopped down on a worm-eaten chair, which creaked and groaned under her weight. 'Is that so?' she said. Every trace of hostility had left her voice.

'It was a case of needs must. I was almost dead from starvation.'

'Why don't you simply run away?'

'I've tried to, but I can't. I don't know how he does it.'

The chair uttered a grateful creak as the Uggly got up again.

'But *I* do,' she said, raising her eyebrows so that her bloodshot eyes protruded still further.

'Really?' Echo pricked up his ears.

'Have you ever gone to sleep in his arms?'

'Yes, right at the start. He carried me up to his castle.'

'There you are, then. It was a spell.'

'A what?'

'A spell. One of Ghoolion's specialities. Not magic, just a post-hypnotic command. Most effective. He must have whispered it to you in your sleep.'

'And there's nothing to be done about it?'

'Yes, I could lift the spell by hypnotising you myself.'

'Would it work?'

'Yes, unless Ghoolion inserted a mental block. If he did, any further hypnosis would render you psychotic. You might spend the rest of your life imagining yourself to be a glass of milk or the town hall at Florinth.'

'We'd better leave it, then,' Echo said quickly.

'I'd advise against it too. Too risky. Ghoolion is an expert hypnotist and he's far too careful to dispense with a blocking mechanism.'

Echo was impressed by Izanuela's self-assurance. She didn't conceal her unlovely features beneath a cowl or in darkened rooms. Hers was a proud, undisguised ugliness that exploited its impact to her own advantage – an ugliness that demanded respect.

'Up is down and ugly is beautiful,' thought Echo. Aloud, he asked, 'You mean it's genuinely impossible for me to run away of my own volition?'

'Yes. Spells of that kind don't expire until their author dies,' Izanuela said in a low voice. 'You'd have to kill Ghoolion to be released from it.'

Although it now seemed quite natural to Echo that Ghoolion meant to kill him, the thought of killing the Alchemaster himself struck him as monstrous.

'I could never do such a thing,' he said.

'It would be the simplest solution, though. There must be enough poisonous stuff lying around in that laboratory to kill a whole horde of Alchemasters. A pinch of something in his coffee, and ...' She blew an imaginary feather off her palm.

'I'm not like that,' Echo said. 'It's out of the question.'

The Uggly sighed. 'That's why you Crats are becoming extinct. You're too nice for this world.'

'Why are *you* still here?' asked Echo. 'I mean, when all the other Ugglies have moved out? Are you also under a spell?'

'No.' Izanuela stared at him until her squint became almost unbearable.

'So why not simply leave this town yourself, given that Ghoolion makes your life such a misery?'

'Why not? I'll tell you. When the other Ugglies had gone I learnt what it means to have a monopoly. In the old days we Ugglies used to be deadly competitors, but all at once I was the most sought-after naturopath and fortune teller in Malaisea. Customers beat a path to my door. You've no idea what a demand there is for alternative medicine in a town full of sick people.'

The Uggly gazed intently at Echo, waggling each of her ears in turn.

'Anyway, Ghoolion leaves me alone most of the time. He knows how important to him my presence is. What town needs a persecutor of the Ugglies if there aren't any Ugglies left to persecute?'

'I see,' said Echo. He stared, spellbound, at her waggling ears.

'And don't imagine that the Ugglies who moved out are faring any better as a result. Most of them are vagabonds. They traipse around Zamonia from one fairground to the next, complete with their donkey carts and cooking pots, sleeping rough and going in constant fear of Corn Demons and Woodwolves. I've got a roof over my head and plenty of regular customers. What more could anyone want?'

Izanuela stopped waggling her ears. 'But what about you?' she said. 'What made you think I could help you?'

'Oh, I don't know,' said Echo. 'Actually, I got the idea from a friend of mine. He thought you Ugglies either know or possess something Ghoolion is scared of.'

The Uggly gave him the sort of look she might have reserved for imbeciles or children who have said something idiotic.

'What gave your friend *that* idea?' she asked pityingly. 'Why should Ghoolion be scared of us, of all people?'

'Not a clue,' said Echo. 'It wasn't my idea, as I say. Perhaps he thought you could brew a potion of some kind.'

'Oh,' Izanuela scoffed, 'if that's all! Brew a potion? No problem. One that would shrink him to the size of a mouse, maybe? Or make him disappear into thin air?'

Echo's jaw dropped. 'Could you do that?'

'Of course not!' she snapped. 'Good heavens, what an exaggerated idea of our powers you have! I mean, look around you. The most effective potion we can administer is camomile tea!'

Echo looked deflated. 'Then it was no use my coming here again, I suppose,' he said with a sigh.

The Uggly's shoulders gave a loud creak as she shrugged them.

'I can't help that, can I? Listen, youngster: Ugglies versus Ghoolion is like a bucket of water against a forest fire, or harmless herbalism against the most dangerous form of alchemy, or fennel tea against the bubonic plague.'

'Yes,' said Echo, 'I understand. Many thanks for hearing me out all the same.'

He turned to go. Izanuela clicked her fingers and the door swung open.

'So why should my conscience be pricking me?' she cried, rolling her eyes. 'Just because I've no wish to put a noose round my own neck? Or because I don't feel suicidal and I'm not as hell-bent as you are on crossing swords with Ghoolion?'

'It's all right,' Echo said as he went down the veranda steps. 'It wasn't my idea, as I say. Goodnight.'

'Hang on,' Izanuela called.

Echo paused on the bottom step and turned. He felt a faint glimmer of hope.

'The thing is,' she said, 'there's another reason why I'm still in Malaisea.'

'What's that?'

'I'm the worst Uggly in Zamonia.'

'What?'

'I mean it. I can't foretell the future, I can't brew love potions – I can't even read cards. I don't possess any Ugglian aptitudes at all.'

'Is that true?'

Izanuela gave another shrug. 'Absolutely. They found that out when I was at school.'

'You mean there's a school for Ugglies?'

'Of course. I came bottom of the class in every subject. You unerringly hit on the most ineffectual Uggly in the whole of Zamonia. That's why I'm here. I wouldn't stand a chance on the open market. When the others were still here I lived on charity.'

'But what about all your customers? Why do they keep coming to you if you're so hopeless?'

'The herbal remedies I sell them consist of one per cent medicine and ninety-nine per cent hope. The more you believe in them, the more good they do you. I simply roll my eyes a bit as well.'

Echo sighed and turned to go.

'I'm sorry,' she said. 'Come back any time, my young friend. I mean, if you feel like a chat or anything.' Izanuela clearly felt relieved to have thought of something consoling to say.

'Many thanks,' said Echo, as he walked off down the lane. 'Maybe I will.'

'There's one thing I'd like you to explain,' she called after him. 'If he's going to kill you anyway in two weeks' time, why are you still on a diet?'

'Nobody understands the Leathermice,' Echo called back.

'The Leathermice?' she asked. 'What on earth do the Leathermice have to do with it?'

But Echo had already disappeared into the darkness.

The Second Nut

Now that he was entirely dependent on himself, Echo had to use his own grey matter to devise a new strategy. After running the equivalent of a marathon up and down the castle stairs, he had retired to his basket for a rest and was communing with himself.

'Where is Ghoolion's weak spot?' he wondered. 'Where is he most vulnerable? He smiles, he laughs, he makes jokes – he even weeps occasionally, so he must have feelings like any other creature.'

He turned over on his back and stared at the ceiling.

'Why does he have such a passion for cooking? Anyone who's so devoted to an art that gives other people pleasure must surely be capable of unselfishness. Could I appeal to his better nature? If so, how?'

The ceiling above him suddenly turned gold and something even brighter materialised at its central point. At first Echo thought it was the Cooked Ghost, but then he recognised it as the Golden Squirrel from the Tree of Nutledge.

'Hello again!' it squeaked. 'Are you prepared to let me help you undertake some important cognitive processes?'

Echo stared at the apparition open-mouthed. He could feel a warmth that suffused his whole body with a sense of serene well-being.

'Those are the sympathetic frequencies that emanate from the Cogitating Eggs,' said the squirrel. 'They transmit those powerful vibrations from the Valley of the Cogitating Eggs so that I can pass them on to you. I'm their telepathic postman, so to speak.'

'Vibrations?' said Echo.

'Yes. You could also call them faith. Faith is essential when one has visions like the ones you're having, otherwise you'd lose your mind.'

'It isn't my mind I'm worried about,' Echo replied, 'it's my survival.'

'That's why I'm here. You're working out a new strategy, aren't you?'

'I've been wondering how to arouse Ghoolion's pity.'

'That won't be easy. He's got a heart of ice.'

'But I've seen him shed tears.'

'Perhaps he had something in his eye. Or toothache.'

'No, there was another reason.'

'Good,' said the squirrel, 'that's a start, but you'd best begin with yourself. Can you remember any incident in your life that moved you deeply? Anything that aroused your pity?'

'No,' Echo replied.

'Then try! Think! Search your memory!'

Echo did his best. Pity? Compassion? No, he'd seldom had recourse to those emotions in his brief existence.

'The only person I've ever felt sorry for is me.'

'That doesn't count!' the squirrel exclaimed. 'Think harder! Maybe something will occur to you.'

Echo racked his brains.

'Have you ever wept, but at someone else's misfortune, not your own?' the squirrel prompted him.

Echo recalled the occasion when he'd pushed a blind mole into a stream. Except that he hadn't wept, he'd laughed.

'That was malicious glee!' the squirrel told him disapprovingly. 'That wasn't pity, it was the opposite.'

'I know,' said Echo. 'I can't think why it popped into my mind.'

'It's a part of your cognitive process,' the squirrel explained. 'Your brain is sorting out suitable emotions. Go on looking. Go back as far as you can.'

A vague memory surfaced in Echo's mind. An incident he'd almost forgotten, it was so long ago.

'I do believe I've thought of something,' he said. Tears sprang to his eyes at the mere recollection. 'It's a story I heard when I was little.'

'Bravo!' the squirrel cried triumphantly. 'Congratulations, my friend. That was your second flash of inspiration. We'll be seeing each other only once more.'

The golden glow faded and the squirrel turned translucent.

'Hey!' Echo called. 'Don't you want to hear the story?'

'No!' the squirrel called back. Its voice was very faint now. 'Don't tell it to me, tell it to Ghoolion.'

Ingotville

'Listen, Master,' said Echo, having devoured the delicious fillet of sole Ghoolion had given him for supper in the kitchen that night. 'This time *I'd* like to entertain *you* for once. By telling you a story.'

Ghoolion proceeded to fill his pipe. 'I didn't know storytelling was your forte,' he said with a grin.

'That makes two of us,' Echo replied, 'but I can at least try.'

'You're full of surprises. What sort of story is it?'

'A love story.'

'Oh,' said Ghoolion. He looked as if he'd swallowed a cockroach.

'Don't worry,' Echo said quickly, 'it's a thoroughly tragic love story. The saddest story I've ever heard.'

Ghoolion's face brightened. 'Go on, then,' he said, lighting his pipe. 'I like tragic stories.'

Echo made himself comfortable on the kitchen table. He sat down on his haunches and supported himself on his forepaws.

'I must begin by emphasising that this story is true in every detail. It's about a very beautiful young woman.'

Ghoolion nodded, puffing away. Dense clouds of smoke ascended into the air.

'Picture to yourself the most beautiful girl imaginable! She was so beautiful that there would be no point, in view of my meagre talent for storytelling, in even trying to put her beauty into words. That would far exceed my capabilities, so I'll refrain from mentioning whether she was a blonde or a brunette or a redhead, or whether her hair was long or short or curly or smooth as silk. I shall also refrain from the usual comparisons where her complexion was concerned, for instance milk, velvet, satin, peaches and cream, honey or ivory. Instead, I shall leave it entirely up to your imagination to fill in this blank with your own ideal of feminine beauty.'

It could be inferred from Ghoolion's expression and the faraway look in his eyes that he had already complied with Echo's suggestion. His thin lips were set in one of those rare smiles that made him look almost likeable. To Echo, the fact that Ghoolion had any kind of ideal of feminine beauty was an encouraging sign.

'Well,' he went on, 'at the time of my story, this beautiful girl lived in Ingotville.'

'Ingotville?' Ghoolion broke in. He was looking taken aback.

'Yes, Ingotville. Anything wrong with that?'

'Er … no, no, not at all.' Ghoolion puffed at his pipe. 'Go on,' he commanded.

'Well, Ingotville, as everyone knows, is the ugliest, dirtiest, most dangerous and unpopular city in the whole of Zamonia. It consists entirely of metal, of rusty iron and poisonous lead, tarnished copper and brass, nuts and bolts, machines and factories. The city itself is said to be a gigantic machine that's very, very slowly propelling itself towards an unknown destination. Most of the Zamonian continent's metalworking industry is based there and even the products it manufactures are ugly: weapons and barbed wire, garrottes and Iron Maidens, cages and handcuffs, suits of armour and executioners' axes. Most of the inhabitants dwell in corrugated-iron huts black with coal dust and corroded by the acid rain that falls there almost incessantly. Those who can afford to – the gold barons and lead tycoons, arms dealers and arms manufacturers – live in steel fortresses, in constant fear of their starving and discontented underlings and workers. Ingotville is a city traversed by streams of acid and oil, and perpetually overhung by a pall of soot and storm clouds in which shafts of lightning flash and thunder rumbles. The grimy air is forever filled with the pounding and hissing of machinery, the squeak of rusty hinges and the rattle of chains. Many of its inhabitants are machines themselves. It's a vile city, perhaps the vilest in all Zamonia.'

Ghoolion nodded again. 'You're doing pretty well,' he said. 'Very atmospheric. That's just the way it looks.'

'You know the place?' Echo asked.

'I do indeed. But go on.'

'Now picture this contrast: the lovely girl and the hideous city. Beauty and the beast. Innocence and a metallic Moloch.'

'I can imagine it,' said Ghoolion. He was gazing into the distance once more.

'She was the daughter of a lead tycoon and lived in his fortress built of precorrodion – that's a very special kind of metal which rusts on the surface but, beneath that deceptive layer, consists of impenetrable steel. The fortress had loopholes instead of windows and, instead of doors, drawbridges spanning a moat filled with acid.'

Echo paused for a moment. His storytelling was quite a success. He'd ignited a spark of interest in Ghoolion, he could tell.

'When our lovely heroine at last reached marriageable age, the lead tycoon invited every young man in the city to take part in a contest for his daughter's hand – provided he had a certain amount of money. Like everything else in Ingotville, the contest involved metal: who could bend the thickest iron bar, who could bring lead to the boil the fastest, who could forge the finest sword, who could throw a gold ball the farthest – that sort of thing. In the end there were only three suitors left. The decision now depended on their mental agility. Our heroine had made it a condition that she would ask each of them three questions and the one who thought of the cleverest answers would be awarded her hand in marriage.'

Ghoolion had grown quite still. He wasn't even puffing at his pipe, just staring at Echo with an inscrutable expression.

'But the questions were so subtle and ingenious that none of the suitors managed to come up with sensible answers to them. The lead tycoon was at his wits' end, the onlookers started to grumble. They felt they'd been duped by our shrewd and beautiful heroine, who seemed unwilling to bestow her heart on anyone at all.'

Echo paused for effect.

'But then another young man entered the arena. He apologised for being late and whipped through the first part of the contest at lightning speed: he bent the thickest iron bar, brought lead to the boil the fastest, forged the finest sword, threw a gold ball the farthest, et cetera, et cetera. Then, at last, he faced our heroine's questions.'

Ghoolion had deposited his cold pipe on the kitchen table. He seemed even more affected by the story than Echo had hoped, yet the climax was still a long way off.

'Well,' Echo went on, 'it was obvious to everyone present that our heroine had taken a fancy to this young suitor. He was extremely good-looking, but I shall refrain from giving a description of him in this case too. Simply picture the handsomest young man imaginable.'

'That's easy,' Ghoolion said in a curiously unemotional voice.

'Really?'

'I need only picture the opposite of myself.'

Echo was surprised by Ghoolion's modest self-assessment, but he took it as a good sign.

'Our heroine put her first question: "How much is one plus one?"'

'A murmur of approval ran round the room, now that it was clear she'd fallen for the young man and wanted to make his path to her heart as easy as possible.

'"Two," he said.

'"And how much is two divided by two?"

'"One," he replied.

'A few people laughed and the lead tycoon heaved a sigh of relief. Our heroine put her third and last question: "If I asked you to do me a great favour, one that would deprive you of your heart's desire, would you do it?"

'Another murmur went up and the lead tycoon looked round in bewilderment. What sort of question was that?

'"Of course," the young man answered gravely.

'"Come with me, then," said our heroine. She took him by the hand and led him from the room, leaving a confused babble of voices behind them. When they came to a secluded part of her father's fortress, she paused and gazed into his eyes.

'"Please listen," she said. "I've taken to you, I must confess – very much so, in fact, but the problem is this: I'm engaged already. My heart belongs to another."

'The young man didn't reply.

'"My father still doesn't know this," the girl went on. "I took part in this contest purely to gain time for my beloved. In order to ask for my hand in marriage, he needs to acquire a hundred thousand pyras. That sum is the basic requirement for anyone hoping to marry a girl of my rank, as you know, but he comes of a poor family and hasn't managed to raise it yet."

'She looked round anxiously, as if afraid of being overheard.

'"Since I know you possess that sum, or you couldn't have entered this contest," she went on, "here is my shameless request: can you lend my beloved the hundred thousand pyras and enable him to ask for my hand? He will definitely repay you some day, with compound interest. You can rest assured of my undying gratitude."

'Although the young man had turned pale, he steadfastly preserved his composure. "Of course," he told her. "Nothing matters to me more than your happiness."

'Our heroine gave him a kiss. "How very unselfish of you," she said. "You must promise that we'll remain good friends and that you'll come to visit me regularly."

'"I promise," the young man said softly and took his leave. The next day he brought her the sum of money in question. She kissed him and extracted another promise that he would come to see her again before long. Then she let him go.

'As soon as he'd gone our heroine clasped the purse to her bosom. She was overjoyed because she didn't have another suitor at all; she had simply wanted to ascertain the true extent of the young man's feelings for her.'

Ghoolion groaned aloud – whether at the story or in physical pain, Echo couldn't tell. The look of distress on the Alchemaster's face might have been caused by either.

'Well,' Echo went on, 'no one could have given a greater demonstration of his love. Our heroine waited for the young man to visit her, as he had promised, so that she could confess her cruel subterfuge and marry him.'

Echo sighed.

'But he never came. A week, two weeks, a month went by. Our heroine became anxious. She eventually took to her bed, sick with worry, and lay there clasping the purse as if it were her beloved. Then messengers came bearing news: after leaving the fortress, the young man had turned his back on Ingotville and joined an army of mercenaries. Not long afterwards he had been killed during the Battle of the Gloomberg Mountains.'

Ghoolion's spindly fingers clutched his cloak in the region of his heart. His eyelids fluttered.

'Our heroine almost went insane when she heard this news. She tore her clothes, scratched her face and wept for a whole month. Then she left Ingotville and roamed the length and breadth of Zamonia. At last, having tossed the purse of money into Demon's Gulch, she settled down in Malaisea, where she mourned her dead love in silence. She led a reclusive life. Whenever she left the house, which she seldom did, she concealed herself in a cloak with a hood, for she remained strikingly beautiful, even in old age.'

Ghoolion gave a sudden start. Echo flinched.

'What?!' the Alchemaster cried in a voice like thunder. 'She's here in Malaisea?'

'No, she doesn't live here any more – she died not long ago. It's a true story, though, I didn't make it up. It's the story of my former mistress's life. She told it to me when I was little.'

Ghoolion went reeling across the kitchen as if someone had dealt him a mighty blow on the head.

'She was here all the time … here in Malaisea …' he muttered, more to himself than to Echo. Then he looked round once more. Echo shrank under his gaze, for it conveyed a despair that bordered on insanity. A tear trickled from the Alchemaster's eye as he tottered to the door.

'She was here all the time,' he whispered again. Then he blundered out.

Echo hadn't been expecting such an emotional outburst. What did Ghoolion's mysterious words signify? He jumped down off the table, fled from the kitchen and hid in his basket till bedtime.

Bee-Bread

Echo slept exceptionally badly that night. He dreamt of Ghoolion, as he so often did, but also of Theodore T. Theodore, the Cooked Ghost and Izanuela the Uggly. He dreamt of his mistress, both as a lovely young girl and as a kindly old woman. He dreamt of the Leathermice and the Snow-White Widow. Of Anguish Candles and the salmon he'd swum with after eating that dumpling. Of Shadowsprites and Leyden Manikins. Of the wild dogs he'd chased as a Leathermouse and the stuffed Demonic Mummies that had come to life in his nightmare. Even while dreaming, he realised that he was being shown the whole of his life to date in a condensed form but completely out of order, like a stage play whose director has got his pages mixed up. The actors performing this farrago of a play swapped voices and roles as they pleased. Ghoolion spoke in the Uggly's voice and vice versa, Theodore was a Leathermouse and the Snow-White Widow his mate. They all gave him conflicting advice and bombarded him with meaningless drivel as he roamed restlessly through the streets of Malaisea and along the castle passages in search of something, not that he could remember what it was. A huge Woodwolf with resin dripping from its open jaws came lurching out of the darkness. 'Don't believe a word an Uggly says,' it declared in the Golden Squirrel's voice, 'especially when it's to do with the Alchemaster! If you have trouble with him, better consult your doctor or pharmacist!'

Echo awoke with those words ringing in his ears. Feeling utterly bemused, he scrambled to his feet. Beside his basket was a bowl of cold milk and a plate containing a slice of bread and honey cut into bite-sized morsels. The handwritten note lying beside it read:

My dear Echo,

I regret my inability to offer you a particularly lavish breakfast this morning, as I will be engaged on a research project all day. However, the honey on the bread is very special. It's made by the Demonic Bees of Honey Valley.

Don't worry about the dead bees in it, they've had their stings removed and they make the honey nice and crunchy. But be sure to chew with care. It sometimes happens, though very rarely, that one of the bees has not had its sting removed. Although a prick in the gum or tongue wouldn't kill you, it would certainly give you an unpleasant time. This risk factor is said to be part of the enjoyment one derives from eating a slice of bee-bread.

Bon appétit!

Succubius Ghoolion

'Well, well,' Echo thought sleepily, 'Demonic Bees from Honey Valley. Whatever. After last night I'd eat a grilled Sewer Dragon, with or without its knilch.' He hurriedly devoured a few morsels and took a swig of milk. The milk tasted odd – soapy, somehow – so he wolfed another piece of bee-bread to take the taste away – and instantly felt a stabbing pain in his tongue.

'Ouch!' he said, but that was as far as he got. The room began to revolve, alternately bathed in light and darkness, and he went plummeting down a black-and-white shaft that spiralled into the depths, losing consciousness on the way.

When Echo came to, he seemed to be looking into a shattered mirror that reflected many little fragments of the world around him. It wasn't long before the tiny images assembled themselves into one big picture, and he saw that he was in a chamber with a huge domed roof composed of cells of yellowish wax. It was dimly lit by the few rays of light that filtered through cracks between the cells. What impressed Echo most of all, however, was not the chamber in which he'd recovered consciousness, but the company in which he found himself. There were bees in front of him and bees to his right and left. He felt sure he would also find bees behind him if he looked round, but he wasn't brave enough. They

206

were Demonic Bees the size of full-grown mastiffs, and there must have been thousands of them.

'Just a minute,' he thought. 'Bees the size of dogs? I must think this over before I get into a panic. What happened before I passed out? The milk tasted odd – Ghoolion probably spiked it with something. If I bit on a bee sting, you can bet he put it there. This can only be one of those trips in another body he so generously arranges for me – a meta-morphotic meal.'

Echo looked down at himself. Bristly black hairs were sprouting from his chest, and his legs – six of them! – were insectile legs of glossy black chitin. And what were those things waving around in front of his eyes, antennae? Yes, they really were.

'I'm a bee,' he thought, 'a Demonic Bee, and these creatures aren't so big at all. It's simply that I've shrunk. This is just a trip,' he went on, trying to reassure himself. 'It'll soon be over. Relax! Enjoy it! After all, you enjoyed being a Leathermouse.'

So this was what a beehive looked like from the inside. The air, which smelt pleasantly of honey, was nice and warm. Oddly enough, Echo felt at home. Except that it wasn't really so odd. After all, he was a bee.

'Just relax,' he told himself. 'Be a bee. See what happens.'

His head was suddenly transfixed by a thought which – he couldn't put it any other way – came from outside himself. A Demonic-Bee thought, it took the following form:

'Gnorkx is great!'

The community of Demonic Bees suddenly stirred. They all took one simultaneous step to the right, then one to the left and ended by turning on the spot. Echo performed the same movements precisely and he knew why he was doing so. These dance steps were a statement in the Demonic Bee language. What was more, he knew what it meant:

'Gnorkx is great!'

He even knew who Gnorkx was – it was common knowledge among Demonic Bees. Gnorkx was the venerable, supernatural being who had created them all. Gnorkx dwelt on the sun and was believed to be immortal. When a Demonic Bee died it went to Gnorkx and lived with him on the sun for evermore.

'Good heavens,' thought Echo, 'not only am I a Demonic Bee; I even think and feel like one, and it doesn't feel strange at all. It feels – well, normal. I wouldn't mind gathering some pollen, and I'm also experiencing an irresistible urge to worship Gnorkx.'

He took one step to the right, one to the left, then turned on the spot. The other bees followed suit. **'Gnorkx is great!'** they danced again.

This bred a reassuring sensation that they'd worshipped Gnorkx enough for the time being. Absolute silence fell. A Demonic Bee somewhat bigger than the rest ascended a low mound in the middle of the chamber.

'This must be our leader,' thought Echo. At all events, he felt bound to obey the insect implicitly. Indeed, he would have been prepared to carry out every one of its orders to the letter.

The big bee broke into a solo dance. It turned in a circle and fluttered its wings, waggled its antennae and shook its head. This meant:

'Gnorkx is great! Gnorkx is immortal! Because we serve him, we too are immortal. We shall be so even when we die, and will dwell on the sun with Gnorkx the Great for evermore!'

To Echo, this seemed absolutely logical. The leader's words were carved in stone and incontrovertible. It would never have occurred to him to doubt them. He felt an overwhelming desire to endorse them.

'Gnorkx is great!' danced the throng of bees and he joined in.

The bee-in-chief crossed its antennae, fluttered its wings twice and nodded its head. This meant:

'Today is a very special day!'

'This is terrific,' thought Echo. 'I'm not only getting to know the life of the Demonic Bees at first hand, I've hit on a very special day as well. Perhaps they're holding a celebration, or something of the kind.'

'Gnorkx is great,' the leader danced. **'His name is sacred, so all who deny Gnorkx must be exterminated.'**

'Hear, hear,' thought Echo. 'All who deny Gnorkx must be exterminated, that goes without saying.'

'We are merciless and pitiless,' danced the leader. **'We ruthlessly annihilate all who dare to oppose Gnorkx the Great.'**

'Yes, sir!' thought Echo. When Gnorkx's interests were at stake, mercy and pity were out. Someone had said it at last. This bee had taken the words out of his mouth.

'And that', the leader danced, 'is why we must die this very day!'

'Eh?' thought Echo.

'The everlasting war against the Elfinwasps requires us to make the ultimate sacrifice, and we shall give up our earthly life willingly for the privilege of dwelling on the sun with Gnorkx the Great for evermore.'

'Hang on a minute,' thought Echo, 'I've got no quarrel with the Elfinwasps.' Besides, he was averse to dying. Surviving for as long as possible was much more to his taste. And what was the point of a war that lasted indefinitely? Anyway, what was all this nonsense about the sun? Nobody could live on the sun, they'd get burnt to a crisp. His Crat's common sense reasserted itself.

'The Elfinwasps fly away from the sun, not towards it. That means they deny Gnorkx's existence!'

'They probably fly away from the sun because it dazzles them,' thought Echo. 'Sensible creatures!'

'We possess a powerful weapon: our stings. But we can use them only once because we die thereafter. Stinging entails dying!'

'Stinging entails dying!' danced the bees. That seemed logical, so Echo joined in.

'But Gnorkx is great, and that is why he summons us to him when we die, to dwell on the sun with him for evermore. Stinging entails dying, but dying entails eternal life!'

'Stinging entails dying, but dying entails eternal life!' danced the bees.

'Nonsense,' thought Echo. 'Dying entails dying.' He was the only bee to have stayed put.

All at once, absolute silence fell. Not a single Demonic Bee dared to move – apart from Echo, who realised that his situation had become awkward. Nervously, he took a step sideways and waggled his antennae. Not that he knew it, this was the beginning of an inadvertent remark in the Demonic Bee idiom:

'Gnorkx is ...'

Still no one moved. He took a step backwards. This meant:

'not ...'

He turned on the spot to see what the other bees were doing. This meant:

'great.'

All the bees waggled their antennae in extreme agitation. Their leader drew himself up to his full height. Echo had just danced an outrageous statement. No inhabitant of the Demonic Beehive would have dared to make such an assertion, namely:

'Gnorkx is not great.'

The next dance routine the leader performed was quite complicated. He fluttered his wings, turned on the spot four times, rubbed his antennae together and shook his head repeatedly. This meant:

'I fear we have a heretic in our midst. Those who are anti-Gnorkx are pro-Elfinwasp. As Gnorkx's champions in the everlasting war, what do we do with those who deny him and side with the Elfinwasps?'

'We sacrifice them to Gnorkx!' the colony replied.

Echo didn't join in. 'It's high time I made myself scarce,' he thought. 'Let's see what I can do with these things on my back.'

He fluttered his wings, rose into the air and went zooming off. The serried ranks of the Demonic Bee army didn't dare move until ordered to do so by their leader.

'I'm managing pretty well already,' thought Echo. 'Maybe my experiences as a Leathermouse are paying off.' And he flew down a narrow tunnel leading off the big chamber in the centre of the hive.

The leader went into another dance routine meaning **'Kill him as painfully as possible!'**. Even before he could add another **'Gnorkx is great!'** the entire colony rose into the air and set off in pursuit.

'Buzzing along like this isn't as nice as flying like a Leathermouse,' Echo couldn't help thinking, despite his panic. 'There's something mechanical about it.'

Just wide enough for two bees to pass one another, the narrow tunnel he was flying along soon ended in a fork. He wondered which way to go, but how did you get your bearings in a Demonic Beehive? He opted for the passage that was more brightly illuminated. Of course, *that* was how Demonic Bees got their bearings: they made for the sun. For Gnorkx.

The chorus of humming behind him grew louder, which meant that his pursuers were gaining on him. He tried to put on speed but found he couldn't fly any faster. He was a bee, not a Leathermouse. Bees flew at a walking pace. The next turning took him along an even brighter tunnel. He could already see sunlight streaming in at the far end – he would soon be out of the hive.

Something would occur to him once he was outside, he thought. There were bound to be places he could hide. Then he would lie low until this confounded trip was over. If only he didn't feel so tired! His pursuers' angry buzzing was growing ever louder.

Echo flew out into the open. Dazzled by the sunlight, he was suddenly overwhelmed by the immensity of the world outside. He was flying over a verdant Zamonian meadow with flowers shedding their pollen all around him. There was life and colour on every side. Rabbits were lolloping across the grass, butterflies sipping nectar, midges darting through the air. Echo looked back. Demonic Bees were pouring out of the hive in droves. He looked ahead again – and saw a gigantic bird swooping down on him.

No, the bird wasn't gigantic, it only seemed so to a tiny insect his size. It was a relatively small bird: a Cyclopean Tuwituwu, in fact. To be more precise, it was Theodore T. Theodore, Echo recognised him by the pale dot over his single eye. The Tuwituwu opened its beak and headed straight for him. It was out hunting.

Echo could neither advance nor retreat. His mind was in a whirl. Was this a form of retribution? Was he to be eaten by Theodore because he'd eaten him? No, that made no sense. How could the Tuwituwu be here if he'd eaten him?

'Echo?' someone called. 'Echo?' It was the Alchemaster's voice.

With his own name ringing in his ears, Echo disappeared into Theodore's open beak. Everything went light and dark, light and dark by turns. Then he bade farewell to his existence as a Demonic Bee.

211

The Banquet

Echo opened his eyes to find himself looking into the Alchemaster's face. Crouching down beside his basket, Ghoolion was just replacing a big hypodermic syringe in his cloak.

'Now you know what collective insanity feels like,' he said. 'That's another experience granted to very few.'

Echo rubbed his eyes and yawned.

'I brought you back from your trip before time because I was worried about you,' Ghoolion went on. 'You were groaning and moaning and kicking like a mad thing.'

'I was a bee,' Echo said reproachfully. 'A Demonic Bee.'

'Yes,' said Ghoolion, 'it was essential, I'm afraid. That's why I put an undeactivated bee in the honey and diluted your milk with Blue Tea. It must have been a fantastic metamorphosis.'

'It certainly was,' Echo said grumpily. 'But why was it essential?'

'For the same reason I turned you into a Leathermouse,' the Alchemaster replied, as if both transmutations were a matter of course.

'There was a reason?' Echo asked, struggling into a sitting position. 'What was it?'

'Well, I still don't have any Leathermouse or Demonic Bee fat in my collection, and I can't get hold of any in the time available. It's quite impossible.'

'Why? You've got a whole loft full of Leathermice and dozens of Demonic Bees in your honey.'

'In order to extract a creature's essential fat, I have to render it down within a minute of its death. Cadavers become useless shortly afterwards. Whenever I come across the corpse of a Leathermouse, it's generally been dead for hours, sometimes days. The most I can do is make it into black pudding. And you know why I don't lay hands on the live vampires in my loft.'

Echo climbed out of his basket,

'As for Demonic Bees, catching them alive is a difficult and extremely hazardous business,' Ghoolion went on. 'Only the beekeepers of Honey Valley have mastered the technique. Unfortunately, dead bees preserved in honey are quite useless for alchemical purposes.'

'But what's that to do with my transformations?' Echo asked.

Ghoolion smiled. 'If I can't obtain the unadulterated fat of those life forms,' he said, 'I can at least preserve their fundamental characteristics: the dogged tenacity of the Leathermouse, the insane fanaticism of the Demonic Bee. That's where you come in. You've experienced them both. They're both in here!' He tapped Echo's little head with a long fingernail. 'I need only extract them.'

'You're really fond of doing deals with animals, especially if they cost you nothing,' Echo grumbled. He proceeded with his morning wash. It was nice to be a Crat again. To hell with Gnorkx!

'Oh, come,' said Ghoolion, 'it must have been interesting, surely? Do the bees really communicate by dancing?'

'Yes. But I was nearly devoured by Th – er, by a bird.'

Ghoolion grinned. 'It's impossible to die during a metamorphosis. Do you really think I'd risk your precious life?'

'Nice to know that after the event,' Echo said sulkily.

'I told you once before: too much information can spoil or even eliminate the hypnotic effect. It must come as a surprise, without any preparation. Anyway, how are you feeling now? I gave you an alchemical injection that curtailed your trip. It also neutralised the other after-effects of the bee venom.'

'I've felt better,' said Echo. 'Still, I'm not as bad as I was after my Leathermouse trip.'

'There are various ways of ending such a trip,' Ghoolion said. 'The commonest is a post-hypnotic command to terminate it if danger threatens; then you either lose consciousness or return to your real body. In this case I summoned you back by alchemical means. You've now experienced all three methods.'

'What I still don't know', said Echo, 'is whether I'm really experiencing these things or only dreaming.'

'Why not ask yourself whether your other dreams are real? You go on trips and undergo the strangest experiences every night. How do you know they only take place in your mind?'

Echo shook his head, which was buzzing with the after-effects of his trip and the Alchemaster's bewildering remarks.

213

'Anyway,' he said, 'I've had enough. I won't eat another morsel unless you promise not to dish up any more metamorphotic meals. I prefer being a Crat.'

'I promise,' Ghoolion told him. 'I already have what I need. It's in there.' He gave Echo's skull another tap. Echo indignantly shook his finger off.

Ghoolion straightened up, looking serious. 'Right,' he said, 'now for something else. That story you told me yesterday evening ...' He hesitated.

Echo pricked up his ears. 'Yes,' he said, 'what about it?'

'It shocked me at first – quite why, you'll learn in due course. But then, after thinking about it the whole night long, I recovered my mental equilibrium. I'd like to thank you for opening my eyes. More than that, you saved me from the clutches of insanity.'

'I did?' Echo looked astonished.

'Yes indeed, and I'll prove it to you. But first I'll tell you my own version of the story, then you'll understand everything better. Come with me, I must show you a part of the castle you haven't been to yet.'

Echo followed Ghoolion with reluctance. They'd gone down to the cellars the last time the Alchemaster had made such an invitation.

Ghoolion hurried on ahead, iron soles clattering, and it was all Echo's aching legs could do to keep up with him. They descended a short flight of stairs and made their way along a passage Echo had never entered because it smelt so odd.

'You may be surprised to hear that I already knew the story,' Ghoolion said. 'It's a strange coincidence.'

'How do you mean?' asked Echo.

'I knew the young man you told me about. He was an alchemy student and a good friend of mine. We attended Grailsund University together. That's why the story affected me so much.'

'I wasn't to know,' Echo said.

'He was one of the most popular students in our year and a very talented alchemist, even as a youth. If *he* had set out to turn lead into gold, he'd probably have succeeded.' Ghoolion laughed. 'I was immensely proud of being his friend,' he went on. 'As I already said, if you want to imagine the diametrical opposite of his good looks, quick wit and natural charm, you need only picture me at that age: ugly, awkward and unsociable.'

Echo could picture him only too well, but he took care not to say so out loud.

'I clung to him like a limpet. I aped his mannerisms, wore the same clothes, studied the same subjects, cultivated his scientific and cultural interests. I *became* him, so to speak.'

They were now descending a spiral staircase. Echo was afraid it led down to the cellars, but they came out in another wing of the castle. The odd smell was stronger here, and he found it more and more disagreeable. The few windows, which were high but very narrow, admitted only a modicum of daylight and fresh air.

'After his finals he went off to Ingotville,' Ghoolion went on, 'to experiment with metals there. I stayed on in Grailsund for financial reasons, but we kept in touch and corresponded regularly. He sent me detailed reports of his experiments. I tried to reproduce them on a modest scale – unsuccessfully, of course, but I was happy to go on sharing in his work. One day he wrote that he had seen the loveliest girl in the world. She was the daughter of a powerful lead tycoon, so he could only worship her from afar. He said he had amassed a certain amount of money, thanks to his successful experiments, but the plutocrats of Ingotville were a caste of their own. Then, after a year's secret adoration, he sent me a letter brimming with optimism. It spoke of a contest whose winner would gain the beautiful girl's hand in marriage. My friend intended to take part and stake all his savings on the outcome. I urged him to go ahead. The rest of the story you know. His last letter informed me that he proposed to join a mercenary army and go campaigning in the Gloomberg Mountains. I wrote back imploring him to reconsider his decision. I learnt of his death not long afterwards.'

Ghoolion had uttered the last few sentences in an uncharacteristically low, hesitant voice. The smell was now so offensive that Echo almost gagged. Had he walled up the corpses of his animal victims here, or was he hiding something still worse?

The Alchemaster came to a sudden halt. He turned and looked at Echo.

'Listen,' he said, 'I'll tell you the whole truth. I've been lying in one important respect, I must confess.'

Echo had absolutely no wish to hear the truth, nor did he want to follow Ghoolion any further. The Snow-White Widow had been waiting for them at the end of their last excursion. Whatever it was that was giving off this stench, it had to be something frightful.

'The fact is, there isn't any "friend" in this story. I was wrong when I said I *became* him. I *was* him and have always been so. *I* am the young man who wooed your late mistress.'

Echo stared at the Alchemaster. He was dumbfounded.

'But that's impossible,' he said. 'He's dead.'

'So was I, to all intents and purposes,' Ghoolion said gravely. He turned and walked on. 'Let me take up the story at the point where I brought my beloved the money. I was already dead inside, but my outer shell had still to meet its end. I was a handsome youth, though I say it myself, but in reality I was just a dead man walking. Having promised my beloved to visit her soon, I went straight to the recruiting office and joined up. We marched off to battle in the Gloomberg Mountains the very next day. I'll spare you the gory details. Suffice it to say, at the end of the battle I found myself lying on top of a mound of dead soldiers, some of whom I'd butchered myself. I'd been wounded scores of times with sword and axe, but I was still alive. An old alchemist who happened to have got mixed up in the fighting found me, gave me first aid and conveyed me back to his laboratory. Since he also had some knowledge of surgery, he patched me up in a makeshift fashion – makeshift being the operative word.'

Ghoolion laughed bitterly.

'The first time I looked in a mirror, I realised I'd become a different person. No one would have recognised me. But my outward appearance was not all that had changed. My once handsome face had become this hideous mask and my scalp was bereft of its golden locks, but my heart had become this cold mechanism that ticks away inside me and my carefree disposition had given way to the restlessness that dominates me today.'

Echo felt almost moved by Ghoolion's astonishing confession, but the vile stench had become so strong that it left no room for any emotion save disgust.

Ghoolion had halted again. They were standing outside some big double doors whose massive hinges were adorned with gold leaf. Echo could tell that the source of the terrible smell must lie beyond them.

'Not a day went by', Ghoolion whispered, 'that I didn't think of my beloved. I cherished the hope that she would some day appear at the castle gates. Under the delusion that I must be prepared for that day, I cooked her a banquet whenever it overcame me.'

He flung the doors wide.

The smell that came wafting towards them was so strong, so throat-catching, that tears sprang to Echo's eyes. He swung round and vomited on the spot.

But Ghoolion strode into the room undaunted. It had no windows and was lit by a few Anguish Candles. The only pieces of furniture were a long banqueting table and two chairs, one at either end.

Having voided the contents of his stomach, Echo could now venture a look. Although the stench was still indescribable, his nausea had subsided. He wiped the tears from his eyes and followed Ghoolion, though only as far as the threshold. That was sufficient for him to take in the full horror of what lay inside.

The table was piled high with food, or rather, with what remained of it. In fact, the table's existence could only be guessed at beneath a revolting welter of rotting meat and fish, stale bread, shrivelled fruit, dusty plates and glasses, dishes and tureens, knives, forks and spoons.

'There it is!' cried Ghoolion. 'My beloved's banqueting table!' It was impossible to tell from his expression what was going on inside him at that moment: whether he was ruled by reason or insanity.

Echo saw meat and fish bones picked clean; an enormous ham – still recognisable by its shape – with maggots crawling out of it; a whole desiccated boar's head, the orange in its mouth blue with mould; semi-mummified poultry; raisins that had once been grapes; shellfish and fish heads in every stage of putrefaction. Insects and worms were swarming everywhere. Clouds of fruit flies hovered above these bizarre ruins of the culinary art and a fat spider lurked in a veal calf's eye socket, ready to catch them if they landed. Rats were gnawing at an old round of cheese and a mouse had made its teeming nest in a heap of bones. Echo had never seen anything more repulsive. He turned away, unable to endure the sight any longer.

'I cooked an elaborate meal whenever the frenzy of love overcame me,' said Ghoolion. 'I dished up those meals and left them to go bad, one after another. *Now* can you imagine my state of mind?'

Echo fled down the passage in the direction they had come from. Ghoolion left the gruesome banqueting table, closed the doors again and followed him.

'It wasn't until you told me the story last night', he called, 'that I was released from that years-old curse. I can see clearly once more. Tomorrow I shall get rid of all that frightful rubbish.'

They were now far enough away for Echo to dare to breathe freely again.

'I'm glad to have been of service to you,' he gasped. 'Especially if it results in the disappearance of that mess.'

'I'm indebted to you, in a manner of speaking,' said Ghoolion. 'You may ask me a favour.'

'How about releasing *me* from a curse and letting me go?'

'Ah,' Ghoolion said with a grin, 'that would be taking gratitude too far! I was thinking more of a culinary delicacy of some kind. What would you say to some fried mouse bladders?'

Echo sighed.

'You could do with a decent meal,' Ghoolion went on. 'I do believe you've lost weight recently.'

They returned to the familiar reaches of the castle. Ghoolion fried some mouse bladders, as he had promised, and Echo manfully ate them to replenish his involuntarily emptied tummy.

That night, as he lay in his basket, he had a certain amount of food for thought. Startling, bewildering and revolting though today's events had been, they did entitle him to feel vaguely hopeful. The secret of Ghoolion's culinary activities had been revealed. So the Alchemaster was capable of emotion, even of love. His gloomy mood had evaporated; in fact, he now made a positively reasonable, approachable impression. Before the night was out, Echo had devised a bold plan, but one he couldn't carry out unaided. He would need help: the help of the last Uggly in Malaisea.

The Botanical Theatre

Echo still hadn't got used to setting foot in Uggly Lane by night. Although he knew the gnarled old houses were unoccupied, he couldn't shake off the feeling that he was being watched as he slunk past them. The mist resembled a living creature, a huge, fluffy, vaporous serpent writhing around the deserted wooden shacks. He padded swiftly along to Izanuela's house and climbed the veranda steps, which seemed – he could have sworn it – to flinch beneath his paws. He'd not made a sound, but the front door swung open.

The Uggly was seated at the kitchen table, stuffing something quickly into her mouth – something alive, it seemed to Echo. Whatever it was, she hurriedly gulped it down.

'Good evening,' Izanuela said in a strangled voice. 'What a surprise. You've taken advantage of your visitation rights sooner than I expected.' She gave an involuntary belch.

'Good evening,' said Echo. 'I have to make the most of the time I've got left. I can't afford to put things off.'

'You really know how to prick a person's conscience, my young friend. I've had trouble sleeping since your last visit.'

'I'm sorry,' said Echo. 'Look, I won't beat about the bush: I've come to ask your help again.'

Izanuela rolled her eyes. 'I guessed as much,' she sighed.

'It occurred to me that we might pool our talents,' Echo began. 'I thought –'

'What are you talking about?' she broke in. 'I don't possess any talents.'

'I don't believe that. You must have some knowledge of Ugglimy. You went to a school for Ugglies. You've got a flourishing business.'

'What of it?'

'If Ghoolion is preventing you from putting your true abilities into practice, you must be able to do something he's afraid of.'

Izanuela grunted. 'So you already said. What are you getting at?'

'Well, I don't think alchemy is that far removed from Ugglimy. If your knowledge of the latter is sketchy, I can put all my knowledge of alchemy at your disposal. We could pool our knowledge and create something.'

'What do you suggest we make?'

Echo hesitated. 'Well, er ... How about a love potion?'

The Uggly rose abruptly to her feet. 'A love potion?'

'Well, yes. Certain recent events have led me to believe that Ghoolion's heart isn't as cold as everyone thinks. He's quite capable of falling in love and I thought that a love potion might –'

'One moment!' Izanuela exclaimed. 'Who is he supposed to fall in love with?'

'Well,' Echo said sheepishly, 'me.'

Izanuela flopped down on her chair again. 'Is *that* your plan?'

'Yes. If he falls in love with me, he may not want to kill me any more.'

'Good heavens,' she said, 'why on earth did I let you in?'

'It's only a request, not a demand,' said Echo. 'If you won't help me, I'll have to accept the fact. I'll simply leave and we'll never see each other again.'

He padded back to the door.

'Hang on,' she said. 'Can't I have a bit of a pause for thought?'

Echo came to a halt. 'You'll think it over?'

'I don't want you haunting my dreams for the rest of my life. Like last night. You were carrying your head under your arm like the Decapitated Tomcat.'

Echo returned to the table.

The Uggly grunted. 'All right, let's think ... A love potion ... Well, yes, that's basic knowledge for an Uggly, but even my basic knowledge is patchy. I'll have to consult the relevant reference books. And we won't be needing just any old love potion, either. We're dealing with Ghoolion. Who knows what he's immunised himself against? It would have to be very potent stuff.'

'That's the spirit,' Echo said appreciatively.

Izanuela cleared her throat. 'There's something else ...'

'What?'

'A minor change of plan.'

'Like what?'

Izanuela's cheeks were burning. 'Well, er ... I don't think it's wise for him to fall in love with *you*.'

222

'Who else?'

'Well … me, for instance.'

'*You?*' Echo exclaimed in surprise.

'Er, yes … If Ghoolion falls in love with you he may never let you leave. If he fell in love with me I'm sure I'd be able to persuade him to release you.' Izanuela gave a little cough. Her forehead was beaded with sweat.

'That sounds plausible,' said Echo, 'in a way.' He stared at her. 'There's something else, though, isn't there? Why are you blushing like that?'

The Uggly stood up and minced around the kitchen table like a little girl. She clasped her hands together and stared at the floor.

'You asked me once why I'm still living in Malaisea,' she said, 'and I told you I stayed because I had the market to myself.'

'Well?'

'That was only the half of it. The truth is …' She hesitated.

'Yes?' Echo prompted.

She raised her head and looked him straight in the eye.

'I'm besotted with Ghoolion. There, now I've said it.'

Echo subsided on to his haunches. He felt as if his legs had been amputated.

'Surely not!' he gasped. 'You're having me on.'

'What can I do?' said Izanuela. 'I'm in love with the old devil. There's no accounting for tastes.' She chuckled. 'I can't help it. It was love at first sight. He walked in, confiscated my library of Ugglian curses, increased the prophecy tax by two hundred per cent, sentenced me to a week's hard labour because my cash box wasn't the regulation distance from my scales, and that was it. I was done for.' She sighed.

'I must confess I find it hard to conceive of a romantic liaison between an Uggly and an Alchemaster,' said Echo. He was still feeling bemused.

'It's a very one-sided relationship, admittedly. I adore him and he detests me, but it's been like that all my life. I always fall for the wrong men.'

'But can you genuinely imagine *living* with Ghoolion?'

'I sit at my window every evening, staring up at the castle and

223

picturing myself washing his socks and so on. *Me*, a dyed-in-the-wool Uggly!'

She opened her eyes wide, squinting horribly.

'I led the Ugglies' historic protest march on Baysville Town Hall. We stripped off our regulation smocks, made a public bonfire of them and marched through the town stark naked, singing as we went.'

Clearly carried away by her youthful memories, Izanuela punched the air with her fist and started singing in a rusty falsetto:

'We are Ugglies, and we're proud
to be members of this crowd.
Sisters, who cares whom we shock?
Take off that unsightly smock!
Be yourself, no more, no less.
Glory in your nakedness!'

'Well?' Echo said hastily, when it dawned on him that the Uggly was really preparing to tear the clothes off her body. 'What happened then?'

Izanuela stopped short. She let go of the hem of her cloak, beaming delightedly.

'People screamed in horror, of course. Just imagine: hundreds of stark-naked Ugglies singing and dancing in the streets!'

The very idea made the fur stand up on the back of Echo's neck.

'That was the end of the Ugglies' smocks, take it from me. We were allowed to wear whatever we liked from then on.'

'We're straying off the subject a bit,' Echo put in.

'I only wanted to show how unnatural I find it myself. I mean, me and Ghoolion! It's like a love affair between a frog and a stork.'

'All right,' said Echo, 'so it's crazy, but never mind. If that's your minor change of plan, I can live with it. So you'll brew this love potion?'

'Just a minute! I said I can try. I'll need various things, your help most of all.'

'Of course. What do you want to know?'

'Not so fast. We must visit my cellar first.'

'Here we go again,' thought Echo. 'Everyone wants me to visit their cellar.' But hey! He knew from Ghoolion's books about the Ugglies that they were strictly forbidden to dig cellars beneath their houses. It was another of those spiteful, nonsensical restrictions the Alchemaster was so proud of.

'I thought Ugglies' houses didn't have cellars.'

Izanuela merely grinned. 'But first,' she said, as if she hadn't heard the implied question, 'we must seal our pact in the traditional Ugglian manner.'

Echo braced himself for some barbaric ritual. 'What's that?' he asked apprehensively.

'We exchange a kiss. A proper one, though. Tongues and all.'

Echo briefly considered taking to his heels and running off down Uggly Lane. Then he pulled himself together and leapt on to the table to get it over as quickly as possible.

The Uggly leant on the table and extended her tongue. Incredibly long and greenish in colour, it protruded from between her crooked teeth like a snake peeking out of a jungle thicket. Echo edged closer, shut his eyes, opened his mouth and wished his own tongue would disappear the way it had when he sampled the invisible caviar. Izanuela clamped her lips to his and thrust her tongue into his mouth. It tasted like an old cleaning rag that had been left in a pickle barrel overnight, but he didn't flinch. Izanuela withdrew it and he opened his eyes.

'Now we're a team,' she cried. 'Iza and Echo, the dauntless duo! Now let's go down to the cellar.'

She took up her position in the middle of the kitchen and stamped her foot three times.

'**Alumbro, jeckel krapstropotznik!**' she cried, flinging up her arms dramatically.

'Open, cellar garden?' Echo translated tentatively.

Izanuela stared at him in surprise. 'You speak Old Ugglian?'

'There isn't a language I *don't* speak.'

'Good heavens, what a little swot you must have been!'

'I didn't have to learn to speak them. I just can.'

The whole house shook and Echo thought she had conjured up an earthquake. Then the floor opened at his feet! But it wasn't a natural disaster; the floorboards themselves had obediently parted to reveal a crooked, rickety staircase composed of tree roots. It led down into the darkness.

'Is that ... a mechanical device of some kind?' Echo asked, filled with wonder. Not even Ghoolion's spooky old castle possessed such a contrivance.

'No,' Izanuela replied curtly, as if that said it all. 'Come with me.' She set off down the uneven steps with Echo following timidly at her heels.

At the bottom of the steps she clapped her hands. Swarms of fireflies awoke and rose into the air, bathing the underground chamber in a multi-coloured glow. It was at least five times as big as the kitchen overhead.

'If Ghoolion knew about this place, he'd have grilled me on his Ghoolio-Ugglian Barbecue long ago, legitimately or not. This is my subterranean retreat. My garden. My secret kingdom.'

Echo gazed open-mouthed at the spacious cavern, whose damp mud walls and ceiling had roots growing through them. The paint was peeling off its multitude of worm-eaten tables, stools, shelves, chairs and benches. Old books and watering cans were lying around here and there, rakes and shovels stood propped against the walls. The pieces of garden furniture were laden with flowerpots and clay vessels, bowls and vases, terracotta jardinières and china mugs, wooden dishes and galvanised buckets. Most of the plants growing in them were unfamiliar to Echo. Although he could have quoted the correct botanical names of a few of them – wild roses, orchids, ferns and cacti – he had never before seen the vast majority of the fungi, berries, mosses, herbs and flowers growing in this subterranean garden. Their colours were as overwhelming as the many different scents that impregnated the air. Izanuela went on ahead, picking her way along the narrow paths between the luxuriant vegetation and pointing this way and that.

'There are the usual plants that everyone knows,' she trilled in the best of spirits. 'Wild garlic and lily of the valley, woodruff and juniper, lavender and poppy, plantain and heptapleuron, saxifrage and soapwort, Auricula and Daggerthistle, Pharsley and Pheasant's Eye. These look like ordinary stinging nettles but are ten times as virulent. That's a Twin-Tongued Adderhead, and those two are Bullfinch Furze and Consumptive's Cough. The blue-and-yellow flower is a Trigonelle. Those are Venus-Hair and Marsh Tea – both deadly poisonous, so don't touch! The two over there are Cat's-Foot and Hound's-Tongue. They shouldn't really be growing side by side, they simply can't abide each other.'

Thick roots were growing out of the floor and walls, and many more were dangling from the ceiling. For some reason he couldn't have explained, Echo balked at clambering over them and tried to give them all a wide berth.

Izanuela addressed herself to another part of her garden. 'This area is more interesting. These are so-called horrificoplants from the Megaforest – few people ever get to see them. You've no idea how hard it is to obtain the things. Ghost Grass, Guillotinea, Graveyard Moss,

Devil's Besom, Trombophonic Toadstool, Executioner's Axe, Dead Man's Finger – the very names are enough to give one gooseflesh, but it's amazing the juices one can distil from them, especially the fungi. I've made cough syrup out of this Corpse-Glove here. It doesn't actually cure a cough, but your hair starts singing so sweetly when you take the stuff, you forget all about it.'

Echo was puzzled. Hadn't Izanuela told him that the most effective remedy she possessed was camomile tea? These plants of hers could create a whole host of hallucinations.

'How can all these plants grow down here?' he asked. 'In the dark, I mean?'

She plunged both hands in a bucket and held some loose soil under his nose. It was teeming with big, long worms that emitted a bright red glow.

'Lava Worms,' she explained. 'I put some in every flowerpot. They give off light and heat, which is all that the sun does. In fact, they're even better than the sun because they radiate heat the whole time, even at night. There's no winter down here, no clouds, no storms, no hail or frost – no bad weather at all. It's a botanical paradise, an Elysium for anything with roots. If I were a flower I'd like to grow here and nowhere else.'

Izanuela went over to a rough old kitchen dresser draped in a red velvet curtain. 'Would you like to see something really special?' she said.

Echo nodded. Of course he would.

'This is my botanical theatre. It's horticulture of the highest order. You could also call it a mobile plant theatre, but that would be a misleading designation. All plants are mobile, but most of them move so slowly their movements can't be detected with the naked eye. These are rather more agile.'

The Uggly drew the curtain aside, pursed her lips together and imitated a brief fanfare.

'Tarantara, tarantara! Allow me to present the Ballerina Blossom!'

She pointed to a plant on the top shelf. It did full justice to its name. A handsome flower with a red calyx, a long green stem and thin, translucent leaves, it launched into a graceful *pas seul*.

'The one beside it is a Cobra Thistle – careful, please, it can strike like lightning!'

The prickly weed made an almost imperceptible movement. Its tense body was vibrating like a coiled spring and Echo guessed how unexpectedly its poisonous barbs could strike home.

'That one there is a Throttlefern. It's capable of strangling creatures as big as a thrush, but I'd advise you to stand back. I'm sure it wouldn't hesitate to attack a Crat.'

The fern lashed the air with several of its tendrils, cracking them like bullwhips. Echo retreated a step.

'On the shelf below is a Twitching Terebinth. Eat a salad made from its leaves and you develop St Vitus's dance. You dance for three days and then drop dead.'

The plant shook its big leaves violently to and fro – so violently that the flowerpot wobbled, scattering soil in all directions.

'It's absolutely insane,' Izanuela whispered, tapping her forehead. 'The billowing stuff in the green bucket is Breezegrass. I like looking at it when I'm in need of relaxation. Watching Breezegrass for five minutes sends me off to sleep.'

Although there wasn't a breath of wind in the cavern, the grass stirred as if a gentle breeze were blowing through its stems. Echo found this had a soothing effect on him too. He was gradually becoming accustomed to his strange surroundings.

'Growing in the yellow flowerpot is a Clapperatus Applaudiens. I can't help it, but it's a bit too obsequious for me.'

When Izanuela pointed to it, the tuliplike flower broke into applause, clapping its leaves together like a maniac.

'I think it's amusing,' Echo said.

'That Asparagus Timidus is the absolute opposite. Another specimen from the Megaforest. It's as shy as a blushing bride.'

The tip of the asparagus turned red at the touch of Izanuela's outstretched finger, then buried itself in the mossy ground and stayed that way.

She sighed. 'Mobile plants are becoming increasingly popular with people who find normal plants boring but are too lazy to keep a pet. Personally, I think they should be declared a protected species. It's cruelty to plants to allow such people to own them. They're bound to start teaching them tricks.'

'Could they do that?' asked Echo.

The Uggly studied her fingernails. 'Well, I must confess I taught that Trampoline Fern down there a little trick. The temptation was too great.'

She clicked her fingers. The Trampoline Fern withdrew its roots from the flowerpot, climbed out of it, turned a somersault and climbed back in again.

'Encore!' Echo cried delightedly.

'Certainly not,' said Izanuela. 'This isn't a circus, it's a serious botanical theatre.' She drew the curtain and looked around. 'Let's see … What else have we got?'

She hurried over to a long red wooden bench. 'This is a collection of especially fragrant plants: Lemon Balm and Thyme, Rosemary and Sage, Poppy Orange and Blossoming Nutmeg, Gingerbread Japonica and Sprouting Vanilla, Marzipan Potato and Cinnamon Citronelle.'

Eagerly, Echo applied his little nose to each plant in turn. They all smelt divine.

Izanuela made her way across to a crude wooden cupboard overgrown with ivy and opened the door. 'I keep the more evil-smelling plants shut up in here,' she said. Echo backed away, repelled by the vile stench that came drifting out of the interior.

'Garlic Breath and Cheesefoot, Sulphurous Sumach and Perspiring Tulip, Horse-Apple Hosta and Common Turdwort, Fernfart and Stinkboot. Pooh!' She fanned herself. 'I have to admit I always speed up a bit when I'm watering this section.' She slammed the cupboard door and went over to a set of shelves. Unlike the others, they were made of some silvery, richly decorated metal.

'Take a look at these beauties instead. They're Crystalline Orchids.'

Echo gazed at the wonderful plants. Their flowers resembled magnified snowflakes, each unique in shape.

'Please be careful of this magnificent cactus. Although it changes colour every second, it fires off its poisonous spines like arrows when it's out of sorts. It hit me in the backside once and I had heartburn for three days. Beautiful, though, isn't it? It glows in the dark.'

Izanuela pointed to various flowerpots and reeled off the names of their occupants: 'Golden Leafling, Ladykiller, Cupreous Rose, Nightingale Crocus – that one can actually sing when it's in the mood. Angel's Hair. Blonde Princess.'

She turned to a tub which seemed to be on fire.

Issuing from the peaty soil was a wonderful, balletically flickering blue flame. 'A Graveyard Ghost,' she said in a whisper.

As Echo and the Uggly looked more closely, he saw that the flame had a childlike face and was whispering softly to itself. It was a while before the two of them could drag themselves away from this mesmeric apparition.

'But where there's light, there's darkness as well,' Izanuela said in a low voice, beckoning to Echo to follow. 'Come with me. I'll show you some plants that aren't as good-looking.'

She led him over to some flowerpots standing on a rustic bench beneath a table. 'I have to confess I keep them hidden,' she said. 'Their appearance tends to depress me.'

Echo looked at the plants. They really were remarkably unattractive. Suppurating sores had developed where flowers once grew. Their leaves were shrivelled or dung-coloured, their stems misshapen and prickly.

'Humpbacked Gnome, Python's Fang, Death Cup, Septic Verruca, Mouldering Morel, Slimy Susan, Athlete's Foot. You can't help feeling sorry for them. The majority were almost exterminated, simply because they're so ugly, but they're highly effective medicinal herbs if administered in the correct dosage. That one cures rheumatism.'

Echo could restrain himself no longer. 'You told me that camomile tea was the most effective remedy you possessed,' he blurted out, 'but this garden of yours is full of the most miraculous plants.'

Izanuela eyed him with a pitying expression. 'You really are gullible. I only said that to get rid of you. I also said I was the worst Uggly in Zamonia. That was another lie, of course.'

'Really?' Echo pricked up his ears.

She pointed to a framed document hanging on the wall 'See that diploma?' she said with a tremor in her voice. 'It was awarded me by the Ugglian Academy in Grailsund. I graduated with five necromantic stars. Do you know what that means?'

'No,' Echo said.

'It means I'm a qualified Uggly with five necromantic stars, that's what! I wrote my doctoral thesis on the capillary system of the Witch's Hat Toadstool. I studied prophosophy for thirty-four terms – that's prophetic philosophy, a subject only Ugglies can study. Only one Uggly in a hundred is awarded five necromantic stars. My mentor was the legendary Kora Kronch. *That's* what it means.'

Breathing hard, Izanuela pointed to a gold cup on a shelf. 'You see that cup? That's the Green Thumb of Watervale, the most highly prized award in the field of floristic botany. Guess who was nominated for it three times and awarded it once! I'll give you a clue: the person who's standing in front of you, bears my name and is the only Uggly left in Malaisea.'

Izanuela had delivered this harangue with her head held high, squinting like mad and waggling her ears excitedly. She still seemed proud of having pulled the wool over Echo's eyes, but that was fine with him. Better a well-qualified Uggly than the worst one in Zamonia.

'Is there anything else I should know?' he asked. 'Now that we're partners, I mean?'

She looked down at him with a smile.

'I really must congratulate you, my young friend,' she said in a condescending tone, 'on your good manners. There's one question you must be itching to ask me.'

'What's that?' said Echo.

'Well, how the staircase works. But you don't dare, eh?'

'It would certainly interest me to know,' Echo admitted.

'Then look around you. Which is the biggest plant down here?'

Echo looked around the cavern.

'That big blue cactus over there,' he said. 'That's the biggest.'

'Wrong.'

'But there isn't anything bigger.'

'You aren't using your eyes properly. Where do you think all these roots in the ground and the ceiling come from?'

'A tree of some kind, I suppose.'

'Well? Have you seen any trees in Uggly Lane?'

Echo thought hard. No, there were no trees at all in Uggly Lane.

'The nearest trees are in the municipal park,' Izanuela said with a laugh. 'That's half a mile away. No trees have roots that long.'

'You mean …' Echo looked up at the ceiling.

'Exactly,' said Izanuela. 'This house is the biggest plant here. All the houses in Uggly Lane are plants and they're alive. Very much alive.'

Picking up a flowerpot, she brought it down hard on the fat black root writhing around her feet. The bark split open in several places and some big, melancholy eyes came to light beneath it.

'An Ugglian oak,' she said. 'One of the oldest plants in Zamonia. Only the Ugglies know of its existence. Which makes you an Uggly too, in a manner of speaking. Can you keep a secret?'

'Of course,' Echo said hurriedly.

'Good. You wouldn't like to hear what would happen if you blabbed.'

Izanuela subjected him to a long, piercing stare and he felt genuinely scared of her for the first time. Her eyes were incandescent with the millennial power of Ugglyism. He grew terribly cold, as if a giant shadow had engulfed him, and for one brief moment he thought he heard the weird music that had assailed his ears the first time he set eyes on her house. Her gaze was like an unspoken threat, a curse. He shivered.

Then the light in her eyes went out.

'These trees existed many thousands of years before Malaisea was founded,' she continued, squinting good-naturedly now. 'Only the Ugglies realised that they were habitable, and they were also the only living creatures the trees would accept as tenants. The Ugglian oaks came to look more and more like houses as the centuries went by, until no one would have guessed they were really plants. The town of Malaisea grew up around the Ugglies' colony, but they kept the secret to themselves and passed it on from generation to generation.'

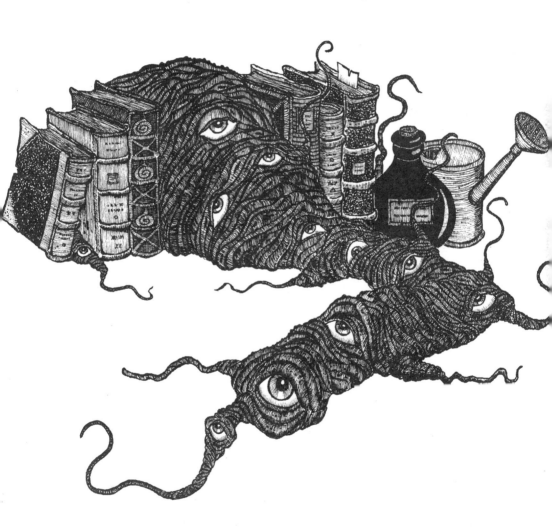

The eyes in the roots slowly closed as if the tree were going to sleep.

'Living inside living plants isn't a bed of roses, believe you me. They have their idiosyncrasies, their moods, their quirks, their habits. You have to be able to put up with them or you'd go mad. Things are in a constant state of flux. Walls become displaced, windows close up, roots suddenly appear where there weren't any before – you trip over them and fall flat on your face. This tree also hums to itself at night, that's why I wear earplugs.'

Echo looked around nervously. It wasn't a very reassuring sensation, being inside a living creature – it was like being swallowed by a giant. He now understood his instinctive fear of the Ugglies' houses.

'Don't be frightened,' Izanuela told him soothingly. 'It's thoroughly good-natured. At least, I've never known it to lose its temper.'

She climbed over the root and went to a big trestle table groaning under the weight of numerous flowerpots. Echo would have liked to hear more about the living houses, but Izanuela seemed to have exhausted the subject.

'This is the medicinal section,' she went on. 'That's another misleading designation, of course, because almost any plant can be used for medicinal purposes, even the most poisonous. These are particularly effective, though. They range from the simple Runny Nose to the Crazy Courgette, but there are many more.' She indicated a cucumber that had tied itself in knots. 'That one can cure serious mental illnesses, but it can also induce them if incorrectly administered. When Ghoolion's castle was still a lunatic asylum, the patients there were fed on it. No wonder it all ended in chaos.'

She pointed to a few inconspicuous plants. 'That's Disinfectant Knotgrass and that's an Anaesthetic Sponge. The juice of this cactus can combat hair loss, but the patient's head grows prickles instead. Turdwort, Thistlegut, Black Uncle … I'd rather not tell you what ailments they're good for.'

Echo was fascinated. This was in every respect a counterpart to the Alchemaster's laboratory. Ghoolion's morbid realm was filled with stuffed corpses and dangerous chemicals, pathogenic substances and preserved death rattles, whereas this was a celebration of life, a living, proliferating, breathing world in which everything served therapeutic medicinal purposes. What a contrast between the Alchemaster's acrid alchemical fumes and the vernal fragrance of Izanuela's flower garden! Echo felt like making his home there right away.

'But that's enough about diseases,' Izanuela said firmly. 'It's an unpleasant subject.'

They came to a big table laden with gadgets, all of which might have come from the Alchemaster's laboratory: flasks and test tubes, phials and mortars, coloured liquids and powders, microscopes and tweezers. Compared to Ghoolion's equipment, however, Izanuela's was just a child's chemistry set.

'This is my distillation plant,' she said with a grin. 'I certainly can't compete with Ghoolion's laboratory, but I can brew a potion or two. Incidentally, about my so-called *Placebo* Wart Ointment: it is, in fact, the most effective wart ointment in the whole of Zamonia. Apply some to a wart and it'll drop off the next morning. There's nothing to touch it anywhere on Apothecary Avenue. Here, this is a cold cure distilled from Snotgrass. Take some and five minutes later your cold will be gone. I'd like to see the doctor who can prescribe such a medicine.'

She held up a test tube containing some green powder.

'There's no such thing as a cure for hangovers, right? You just have to let them wear off, right?'

Echo thought of his wine-tasting session with Ghoolion and nodded.

'Wrong!' cried Izanuela. 'A spoonful of this powder in your coffee and you'll be as clear-headed as a teetotaller. This tincture cures any migraine. That pill banishes any toothache. Here's a liqueur that will heal stomach ulcers. Appendicitis? Chew this root and your appendix disinflames itself. Chickenpox? Simply rub my chickenpox ointment on your spots and they stop itching within seconds. Jaundice? Drink this potion and your liver will be back in order immediately.'

She spread her arms wide.

'Down here I've devised remedies for most of the diseases Ghoolion is concocting up there. Not that he knows it, the two of us are engaged in an everlasting duel.'

Echo had been carried away by her enthusiastic recital. 'Let's get down to work!' he cried. 'When are we going to brew this love potion? Now?'

The Uggly made a soothing gesture.

'Not so fast,' she said. 'First I have to familiarise myself with the relevant literature.'

She picked up a huge leather-bound tome and slammed it down on the tabletop so hard that it set all the retorts and test tubes around her jingling.

'The Ugglimical Cookbook,' she explained. 'It contains every Ugglimical recipe in existence. In Old Ugglian.'

She opened the book at the title page and read out the motto:

'"**Nyott stropstnopirni hapfel zach; hapfel zach stropstnopirni!**" Can you translate that too?'

'We don't live to learn; we learn to live!' Echo replied.

'Correct,' she said. 'Let's see now ...'

She turned over the pages for quite a while.

'Toadstool Soup ... hm ... Henbane Rissoles ... Crab-Apple Cocktail ... hm ... Muddlewater Cordial ... Adderthistle Salad with Larkspew Dressing ...'

She tapped a page with her finger and uttered a triumphant cry. 'Here we are! Ugglimical Love Potion, Extra Strong!'

'Have you found it?' Echo asked excitedly. 'Is it really in there?'

'Phew,' Izanuela said to herself, 'this is a tall order. We need some Gristlethorn ... some Treacletuft ... a spoonful of Champagne Rennet ... a Clubfoot Toadstool ... some Prickly Wormfern ... a Twelve-Leafed Clover ... a Graveyard Marsh Anemone ... Arctic Woodbine ... a pinch of Old Man's Scurf ... some chopped Toadpipe ... a pound of Pond Scum ... some Sparrowspit ...' She mopped her brow. 'Heavens, what next! A Funnelhorn ... Quail's-Eye Wheat ... Tuberous Stinkwort ... Devil's Clover ... Inflorescent Cabbage ... some Ranunculaceous Nectar ... two Shadow Shallots ... hm ... hm ...'

She looked up at last.

'It's as I feared, my friend: this isn't going to be a stroll in the park. All right, I've got most of the ingredients here and the rest I can get from Ugglies of my acquaintance. But there's one that's almost impossible to obtain. It's a plant that has become almost extinct. No Uggly knows where it's still to be found.'

Echo's heart sank. All his elation had gone. 'What's it called?' he asked dejectedly.

'Cratmint,' she said. 'An extremely potent herb.'

'Cratmint?' he exclaimed. 'I know where to find some!'

'Really? Where?'

'On Ghoolion's roof. A big clump of it. In full bloom.'

Izanuela looked relieved. 'That's wonderful. I thought we'd had it.'

'I can pick a few leaves and bring them to you. No problem.'

She perused the book again.

'Hm ...' she said. 'A few dead leaves won't do. I need the whole plant – alive. You'll have to dig it up, roots and all.'

'But I can't,' Echo said miserably. 'It's far too big for a Crat to manage.'

Izanuela gave him a long look. Echo stared back. Profound silence reigned for a while. Everything was so quiet, the Graveyard Ghost could be heard whispering to itself.

'No,' Izanuela said, 'you can't be serious!'

'Yes,' said Echo, 'there's no alternative: you'll have to come up on the roof with me.'

Cratmint

There was only one time of day when Echo and Izanuela could risk an excursion to the mother of all roofs, and that was when the Alchemaster was at work on his dinner menu in the kitchen. He would be so preoccupied that they could sneak through the laboratory unobserved. The Leathermice would already have left at twilight.

The following evening found Echo waiting impatiently at the castle entrance, ready to guide the Uggly to the roof. She turned up late, as he'd feared she would. There was something different about her when she finally walked in. Her lips looked glossier than usual and her complexion less greenish.

'What took you so long?' Echo demanded.

'I spruced myself up a bit,' she said sheepishly.

'For whose benefit? This isn't a date, you know. You're here to snaffle a plant.'

'I was almost ready before I remembered that. I'm always in such a spin where Ghoolion's concerned.'

Echo went on ahead. Izanuela followed him along one of the galleries in which the Alchemaster had hung his disaster paintings. The scenes looked almost lifelike in the wildly flickering candlelight. 'This is even more of a madhouse than it looks from outside,' the Uggly said wonderingly. 'Who painted all these pictures?'

'Ghoolion,' said Echo.

'He's a man of many talents,' she whispered. 'I'd never have believed he could paint as well. These pictures are absolutely –'

Echo came to a halt and swung round abruptly. 'Listen,' he said, 'you're besotted with Ghoolion already. You aren't here to indulge your passion for him; you're here to make *him* fall in love with *you*. Can we please concentrate on the matter in hand?'

'Of course,' said Izanuela. 'But these pictures really are something!'

They climbed the stairs to the floor on which Ghoolion had displayed most of his stuffed mummies. Echo deemed it advisable to issue a warning.

'Don't get a fright when we turn the next corner,' he said. 'There's a Corn Demon there, but it isn't alive. It's stuffed.'

'Ghoolion stuffs Corn Demons?'

'Yes.'

'He's a man of many talents,' she repeated admiringly. 'Really multitalented!'

A chorus of whispers floated past their ears. It sounded as if a host of disembodied spirits were flying down the passage.

Izanuela shivered. 'Eerie here, isn't it?'

'Yes,' said Echo, 'but you get used to it.'

When they rounded the corner the Uggly uttered a piercing shriek. 'Aieee!' Her cry re-echoed from the lofty walls.

'Are you mad?' Echo hissed. 'I did warn you!'

'But it looks so lifelike,' Izanuela whispered as she squeezed past the horrific figure. 'Goodness me!'

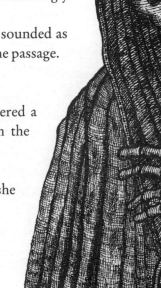

'Pull yourself together! Here are some more of the brutes.'

They slunk past Woodwolves, Hazelwitches and more Corn Demons lurking in niches or mounted on pedestals as if preparing to pounce. Izanuela pulled a face whenever she caught sight of one.

'This is a regular chamber of horrors,' she gasped. 'It'll be the first thing to go once I've got Ghoolion under my thumb.'

They were now climbing the stairs to the floor on which the kitchen was situated. Ghoolion could be heard at work in the distance. Saucepan lids were clattering, fat sizzling. He was obviously going full speed ahead and hadn't heard Izanuela shriek over the noise of the bubbling saucepans and crackling flames. It was now or never!

'Quiet as a mouse,' said Echo, 'and as quick as you can.'

Now came the critical moment. They had to steal past the kitchen. If Ghoolion needed something from the larder and came out just at that moment, it would be curtains!

Echo padded on ahead and the Uggly followed on tiptoe. The kitchen door was open a crack and Ghoolion's clattering footsteps could be heard. The air was filled with delicious smells: roast duck, red cabbage, nutmeg … Echo spotted a hole in the carpet and leapt lightly over it, but he was too late to warn Izanuela, who caught her foot in it. She tripped, lost her balance, flailed her arms wildly and measured her length on the floor. There was a dull thud as she landed.

'Unk!' she went, and Echo seemed to hear a high-pitched giggle coming from the gloomy reaches of the passage.

Ghoolion's metallic footsteps ceased. For the space of a few heartbeats nothing could be heard but his bubbling saucepans.

'Hello?' Ghoolion called. 'Anyone there?'

Izanuela flinched as if she'd been struck by lightning.

'Hello?' Ghoolion called again.

'Miaow!' said Echo. 'Miaooow!'

The Alchemaster laughed.

'Be patient for a little while longer, Echo!' he called. 'This is a pretty complicated dish I'm making. It'll be worth the wait, I promise you.'

Izanuela scrambled to her feet. They made their way along the passage and up the next flight of stairs. This brought them to the sinister room filled with cages.

'He's got a nice voice, in my opinion,' Izanuela said as they threaded their way between the cages of wood and iron. 'To think he can cook as well!'

'You're sweet on someone who collects cages,' Echo hissed. 'Doesn't that make you think twice about him?'

'Why should it?' she demanded. 'Every man needs a hobby.'

They entered the laboratory. Izanuela stood rooted to the spot. She put her hands on her hips and looked around.

'Well, well,' she said, 'the holy of holies, Ghoolion's poison kitchen! You've no idea how often I've fantasised about it. Good heavens, so that's his Ghoolionic Preserver. What a beauty!'

She went over to the alchemical device and fingered its controls.

'Yes, yes,' Echo groaned impatiently, 'but get a move on. And don't touch anything! We've got to get to the roof.'

Izanuela minced around the laboratory. 'So this is where he works, where he does his research! To think I'm seeing it at last!' She couldn't tear herself away.

A gust of wind blew in through an open window, swept up some notes lying on a workbench and sent them whirling through the air, riffled the pages of an open book, stirred up a dancing dust devil of blue powder, then went howling up the laboratory chimney. It was as if Ghoolion himself had crossed the room in spirit form. Izanuela shivered with delight.

'Come on!' Echo called, and she followed him obediently up the ramshackle stairs to the Leathermousoleum.

'This place is far sexier than I ever imagined in my wildest dreams,' she burbled excitedly. 'The decor isn't quite my taste, but it's got class. What's needed here is house plants – masses of house plants. And lilac wallpaper. The windows must be glazed, every last one of them – my flowers would die in this draught. We'll need curtains, too. Lilac curtains.'

'This is where the Leathermice sleep,' Echo explained. 'They're out at present, drinking blood.'

'Nobody understands the Leathermice,' Izanuela whispered, looking around the loft. 'Isn't that what you said?'

Echo didn't reply. They left the Leathermousoleum and came out on to the roof. Echo was eager to see how impressed his companion would be by the fantastic panorama. He was as proud of the view as if the old castle and its roof were his personal property.

'Oooh!' Izanuela said and froze.

'Great, isn't it?' said Echo, going to the very edge of the roof. 'You can see all the way to the Blue Mountains – there are supposed to be some female Crats living on the far side. Look, that's Malaisea down there. Like a collection of dolls' houses, isn't it?'

Receiving no answer, he turned round.

The Uggly was standing there transfixed, clutching her cloak in the region of her heart. Her eyes were alight with terror, her ears fluttered in the wind.

'What's wrong?' Echo demanded. 'What do you think of the view?'

'Oooh!' Izanuela said again.

Echo came closer. 'What's the matter?' he asked. 'Aren't you feeling well?'

'I suffer from acrophobia,' she said between clenched teeth.

'What?'

'Acrophobia. Fear of heights.'

'Why didn't you say so before? This is the highest point in the whole of Malaisea.'

'I didn't know it myself. I've never been so high before. The highest I've ever been is the veranda of my house. Can we go now?'

'What are you talking about?' said Echo. 'You've got to help me dig up that Cratmint.'

'Impossible, I can't take another step. I'd no idea. I'm sorry, but it's just not on.' Izanuela didn't even move her lips as she spoke. She was utterly rigid except for her eyes, which were darting to and fro, and her eyelids, which quivered like the wings of a hummingbird.

Echo hadn't allowed for this. Precious time was going by. Ghoolion would soon be serving dinner and their return route would be cut off. He would have to think of something quickly.

'Listen,' he said, trying to sound firm and confident. 'Evaluate your acrophobia on a scale of one to ten.'

'What?'

'Just do it.'

'All right, but I'm not taking another step.' Izanuela remained rooted to the spot.

'Good. One means a touch of acrophobia, two a touch more and so on. Ten signifies maximum intensity. Got that?'

'Yes.'

'Fine. If you had to define your present fear of heights in terms of that scale, what would it score?'

'Twelve,' she said.

'The scale only goes up to ten. Please!'

'All right. Ten, then.'

'Good. Now let's wait for a moment. Breathe deeply.'

'I can't breathe. I'd sooner hold my breath.'

'Come on, take a deep breath! You've no need to move, after all.'

'Hhh ...' she went.

'You see? And another.'

'Hhh ...' she went.

'And again!'

'Hhh ...' Izanuela opened her mouth.

'Well done,' Echo said approvingly. 'Right, now define your present fear of heights in terms of that scale.'

'Still ten,' said Izanuela.

Echo nodded. 'Good.'

'What's good about it? It's the maximum.'

'But it's still ten. That shows your acrophobia can't get any worse, and that you can stand it.'

'True,' she said, sounding rather surprised.

'Now take another deep breath.'

'Haaa ...' she went. Her left hand let go of the cloak and returned to her side.

'And now?' Echo asked. 'How would you rate your fear now? But be honest!'

'Well,' she said. Her voice sounded slightly less panic-stricken and she managed to prise her teeth apart. 'Nine, say?'

'There you are!' cried Echo. 'Your fear is subsiding – fear always does when a person overcomes it. It's a law of nature.'

'I still think nine is pretty high,' she said.

'Now listen,' said Echo. 'I know a route to the Cratmint that's all flights of steps. It's a bit longer than the one I usually take, but you don't have to clamber over any slippery tiles. The steps are absolutely safe – solid stone. I'd like you to follow me along that route, calibrating your fear on the scale. Will you do that for me?'

'I should never have opened the door to you,' she said hoarsely. 'It was the biggest mistake I've ever made in my life.'

'This business will be over in no time,' said Echo. 'Willpower, that's all you need.'

He set off up the steps. 'Come on! Keep your eyes fixed on me. Don't look down, don't look at your surroundings, concentrate on overcoming your fear.'

The Uggly followed him, knees trembling, arms flailing. 'This is the end!' she cried. 'I can see it now: this roof spells my doom.'

Echo waited for her at the top of the first flight.

'Well?' he said. 'You've not only taken a step, you've climbed a whole flight of steps. How's the acrophobia? On the scale, I mean?'

'Ooof!' she went. Sweat was streaming down her face. 'Well ... Eight, maybe?'

'We must hurry,' he said. 'Time's running out.'

They climbed the next flight of steps. Izanuela grunted, groaned and cursed him terribly, but she persevered.

'And now?' Echo asked after three more flights.

'Seven,' she replied. 'No, six.'

Izanuela's cloak billowed out in a sudden gust of wind, but she doggedly went on climbing. 'You've no need to be scared of Ghoolion,' she said. 'When this is over I'll wring your neck with my own hands.'

'Only one more flight and you'll be able to see the Cratmint,' Echo said coaxingly. 'What's the score?'

'Five, I'd say. Or even four.'

'You see? Your fear is subsiding.'

Izanuela reached the top step and stared at Echo in astonishment. 'How did you do it? Is it a trick you've learnt from Ghoolion?'

'No, just a little applied Cratology. Or Echoism, if you prefer.'

'Now you're poking fun at me. Stop it, or I'll –'

'There it is!' Echo broke in. 'The Cratmint!'

The plant was still in full bloom. In the moonlight its stems looked white as milk and the flowers silver. Nocturnal insects were buzzing round it, attracted by its powerful scent.

Izanuela sighed. 'It's superb!'

'Is it big enough for your love potion?' Echo asked.

'The Cratmint won't be an ingredient of the potion. It doesn't work like that. I shall distil my perfume from it.'

'Your perfume?'

'The erotic spell depends on two factors. The drink itself will merely cause Ghoolion to fall in love. In that state he could fall in love with anything or anyone: with me, with you, even with a tree. Only the perfume I distil from the Cratmint will point him in the right direction. If I drench myself in it, he'll fall head over heels in love with me.'

Echo nodded. 'I see. Then let's dig it up.'

They went over to the plant. Izanuela produced a trowel from her robe and proceeded to dig.

'I'm quite carried away,' she said breathlessly. 'It smells divine. It's the loveliest scent I've ever smelt.'

Echo grinned. 'It's the same with me. I love that fragrance.'

'Look at all the insects,' she said. 'They're absolutely besotted with the plant.'

It was true, the beetles and moths whirring around the Cratmint were displaying almost lovesick behaviour. They kept diving into the flower cups and bathing in the pollen.

'Your fear of heights,' Echo remembered to ask, 'what's the score?'

'Oh, I don't know,' Izanuela said absently. 'No idea. One or two, maybe.'

She dug up the plant with surgical precision. 'One can't afford to damage the smallest root hair,' she pontificated. 'Flowers feel no pain, but they feel something else. There isn't a word for it in our language, which shows you how ignorant of plants we are. You can hurt them in many different ways.' Having finally detached the clump of Cratmint from the surrounding soil, she held it up in the moonlight.

'I love this plant – I could sniff it for ever. It's wonderful.'

'We must go now,' Echo said. 'How's the acrophobia?'

'Acrophobia?' Izanuela retorted. 'What's acrophobia? I feel like dancing in the moonlight with this plant. I'd like to marry it!'

She clasped the Cratmint to her bosom and drew its scent deep into her lungs. 'Aah!' she cried. 'Come, dance with me!' Rising on her toes like a ballerina, she tittuped off the steps and on to the sloping tiles. Echo was seized with panic.

'Come on now!' he hissed. Izanuela was utterly enraptured. There would be a nasty accident if he didn't take her home. 'Get back on the steps!' he said sharply. 'Move!'

'Acrophobia?' she cried exuberantly. 'Acrophilia, you mean! I'm fearless. I'm like a feather in the wind. I'm lighter than air!'

She leapt boldly over several tiles. When she landed on them with her full weight, they disintegrated like stale piecrust. Her left leg went through and sank in up to her crotch.

'Ow!' she wailed. 'Ow, my leg!'

Echo jumped on to the roof and went over to her. 'I told you to stay on the steps,' he grumbled. 'Come on, we've got to get out of here.'

Izanuela had come down to earth. 'Ow,' she wailed, 'my leg's stuck.' Holding the Cratmint in one hand, she tugged at the imprisoning tiles with the other. One of them came away, then another, then a full dozen. The whole roof started to slide. Echo tried to leap to safety, but it was too late. It was like jumping from ice floe to ice floe while plunging down a waterfall.

'Whoa!' cried Izanuela. With a sound like thunder, the whole avalanche of tiles cascaded over the edge of the roof with her and Echo on board.

Then they were in free fall. This time, Echo possessed no Leathermouse wings he could have deployed at the last moment. Quickly, far too quickly, Malaisea came rushing up to meet him. It would be all over in a few seconds. Was this his punishment for trying to redirect his destiny: an even swifter death than at Ghoolion's hands?

He was almost on a level with the Uggly, who was plummeting to earth in a shower of tiles. Her face betrayed no fear, just bewilderment.

A moment later they were suddenly surrounded by darting shafts of black lightning – by hideous, wrinkled faces and bared teeth: Leathermice, hundreds of them! They sank their teeth in Echo's tail, buried their claws in his fur and gripped him by the neck.

Then he noticed that his rate of descent was slowing. The same thing was happening to Izanuela, he could see this through a flurry of black bodies. The vampires had fastened their teeth and claws on her in many places and were bearing her slowly downwards, vigorously flapping their membranous wings.

Echo was gently deposited on the path that led up to the castle. Izanuela landed just beside him, the Cratmint still in her trembling hand. The creatures of the night were fluttering overhead.

Echo looked up at them. 'Why did you do that?' he called. 'You're under contract to Ghoolion. I don't understand.'

'Nobody understands the Leathermice!' came the reply, doubtless from an individual whose first name was Vlad. 'Not even the Leathermice!' Then the vampires, in close formation, went soaring into the sky and darkened the moon.

Echo felt himself all over. He had escaped without a single scratch.

'Please excuse me,' he said to Izanuela. 'Ghoolion is bound to be waiting dinner for me.'

The Cheese Museum

When Echo paid a visit to Izanuela's house the next day, the door opened even before he set foot on the veranda steps. It was as if the house had seen him in the distance and invited him in. He was flattered by this mark of esteem on the part of a centuries-old plant and tried to tread with special care once he was inside the house. Izanuela wasn't in the kitchen, but the stairway to the subterranean garden was open.

'Hello!' he called. 'Iza? Anyone at home?'

'I'm down here!' she called back. 'Come and join me!'

He found her at her distillery, which was surrounded by unfamiliar plants in clay pots. Translucent coloured liquids were bubbling away, and the air was filled with many new smells.

'Some job you've landed me with!' she groaned. 'Thanks a lot. Have you any idea what a business it is, extracting the chlorophyll from a Dragonthistle? I have to ugglimise almost every plant I need. That's a particularly economical way of isolating its active substances, but you've no idea how much work it entails. And my suffragatoi has just broken down. Now I'll have to suffragate everything by hand.'

'Well, how's it going?' Echo asked diffidently.

The Uggly put her hands on her hips and squinted at him.

'Is that the only reason why you've come, to hassle me? What comes next, the "I've-got-so-little-time-left" act? The "poor-little-Crat-in-distress" spiel? You can save yourself the trouble, my friend! I've been slaving away – didn't sleep a wink all night. My heart has

249

been beating like a tomtom ever since we fell off that roof – it just won't stop. I feel as if I'd drunk fifty cups of coffee and I never touch the stuff.'

'I was only asking,' said Echo.

'Thanks for the enquiry, then. Yes, I'm making progress. I've been distilling the Cratmint oil for twelve hours. It's a remarkably productive plant. The perfume will be very strong.'

The Cratmint, Echo saw, was immersed in a big glass balloon filled with some kind of clear, pale-green liquid. It had lost none of its beauty.

'The Gingerbread Japonica has already been etherised,' Izanuela said with a sigh, 'and I immersed the Toadmoss in a marinade of Crocodiddle's tears overnight. It should soon be chattified.'

'Chattified?' said Echo.

'Yes, chattified, the opposite of unchattified. You're surely not suggesting we lace our love potion with *un*chattified Toadmoss?'

'No,' Echo said uncertainly, 'of course not.'

She grinned at him.

'You don't have the faintest idea what I'm talking about, do you? That's because I'm a qualified Uggly and you aren't. It doesn't matter how much you know about alchemy; Ugglimy is a science in its own right. Ghoolion may cook ghosts or transform sugar into salt or heaven knows what, but he can't concoct a decent love potion – not him! And I'll tell you why: because alchemy doesn't give a fig for the emotions, that's why! Because he's too busy trying to construct perpetual-motion machines or looking for the Philosopher's Stone to trouble his head about anything as stupid as love. But the thing that makes the world go round isn't in here.' She tapped her forehead. 'It's in here!' She thumped her chest twice with her fist.

Echo didn't reply, but he wasn't displeased by Izanuela's vehemence. It showed how motivated she was.

'My colleague, Sister Crapanthia Urgel, is sending me some Goat's Gristle and Old Man's Scurf from Florinth,' she said. 'The Treacletuft and the Toadpipe I'm getting direct from the Impic Alps. The Devil's Clover is coming from Grailsund.'

'Are you really planning to get them from so far away?' Echo was shocked. 'It'll take weeks. I don't –'

'– have that much time left!' Izanuela broke in, casting her eyes up to heaven. 'I know, I know. They're coming by airmail.'

'Airmail?'

'Yes,' she said. 'That's one of the advantages of being on good terms with Zamonia's flora and fauna. We Ugglies have an efficient airmail service at our disposal. Pigeons and seagulls mainly, but also eagles, vultures and swallows. Sparrows for short-haul flights, condors for freight.'

Echo looked surprised. 'You've got trained birds?'

'Our birds aren't trained,' she said indignantly. 'They work for us on a voluntary basis.'

'You don't say!'

'Yes, a long-standing relationship of mutual trust with the natural world can sometimes pay off,' said Izanuela. 'We refrain from polluting the birds' air space with sulphurous fumes from alchemical furnaces, provide them with medical treatment free of charge and hang up bird feeders in the woods in winter. In return, they deliver an occasional express letter or parcel. I'm expecting those consignments as early as tomorrow morning.'

Echo looked relieved. 'Oh, that's all right, then.'

'Meantime, you can make yourself useful. I need your help.'

'Of course, that's why I'm here. What shall I do? Do you need some alchemistic advice?'

'Not yet. I haven't got enough chattified Toadmoss, but I don't have time to roam around in the Toadwoods. You could do that for me.'

'You want me to fetch some moss from the Toadwoods?'

'Not just any old moss, *Toad*moss. As much as you can carry in your mouth.'

Echo swallowed hard. 'I've never been that far from town.'

'The Toadwoods are still inside the city limits,' Izanuela said. 'They're quite civilised, really. People only avoid them because the Incurables live there.'

The Incurables … Echo felt uneasy. You didn't venture into the Toadwoods unless you had some fell disease: you went there to die.

'"*You're feeling terminally sick? Off to the Toadwoods with you, quick!*"' Izanuela recited. 'You know the poem by Knulf

Krockenkrampf?' She gave a hoarse laugh. 'I told you this wouldn't be a stroll in the park, my friend, but we need that Toadmoss badly.'

'All right,' said Echo, 'I'll go. How do I recognise it?'

'By its smell: it smells of toad.' Izanuela removed the lid from a clay pot and held it under Echo's nose. The Toadmoss floating in the Crocodiddle's tears stank appallingly.

'Got it,' he said with a shudder. 'I'll find some.'

Izanuela laid the pot aside. 'Pooh!' she said. 'I could do with a break. A little snack wouldn't come amiss, either. Like to join me?'

'What have you got?' he asked.

She stared at him in astonishment. 'Cheese, of course, what else?'

Echo wrinkled his nose. 'Cheese is for mice,' he said disdainfully. 'I never eat the stuff.'

She went stomping up the stairs to the kitchen. 'Really?' she said. 'What possible objection could anyone have to cheese?'

'It stinks. Besides, it's all much of a muchness.'

'Cheese doesn't stink,' she retorted. 'It's fragrant. It isn't all much of a muchness, either; it's possibly the most varied food there is. Do you know how many varieties of Zamonian cheeses there are?'

'No.'

'Nor do I. That's because there are so many, nobody has ever tried to count them, and new varieties are appearing every day. Me, I eat nothing but cheese.'

'Really?'

Izanuela nodded proudly. 'I'm a fanatical Caseinian. We Caseinians are convinced that cheese contains all the essential nutrients. Fat, salt and calcium, that's all one needs.'

She drew herself up.

'Look at me! I've been on a strict cheese diet nearly all my life. Does my physique give you the impression that it may have been impaired in some way?'

Echo had to bite his tongue to prevent himself from making some injudicious remark that might have jeopardised their budding friendship.

'Do you eat no meat?' he asked instead. 'No fish? No vegetables? No fruit?'

'I could never eat an animal,' said Izanuela, shaking her head vigorously. 'As for vegetables … Being a holder of the Green Thumb, how could I bring myself to eat plants? They're rational, sentient beings like you and me.'

'How about bread? Or cakes?'

'They both contain flour. Flour is a product that comes into being when innocent vegetable matter is ground to death between millstones. Can you conceive of a more barbarous method of execution? No, I eat nothing but cheese. We Caseinians worship it almost like a god.' She flung open both doors of the kitchen cabinet and performed an elaborate bow.

Echo was totally unprepared for the tidal wave of odours that burst from the interior and surged over him. The garden cupboard containing the 'more evil-smelling' plants had smelt like a perfumery in comparison. But this was not a wholly disgusting smell like that of Ghoolion's banqueting table. What came wafting out of Izanuela's cheese cupboard was of a quality and variety all its own. It smelt not of death and decay, but of life. A very peculiar form of life, admittedly.

'In this cupboard,' Izanuela declared in a tremulous voice, 'three hundred and sixty-five cheeses are ripening to perfection. One for every day of the year, yet this choice assortment is far from complete. It's a very subjective selection. Cheese is a matter of taste, you know.'

His curiosity aroused, Echo peered into the cupboard. He saw big rounds of cheese, plump balls, pointed cones and pyramids, and countless wedges. Many were wrapped in greaseproof paper, others dipped in ash or sealed with varnish, and still others encrusted with mildew or mustard seeds. It was a veritable cheese museum.

The Uggly clapped her hands in anticipation and craned far into the cupboard.

'What shall we have today? Some Gloomberg Gorgonzola? A smidgen of Cape Coldfinger Camembert? A Bookholm Blue? Some creamy goat's cheese from the Impic Alps? A slice of Murkholmian Mumblecheek? A tasty Florinthian Slithercurd, which melts on the tongue like butter when ripe? Or would you prefer something more powerful, for instance a Double Magma from the slopes of Mount Molehill, which is rolled in volcanic ash? Some Demon's Gulch Gouda? Some Druid's Delight, complete with wax coating? Or how about some Dullsgard Diarrhoeic?'

Izanuela grinned at Echo over her shoulder.

'Didn't you just tell me that all cheeses were much of a muchness? Quote me another food that exists in as many different varieties.'

Echo shrugged. 'All right, you win. Cheese is the greatest.'

She reached into the cupboard and brought out a small glass jar with a screw cap.

'This is Grailsundian Miner's Breath,' she said reverently. 'Look at it.' She held the jar under Echo's nose.

'I can't see anything. The jar's empty.'

'But it's in there. You can't see it, that's all.'

'You mean it's invisible, like the caviar Ghoolion gave me once?'

'No. I should make it clear that Grailsundian Miner's Breath exists only in Grailsund, and there's only one example of it – a pretty big one, mark you. Grailsund is Zamonia's cheese capital, the fragrant metropolis of Caseinism.'

Izanuela lowered the jar and stared into space.

'Ah, Grailsund! Every Caseinian has to make a pilgrimage there once in his or her lifetime, to pay homage to the great Grailsundian Miner's Breath. A cheese of monumental proportions, it's as big as several houses piled on top of one another.'

She made a sweeping gesture, and Echo pictured a cheese towering into the sky.

'Miner's Breath has to ripen in a mine, of course, so the Grailsundians dug the deepest cheese mine ever excavated. The cheese has been maturing down there for over a thousand years and is still far from fully ripe. No one may eat any – it's prohibited on pain of death! – but one can smell it. And believe me, that's quite enough for anyone.'

Izanuela smiled ecstatically.

'I was only permitted to sniff it for a few brief moments when I made my own pilgrimage to Grailsund, but I was completely glutted for several days. I even put on a pound or two. I couldn't so much as look at a cheese for a whole week, I was so full.'

She unscrewed the lid.

'Although it's forbidden to eat any Grailsundian Miner's Breath, every pilgrim is permitted to fill a preserving jar with its aroma and take it away. Here, have a sniff!'

Echo reluctantly sniffed the jar and Izanuela promptly screwed the lid on tight again.

For a moment he thought he would choke. The smell was so intense, so physically palpable, it threatened to cut off his air supply. Then the alarming sensation subsided and he felt as if his stomach were full of hot olive oil. He became as warm and sleepy as he did after one of Ghoolion's lavish meals.

'Phew!' he said. 'Thanks a lot. You've ruined my diet for at least a week.'

Izanuela smiled. 'Yes, quite something, isn't it? Mind you, it's really only for special occasions.' She replaced the jar. 'I think I'm going to treat myself to a little Ornian Crumblecrust.'

She removed a primitive-looking farmhouse cheese from the cupboard. As she did so, Echo thought he glimpsed a movement on one of the shelves inside.

'What was that?' he asked.

She instantly slammed the cupboard doors.

'I don't know what you mean.'

'I saw something move in there.'

Echo noticed only now that the worm-eaten cupboard itself resembled a gigantic cheese.

Izanuela gave a little cough. 'You're imagining things.'

'Come on,' he said, 'what are you hiding in there?'

She blushed. 'Nothing,' she mumbled. 'Nothing at all.'

'Something moved. I saw it with my own eyes.'

Izanuela shuffled from one foot to the other. 'But you must promise never to tell anyone,' she said.

'I promise.' Echo raised one paw.

She deposited the Crumblecrust on the kitchen table, opened the cupboard again and reached for the shelf on which Echo had seen something moving.

'Come here, you ...' Izanuela made several attempts to grab something, but it appeared to evade her every time. Could it be a mouse?

'Got you at last!' she cried eventually.

Turning round, she held out a cheese the size of a clenched fist. It had numerous legs, all of which were waggling furiously.

'A … a *live* cheese?' Echo looked dumbfounded.

Izanuela shrugged her shoulders.

'All cheeses are alive, strictly speaking. They mature like other living creatures. I simply give the process a helping hand – in a spirit of Caseinian fun, so to speak.'

She held the kicking cheese close to her face. It emitted a fretful whine.

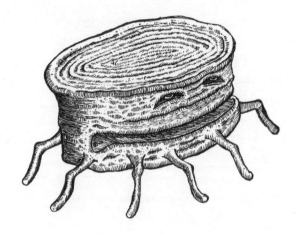

'I've christened it Inazuelan Brie – in my own honour. It's my personal Caseinian creation. Live yoghurt cultures are partly responsible for its animation, as you can imagine, but I also use some Ugglimical essences strictly prohibited under the provisions of Ghoolion's Municipal Ordinance No. 52736.' She laughed.

'What put the idea into your head?'

Izanuela sighed. 'If you abstain as rigorously as I do from foods that used to be alive, you sometimes feel the urge to eat something that moves as much as possible while you're eating it. It's like that with me, anyway.'

'I understand.'

'If that brings me down to the level of a Demon's Gulch Cyclops, so be it. But I should point out that the cheese feels nothing while you're eating it. It resembles a Leyden Manikin in possessing no nervous system, so it can't feel pain.'

As though in contradiction of the last statement, the cheese uttered a high-pitched whimper. Izanuela stuffed it into her mouth and devoured it in a few bites.

'Mmm!' she said, looking at Echo. 'Yes, I know it's a blot on my Ugglian escutcheon.' She shrugged. 'But who is free from guilt?'

'So everything is alive in this place,' he said. 'Even the cheeses.'

'Would you like one?' Izanuela asked. 'There are some more in the cupboard. They taste really delicious.'

'No thanks,' he said, 'that Miner's Breath was quite enough for me. Besides, I'd like to get my trip to the Toadwoods over before dark. It's getting late.'

Izanuela recited again in vibrant tones:

> *'You're feeling terminally sick?*
> *Off to the Toadwoods with you, quick!*
> *All alone you there will be,*
> *with no one else around to see.*
> *So dig yourself a grave to fit*
> *and then, my friend, lie down in it.'*

Echo left the house as fast as he could.

The Toadwoods

The foliage in the Toadwoods was so dense that a kind of permanent twilight prevailed at ground level. Moreover, visibility was further reduced by the thin skeins of mist forever rising from expanses of marshland and drifting around the blackened trunks of the ancient trees.

'Well, I suppose I'll have to press on,' Echo said to himself. 'I opened my trap too wide, so I deserve to have it stuffed with Toadmoss. I can already smell the stuff, fortunately. I must head in the direction of those fallen tree trunks.'

The fallen tree trunks resembled the backs of gigantic lizards lying in wait for him in the grass. His progress was hampered by the prickly weeds and stinging nettles proliferating everywhere. Izanuela had a nerve, sending a little Crat off into a wilderness like this. Still, she'd risked her life on the mother of all roofs and he wanted to repay her. It would be shameful to return with nothing to show for his trip. He sniffed the air again.

'I must go deeper into the woods. I'd better follow that mist.'

A wisp of vapour was drifting ahead of him. It reminded him of the Cooked Ghost and their joint excursions along the passages in Ghoolion's castle. Ah, the castle! The Alchemaster's sinister old ruin seemed like a luxury hotel out here. The trees appeared to be drawing ever closer together the further he went. He could see plump beetles and outsize ants and spiders crawling around on their bark.

It was Echo's first time in a forest. 'I suppose I'm the urban type,' he thought. 'Forests aren't my bowl of milk.' Twigs snapped, leaves rustled. Trees bent over him like hunchbacks, groping for him with their gnarled branches. The agonised cry of some animal rang out in the distance. Something drummed on a hollow tree trunk. Then absolute silence returned. 'I can't understand what people see in forests,' Echo muttered to himself. 'Personally, I'd sooner have a nice, well-kept municipal park.'

He heard a low, throaty sound, possibly made by a fat frog. It came from the direction in which his nose was taking him.

> *You're feeling terminally sick?*
> *Off to the Toadwoods with you, quick!*

The Uggly's words rang in his ears. Did the Incurables really exist, or were they just another old wives' tale concocted by grown-ups to dissuade their children from wandering off into the woods?

> *All alone you there will be,*
> *with no one else around to see.*

'Precisely,' thought Echo. 'No one wants to be here, least of all yours truly! Where's that confounded moss?' He lifted his little nose and sniffed the air. The scent of Toadmoss was growing stronger. For the first time in his life, he cursed his acute sense of smell for leading him ever deeper into this wilderness.

> *So dig yourself a grave to fit*
> *and then, my friend, lie down in it.*

'Rhyming is one thing,' Echo reflected, 'digging your own grave is quite another.' What a gruesome thought! Who dreamt up these ideas? Poets were strange creatures. That Knulf Krockenkrampf needed his head examined.

The sun was sinking. Just to make matters worse, the forest was now populated by shadowy figures that stole through the trees and waved to him from the topmost branches. 'No,' he told himself bravely, 'the branches are simply stirring in the evening breeze. There aren't any shadowy figures. Or Incurables.' All that was incurable was his own lively imagination.

In the distance he heard again the low, throaty sound. The trees thinned and he eventually came to a narrow path, a beaten track leading in the direction from which the scent of Toadmoss was drifting towards him.

'Ah, civilisation,' he thought, feeling relieved. Well, only what might be regarded as civilisation in such surroundings: a boggy path dotted with puddles and stumbling blocks in the shape of tree roots and boulders. Still, no more thistles and stinging nettles. A rough aid to direction, at least. Presumably, this was the path Izanuela herself had taken when gathering Toadmoss.

Echo was further reassured by the protracted drum roll of a woodpecker. 'There are only harmless little forest creatures here,' he told himself. 'Woodpeckers and frogs, beetles and squirrels.' He rounded a bend in the path half hidden by the massive root of an oak tree. What awaited him beyond it made his heart stand still for a moment. He stood there transfixed. Seated with its back against the oak tree's blackened trunk was the skeleton of a man. His white bones had been picked clean by ants and were cocooned in spiders' webs. Wild ivy was growing around his thigh bones and between his ribs. A red forest rose was flowering on his lower jaw, which had dropped open. Echo fluffed out his tail and hissed.

You're feeling terminally sick?
Off to the Toadwoods with you, quick!

A butterfly landed on the skull and folded its wings. This had been an Incurable, no doubt about it, but he was dead. 'It isn't a pleasant sight,' thought Echo, 'but it's less alarming than being ambushed by someone with an incurable disease.' The poor man hadn't even had time to dig himself a grave. Echo's tail resumed its normal appearance.

> *All alone you there will be,*
> *with no one else around to see.*

Echo found it awful to picture the man dying all by himself in the woods. On the other hand, wasn't it awful to die anywhere? And wasn't everyone alone when the time came? He shook off the disagreeable thought and walked on along the path. Really nice of Izanuela to send him blithely off into a wood with a skeleton lurking in it!

A skeleton? Echo froze once more. Another one was lying a few paces further on. A miaow of alarm escaped his lips, but he didn't hiss or fluff out his tail. This man's remains were lying full length in the grass. Busy bees and bumblebees were droning around a whole garden of weeds and wild flowers that had sprouted from between his bones. 'A peaceful sight, actually,' Echo thought to himself. Why were people so scared of skeletons? Nothing could do one less harm than a skeleton and in this particular case, dead was really better than alive.

He walked on, keeping his eyes peeled so as not to be startled by another dead Incurable. Wisely so, because it wasn't long before the next one came into view. Like a knight on a medieval tomb, he was lying on a huge boulder with his eye sockets directed at the canopy of foliage overhead and his skeletal arms folded on his chest. Whether or not he hadn't liked the thought of flowers growing through him, he couldn't defy the moss, which had spread from the boulder to his bones.

Moss ... Of course, thought Echo, that's why he was here, not to view the Incurables' mortal remains. He sniffed the air once more. Yes, the smell of Toadmoss was growing steadily stronger.

Again he heard that low, throaty sound issuing from the depths of the forest. No doubt about it: Toadmoss and the author of the sound shared the same location. He walked on along the path, undistracted by the skeletons lying or sitting here and there. One Incurable was staring down at him from his perch in the fork of a large tree; another, who had presumably wanted to cut his sufferings short, was hanging by his neck from a branch.

One part of the forest consisted almost entirely of willow trees whose foliage, which resembled strands of pale-green hair, hung down to the ground. The smell of Toadmoss was now so intense that Echo caught it every time he drew breath. Mingled with it were other smells – unpleasant ones! – that prompted him to slacken his pace. Was that a clearing up ahead?

Although the sun had already set, the sky was still faintly tinged by its afterglow. The moon was three-quarters full. Echo came to a halt. Yes, it was a clearing. More than that, however, it was one of Nature's marvels.

Jutting from the ground was a forest of tall slabs of stone. What kind of wood was it in which rocks grew instead of trees? It seemed unwise to approach them, but the smell of Toadmoss was coming from their direction. Having come this far, Echo wasn't about to return without achieving anything.

He ventured a little nearer the slabs, which looked old and weather-worn. Many of them overgrown with creeper, they differed in shape and colour. Some were bigger, some smaller, some paler, some darker, some jet-black, others streaked with red and white veins. One slab was thick and composed of dark-brown porous stone, another was thin, with a white, mirror-smooth surface. Echo now saw that some of the slabs bore inscriptions. No, not just some, many – possibly all of them! This was becoming more and more mysterious. What was written on them?

He took a close look at one of the monoliths. Black marble. An engraved name. A date. Another date. The next bore another name, another date. He began to doubt that the rocks had grown here naturally. They had been embedded in the ground, but by whom? And when? Were they a work of art? A monument? An artefact from another age? He felt ashamed of his naivety in mistaking them for plants.

He read some more inscriptions. They always comprised names and dates. Some of the surnames were familiar to him from Malaisea. Many were emblazoned on the fascia boards of pharmacies and bakeries, opticians' and butchers' shops. And then he read one that affected him so deeply that he couldn't suppress a sob:

261

FLORIA OF INGOTVILLE

It was the name of his former mistress.

Echo grasped the truth at last: this was a graveyard! He hadn't recognised it at once because he'd never been to one before, only heard tell of such sinister places. The townsfolk of Malaisea had consigned their burial place to the depths of the forest because they couldn't endure the sight of it. They were too preoccupied with their ailments to tolerate a perpetual reminder of death, so they came here to bury their nearest and dearest, not to mourn them.

This was the kingdom of death. His late mistress's mouldering corpse was down below, together with countless others. He now knew where the unpleasant smells were coming from: the ground itself.

He found it only too easy to imagine the dead breaking through the surface, as they had in Ghoolion's story of the accursed vineyard, and grabbing him with a view to dragging him down into their damp, worm-infested world below ground. He must get out of here fast! He was still on the outskirts of the cemetery; he had only to turn and go.

But he stayed where he was. The smell of Toadmoss was stronger than ever. It was luring him straight into the stone forest.

What should he do? He shuffled irresolutely from paw to paw. Why should that confounded moss be growing in the middle of a cemetery, of all places? Why had that stupid Uggly failed to mention the fact? It wouldn't have hurt her to give him a little prior warning.

On the other hand, would he have gone at all? Izanuela knew only too well what she was doing and what was better left unsaid. He pulled himself together. She wanted some Toadmoss and Toadmoss she should have. He had no wish to give her the satisfaction of calling him a scaredy-Crat. If she herself had crossed this graveyard unscathed, why shouldn't he be able to do the same? He set off, heading for the heart of the burial place.

Many of the graves looked very old; others, judging by the look of the soil, had been dug not long ago. Here and there, empty graves without headstones awaited their future occupants. Rainwater had turned one of them into a big puddle whose surface reflected the moon. Echo shivered.

The stench of Toadmoss was now so strong that he must be getting very close. He took another few steps. Sure enough, the penetrating smell was coming from an open grave just ahead of him. He went up to the edge and peered into it.

Ensconced in the grave was a gigantic frog. Its dark-green body, which was covered with black warts, was so big that it occupied almost half the pit. Staring up at Echo with turbid yellow eyes, it opened its slimy mouth and uttered the throaty sound he'd already heard more than once.

'A cat?' the creature muttered to itself. 'What's a cat doing here?'

Echo took advantage of this to strike up a conversation. 'I'm not a cat,' he said, 'I'm a Crat.'

'You speak my language?'

'Yes,' said Echo. 'My, you're a frog and a half!'

'You're wrong there. I'm not a frog, I'm a toad.'

Echo's head swam. If this was a toad, there probably wasn't any Toadmoss here at all. He'd been following the smell of the toad, not the moss. That was logical. What smelt more like a toad than a toad?

'I'm sorry,' he said, thoroughly disconcerted. 'I was looking for some Toadmoss. You smell so much like that plant, I thought –'

'Wrong again,' the toad broke in. 'I don't smell like Toadmoss, Toadmoss smells like me. There's a subtle difference. This forest is called the Toadwoods, not the Toadmoss Woods.'

'You're right,' Echo said politely. 'I made a mistake, as I said.'

'Wrong yet again. You didn't.'

'Didn't I? How so?'

'See this green stuff on my back? What do you think it is?'

'You mean it's …'

The toad nodded.

'Toadmoss. The only Toadmoss growing in the Toadwoods.'

Echo didn't know what to think. On the one hand he had found some Toadmoss at last; on the other it was growing on the back of a monstrous and rather vicious-looking creature residing in a grave. He had hoped to scrape some off a root somewhere, but it now looked as if obtaining the stuff would present certain problems.

'You'd like some of my moss, is that it?' asked the toad.

'Yes indeed!' said Echo, relieved that the monster had broached the subject itself.

'No moss would be your loss, eh?'

Echo forced a laugh.

'Sorry,' said the toad, 'I couldn't resist that. It's the only joke I know.'

'That's quite all right,' said Echo. 'I'm afraid it's only too true. Without your moss I'm completely stumped. It's a bit difficult to explain, but the long and the short of it is that unless I take some of your moss home I shall lose my life in the very near future.'

'Oh,' said the toad, 'that's sad. Is it for the old crone who keeps scraping it off my back?'

'Exactly,' said Echo. 'You know her, then?'

'I most certainly do. She always squirts some stuff up my nose before she scrapes it off. It makes me go all dizzy and my head swims for days afterwards. There's absolutely no need for her to do that – I'd gladly give her the stuff of my own free will. I'm only too delighted when someone scrapes some off from time to time. It itches, that's why, but I can't tell *her* that because I can't talk to her the way I can to you.'

'I could drop her a hint,' Echo said.

'Would you?'

'Of course. So you wouldn't mind if I took a little of your moss?'

'No, no,' said the toad, 'help yourself.'

'You mean I can jump down on to your back?'

'Well, *I* can't scrape it off for you – I can't reach the stuff myself.' The toad looked over its shoulder and raised its short front legs with a tormented croak.

Echo debated with himself. The toad was big and ugly, but did that mean it was dangerous? It certainly didn't make a devious impression. On the other hand, if you spotted a trap it ceased to be one. He grunted irresolutely.

'What's the matter?' the toad demanded. 'Changed your mind?'

What had he got to lose? He was under sentence of death in any case. His only means of extricating himself from his predicament was growing on the back of this warty monster. He leapt boldly into the grave.

'Ah!' the toad said blissfully. 'That feels good. Would you mind marking time on the back of my neck for a while? I think I'm suffering from muscle cramp.'

The old creature smelt truly frightful at close range. Echo had landed plumb on its back between some huge warts and a clump of Toadmoss. He would have preferred to get the business over in double-quick time, but he didn't want to seem discourteous, so he complied with the toad's request.

'Ah!' it said again. 'You've no idea how good that feels. What's your name, by the way?'

'Echo. And yours?'

'Just Toad. I'm the only toad left in this forest, so any more names would be superfluous.'

265

'I see,' said Echo.

He stopped marking time.

'I'd like to scrape off some of your moss now,' he said, 'if it's all right with you.'

'Of course,' said the toad. 'I'm wasting your precious time. Help yourself.'

Echo drew a deep breath and took a big bite of Toadmoss. He wrenched it off with his teeth, gagging despite himself. It tasted even more revolting than Izanuela's tongue.

'There,' said the toad, 'now you know what Toadmoss tastes like. Shall I tell you what *I'd* like to know?'

'Mm?' Echo said with his mouth full.

'I'd like to know what a Crat tastes like.'

The toad opened its slimy jaws as wide as they would go and put out an enormous tongue at least three times the length of its body. Reaching back over its shoulder, the tongue wrapped itself round Echo and popped him into the creature's gaping mouth, which promptly closed again – all within the bat of an eyelid.

Just as he had been when falling from the castle roof, Echo was far too astonished to feel scared. 'Ghoolion's going to be mighty disappointed,' was the only thought that occurred to him.

But the toad didn't swallow him.

It opened its mouth and extended its tongue, Echo and all. Having deposited him on the edge of the grave, the creature retracted it again.

'You taste of absolutely nothing,' it observed in a reproachful voice.

'The Leathermice said that too,' Echo thought dazedly. He was covered in toad slobber from head to foot, but he still had the Toadmoss in his mouth.

'So I haven't been missing anything,' said the toad. 'I apologise, my friend. Don't take it personally, it was only an experiment.'

Echo retreated a few steps for safety's sake.

'Best of luck with that moss!' he heard the toad call. 'And look in on me again some time. I could use a massage like that occasionally. It would be nice to see you again.'

Echo turned and made his way out of the forest as fast as his paws would carry him.

Alchemy and Ugglimy

'Now the Alchemist's away
I'm at liberty to play,
and shall now, for good or ill,
bend his spirits to my will.
Having marked his words and ways
carefully these many days,
ready to perform am I
miracles of alchemy.'

The old poem by Aleisha Wimpersleak, which Izanuela was now reciting, could not have been more appropriate to the occasion. Echo had returned to the Uggly's house late that night to assist her in preparing the love potion.

'Copious streams of sweat shall flow
from my overheated brow,
as I brew the magic broth
that will help me plight my troth,'

said Echo, who had been reminded of another poem.

'Ah!' Izanuela exclaimed. 'You're familiar with the Zamonian classics, I see. That was from "Love Soup" by Wamilli Swordthrow, wasn't it? We're really getting into the swing of things! There's nothing more essential to Ugglimical potion-brewing than sympathetic vibrations.'

They were standing beside the distillation plant in the secret underground garden, where Izanuela had installed an apparatus quite the equal of any in Ghoolion's laboratory. Echo jumped up on to the big table by way of a chair. Translucent coloured liquids – green, yellow, red, orange, blue and violet – were standing or bubbling away in glass balloons. The vessels were linked by thin tubes of copper, silver or glass, and methane-fed flames were burning brightly. Echo was surprised to see a pair of bellows pumping away steadily, apparently under its own power.

'It contains earthworms in peat,' Izanuela explained in a low voice.

'It pays to harness the energy of Mother Earth. By the way, thanks for the Leyden Manikin formula. I've already animated one. We'll be able to test the efficacy of the love potion on it.'

The Leyden Manikin was seated in a big-bellied flask, apathetically dabbling its feet in nutrient fluid. Echo took little notice of the creature, being far too eager to inspect Izanuela's apparatus. He darted here, there and everywhere, sniffing and marvelling. Violets and rose petals were floating in pale-pink liquid, clumps of eelgrass waving around in alcohol. Some treacly dark-green substance was bubbling over a Bunsen burner. The air was filled with a smell reminiscent of flower gardens in springtime and stormy nights in the jungle, poppies and freshly mown grass, intoxicating orchids and poisonous tropical fungi, roses in full bloom, lemon balm and rosemary, fresh peat and wet straw.

Incandescent red Lava Worms wriggled along a spiral glass tube, heating up a flask in which a solution of chlorophyll was simmering. A column of big, black soldier ants marched across the table, transporting fragments of leaves and roots to a mortar. Stag beetles dragged whole flower heads over to a copper and dropped them in.

'I see we've got plenty of busy little assistants,' Echo remarked.

'Oh,' Izanuela said dismissively, 'they're just being neighbourly – paying me back for pinching my sugar and eating my spinach.'

The roots growing out of the floor and walls were unusually animated. The eyes in the knotholes kept opening and shutting as if aware that some crucial event was in the offing. For the first time, Echo took a closer look at the colourful butterflies fluttering through the subterranean vegetation.

'What are all these butterflies doing down here?' he asked when one of them settled on his head.

'Generating atmosphere,' said Izanuela, tossing a handful of pollen into the air. 'Can you imagine brewing a love potion without any butterflies around? I can't.'

'You've really thought of everything,' Echo said admiringly. 'When does the balloon go up?'

'Soon,' she said. 'I've still got to regulate my hop dispenser.' She adjusted the control knobs on a big wooden box in which something was rumbling around and banging against the sides. 'There,' she exclaimed, clapping her hands. 'All we need now is some **twitchstik**.'

'Music?' Echo translated.

The weird, rhythmical humming he'd heard on his first visit to the Uggly's house started up again. He now realised that its source was the house itself, the roots and vegetation all around them.

'The Song of the Ugglian Oaks,' Izanuela said enthusiastically. 'There's nothing better.' She put a jar on the table. At once, the Twitching Terebinth inside it began to sway ecstatically to and fro in time to the music. The Leyden Manikin also came to life. It stood up and started drumming on the side of its glass container.

'Atmosphere is all!' cried Izanuela. 'Now let's get down to work.'

She took various flasks filled with liquid from beneath the table and put them down beside a small cast-iron saucepan.

'First we must dispense the vegetable essences in the correct quantities,' she said.

'Have they been chattified?' Echo asked sternly.

'With a vengeance,' Izanuela replied with a grin. 'More chattified than them you can't get.'

She added minute amounts of the essences to the saucepan, consulting her Ugglimical Cookbook as she did so.

'One ugg of Gristlethorn ... two uggs of Treacletuft ... five uggs of Clubfoot Toadstool ... twenty-four uggs of Twelve-Leafed Clover ... Yes, we can use some good luck ...'

'Why so little?' Echo put in. 'Why not tip the lot in? The more the merrier, no?'

'Keep out of this!' Izanuela hissed. 'It's over your head. Everything depends on the correct dosage. One ugg too many or too few and it's completely ruined, so don't distract me!'

Echo bit his tongue.

'Eighteen uggs of Arctic Woodbine ... two uggs of Old Man's Scurf ... four-and-a-half uggs of Pond Scum ... one ugg of Sparrowspit ... two uggs of Funnelhorn ... one hundred and seventy-one uggs of Tuberous Stinkwort ...'

And so it went on until all the essences had been added in the quantities prescribed. Izanuela placed the saucepan over a low flame and suspended a thermometer from the rim. 'Now we heat it to exactly seventy-seven uggs,' she said. 'It mustn't boil under any circumstances!'

'What *is* an ugg?' Echo asked.

'An ugg can equate to a gramme or a degree – sometimes to a millimetre. It all depends,' said Izanuela. 'Why?'

'Oh, nothing,' said Echo. Having already gained the impression that Ugglimy wasn't a particularly exact science, he was now, for the first time, struck by the disturbing thought that Izanuela might merely be blinding him with science.

'Seventy-seven uggs on the button,' she muttered after a glance at the thermometer. She consulted the cookbook again. 'Now for the infusion of Witch's Purslane.' She produced a big, rusty syringe from a cupboard and went over to a glass container. Once there, she froze. The syringe hit the ground with a clatter.

'By all the … Oh, no!' she exclaimed.

Echo hurried over to her. 'What's wrong?' he asked anxiously.

'The Witch's Purslane essence,' she groaned, 'it's gone off. How could *that* have happened?'

The liquid in the glass container looked brackish and slimy. Fat bubbles of gas were rising to the surface, on which limp, greenish-brown leaves floated like victims of drowning. The rhythmical music ceased.

'Oh dear,' Izanuela wailed, 'I turned off the filter by mistake and left it overnight. The essence has become polluted.'

'So?' said Echo. 'It's only a salad vegetable. I'm sure you can get some more.'

'That's just it. This was a very rare variety from a farm on Paw Island. Have you any idea how far away that is? It would take a week to get hold of another batch and by then the other essences would have lost their potency. Don't you understand? This is the moment to brew the potion. Here, today, tonight! It's now or never! Damnation!' She thumped the glass container.

Echo feverishly searched his knowledge of alchemy for a solution. 'What is in the plant?' he asked.

'Well,' she said, 'nothing special, really. Iron, zinc, alkaloids – the stuff plants usually contain. But this was *Witch's* Purslane and it contained an exceptionally effective kind of mucilago. That's a gum designed to bind the ingredients of our potion tightly together. It's like

a soufflé, my young friend. Unless you follow the recipe exactly ...'
Izanuela subsided weakly on to a chair.

Gastropoda, Echo heard the Alchemaster saying. *Fossaria modicella. Radix auriculata. Stagnicola caperata. Aplexa elongata. Physella vigata. Gyraulus deflectus. Planorbula trivolvis. Planorbula armigera ...*

'Planorbula armigera!' he exclaimed.

'What?'

'It's a snail. A very rare one.'

'What about it?'

'Ghoolion rendered one down and preserved its fat.'

'Well?'

'The fat of Planorbula armigera contains remnants of the slime the snail excretes and leaves behind it, and this slime has the same chemical composition as mucilago.'

The Uggly looked astonished. 'How do you know that?'

'It's part of the alchemical knowledge Ghoolion has been drumming into this.' Echo raised a forepaw and tapped his head.

'Off you go, then!' cried Izanuela. 'Run back to the castle and fetch some of this snail fat. In the meantime, I'll –'

'No can do,' said Echo.

'Why not?'

'There are several locks on the door of the cellar where the fat is stored. I can't get them open by myself.'

Izanuela rose from her chair and drew herself up. 'Oh, no,' she said, folding her arms, 'not again. Count me out.'

'I went into the Toadwoods all by myself,' said Echo, 'and you didn't warn me about the toad. You owe me one.'

'No, I don't!' she said defiantly.

'They're pretty sophisticated locks,' Echo said thoughtfully, 'but we should be able to open them between the two of us.'

The Uggly had fallen silent.

'Have you forgotten what you said just now? "This is the moment to brew the potion. Here, today, tonight! It's now or never!"'

Izanuela groaned.

'"Copious streams of sweat shall flow from my overheated brow ..."' Echo reprised.

'Yes, yes,' she groaned again, '"as I brew the magic broth that will help me plight my troth!"'

'That's the spirit,' said Echo. 'Do you by any chance have a flute in the house? And a picklock? We'll be needing a candle, too.'

The Burglary

Having satisfied himself that the Alchemaster was busy in his laboratory, Echo hurried back to the castle entrance, where Izanuela was already waiting for him. Then they set off for the cellars.

'There's something else I should tell you,' Echo whispered as they were creeping down the long, dark stairs.

'What's that?'

'There's a Snow-White Widow down there.'

The Uggly stopped short. 'He's got a Snow-White Widow?' she hissed. 'In the cellars?'

'She's shut up in a glass cage.'

'How do you know?'

'I've seen her.'

'That's very reassuring. Thanks for telling me, I feel much better now.'

'It's all right, we won't be going anywhere near her,' Echo whispered. 'She's in a remote part of the cellars.'

Izanuela reluctantly continued to descend the stairs. 'A Snow-White Widow on top of everything else!' she grumbled. 'A few days ago I was leading a peaceful Ugglian existence. A client would occasionally complain that one of my predictions hadn't come true, but that was the worst that could happen. Now I'm breaking into Ghoolion's castle and working on a love potion. I steal plants, I almost fall to my death, I break one regulation after another, I risk my life as well as my fortune teller's licence. And who am I doing all this for? A stray Crat. Can you give me one good reason why I should?'

They had reached the foot of the stairs.

'We need some light,' said Echo.

Izanuela lit the candle she had brought with her. To Echo, the dark, vaulted ceilings looked as menacing and close to collapse as they had the

272

first time. He had never thought he would pay another visit to this loathsome part of the castle, still less of his own volition.

They made their way in silence through the series of underground chambers, which teemed with insects that shunned the light of their candle. Echo couldn't help recalling Ghoolion's memorable account of the ancient building's gruesome history, but he refrained from sharing it with the Uggly, who strangely kept a bridle on her tongue for once. Whether this was because of their oppressive surroundings or the Alchemaster's proximity, he couldn't tell. It was probably a mixture of both – of awe and unrequited love – that had reduced Izanuela to silence. When they came to the door of the fat store, as they eventually did, she shone the candle on its numerous padlocks.

'The one at the top is an acoustico-elemental lock,' Echo said in a whisper, although no one could possibly have heard him. 'That's probably the hardest.'

'Oh, I know those things of old,' Izanuela said with a grin. 'The Grailsund University authorities used one to secure the door of the room in which they kept their coveted Ugglimical diplomas. They're child's play to open.'

'Just a minute,' said Echo. 'Are you telling me you stole your diploma?'

Izanuela blushed furiously. 'Whoops!' she said. 'It just slipped out.'

'I won't tell anyone,' Echo promised, 'but only if you get that thing open.'

'If you recite the correct names of the elements in the correct order – and you must know them if he opened the lock in your presence – it's quite simple.'

Echo whispered the names in her ear.

'Bismuth, niobium, antimony!' cried Izanuela, and the lock sprang open.

'Hey,' said Echo, 'how did you do that? The words kept getting twisted up on my tongue.'

'The trick is to use your tongue to rearrange the individual syllables,' she said. 'I expect you remember what a talented tongue I have, don't you?' She extended the long green thing in question and Echo gave a reminiscent shudder.

'Oh dear,' she said, rattling the next padlock, 'this is a numerical lock. I've no head for figures.'

'This one's mine,' said Echo. 'I made a note of the numerals Ghoolion spoke into it. Eighteen … twelve … six hundred and sixty-six … four thousand one hundred and two … seventeen million eight hundred and eighty-eight thousand five hundred and sixty-four …'

He reeled off the long series of numerals effortlessly. The padlock sprang open just as he finished.

'You really do have a fabulous memory,' Izanuela said admiringly. 'You could make money out of it. Me, I can hardly remember my own birthday.'

'Ghoolion used an invisible key for the next lock,' Echo recalled. 'Where are we going to get an invisible key?'

'No need. Pedlars sell them to gullible yokels at country fairs. They're rubbish. The key is invisible so no one can see it only has two wards, that's all. I'll get it open with the picklock.'

She produced the burglar's tool from her cloak and poked around in the padlock. It sprang open almost at once.

'Great,' said Echo. 'Now we need the flute. The next one is an unmusical lock made of cacophonated steel.'

'Child's play,' Izanuela said scornfully. She brought out the flute and played exactly the same discordant notes as Ghoolion. The padlock opened by itself.

'Well, I never!' Echo exclaimed. 'How come you knew that frightful tune? I thought you'd have to toot away for ages.'

'It wasn't hard to guess,' said Izanuela. 'Ghoolion has given me earache more than once by playing that tune. It's his favourite way of tormenting Ugglies.'

She applied herself to the next lock. 'Hm,' she muttered. 'A Florinthian shamlock with triple tumblers. This is another kettle of fish altogether.' Methodically, she set to work with the skeleton key and had it open within minutes.

'Wow!' said Echo. 'Where did you learn to do that?'

'Listen, my friend,' Izanuela said sombrely, fixing him with the piercing gaze that had unnerved him once before, 'I'm an Uggly. My sisters and I belong to a downtrodden race. People have always found fault with us. Once upon a time they used to lock us up or put us in the stocks – in fact they even burned us at the stake, although no one likes to mention that nowadays. Over the centuries, we were forced to acquire certain skills that aren't in full conformity with the laws of Zamonia. Picking locks is the most innocuous of them. Now ... Do you want me to get this door open, or would you prefer to go on asking stupid questions?'

'All right,' said Echo, thoroughly intimidated, 'I'll keep quiet.'

The Uggly gave him another piercing stare and went back to work. Sometimes she manipulated the picklock, sometimes she used a hairpin or a piece of wire conjured from the depths of her cloak. Padlock after padlock yielded to her deft touch.

'That's it,' she said when the last one sprang open. 'The way is clear.'

They entered the fat cellar. It was as dry, cool, clean and tidy as it had been the first time. The Alchemaster's balls of fat were neatly arrayed in long rows.

'This', Echo said as he walked past the shelves, 'is where Ghoolion stores the fat and the death rattles of the rare animals he tortures and renders down. How do you feel about him now you've seen this place?'

Izanuela sighed. 'That's the trouble with feelings,' she said. 'They're hard to reconcile with common sense. Believe me, I'm just as horrified by Ghoolion as you are. I'd really sooner poison him than brew him a love potion, but what can I do?' She cast her eyes up at the ceiling.

Echo read out the names on the labels: 'Porphyrio veterum ... Numida meleagris ... Python molurus ... Nyctibius grandis ... Stenops gracilis ... Moloch horridus ... Testacella halotidea. Ah, here are the snails! And there it is: Planorbula armigera!'

Izanuela snatched the ball of fat and stowed it in her cloak.

'What if he notices it's gone?' she asked.

'He's far too busy at present to count his balls of fat, and even if he did, what ...'

Echo broke off. His sensitive ears had alerted him to something.

'What is it?' asked Izanuela.

'Ghoolion's coming!' Echo could definitely hear the clatter of his iron-shod feet.

'Then let's get out of here, quick!' Izanuela's convulsive movements suggested that she was trying to run in all directions at once.

275

'Too late! He'll be here in no time.'

'What shall we do?' Izanuela whispered anxiously. 'What on earth shall we do?'

'We'll simply have to hide.'

'But he'll see there's been a break-in. The open padlocks! He'll search the place.'

'Leave it to me,' Echo said. 'I've had an idea. Get down behind that cupboard and keep still. And blow out that candle.'

Izanuela complied. She too could now hear Ghoolion's footsteps. Echo groped his way to the back of the cellar and crouched down in a corner just as Ghoolion appeared in the doorway. The cellar was suddenly bathed in multicoloured light by the will-o'-the-wisp lantern in his hand.

'Who's there?' he called sternly. 'Who has been suicidal enough to break into my cellar?'

There was a moment's absolute silence. Echo's heart was racing. At last he plucked up all his courage.

'It's only little me, Master,' he called jauntily. 'Echo.'

He emerged into the light of Ghoolion's lantern.

'What are you doing down here?' the Alchemaster demanded sharply. 'How did you get those locks open?'

'What, *me* open them?' Echo sounded mystified. 'I'm only a little Crat. The door was wide open when I got here.'

'It was open?' said Ghoolion. He looked dumbfounded.

'How else could I have got in? I thought *you'd* left it open for me, the way you do the door to the roof.'

Ghoolion seemed to lose his balance for a moment. He lurched sideways, swinging the lantern to and fro.

'I must have forgotten to lock up,' he muttered. 'I'm thoroughly overworked, I suppose.'

'I know you are,' said Echo. 'I hardly ever see you these days.'

The Alchemaster gave a sudden start. His face stiffened.

'You didn't answer my question,' he said sharply. 'What are you doing down here? I thought you were afraid of these cellars.'

Echo sighed. 'Oh, nobody with a future as limited as mine wastes time on silly phobias. An idea occurred to me recently, while I was paying my first visit to the Toadwoods. I don't know what you propose to do with my remains once you've boiled off the fat, but one thing's for sure: I don't want to be buried there.'

Ghoolion lowered the lantern.

'I see,' he said. 'In that case, where?'

'Well, this cellar is a nice, cool, clean place. The insects and rats can't get in, and if my fat is going to be stored here anyway, I thought ...' Echo broke off.

'You want to be buried down here?' asked Ghoolion.

'Yes, in a manner of speaking. If it isn't too much trouble, you could stuff me like those mummies of yours. Then you'd have a nice memento of me and I wouldn't be so completely cut off from the rest of the world.'

Ghoolion grinned. 'Oh, is that all? You're going to make a pretty demanding corpse. Anything else?'

'Yes, there is,' said Echo, 'while we're on the subject. I'd like you to put me in a particular spot. Would you mind coming with me?'

He now had to lure the old man further into the cellar so that the Uggly could sneak out behind his back.

'The thing is,' he said, leading the way, 'I wouldn't want to be on display among the balls of fat extracted from loathsome creatures like Throttlesnakes or Spiderwitches, or whatever they're called.'

'That's understandable,' said Ghoolion.

Glancing over his shoulder, Echo saw Izanuela emerge from her hiding place and tiptoe towards the door. He could imagine how terrified she was.

'I'd like to be displayed back here beside the elements,' he went on, 'in a nice, dignified position.'

'I think that could be arranged,' Ghoolion said.

'I've already chosen a spot: here, just beside the zamonium.'

Ghoolion gave another grin. 'You want to be displayed beside the zamonium? Not a very modest request.'

'But not presumptuous either, I hope. You told me yourself what an important role my fat is going to play in the development of Zamonian alchemy, so I thought, well ...'

Echo was doing his utmost to prevent the old man from looking in Izanuela's direction. He spoke as loudly as possible to drown any telltale sounds.

'Well,' Ghoolion repeated magnanimously, 'I think that could be arranged. It's not without a certain logic.'

Echo glanced over his shoulder again. The Uggly's backside was just disappearing round the doorpost. Now he could relax. He would have to detain Ghoolion a little longer, that was all. He could picture Izanuela hurrying back along the underground passages, panting and sweating and cursing him under her breath. He hoped she would take good care of the stolen ball of fat.

'Did you know', he asked, 'that there's a monstrous great toad living in a grave in the Toadwoods and that it's the last of its kind?'

The Love Potion

It was late that night – just before dawn, in fact – when Echo ventured out of the castle and hurried off to Uggly Lane to help Izanuela put the finishing touches to her potion. The front door admitted him of its own accord and he made his way down to the cellar, only to find the Uggly fast asleep beside her distillation plant. She was snoring with her head on the table top, surrounded by utter chaos. Dozens of flasks and test tubes, phials and beakers were standing there. Some of them had overturned and butterflies were sipping or bathing in the mingled liquids that had spilled from them. The glass flask of chlorophyll solution was boiling over, the hop dispenser rattling away and spitting out hop pellets, the Twitching Terebinth dancing a fandango in the midst of this mess.

Echo jumped up on the table and went over to Izanuela. She was talking in her sleep.

'No ... Please don't ... Ghoolion, I'm innocent ... Don't barbecue me, I beg you ...'

Echo tapped her gently on the head with his paw. She sat up with a jerk and waved her arms around. Then she saw who it was and relaxed.

'Good heavens ... er ... I must have dozed off ... Sheer exhaustion, I'm afraid ...' She yawned prodigiously.

'Can we carry on now?' Echo asked.

'Carry on?' Izanuela said sleepily. 'What with?'

'The love potion, of course.'

'Oh, the love potion.' She grinned. 'It's done already.'

'You went ahead without me?'

'Of course, we don't have much time. I worked all through the night. Four disasters. The fifth time, bingo! Then I collapsed. There it is.' She pointed to a small, unremarkable-looking flask on the table. It contained some clear, pale-green fluid.

Echo sniffed the cork inquisitively.

'It smells and tastes of nothing at all,' said Izanuela, 'but it would rip the heart out of your body and squeeze it dry. A single drop of the stuff and you'd be miaowing at the moon for the next three nights.'

'What do we do with it now?'

'Well, we …' She broke off. 'I mean, *you* administer it to Ghoolion. The whole batch. Preferably in a glass of red wine. He does drink red wine?'

'Certainly,' said Echo, remembering their carousal.

'Good. I've made you a receptacle we can tie round your tummy. We'll practise how you uncork it in a minute. Tip it all into his wine and don't even dream of sampling any yourself.'

'I'm not that stupid.'

'Don't be too sure. The potion may smell and taste of nothing, but it exerts an immense attraction when it's uncorked. I had to struggle to stop myself from drinking the lot. It was all I could do to cork it up.'

Izanuela rose and stretched. She turned off the hop dispenser and removed the boiling chlorophyll solution from the heat.

'I'm almost as proud of the choice perfume I've distilled from the Cratmint,' she said, indicating the glass retort containing the mint. Its grey leaves, now completely desiccated, were drooping limply.

She reached inside her cloak and produced another flask. 'Cratmint perfume, the most potent scent in existence. Its effect on someone who has drunk the love potion is as powerful as that of the moon on the tides or a magnet on a piece of iron. Or a clump of Cratmint on a Crat. Only a hundred times stronger.'

She deposited the second flask beside the first.

'Those two together', she said, 'constitute the bottled essence of true and everlasting love.'

'Are you quite sure?' Echo hazarded.

Izanuela glared at him.

'You doubt me?' she said coolly. 'Then let's test some on the Leyden Manikin. A waste, in my opinion, but it's better to be safe than sorry. We don't want to leave anything to chance.'

She took the flask of love potion and went over to the jar containing the Leyden Manikin, which was still languishing apathetically in its nutrient fluid. Then she removed the cork. Her expression changed in a flash. Her eyes widened, her lips trembled.

'Aaah!' she cried.

Now Echo, too, felt the mysterious power of attraction. He saw nothing and smelt nothing, but he experienced a fierce desire to snatch the flask from the Uggly's hand and drain it.

'Oooh!' cried Izanuela as she dribbled a few drops of the precious liquid into the Leyden Manikin's glass jar.

She clearly found it a great effort to replace the cork.

'Phew,' she said, 'that was powerful.'

Echo, too, breathed a sigh of relief.

The Leyden Manikin got up and toddled around in its nutrient fluid.

'It'll take a little while,' Izanuela explained. 'It's absorbing the potion through its feet. It'll go to its head before long.'

Echo had gone right up to the jar. The Leyden Manikin was beginning to splash around in a more exuberant fashion.

'It's beginning to work,' Izanuela said with a grin. 'Pretend the little creature is really Ghoolion.'

The Manikin started to dance. Clumsily, it turned on the spot and waved its arms around.

Echo stared at it open-mouthed. 'It looks drunk.'

'It's lovesick,' said Izanuela, 'but it still doesn't know who it's in love with. We'll soon see about that.'

She took the flask containing the Cratmint perfume, unscrewed the top and dabbed a single drop of it on her neck. The underground chamber was instantly suffused with a glorious scent that filled Echo with a profound sense of happiness. He jumped down off the table and wound round Izanuela's legs.

'And you haven't even drunk any of the love potion!' she said with a laugh. 'Come, see what the Leyden Manikin is up to.'

Echo found it hard to tear himself away from her legs. He jumped back on the table and looked at the manikin in its jar.

The little thing was behaving quite dementedly. It kept butting its head against the glass in an attempt to get at Izanuela, pausing occasionally to sing to her in a high-pitched, piping voice.

'It's completely infatuated with me,' she said with a touch of satisfaction. 'And it's only an artificial, alchemical creature without a heart or genuine feelings. Imagine what our potion could do to a real, live, sentient person!'

'This is fantastic!' Echo cried enthusiastically. 'It works!'

'Of course it works,' Izanuela said loftily. 'I told you it was silly to waste the stuff on the manikin. Now I'll show you what I've made for you to use when emptying the potion into Ghoolion's wine glass.'

It was a little wineskin which the Uggly had adapted by sewing two leather straps to it. These would be secured round Echo's body. He would have to support himself carefully with his forepaws on the rim of the glass, then remove the cork with his teeth and apply pressure with one paw, squirting the potion into the wine. It became clear to him that this would entail a feat of acrobatics for which a Crat was not exactly predestined. There was a risk that the wine glass might fall over and spill its precious contents, so they practised this technique until he had mastered it perfectly.

It was early morning by the time Echo was ready to return to the castle at last. It occurred to them that they had completely forgotten about the Leyden Manikin.

They bent over the jar together. The little creature was floating on its back in the nutrient fluid, motionless. Its tiny mouth was wide open.

'It must have fractured its skull,' said Echo.

'It loved me too much,' Izanuela said with a sigh.

Echo couldn't decide whether the Uggly's tone of voice was dictated by compassion or pride.

'Well,' she said, straightening up, 'I've fulfilled my part of the bargain. I've brewed the love potion and distilled the Cratmint perfume. Now it's up to you to keep your promise.'

Echo nodded. 'That's only fair,' he said.

'Off you go, then.' Izanuela flopped down on a chair. 'But first,' she commanded, 'tell me about the distillation of thoughts that rotate clockwise and the preservation of volatile substances. I want to learn all of Ghoolion's alchemical secrets. All of them!'

Ghoolion Gets Busy

While the moon was growing steadily rounder, night after night, Echo's strict diet and his recent exertions enabled him to shed another few pounds. He and Izanuela had agreed to wait until the day before the moon was full. They wanted to catch the Alchemaster at a moment when he was at his busiest. That would make it easier for Echo to administer the love potion unobserved.

So all that remained for him to do was to kill time in a state of anxious suspense. He wandered around the castle with the Cooked Ghost and roamed the roof by himself or sat at the foot of Theodore's chimney, waiting in vain for him to return. But his favourite diversion was secretly watching the Alchemaster at his many and various activities. Ghoolion hurried to and fro between the laboratory and the cellar with increasing frequency, fetching balls of fat and boiling them up, concentrating or mingling elements and gases, vital essences and dying sighs. Echo could scarcely endure the smells that prevailed in his laboratory, so caustic and poisonous were the substances he processed there. Ghoolion himself didn't seem to mind them. On the contrary, the more stifling and unhealthy the atmosphere, the livelier he became. His feverish condition developed into a frenzy, his passion for work into a kind of ecstasy. Having formerly waltzed around his pans in the kitchen, he now danced a tarantella around the alchemical equipment in his laboratory. Sometimes he would abruptly clutch his head or his heart, reeling around and trembling as if about to measure his length on the floor. Whenever Echo saw this he hoped the Alchemaster was about to have a stroke or a heart attack, but Ghoolion recovered every time, pulled himself together and resumed his frantic activities.

It became ever clearer to Echo that a life's work was nearing its culmination just as the moon was coming to the full. Ghoolion had spent a lifetime hunting and collecting things, killing and mummifying them, preserving and hoarding them, arranging them systematically and possessing his soul in patience. Now the moment was at hand: a narrow window of opportunity which had to be opened in order to weld his collection together correctly and condense it into the one true substance: Prima Zateria. Ghoolion was every inch the master chef once more, but the soup he was preparing would be anything but wholesome, least of all from Echo's point of view.

The fat store, which Echo now visited more often because Ghoolion left the door open all the time, was steadily emptying. The Alchemaster kept hurrying upstairs with basketloads of balls of fat for processing in the laboratory. To Echo, the most terrible times of all were when he boiled up the sighs of the dying. It broke the little Crat's heart to hear the sounds that then arose from the bubbling saucepans, but to Ghoolion's ears they were the sweetest music, and he danced to it more and more ecstatically. The old alchemist had always got by on a minimum of sleep, but he now needed none at all. The more recklessly he squandered his energies, the more abundantly strength seemed to flow into him. He drove himself on with various beverages including coffee and tea, wine and bitter mineral water. Often, too, he brewed a black, treacly concoction which he drank greedily, only to work twice as hard thereafter. Echo had sniffed it once, and a mere whiff had made his heart race for hours. It smelt of eucalyptus and resin, ether and petroleum.

The Alchemaster scarcely noticed his prisoner any more. He plunked Echo's meals down in front of him, usually tinned food or precooked stuff from the larder, and didn't seem to care whether he ate it or not. This helped Echo to discipline himself and stick to his diet. Although he wasn't quite down to his old, ideal weight, he had considerably improved his agility and staying power.

One night, as he was sitting on the roof and looking down at Malaisea just as the lights were coming on in the houses, he thought: 'Those people have no inkling of the drama in progress up here. On the other hand, I have no inkling of the dramas in progress in their living rooms. People die every day and they all get buried in the Toadwoods. Where's the sense in that?'

283

His eyes strayed to the forest itself, which looked from up above like a huge, sleeping beast. Somewhere in its depths a plump toad was lurking in a grave, waiting for him. 'You're in for a long wait!' Echo called down from the roof. 'I'm not going to wind up in the Toadwoods, nor in Ghoolion's cellar! I'm going to the Blue Mountains and far beyond them!'

He shouted the words as loudly and confidently as he could, but his voice trembled all the same.

Green Smoke

One morning Echo saw a thin plume of green smoke rising into the air from Izanuela's chimney. This was the prearranged signal that the day had come. He set off at once for Uggly Lane.

'We can't wait any longer,' Izanuela told him as she strapped the little wineskin to his body. 'Tomorrow is full moon. You must find an opportunity to slip the potion into his wine before the day is out. When you've done that, come back here and I'll release you from the wineskin. And don't get caught, my young friend, not by Ghoolion or anyone else!'

'I feel sick,' Echo said plaintively, 'sick with fear. Don't pull that strap so tight.'

'How do you think *I'm* feeling?' said Izanuela. 'I didn't sleep a wink all night, and sheer nerves made me eat a whole slab of Troglotroll cheese. What if Ghoolion sets eyes on me and the perfume doesn't work?'

'*Now* you tell me!' said Echo. 'You were so certain before.'

'Nothing in life is certain, especially when you're dealing with someone like Ghoolion. Oh dear, what have I let myself in for? We'll both end up grilling on that barbecue of his.' She waggled her ears nervously.

'You really know how to buoy a person up,' said Echo. 'Hold yourself in readiness and don't leave the house. I've no idea when I'll be back. Possibly in an hour's time, possibly not till tonight. If the worst happens, never.'

Echo left Uggly Lane and turned off down the next street. This time, on the spur of the moment, he decided to take a short cut. He was less likely to encounter any wild dogs on the longer route through the busier streets, but the wineskin was heavy and conspicuous – someone might take a fancy to it and try to catch him. That being so, he went by way of the backyards in Hospital Lane, where the stench of disease was so repulsive that few people cared to linger.

That this was a mistake did not dawn on Echo until he had turned into the alleyway adjoining Hospital Lane. He rounded the corner and there they were: the pack of wild dogs he'd harassed as a Leathermouse – all of them except the one that had run full tilt into a wall. Perhaps it had given up hunting little animals.

'Look, boys,' said the leader of the pack, a jet-black bull terrier as chunky as a blacksmith's anvil. 'Our meal has brought us the wine to go with it.' The other three tykes yapped appreciatively.

Without a moment's hesitation, Echo turned tail and sprinted back down Hospital Lane.

'Come on,' barked the black dog, 'after him!' And the whole pack set off in pursuit.

Echo felt as if the wineskin had ceased to exist. It amazed him how nimbly he could run and what good shape he was in. His training had clearly paid off. He no longer needed to *pretend* to be chased by wild dogs; he really *was* being chased by wild dogs.

The lane ran downhill. Echo went bounding along it, then paused for an instant and drew a deep breath. Vaulting over the kerb, a dustbin and a low wall, he disappeared into an overgrown garden. The dogs, who had been brought to a halt by the wall, milled around barking angrily. Then it occurred to them to look for another way in.

Echo looked around. He was in the hospital garden. Refuse bins brimming with bloodstained dressings were standing in the tall grass. A few patients were hobbling about on crutches. There! The hospital's rear entrance. No use, locked. He was trapped.

The mongrels had found their way into the garden. They came crashing through the hedge and got caught up in some bramble bushes, which made them twice as furious. Echo heard human voices and a creaking sound. He looked back at the rear entrance. Two orderlies were carrying someone out on a stretcher. The door was wide open. Now was his chance!

A few vigorous strides took him out of the long grass and on to the gravel path. Keeping low, he darted under the stretcher, between the orderlies' legs and into the hospital. In his Leathermouse guise he had found the smell that hit him thoroughly inviting; now it almost made him turn back and provide the dogs with a free meal. Blood, ether, iodine, ammonia … Nauseating! Heedless of the screams and groans issuing from the wards and threading his way between patients on crutches, Echo pressed on into the hospital.

The dogs continued to pursue their quarry. They knocked over the orderlies, together with the stretcher and its badly injured occupant, and rampaged along the corridors like a gang of noisy drunks. Patients hurled themselves aside in panic, a nurse shouted for help.

Following a powerful scent of blood, Echo went racing up some stairs with the dogs in hot pursuit. A patient hobbling towards them on a stick went flying. Just then, a door opened and a nurse came out. Echo stopped dead, then darted between her legs and into the big room beyond.

He had guessed correctly: it was the hospital's operating theatre. He came to a halt. Even before any of the surgeons and nurses engaged on the current operation had time to notice him, pandemonium broke out.

The dogs upended the nurse in the doorway and stormed into the hospital's holy of holies. Hadn't they seen the notice on the door, which strictly forbade unauthorised persons to enter, or couldn't they read? Echo grinned to himself.

Confronted by several surgeons with bloodstained scalpels and scissors in their hands, the dogs suddenly stopped barking. Before they could gauge the full extent of their mistake, orderlies armed with broomsticks came rushing in. One of them was even carrying a fire axe.

Echo took advantage of the tumult to slip between their legs and escape through the nearest door. He heard the dogs howling in pain as he scampered down a flight of stairs to the main entrance, which was wide open.

He went out into the street and looked down at his chest. The wineskin containing the love potion seemed to be intact. And so was Echo himself.

Red Wine

Ghoolion was in his laboratory. There were several old tomes lying open on the workbenches and he was consulting them all in turn. He bustled from one book to another, muttering arithmetical calculations and alchemical formulae. Echo watched him from the doorway without showing himself. The Alchemaster wasn't drinking wine at present, but it would have been unusual for him to do so at this time of day.

Echo went off to a room Ghoolion seldom visited and lay down on the threadbare carpet. He would have to be patient and wait for a more opportune time. The Crat hunt had tired him out. He shut his eyes. A minute later he was asleep.

He dreamt that he himself was the Alchemaster's castle and that all the Ugglies in Zamonia had moved into it in order to hold a curious celebration of some kind. They tore off their clothes and went cavorting along the passages, which were his own intestines, tickling the inside of his tummy with their dancing feet until he was awakened by his own laughter.

The sun was already low in the sky. 'Oh dear,' he thought, 'I've slept through half a day's worth of opportunities to slip the potion into his drink.'

He hurried back to the laboratory and peered in. It stank abominably of sulphur and phosphorus. Ghoolion was nowhere to be seen, but there beside an open book on a workbench stood a glass of red wine. It was half full.

What should he do? It was growing late and this might be his last chance of the day. Perhaps Ghoolion hadn't liked the wine and wouldn't touch it again. Where was he, anyway, and when would he return? In an hour? Any minute? A hundred questions raced through Echo's mind. What would Izanuela do in his place? That was beside the point, though, it was up to him to decide. Why hadn't she brewed enough of the potion for more than one attempt? Now it was all or nothing!

He jumped up on the workbench and circled the glass irresolutely. Was there anything wrong with the wine's appearance? Not that he could see. He went closer and sniffed it. Hm, not bad. Or was it? He didn't possess Ghoolion's powers of discrimination, his nose or palate, his familiarity with the noble juice. This might be absolute rotgut or a superb vintage wine. He didn't know.

He sat up on his haunches and rested his forepaws on the rim of the glass. They had practised this manoeuvre often enough. Right, now to remove the stopper from the wineskin with his teeth. Careful now … Pop! Done it!

The potent effect of the love potion caught Echo wholly unprepared. He'd forgotten all about it! The strangest sensation came over him. Must he really waste this precious nectar on an old bogeyman like Ghoolion? Out of the question! It was his alone!

His head swam. He swayed, the glass wobbled, the wine slopped to and fro. He came within an ace of falling over complete with the glass and the unstoppered wineskin, but he let go and came down on all fours. A drop or two of the precious fluid splashed the tablecloth.

'That's a good start,' he thought. 'I nearly botched the whole thing. Pull yourself together! This potion is for Ghoolion, nobody else.'

There! He could hear the Alchemaster's clattering footsteps – he was coming up the stairs already! 'Start again from scratch!' he told himself. 'Up on your haunches, one forepaw on the rim of the glass, the other on the wineskin. Now squeeze!' A thin, arcing jet of clear liquid spurted into the glass.

'But not all of it, surely?' he thought. 'Surely I'm allowed a taste? Just a taste?'

He put out his tongue and craned his neck. Instantly, everything went haywire again: Echo himself, the glass, the whole of their well-laid plan. He thrust himself away, and the last few drops of potion spurted into the air. The glass wobbled on its circular base, the wine sloshed against the rim. Then the glass came to rest in its original position.

Echo listened with a pounding heart. Ghoolion was just outside the door now. Mission accomplished! Only a little of the love potion had been wasted, but it was too late for him to beat a retreat. He mustn't be seen with the wineskin strapped to his body, so he would have to hide somewhere in the laboratory itself. He jumped down off the table and darted over to a bookcase he knew Ghoolion seldom used. Squeezing between two thick tomes, he lay down flat in the space behind them. Then he cautiously peered through the crack between the books. The Alchemaster was just coming in – with a bottle of wine in his hand.

'Damnation,' thought Echo, 'he didn't like that wine. I knew it! He's gone and fetched himself another bottle.'

Ghoolion went over to the wine glass. Held it up to the light of an Anguish Candle. Sniffed it.

'Surely his sensitive snout won't detect the love potion?' Echo thought. 'Please not!'

Ghoolion's face betrayed no reaction of any kind. He put the glass down again. Held the bottle up to the light. Read the label. Put the bottle down beside the glass. And came straight over to the bookshelf where Echo was hiding.

'He's spotted me!' thought Echo. He only just suppressed an urge to make a dash for it.

Ghoolion bent down, took hold of a thick book just in front of Echo's hiding place and pulled it out. If he had bent a little lower, they would have been looking into each other's eyes. But he turned away, browsing through the old encyclopedia.

In the hours that followed Ghoolion made no move either to drink the wine or to leave the laboratory. He checked the temperature of his bubbling cauldron with a thermometer several times, studied some slides under the microscope, walked up and down reciting numerical tables, and made notes. He also drank all kinds of beverages. Tea, water, coffee, his revolting slimy black concoction. But no wine.

The longer Echo persevered in his hiding place, the more exasperated he became. 'Drink that confounded wine, you old devil!' he felt like shouting. 'You're only doing all this to torment me. You know perfectly well I'm here.'

But he controlled himself with difficulty. He endured the disgusting stench Ghoolion created by boiling up his balls of fat. He endured the sighs of the dying, his uncomfortable position, his fear and uncertainty. An hour went by. Two hours. Three. Now he was having to fight off fatigue. The stifling atmosphere and his physical immobility were making him sleepy.

'For goodness' sake don't go to sleep!' he commanded himself. Nobody snored louder than a sleeping Crat.

There! Ghoolion was going over to the wine glass at last. He picked it up again and put it to his lips. Then he had a sudden idea. He put the glass down and hurried over to a blackboard. Quickly covered it with formulae. Wiped them out and scrawled some more in their place. Stepped back and submitted them to lengthy scrutiny. It was enough to drive anyone mad! Echo writhed with impatience in his hiding place.

Then Ghoolion walked briskly back to the wine glass. Picked it up. Put it to his lips. And drained it at a gulp!

Echo gave a delighted start and hit his head on the shelf above. A book fell over. Ghoolion pricked up his ears. His face registered no reaction to the love potion. He took a ball of fat and tossed it into a saucepan. Picked up a basket and hurried out to fetch some more supplies from the cellar.

With a groan, Echo scrambled stiffly out of his hiding place.

The Wedding Gown

Rather than risk another encounter with feral dogs, Echo returned by way of the busiest streets in Malaisea. A few passers-by stared uncomprehendingly at the empty wineskin strapped to his chest, but most were too preoccupied with themselves, their aches and pains, heartburns and gastric disorders, coughs and colds. Not for the first time, Echo realised how little he had missed these universally diseased surroundings.

When he reached Izanuela's house he found the entrance to the cellar open. The usual weird music could be heard, but this time it had taken on a solemn, uplifting quality.

'Down here!' Izanuela called. 'Come and kiss the bride!'

'But no tongues!' Echo insisted as he made his way down the stairs. 'Good news! Mission accomplished! I managed to administer the love potion!'

'I expected no less,' she said. 'Mind you, I haven't been idle in the meantime.'

A long cord had been suspended below the roof of the subterranean garden, and draped over it like a curtain was a big length of red cloth. Izanuela had concealed herself behind this.

'Just a moment,' she trilled. 'I'm nearly ready.'

'Ready for what?' Echo demanded. What had the demented creature dreamed up this time?

'Twitchstik!' she cried, and the Song of the Ugglian Oaks rose in a dramatic crescendo. The curtain was drawn aside and Izanuela stood revealed.

'Tadaaa!'

She wasn't dressed in her usual attire. Instead of her shabby old cloak she now wore a gown like none that Echo had ever seen before. It was completely woven out of flowers and other plants: red and black roses, white and yellow tulips, marguerites and poppies, pale-pink marbled carnations, flame-red orchids, blue violets and violet hyacinths, daisies and plum blossom, snowdrops and lilies, asters and bleeding heart, lavender and lotus blossom, deadly nightshade and eyebright. Also woven into the gown's elaborate ornamentation were herbs, grasses and foliage: celandine and love grass, clover and cardamine, myrtle and melissa, oat grass and silver sage. On her head Izanuela wore a shady, broad-brimmed hat woven out of white waterlilies. Butterflies were fluttering round her and settling here and there to sip at a blossom. To Echo, it looked as if an entire meadow were advancing on him. She smelt like a day in springtime.

'Well, what do you think?' she demanded coquettishly, performing a pirouette that made the leaves rustle. 'Is it worthy of the occasion? I originally intended to make my wedding dress out of red cabbage leaves, but cabbage smells so strong.'

Echo couldn't tear his eyes away from her. She was still the same old Uggly underneath, admittedly, but she seemed transformed. She smelt better. Her movements were more majestic. She radiated a kind of inner beauty. The glorious flowers blinded the eye to all her shortcomings.

'You're a knockout,' said Echo.

'Thank you. And I still haven't put any perfume on.'

'You'll bowl the old man over.'

'How did he react to the love potion?' she asked, patting her dress down.

'Hard to say. He didn't react at all, to be honest, but I scarcely had time to watch him. He drank it and left the room at once.'

'The potion takes time to develop its full effect. An hour or so should do the trick.'

Izanuela proceeded to relieve Echo of the wineskin. 'Was it difficult?' she asked as she unbuckled the straps.

'He took an age to drink the stuff,' Echo replied, 'but then he downed it in one.'

'That's good.' She shivered ecstatically. 'I'm so excited.'

'It's all gone swimmingly up to now.' Echo stretched and yawned, glad to be rid of the cumbersome wineskin. 'Still, we ought to be prepared for any eventuality. What if the potion doesn't work?'

'I've given the matter some thought,' said Izanuela. 'If Ghoolion doesn't react to my appearance as we hope he will, I'll simply tell him

I've come to pay my respects. On the occasion of the ... er, full moon. An old Ugglian custom which I'd like to revive, hence my ceremonial attire. Something along those lines. He can hardly grill me on his barbecue for that, can he?'

'That would let you off the hook,' said Echo. 'Where would it leave me, though?'

'Hm ...' she said. An awkward silence fell.

Her 'Hm ...' hung in the air for a moment or two. Then she threw up her hands and cried, 'No more dire imaginings, everything's going to be fine! I only have to titivate myself a bit more and put on some perfume.'

She vanished behind the curtain, humming to herself like a beehive, while Echo waited patiently. Izanuela looked even more attractive when she reappeared. Her glossy lips were a dark shade of red, the worst of her warts had been masked by make-up and she was wearing a pair of long, silky eyelashes Echo had never seen before. Her cheeks were a healthy pink.

'There,' she said brightly, 'now comes the finishing touch. The icing on the cake, so to speak!'

She took the flask of Cratmint perfume and dabbed a few drops on her cleavage.

Echo was suddenly overcome by a feeling of boundless affection for her. He wound round her legs the way he'd always wound round the clump of Cratmint on the roof, purring and miaowing with delight.

'Off we go, then!' she cried. 'Let's storm Ghoolion's castle!'

The unusual spectacle presented by the strange pair created quite a stir in the streets of Malaisea. The crowds of gawping, uncomprehending pedestrians grew steadily thicker as they walked down Apothecary Avenue, but Izanuela refused to quicken her pace and strode on with head erect. Unlike Echo, she seemed to be enjoying the attention.

'Take no notice of them, my friend,' she said. 'They're nothing but ignorant boors.'

No one ventured to follow them up the lane to the castle.

'They're gutless, too,' she said contemptuously. 'Heavens,' she went on, clutching her bosom, 'my heart's in my mouth.'

They didn't stop till they reached the castle entrance. Izanuela gazed up at the building, which looked even more dilapidated at close range than from a distance.

'Where do you think he is?' she asked.

'Ghoolion? In his laboratory, at a guess,' Echo replied.

'Then let's get it over.' Izanuela's throat was so dry that she could only utter the words in a hoarse croak.

The Proposal

All the pride and self-assurance Izanuela had displayed in the streets of Malaisea swiftly evaporated in the atmosphere of the castle. She climbed the stairs on trembling legs and stared fearfully at the stuffed mummies like a little girl on her first ride in a ghost train. Sweat streamed down her cheeks, dissolving her make-up and washing it into her cleavage.

Halfway up the stairs she stopped abruptly.

'I can't,' she wailed. 'I can't go through with it.'

'Come on,' Echo said encouragingly, 'we've got this far.'

'But I'm scared.'

Echo thought feverishly. How could he reassure her?

'What score would you give your fear on a scale of one to ten?' he asked.

'A hundred. No, a thousand. No, a million. No, a hundred million.' She was breathing heavily.

He wouldn't get anywhere like that this time, he could tell. 'Come on,' he said again. 'We'll make it. You look ravishing.'

'Yes,' she said, 'I can understand why *you're* bound to believe that, it's your only hope. But *I* don't have to do this. I need only go back home and everything will be the way it was.'

'But you've got Plan B in case things go wrong. You simply spin him that yarn about an old Ugglian custom and make yourself scarce.'

'It's nothing to do with that. You think I'm scared of Ghoolion or those gruesome figures there? Bah!' She made a dismissive gesture.

'What do you mean?'

She gave him a long look of genuine despair. There were tears in her eyes.

'It's myself I'm afraid of,' she said in a trembling voice.

'You're talking in riddles. This isn't the time.'

Echo was bewildered. She infuriated him, yet he felt sorry for her.

'I've only just realised,' she went on. 'It's like my acrophobia on the roof, don't you understand? This isn't just *your* last chance, it's *mine* as well.'

'I don't follow.'

'Do you know how old I am? No, you don't, thank goodness, and I'm not going to tell you. Nor am I going to tell you how many chances of romance I've ruined in my lifetime. There's only one certainty: this is the last.'

She wiped away her tears.

'This time I'm staking all I possess: the love potion, the perfume, this gown, myself. If I fail to conquer a man's heart this time, I shall never pluck up the courage to try again.'

Echo was beginning to understand.

'If I go home now,' Izanuela whispered, 'at least I can always tell myself I *might* have succeeded. Surely that's better than the bitter certainty of failure?'

'I can't judge,' said Echo. 'I don't have the experience. I've never ruined a chance of romance because I've never had one.'

A long, melancholy silence ensued.

'All right,' he said, 'let *me* wear the perfume. Just tip it over my fur and push off. I'll risk it.'

'You know that won't work, he'll be twice as anxious to keep you at his side. And when the effect of the perfume wears off, tsssk!' She drew a long fingernail across her throat.

Another awkward silence.

'Very well,' she sighed at last. Her bulky frame came to life with a jerk that made her leafy gown rustle. 'I'll do it, but don't imagine I'll lift a finger to help you if it all goes pear-shaped.' She went stomping up the stairs with Echo at her heels.

When they got to the laboratory he cautiously peered inside. The cauldron of fat was bubbling away. No sign of Ghoolion, though.

Izanuela peeped round the corner.

'Oh, he isn't here!' she exclaimed in relief. 'Too bad. Come on, let's go.'

'Not on your life, we'll wait. He's bound to be fetching some more balls of fat from the cellar. He'll be back any minute.'

Echo went into the laboratory and Izanuela reluctantly followed him.

'Where do you think I should stand?' she asked. 'Where would I look my best?'

'Stand beside the window. The smells aren't as bad over there, so they won't overwhelm the perfume.'

Izanuela went over to the window and carried out some running repairs. She mopped her sweaty face and applied some more rouge. Then she took out the flask of Cratmint perfume and sprinkled herself liberally with it.

'Just to be on the safe side,' she said with a nervous laugh.

'You're being very extravagant with that stuff,' said Echo. 'What'll you do when it's all used up?'

'It'll last for a while yet. Meantime, I'm hoping to obtain some more Cratmint. I've already asked my colleagues to keep their eyes open.'

Echo pricked his ears. 'I can hear him coming. He's halfway up the stairs.'

Izanuela tweaked her gown straight.

'Tell me something,' she said. 'When should I ask him to let you go?'

'I don't know yet,' Echo replied. 'Let's wait and see what he does. We don't want to rush things before we're absolutely sure you can twist him round your little finger.'

Ghoolion's metallic tread could be heard in the passage.

'There he is!' Echo whispered. 'Now for the moment of truth.'

The Alchemaster appeared in the doorway. And froze.

'Er, good evening, Sir Alchemaster,' Izanuela blurted out. 'Please forgive me for barging in here uninvited, but it's an ancient Ugglian custom which has fallen into disuse, and I'd very much like to revive it. That's to say, it's not an ancient Ugglian custom to barge in uninvited, but to call at the castle on the eve of the full moon and pay our respects to the Alchemaster in ceremonial attire. Hence this floral gown of mine.'

It looked for one moment as if she were about to faint. The Alchemaster stood there transfixed, staring at her like a snake mesmerising a rabbit. He didn't spare so much as a glance for Echo. As if towed across the laboratory on a string, he walked slowly, very slowly, over to Izanuela, who was swaying unsteadily beside the window. To

Echo, those few seconds seemed longer than all the hours he'd endured in the bookcase. Ghoolion came to a halt just short of the Uggly, gazing at her with an expression Echo dared not interpret. Then he fell to his knees, bowed his head and whispered: 'Will you marry me?'

'Yes,' Izanuela whispered back. So saying, she lost consciousness and subsided into the Alchemaster's outstretched arms.

The Engagement Party

'You can always tell a good chef by his puddings,' said Ghoolion. 'Isn't that what people say? All the time they're ploughing their way through a menu, isn't it the sweet they're really waiting for?'

Echo and Izanuela nodded eagerly. This had been their invariable response to everything he'd said in the last few minutes. No sooner had the Uggly regained consciousness than he plied them both with flattering compliments and conducted them to the castle kitchen, where he laid the table and proceeded to heat the oven.

'That', he went on, 'is why I should like to celebrate this day by creating a menu composed entirely of puddings. A symphony of rousing finales. One sweet sin of self-indulgence after another. Nothing but the best from first to last. Do you agree, my blossom? Do you agree, Echo, my honoured guest?'

Izanuela was sitting stiffly at the end of the table while Echo occupied his usual place on top of it. They both watched, fascinated, as the Alchemaster busied himself at the stove.

Ghoolion seemed a different person. He was behaving for all the world like a husband of many years' standing, but one who was still as enamoured of his wife as he had been on their wedding day. He missed no opportunity to pay Izanuela compliments and fire off ardent glances in her direction.

'I thought you ate nothing but cheese,' Echo whispered to her when Ghoolion had hurried out of the kitchen to fetch some additional ingredients from his storeroom.

'For his sake I'd eat a plate complete with cutlery,' she whispered back. 'And the tablecloth into the bargain. Stop needling me!'

'There's no need to abandon your principles just because he's besotted with you. Keep him on a tight rein. We want *him* eating out of *your* hands, not the other way round.'

'Isn't it fantastic, though?' she demanded, clapping her hands. 'The potion is working far better than I thought it would.'

'But please remember our ultimate objective,' Echo reminded her. 'We haven't got there yet.'

Ghoolion returned carrying two baskets filled with flour, sugar, butter, eggs, chocolate, dried fruit and vanilla pods.

'I want to prepare everything freshly, my dearest,' he called, 'that's why I must ask you to be patient. Permit me to pass the time by telling you a charming story while I toil away at the stove. It's about the finest pastry cook in Zamonia.'

Echo and Izanuela nodded eagerly again.

'Hm,' thought Echo. 'A charming story about a pastry cook, eh? The old boy really has changed his spots.' All Ghoolion's stories in the past had been about vampires and demented mass murderers, Snow-White Widows and lethal wines that choked those who drank them.

The Alchemaster proceeded to beat up some white of egg in a large bowl.

'Very well,' he said. 'At first this pastry cook was a rather crabbed individual. He despised sweet things of all kinds, detested cakes and puddings, abhorred meringues and biscuits. Puddings were an abomination to him and whipped cream he found loathsome. What he liked best were pickled gherkins and rollmops, smelly cheeses and salt cod, hard roe and sauerkraut from the Sourwoods swimming in sour cream.'

'Ah,' thought Echo, 'that's more like the old Ghoolion. At least his story's beginning on a sour note.'

'Best of all, however,' Ghoolion went on, 'he preferred to eat nothing at all. He was as tall and thin as a beanpole.'

'Sounds familiar,' thought Echo.

'By the way,' said Ghoolion, using a cut-throat razor to dissect an apricot into slices so thin one could have read a book through them, 'I forgot to mention that my story takes place in Ingotville.'

'Ingotville?' Echo exclaimed in surprise.

'Yes,' said Ghoolion. 'Anything wrong with that?'

'Yes,' Izanuela chimed in, 'what's wrong with Ingotville?'

'Absolutely nothing,' Echo said hastily. 'Please go on.'

'Well, Ingotville, as everyone knows, is the ugliest, dirtiest, most dangerous and unpopular city in the whole of Zamonia. It consists entirely of metal, of rusty iron and poisonous lead, tarnished copper and brass, nuts and bolts, machines and factories.'

'Strange,' thought Echo. 'Those are precisely the words I used in my own description of Ingotville.'

The Alchemaster was now stewing some green tomatoes in a cast-iron saucepan, together with raisins, orange peel, brown sugar and sherry vinegar.

'Yes,' he went on, 'the city itself is even said to be a gigantic machine that's very, very slowly propelling itself towards an unknown destination. Most of the Zamonian continent's metalworking industry is based there, and even the products it manufactures are ugly: weapons and barbed wire, garrottes and Iron Maidens, cages and handcuffs, suits of armour and executioners' axes. Most of the inhabitants dwell in corrugated-iron huts black with coal dust and corroded by the acid rain that falls there almost incessantly. Those who can afford to – the gold barons and lead tycoons, arms dealers and arms manufacturers – live in steel fortresses, in constant fear of their starving and discontented underlings and workers. Ingotville is a city traversed by streams of acid and oil, and perpetually overhung by a pall of soot and storm clouds in which shafts of lightning flash and thunder rumbles. The grimy air is forever filled with the pounding and hissing of machinery, the squeak of rusty hinges and the rattle of chains. Many of its inhabitants are machines themselves. It's a vile city, perhaps the vilest in all Zamonia.'

'Those are my own words, syllable for syllable,' thought Echo. It was amazing how well the old man had memorised them. Where was this leading?

'Well, one day, in the midst of this hideous city, our ill-natured hero encountered the most beautiful girl he'd ever seen.'

'Ah,' Izanuela exclaimed, clapping her hands, 'a love story!'

'This sounds familiar too,' thought Echo, but he said nothing.

'Picture to yourself the most beautiful girl imaginable!' said Ghoolion. 'She was so beautiful that there would be no point, in view of my meagre talent for storytelling, in even trying to put her beauty into words. That would far exceed my capabilities, so I'll refrain from mentioning whether she was a blonde or a brunette or a redhead ...'

'He's telling another story but in my words,' mused Echo. 'What's he up to?'

'... or whether her hair was long or short or curly or smooth as silk,' Ghoolion pursued. 'I shall also refrain from the usual comparisons where her complexion was concerned, for instance milk, velvet, satin, peaches and cream, honey or ivory. Instead, I shall leave it entirely up to your imagination to fill in this blank with your own ideal of feminine beauty.'

Echo inferred from Izanuela's downcast eyes and stupid smirk that she had substituted her own likeness for that of the beautiful girl.

'If he's memorised it to this extent,' he reflected, 'my story must have left a far deeper impression on him than I thought.'

Ghoolion was now, with the deft and graceful movements of a head waiter, serving the first course. A warm salad of gossamer-thin slices of apricot on a bed of puréed green tomatoes, it was topped with a remarkably firm dollop of whipped egg white flavoured with vanilla. He gave Izanuela a fiery glance that would have melted the ice in the Cold Caverns of Netherworld, then went on with his story.

'Well, it was widely known that, besides being the loveliest creature in Ingotville, this beautiful girl had an absolute mania for sweet things. She adored bonbons and pralines, chocolate and marzipan, nougat and Turkish delight. She was crazy about pastries and whipped cream, *millefeuilles* and lemon cheesecake.

'The ill-natured young man cursed his lot. "I work in a vinegar factory," he grumbled, "where I skim the scum off the gherkin tubs. How can someone like me win the affections of so sweet a girl?"'

Echo felt relieved. 'He's getting around to it at last,' he thought. 'In his own words, too.'

The Alchemaster peeled a pear while some crystallised chestnuts were simmering in cream in the saucepan in front of him.

'I must say,' trilled Izanuela, 'this tomato compote is a dream. As for the vanilla foam, you could positively chew the stuff! How do you get it like that?'

'Many thanks, my blossom,' Ghoolion replied with a smile. 'One simply has to beat it hard enough. But that's just an appetiser designed to loosen your delightful tongue. I'm producing the other courses as fast as I can.'

He removed the chestnuts from the stove and proceeded to mash them with a fork.

'One day,' he went on, 'when the young man was strolling along, sodden with acid rain and lost in his own gloomy thoughts, he passed a patisserie. It was a rare sight amid the ubiquitous rust and soot and metallic greyness of Ingotville: a shop window filled with colourful, cream-topped pastries, chocolate gâteaux, cinnamon rolls, crystallised fruit and glazed tartlets. To anyone else that shop window would have seemed like an oasis in the desert, a starving man's hallucination, but its effect on our young man was diametrically different. The sight of all those sweet things revolted him.'

Ghoolion tossed some flakes of white chocolate into a saucepan to melt, then added some cream and spiced the result with cinnamon.

'The young man was about to walk on quickly when he caught sight of his beloved inside the shop, her eyes shining with anticipation as she pointed to the various items she wished to purchase. He was quite convinced he had never seen her look as beautiful as she did at that moment.'

Ghoolion removed the white chocolate sauce from the stove. It smelt tempting.

'A strange kind of rage welled up in the young man's breast. He was disconcerted to note that he was jealous of a slice of gâteau. Envious of a strawberry tartlet. Infuriated by a chocolate wafer.

'"Just wait," he said to himself. "I shall be able to make her delicacies far superior to that sugary muck in there. I shall become the best pastry cook, the most famous confectioner, the greatest exponent of seduction by sugar in the whole of Zamonia! I shall produce the most delicious puddings and elaborate gâteaux ever devised. I shall create pralines to break a person's heart. Fondants to fight over. Meringues to kill for. A bitter chocolate velouté that will make her love me to the point of idolatry."'

Ghoolion broke off because he was removing something from the oven and dishing it out on the plates. It smelt of baked pears and marzipan.

'I must say,' Izanuela whispered to Echo, 'I think he's doing terribly well. Did you know he was such an expert storyteller?'

'Yes,' Echo whispered back.

'He's a man of many talents,' she said under her breath.

Ghoolion served the next course. Baked to a pale golden brown, it was a pear-and-marzipan strudel afloat in a warm sea of melted white chocolate.

'Enjoy,' Ghoolion said with a bow.

What impressed Echo most was not the sophistication of the food they were being offered – he was only too accustomed to that – but the fact that Ghoolion was so unpardonably neglecting his real work in the laboratory. Indeed, he seemed to have forgotten about it altogether. Tomorrow was full moon, the night he had been working towards for so long, and here he was, telling stories and cooing at Izanuela. To Echo, this was the surest proof of the love potion's potency.

'Aah! Mmyummm ...' said Izanuela as she took her first mouthful of the strudel. 'This is simply in-cred-ible! It tastes like ... like ...'

'Like love itself?' Ghoolion amplified with a seductive wink. 'That brings me back to my story. It was love that had wrought such a complete change in our young man. His gloom gave way to good cheer, his sourness to sweetness, and Ingotville to Florinth. He realised that he must become an utterly different person if he was to win his beloved's affections. Ingotville being a place where a man might learn how to cast a cannon but not how to make a perfect crème caramel, he left there and went to Florinth, where culinary decadence was then at its height. The reigning Zaan of Florinth had proclaimed cake-making to be an art form in its own right and nine of his cabinet ministers were former pastry cooks. If anyone wished to achieve success in that field, Florinth was the ideal spot to choose. The cherry on the trifle, so to speak.'

Izanuela laughed rather too loudly at Ghoolion's feeble joke for Echo's taste. Meanwhile, the Alchemaster set to work on the next course. He squeezed some blood oranges and limes and chopped up a handful of almonds.

'Our hero began by renouncing all things sour,' he went on, 'and devoted himself to all things sweet. He became a member of the Mielists, a secret society that worshipped honey and believed in a god named

Gnorkx who was reputed to live on the sun and be immortal. They bathed in honey every time the moon was full.'

Echo gave a little start at the mention of Gnorkx's name. Ghoolion glanced at him conspiratorially as he brought a pudding to the boil.

'He learnt his trade from the bottom up. At first he worked in a sugar beet factory, then in a dairy and finally in a cocoa mill. Having enrolled in the cake- and candy-making courses at the Culinary College in Florinth, he completed an apprenticeship at the biggest confectioner's in the city. He also did a three-year course in Advanced Patisserie under Maître Gargantuel, the Zaan of Florinth's pudding and pastry chef. Gargantuel, who recognised the young man's exceptional talent, made him his star pupil and initiated him into the mysteries of the pastry cook's art.'

Ghoolion cleared away and served the next course at once: cold blood-orange soup with gingerbread blancmange and lime-infused butter. Izanuela fell on it as if she hadn't eaten for days.

'For the Zaan's birthday party he produced the longest Swiss roll ever baked. Then he opened his own patisserie, with the result that most of the other patisseries in Florinth went bankrupt because people wanted to eat his pastries and no one else's. The Zaan offered our young man the post of Minister for Desserts, but he declined because he thought the time had come for him to return to Ingotville and win his beloved's heart with a trayful of his most daring creations. When he eventually set eyes on her she was five times fatter and married with three children. Our young man threw himself into the city's most polluted river and died of mercury poisoning before he could drown.'

Echo and Izanuela stared at the Alchemaster, dumbfounded.

'Is that it?' Echo asked.

'Well, yes,' said Ghoolion. 'All Zamonian stories end tragically, as you know. There are two lessons to be drawn from it: first, don't wait too long before marrying your beloved, and secondly, too many sweet things make you fat.'

'Yes, yes,' said Echo, 'and the more courses you eat, the thinner you get. What a stupid story.'

'Well, *I* thought it was *lovely*,' Izanuela said defiantly. 'The ending was a bit abrupt, but it went perfectly with this pudding. The lime-flavoured butter is simply fantastic!' She extended her outsize tongue and proceeded to lick her plate.

'Oh, don't mind him, my blossom,' Ghoolion said. 'Echo's tired of my stories. I sympathise with him, but he'll soon be spared them and left in peace. For evermore.'

Echo's blood ran cold. This might be Izanuela's engagement party, but for him it was the equivalent of a condemned man's last meal. He'd forgotten that for a moment.

Izanuela was equally dismayed by Ghoolion's tactless remark, Echo could tell that from the way her false eyelashes quivered. She stopped licking her plate and put it down.

Ghoolion threw himself at her feet. 'I, at least, intend to take my cue from the story and marry you as soon as possible. Let's tie the knot before the week is out!'

Izanuela turned crimson and struggled for words. 'If you're really sure ...' she said eventually.

Ghoolion jumped up. 'Then let's go on celebrating! I shall make you all the heavenly things our unfortunate pastry cook was unable to create for his beloved.'

He hurried back to the stove. Judging by the symphony of sweets he produced in the hours that followed, Ghoolion himself might have studied in Florinth under Maître Gargantuel: raspberry *millefeuilles* with champagne cream, rennet mousse with chocolate-flavoured zabaglione and cinnamon dumplings, coconut parfait with strawberry fritters, lemon sorbet tinged with saffron, doughnuts stuffed with cherries soaked in port, elderflower pastries topped with creamed pistachio nuts, hazelnut chocolate fingers on a bed of passion fruit and gilded Demonberries.

Echo's dark thoughts were soon dispelled by all these delicacies. He and Izanuela had never been so stuffed with food in their lives, yet they felt as light as air and extremely cheerful – probably because of the various liqueurs and brandies in the puddings they'd consumed. Izanuela had hiccups and Echo was just about to break into song when Ghoolion suddenly said, 'Well, my blossom, it's growing late and the journey from Ingotville must have been long and tiring. I shall now show you to your sleeping quarters.'

'Ingotville?' thought Echo, but he refrained from saying the word out loud. Izanuela was equally puzzled.

Echo was on his guard. Whenever Ghoolion had conducted him to a remote part of the castle, a nasty surprise had been waiting there. Although the Alchemaster was now under the spell of the love potion, he was still dangerous and unpredictable.

'I told you that story, my dearest,' Ghoolion said suddenly, 'because it bears a certain resemblance to our own.'

'Really?' Izanuela looked mystified.

'Yes, in some respects. Our love, too, began in Ingotville. I also lived there as a young man, then went to another city and became a completely different person. But there the resemblance ends. Our own story has a happy ending.'

The Uggly gave Echo a look of enquiry and shrugged her shoulders. She clearly had no idea what Ghoolion was talking about.

He paused outside a massive door. The frame was of polished steel, the door itself of solid iron. It looked like the entrance to a strongroom. 'Or a prison,' thought Echo.

Ghoolion produced a big key from his cloak and unlocked it.

'Here it is, my blossom,' he said solemnly. 'Your bedchamber. I trust you'll find everything to your satisfaction.'

He pushed the door open and went in. Echo and Izanuela followed.

Echo was flabbergasted. There wasn't another room like it anywhere in the castle. The walls, floor and ceiling were of rusty iron, the furniture of polished steel trimmed with copper. The chamber was windowless but brightly lit by Anguish Candles. The pictures hanging on the walls in gold and silver frames had probably been painted by Ghoolion himself. They were gloomy views of Ingotville: factory chimneys wreathed in fog, rain beating down on rusty machinery, cogwheels the size of millstones. Even the roses in a vase were made of iron.

'I want you to feel thoroughly at home,' Ghoolion said with a smile. 'Welcome to your new abode, Floria!'

'FLORIA,' thought Echo.

FLORIA OF INGOTVILLE ...

He had a sudden vision of his late mistress's grave in the Toadwoods.

'Floria?' Izanuela asked in a puzzled tone of voice. Echo gently prodded her foot with a forepaw.

He understood it all now. The love potion's sweet poison, coupled with the potency of the Cratmint perfume, had deluded Ghoolion into believing that his long-lost love, Echo's late mistress, had found her way to him at last. Floria of Ingotville ... His ideal of feminine beauty, which he'd cherished within him since his youth, had become identified with Izanuela, whom he now regarded as the love of his life.

The Uggly interpreted Echo's nudge correctly and asked no more questions. 'This is, er ... incredible ...' she said haltingly. Ghoolion smiled.

'It's all falling into place now,' thought Echo. They said love blinded a person, but in this instance it had driven someone mad. Maybe it had all started when he told Ghoolion the story of his mistress's life, maybe long before that. The Alchemaster had finally flipped. He had told his story in Echo's words because he believed they were his own. He thought he was face to face with his beloved because he mistook Izanuela for Floria. When he looked in a mirror, perhaps he saw the young man he used to be. Ghoolion's sick brain had turned time and space, emotion and reason upside down.

'Up is down and right is wrong,' thought Echo. *Was* it the effect of the potion? If so, the potion was probably just the last straw. The Alchemaster had doubtless begun to lose his wits a long time ago.

'Come now, Echo,' he said. 'Floria needs her beauty sleep and we've got a big day tomorrow.'

The Last Breakfast

Something was restricting Echo's breathing when he awoke the next morning. He felt his throat with his forepaws and was horrified to find a chain encircling it. Ghoolion, standing beside his basket, was smiling benevolently down at him.

'Good morning,' he said. 'Our great day has dawned! The moon is full at last! I hope you'll understand why I can't let you roam around at liberty any more, not on such an important occasion. I don't want to have to go looking for you in the castle's ventilation system just when I need you most.'

The collar that had been slipped over Echo's head while he was asleep was composed of links of solid steel, and it was attached by another chain to the Alchemaster's wrist. Now he was physically as well as hypnotically debarred from trying to escape.

'If you refrain from tugging so hard at that necklace of yours,' said Ghoolion, 'it won't restrict your breathing. I took great care to make it a perfect fit.'

He led Echo to the Uggly's metallic bedchamber, where some breakfast was waiting for him. Izanuela was sitting up in bed in her floral gown with a huge tray on her knees. Discounting a few crumbs, the plates on it were empty. So was the cup in her hand.

'Oh,' Ghoolion exclaimed delightedly, 'you obviously enjoyed your breakfast, my blossom. May I fetch you some more coffee?'

Izanuela nodded demurely.

'It was excellent,' she whispered.

Having secured Echo's chain to the brass bedstead with a small steel padlock, Ghoolion put a bowl of milk down for him, together with a plateful of seared tuna cut up into bite-size portions. Then he left the room.

'What, eating again?' said Echo when the Alchemaster was out of earshot. 'I simply couldn't. All that sweet stuff is lying on my stomach.'

Izanuela brushed some crumbs from the corner of her mouth.

'My,' she said, 'do ham omelettes taste good! Not to mention croissants with melted chocolate. Have you ever tried strawberry jam and peanut butter on white bread? It tastes divine! As for smoked salmon with dill remoulade and beef tartare on pumpernickel ... I had no idea! I could become addicted to all this stuff. If it weren't for Ghoolion, I'd never have eaten anything but cheese all my life, can you imagine?'

'Beef tartare?' said Echo. 'You mean you've been eating raw meat already? At this hour of the day? Has it really come to this?'

'Don't tell me you wouldn't eat all those things,' she retorted, pouting.

'Yes, but I wasn't a devout cheese eater until yesterday, like you. What next? Will you be renouncing your Ugglian beliefs?'

307

Izanuela bowed her head. 'I can't help it if he cooks so well. He's a man –'

'– of many talents,' Echo broke in. 'Yes, yes, I know, but he's still the confounded Alchemaster. He's your arch-enemy, or had you forgotten?'

She stared down at the crumb-strewn counterpane. 'A person must also be capable of forgiveness,' she said softly.

Echo rolled his eyes. The situation was taking a turn he hadn't expected. Izanuela was becoming more and more infatuated with Ghoolion, and time was running out. He had only minutes and hours left, not days and weeks.

'Doesn't it worry you that he calls you Floria and thinks you come from Ingotville?' he demanded.

'I couldn't care less where he thinks I come from,' she said pertly. 'And, heavens alive, he can call me whatever he likes as long as he waits on me hand and foot like this. Anyway, Floria is a nice name! Floria, his blossom. It suits me better than Izanuela. I always thought Izanuela sounded silly. I'm starting a new life today. Why shouldn't I do so under a new name?'

Echo didn't have the heart to point out that Ghoolion wasn't really in love with her, he'd simply lost his wits. She wouldn't have believed it anyway, she was so besotted, and he might even have driven a wedge between them. This was a tricky situation. Ghoolion was insane, Izanuela infatuated, and he himself had one paw in the grave. It was impossible to carry on a normal conversation with the Uggly. He would have to weigh every word with the utmost care.

'We must work out the best way of putting your request to Ghoolion,' he said cautiously.

'Eh? What request? Oh, you mean the lilac curtains. Never mind about them, there's no real hurry, I –'

'No, I *don't* mean the lilac curtains! I mean your request that he should spare my life and let me go! *That's* the request I mean!' Echo's voice broke.

'Oh, *that* request. I'd almost forgotten, but there's no reason to get so heated.'

'He's chained me up!' Echo hissed. 'Tonight he intends to cut my throat and boil off my fat! Forgive me for being a bit on edge!'

Dismayed that he'd blown his top after all, he did his best to calm down.

'It's all right,' Izanuela said awkwardly. 'I'm rather flustered, that's all. This has never happened to me before. Emotional turmoil ...' She gave an embarrassed little laugh.

'All right,' said Echo, 'but we must keep a clear head. Time is running out.'

'I know,' she said. 'Should I ask him as soon as he comes back?'

'No, we mustn't jump the gun. Listen, I've got a plan ...'

'Really?'

'Yes. I think we should lure him out on to the roof.'

'The roof? Must we?' Izanuela shuddered.

'I'm sure it would have a beneficial effect on him. Ghoolion is completely off his ... I mean, he's under considerable pressure at the moment. We must get him away from this unhealthy environment. All those acrid fumes and intoxicating gases. All that hard work and stress he subjects himself to.'

'Good idea. He *is* looking rather pale.'

'The roof has always had a liberating, soothing effect on me. The fresh air. The light. The view. It's another world up there. You develop a new outlook on things. It helps you to see what really matters. In short, it's therapeutic. That's where we should present him with your request.'

'You think I should ask him to show me the roof?' asked Izanuela.

'Better not. It might sound odd – he'd smell a rat. No, *I'll* do it. I'll ask him to take me up to the mother of all roofs one last time. Before he ... well, you know what I mean. He's already gathered how much I like it up there. It'll sound more convincing, coming from me.'

'All right. What then?'

'You must come too, that's all. Once we're up there, you douse yourself in some more of that perfume.'

'What, *more*? I must be economical with the precious stuff if I want a long-term relationship with –'

'Izanuela!' Echo hissed the name so loudly that she flinched. 'My life is at stake! Kindly spare a thought for something apart from your flirtation with the Alchemaster!'

'I'm sorry.' She blushed. 'So I put on the perfume –'

'– and then you ask him. As casually as you can. You don't beg or implore, you simply ask him the way you'd ask for a kiss.'

The Uggly giggled like a teenager, then froze. Ghoolion's metallic footsteps were approaching: he was hurrying back with her coffee. He appeared in the doorway a moment later.

'What a glorious day!' he exclaimed. 'The wind is getting up and it's growing steadily warmer. There could well be a thunderstorm tonight.'

'How nice,' said Echo.

'Breakfast with the two individuals I care about most,' Ghoolion purred as he refilled the Uggly's cup. 'You wouldn't believe how much this means to me.'

'Too true,' thought Echo. 'I wouldn't.'

Ghoolion laid the coffee pot aside and drew himself up to his full height.

'This is a special day from many points of view,' he said. 'Let's start it off in a worthy manner. How would you like me to show you both the best-kept secret in this ancient building?'

The Treasure Chamber

Echo kept wondering what secret he could mean. The Snow-White Widow? The fat cellar? But they didn't go down to the cellar, they climbed the stairs to an upper floor.

'Before a man of honour marries his beloved,' said Ghoolion, 'he discloses his financial circumstances.' He was going on ahead as usual, leading Echo by his chain with Izanuela following obediently behind. 'Well, in my case that's quickly done. I'm merely the municipal Alchemaster of a small and impoverished town. I don't even receive a salary and my meagre inheritance was soon used up. True, I own the biggest property in Malaisea, but who would care to live here apart from me and the Leathermice?'

'I would!' Izanuela said softly.

Echo suppressed a sigh.

Ghoolion smiled. 'Yes,' he said, '*you* would, and for that I'll be eternally grateful to you. But who else? The castle may look impressive from a distance, but any potential purchaser who inspected it more closely would run off screaming, especially if he learned of the building's gruesome history. Fundamentally, therefore, I'm just a poor devil living in a dilapidated ruin. Right?'

'What if you are?' said Izanuela. 'Money isn't everything.'

They came to a halt in a room Echo had already visited dozens of times before. It contained nothing special, just some dusty pieces of furniture.

Ghoolion went over to a bare wall of blackened brick and paused in front of it. For a few moments he seemed to be collecting his thoughts or trying to remember something. Then he proceeded to press various bricks like an organist manipulating the stops of his instrument.

'He's crazy,' thought Echo. 'Even Izanuela should be starting to realise that by now.'

Ghoolion stepped back. There was a sound like an enormous clock beginning to tick. Clickety-clack it went. Metal springs contracted and expanded with a whirring noise. The bricks in the wall started to move in and out and behind one another, grating together as they rearranged themselves to form a steadily widening aperture of triangular shape.

'An ancient mechanism left behind by the Rusty Gnomes,' Ghoolion explained. 'It still works, but I don't know how.'

So he knew of the existence of the dwarfish race whose skeletons Echo had discovered in the building. Echo made no comment because he was far too fascinated by what was happening now. Light was issuing from the aperture. Only a little at first, but the bigger it got the brighter the light became.

'What's that?' Izanuela enquired nervously.

'It's the entrance to my treasure chamber, my blossom,' Ghoolion replied. 'Or should I say, to *our* treasure chamber? Your assumption that you were being wooed by a poverty-stricken wretch wasn't entirely correct, so the fact that you accepted my proposal notwithstanding does you twice as much credit. It has intensified my love for you to an immeasurable extent! I should now like to acquaint you with my true financial circumstances. Kindly follow me, my dears, and feast your eyes on a thing of beauty: the greatest treasure in Malaisea!'

He ducked through the opening, which had now attained the dimensions of a doorway, gently pulling Echo after him. Izanuela hesitantly followed. They were suddenly bathed in a golden glow that seemed to come from all directions at once. The chamber was as spacious and high-ceilinged as several others in the castle, but this one was unique. It consisted entirely of gold. A gold floor. Walls papered with gold leaf. A gold ceiling composed of massive gold panels. A huge, thick carpet woven out of gold thread. A candelabrum of gold with gold candles. A gold fireplace with gold coals in a gold grate. Gold pictures in gold frames on the walls. A gold library comprising thousands of gold books. Cupboards, armchairs, upright chairs and a long refectory table, all of gold. A gold pipe in a gold ashtray. Even the knocked-out ash and the charred match were of gold. Beside them were a half-eaten apple and an open book with a pair of glasses lying on top of it. They, too, were of solid gold.

Echo and Izanuela were dazzled by all this splendour, and even Ghoolion shaded his eyes with his hand. The chamber was invested with its magical refulgence by the dozens of Anguish Candles that were creeping or standing around on tables, shelves and cabinets.

'Isn't gold the loveliest of all the elements?' Ghoolion asked without waiting for an answer. 'Not the rarest, nor the most useful, nor the most effective, but the loveliest.'

Echo tried to tread on the carpet, but the pile pricked his paws like needles. He swiftly removed them.

'You gilded the whole room?' said Izanuela. 'Why?'

Ghoolion smiled. 'I didn't *gild* it. Everything here is made of solid gold. The table, the shelves, the books, every stone in the walls. Go and touch it.'

Izanuela went over to the table and picked up the apple. It was quite an effort.

'My, that's heavy!' she gasped. 'You're right, it's solid gold!'

Ghoolion walked across the chamber with his arms outstretched. 'Yes indeed!' he exclaimed. 'Tons and tons of it. More than a hundred men could carry.'

'Was it always here?' Echo asked. 'Did you discover this chamber?'

'The chamber and its secret mechanism, yes. I found an old parchment in the cellar and managed to decipher it. It bore the formula required to open the door, the language of the stones. But the walls and furniture, floor and ceiling, carpet and books – they were still composed of the materials such things are usually made of. Stone, wood, iron, wool, leather, paper.'

'I don't understand,' said Izanuela. She was admiring her own reflection in a pot-bellied gold vase. 'How did all these things turn into gold?'

'Echo,' Ghoolion commanded, 'quote me alchemy's four supreme objectives.'

Echo didn't have to think for long. 'To find the Philosopher's Stone. To construct a perpetual-motion machine. To attain immortality. To transform lead into gold.'

Ghoolion nodded proudly as the last words were uttered.

'Can you really transform lead into gold?' asked Izanuela.

'Not only that!' Ghoolion said triumphantly. 'I can transform almost anything into gold. Any relatively solid substance. Any metals, of course, apart from quicksilver. Wood, too. Stone. Dust. Wax, as long as it's firm. Lead too, naturally.'

'You told me once it was impossible,' said Echo.

'I had to keep it a secret, of course. You have a nimble tongue, my friend, not to mention a command of every language in existence. Imagine what would happen if it became known that I can manufacture gold – any amount of it! This castle would be under siege! Every mercenary in Zamonia would be at the gates. Every criminal would be after me, hoping to torture me into revealing the secret. Every royal megalomaniac would send his myrmidons to get me.'

Ghoolion gave a mirthless laugh.

'That's why I confined my gold-making activities to this secret chamber. At first I transmuted small objects into gold: a book, a plate, a stone in the wall. Then bigger and bigger articles – chairs, benches, tables – until everything in here was solid gold. I still bring things here and transmute them from time to time, but it became boring in the long run.'

'Why are you telling us all this now?' Echo asked.

Ghoolion smiled. 'Where my future wife is concerned, I consider it my duty.' He gave the chain a gentle tug. 'As for you, my dearest Echo, you're past being able to betray my secret. You'll soon be taking it to the grave with you.'

'Many thanks for reminding me,' thought Echo. The sight of all this splendour had almost made him forget how quickly time was speeding by.

'I only came upon the formula by chance,' Ghoolion went on. 'It probably won't surprise you, Echo, to learn that I discovered the solution to one of alchemy's greatest secrets in the smallest of objects: a dried leaf from the Miniforest, it was the size of a grain of dust. I had only to interchange a few molecules, but one has to know which ones. Moreover, interchanging molecules is an art in itself.'

'So you're a very wealthy man, Master,' said Echo. 'You never cease to surprise me.'

'I have acquired a certain degree of financial independence, it's true.' Ghoolion smirked. 'But take it from me, the two of you: all this gold means nothing to me in comparison with what I hope to achieve tonight. If I could exchange it all, together with my gold-making formula, for the certainty that I shall be successful, I would do so on the spot. For what is wealth compared to immortality? What good is all this loot if I'm doomed to die? And that brings me to the reason for your presence here, Echo.'

'What do you mean?' asked Echo.

'I've filled your little head with all my alchemistic knowledge, but I've left this last piece of information, the formula for making gold, until last. Your brain must, of course, have absorbed it by the time I render you down.'

Ghoolion produced a sheet of parchment from his cloak and held it under Echo's nose. It was covered with alchemistic symbols.

'Would you be kind enough to memorise this?' he asked.

'Hm …' said Echo, scanning the document. It dealt with cohesive and adhesive forces, chlorophyll atoms, graveyard gas, lime, Leathermouse blood, fivefold distillation processes.

He didn't understand the first thing about the formula he was memorising, but by the time he'd finished he knew how to make gold.

'All done,' he said. His head was buzzing.

Ghoolion took the parchment and tore it into tiny little pieces.

'He must feel pretty sure I'm going to die if he entrusts me with such a secret and then destroys the formula,' Echo reflected.

The moment had come at last.

Echo cleared his throat. 'But now, Master, *I've* got a request for *you*.'

Ghoolion stiffened. 'What is it?' he demanded sternly.

'I'd like to visit the mother of all roofs again. For the very last time.'

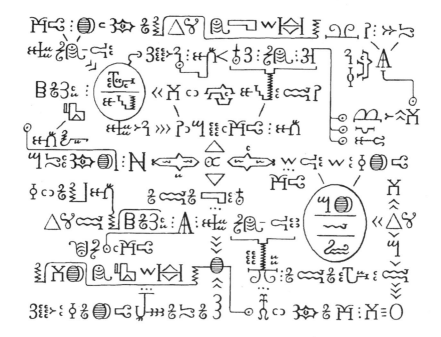

'Oh,' said Ghoolion, relaxing, 'if that's all it is, of course you may.'
He turned to Izanuela. 'I meant to show you the view from up there in
any case, my blossom. It's absolutely breathtaking.'

True Love

The three of them climbed the stairs to the Leathermousoleum. The
vampires were fast asleep at this time of day, so they were
accompanied on their way by the sound of a thousand snores. The stench
was so appalling they couldn't get out on to the roof fast enough.

Once outside, Izanuela froze just as she had the first time. She
clutched her bosom.

'Isn't this wonderful?' said Ghoolion. 'You can see all the way to the
Blue Mountains. You'd think they were close enough to touch.'

'Yes, it's wonderful,' Izanuela gasped. She swayed, her false
eyelashes quivering.

The view was as impressive as ever, but this time it left Echo cold.
With so much at stake, how could he be expected to enjoy it?

'It isn't until one has climbed through that stuffy Leathermousoleum that the view exerts its full effect,' said Ghoolion. 'The best things in life are free. I feel a different person every time I come up here. Lately, alas, I've scarcely had time to do so.'

'It's, er ... glorious.' Izanuela croaked the words, digging her fingers into her floral gown.

'She must get over her fear before she asks him,' thought Echo. 'She must put her request in a self-assured tone of voice, not with a dry throat.'

Ghoolion drew several deep breaths, then pointed downwards. 'You see Malaisea?' he said to Izanuela. 'The town makes such a tranquil, benevolent impression from up here, yet every house is occupied by people who hate me.'

He laughed.

'And why do they hate me? Because they're afraid of me. I have to put the fear of God into them in order to control them, otherwise they'd march up the hill and tear me to pieces. It's an endless vicious circle. If you only knew how tired of it I am. How weary it makes me.'

The Alchemaster was clearly in a philosophical mood, just as Echo had hoped. But they must keep their nerve and take care not to rush things. The Uggly must calm down first. They must wait for the ideal moment.

'May I take a last look at the lake of milk?' Echo asked diffidently.

Ghoolion looked down at him.

'You liked that, didn't you?' He grinned. 'I thought you might like to visit it again, so I refilled it with fresh milk.' He turned to Izanuela. 'Would you care to accompany us, my blossom? It's a bit of a climb.'

'No thanks,' she said hastily. 'I'd sooner stay here and, er, enjoy the view.'

'Let's go, then.' Ghoolion relaxed his grip on the chain and allowed Echo to precede him up the steps. The wind had got up and it was growing warmer, just as he had predicted.

'You may not believe me,' he said, 'but I shall miss your company. Your presence has a beneficial effect on me. I'm reluctant to dispense with it.'

'Very flattering,' said Echo. 'You could always change your mind, of course.'

'If only it were that simple,' Ghoolion sighed. 'The die is cast, I'm afraid. Tonight's the night!'

'Are you really sure it'll work? The experiment, I mean?'

'One can never be absolutely sure. Every venture contains the seeds of failure. Any experiment can go wrong.'

Echo recalled Izanuela's moment of weakness on the stairs. She had said something very persuasive.

'Well,' he said, 'sometimes it can be better to abandon a venture than come to grief. Better not to climb a mountain than fall to your death. Better not to cross a desert than die of thirst. You can still tell yourself you *might* have succeeded.'

'That's an overly convenient attitude to doing one's duty.' Ghoolion laughed. 'It isn't mine. I'd reproach myself for ever if I didn't try it. No, you can't change my mind. Not you, my young friend!'

'Not me,' thought Echo, 'but maybe someone else can.'

They had reached the lake of milk. This time Echo had no eyes for the idyllic beauty of the spot, still less any appetite, but he pretended to drink greedily. He even fished out a crispy roast quail and nibbled it. He had to gain sufficient time for Izanuela to regain her composure.

'I almost degenerated into a vampire myself,' said Ghoolion, leading Echo around on his chain, 'but I eventually realised that day existed as well as night. I want to make it up to Floria. It would really mean a lot to me if you gave us your blessing.'

'What a nerve!' Echo thought. 'He intends to do me in, but he wants my blessing first.' But he played along with the Alchemaster's cruel game and said, 'You can have it.'

'Thank you,' said Ghoolion. 'That means a lot to me. In another world I'm sure we would have been good friends.'

Echo nodded. 'Yes, in another world.'

The sun was now beating down and hot gusts of wind were ruffling the grass. Conditions on the roof were becoming steadily less pleasant.

'Well,' said Ghoolion, tugging at Echo's chain, 'time's up. We must go back inside now. Duty calls.'

When they made their way back to Izanuela, Echo could tell from afar that a change had come over her.

Gone were her darting glances and nervous movements. But there was something else. The overpowering scent of Cratmint was stronger than ever before. She had positioned herself so that the wind carried it to Ghoolion's nostrils when he and Echo were still halfway down the steps.

'At last,' thought Echo. 'She's recovered her wits.'

'One!' said the Uggly, just as they reached her.

'One on a scale of one to ten,' Echo amplified in his head. 'Good, she's conquered her fear.'

'What was that?' Ghoolion asked.

'Er, one ...' Izanuela stammered. 'One, er, can only describe the view from up here as unique – genuinely uplifting. It's as if all one's cares had been blown away by the wind.'

Ghoolion was standing directly in the current of air that was transmitting Izanuela's perfume from her to him. He looked mesmerised. His eyes were glazed and he was swaying slightly. His face wore a blissful smile.

'Now it's *my* turn,' Echo told himself. 'I must appeal to his emotions and arouse his sympathy.'

'It must be a glorious feeling,' he said shyly, 'to stand up here in the throes of a new-found passion. I wish I knew what it was like. I've never been in love myself.'

'What, never?' said Izanuela. 'How sad.'

Echo gazed into the distance and sighed.

'I've heard it said that, over there beyond the Blue Mountains, there's a kind of Crat that could teach me the meaning of love. But I suppose it's too late for that now.'

He cast a surreptitious glance at the Alchemaster. Ghoolion was standing motionless. Was he really unmoved or in an emotional turmoil? Were insanity and compassion, love and malevolence fighting for the upper hand within him? Or had he seen through their amateur dramatics long ago, and was he merely thinking of some alchemical formula to do with the extraction of his, Echo's, fat? It was impossible to tell, but that didn't matter, Echo decided. The moment had come. The perfume must now have taken full effect. It was now or never! He gave Izanuela a meaningful nod.

'I'd like to ask a favour of you,' she said, turning to Ghoolion.

He pricked up his ears. 'Ask away, my blossom. Your wish is my command.'

'I'd like you to let the Crat go. I couldn't bear anyone to die on such a happy day.'

'Perfectly put,' thought Echo. 'Boldly and self-confidently phrased in full reliance on the potent effect of the Cratmint.'

The Alchemaster gave Izanuela a lingering look.

Echo's heart was in his mouth. What would Ghoolion do next? Laugh hysterically? Fall on his knees? Turn into a raven? In his case one had to be ready for anything.

'So that's what you want?' he said. 'That I let Echo go?'

Izanuela nodded, looking him steadfastly in the eye.

'Yes,' she said.

'No,' Ghoolion cried, drawing himself erect. 'With respect, my blossom, you cannot gauge what that would mean – no one could. You might as well ask the sun to stop shining or forbid a storm to break. My whole life, my whole life's work would forfeit its meaning just like that!' He clicked his fingers. Izanuela gave a start.

'It would be like ripping the heart from my body and devouring it before my eyes. Would you really do that to me? Is that really what you want?'

The Uggly, who hadn't been expecting such a reaction, was utterly at a loss. She didn't even dare glance at Echo in search of support, she merely continued to stare at Ghoolion, doing her best not to faint.

A long, awkward silence fell. Echo didn't dare breathe.

'However,' Ghoolion said gravely, 'that's precisely why I shall do as you ask. I'll show you what true love means. I already lost my true love once in my life and nearly went mad as a result. This time I shall hold on to her at the expense of my life's work. So be it.'

He took the little padlock key from his cloak and bent down. 'Well,' he whispered to Echo, 'how was it?'

Echo was bewildered. 'How was what?' he asked.

'My monologue, of course!' Ghoolion said in a low voice. 'I'm not a trained actor, after all.' Straightening up again, he said loudly, 'Did I sound relatively convincing? What do *you* think, Izanuela?'

The name jolted Echo like an electric shock. He had addressed the Uggly by her real name! No more 'blossoms'. No more 'Florias'.

Ghoolion suddenly underwent a remarkable transformation. All the loving kindness and compassion left his voice and demeanour. He reassumed the callous, tyrannical expression he wore in his darkest moments. This was the Alchemaster in his true persona.

'Do the pair of you know how people of the Middle Ages discovered whether an Uggly was innocent or guilty?' he asked. 'They hurled her off a roof. If she survived by flying through the air, she was guilty. If she fell to her death, she was innocent. Simple but just.'

He went right up to Izanuela and gave her a push. Only a gentle one, but enough to throw her off-balance.

'Whoops!' he said.

Izanuela took a few clumsy little steps down the sloping roof and tumbled over the edge without a sound. Not until she had completely disappeared from view did Echo hear her long-drawn-out, high-pitched scream, which must have been audible all over Malaisea.

He dashed to the edge of the roof himself, only to be brought up short by the chain in Ghoolion's hand, and stared down in horror. Izanuela was plummeting into space like an enormous wedding bouquet, leaving a long, multicoloured trail of flowers behind her as she spun and somersaulted through the air. She plunged into Malaisea's expanse of rooftops and her scream died abruptly. All that could be heard thereafter was the whistle of the wind.

'So she was innocent!' Ghoolion exclaimed, looking perplexed. 'Who would have thought it?' He pocketed the key again, then dragged Echo away from the edge of the roof. 'I must advertise for another Uggly at once,' he said. 'What's the use of a municipal Alchemaster if he doesn't have a single Uggly to torment?'

The Wrong Heart

'I can't make up my mind which was your biggest insult to my intelligence: the belief that I wouldn't have rendered myself resistant to that herbal potion of yours, or the childish expectation that an Uggly could triumph over an alchemist. I really can't decide between the two. And to think of all I've taught you about alchemy, the mother of all sciences! I'm immensely disappointed in you.'

Ghoolion had chained Echo to the alchemical furnace. He was striding back and forth across the laboratory and fiddling with various pieces of equipment while he lectured his captive. The clouds that could be seen racing past the windows grew steadily thicker and darker until they were pierced by only an occasional ray of sunlight. The room was fitfully illuminated by Anguish Candles, of which Ghoolion had lit several dozen.

'Who do you think planted that Cratmint on the roof?' he demanded. 'Do you honestly think I haven't familiarised myself with the Ugglimical Cookbook from cover to cover? What do you take me for? Eighteen uggs of Arctic Woodbine! Two uggs of Old Man's Scurf! Four and a half uggs of Pond Scum! One ugg of Sparrowgrass! Floral mumbo-jumbo! Botanical hocus-pocus! Don't make me laugh!'

Echo didn't speak. Scarcely aware of Ghoolion's presence, he seemed to hear the Alchemaster's voice through a layer of cotton wool. He was still too much in shock to feel either fear or anger. The same scene continually unfolded before his inner eye: Izanuela in free fall, leaving a multicoloured trail of flowers behind her.

'I thoroughly enjoyed watching you through my telescope,' Ghoolion went on, 'when you slunk off to your stupid conspiratorial meetings. Did you imagine I wasn't aware that the two of you were skulking on my roof? And as for that ludicrous scene in the fat cellar! You must have thought me totally insane if you believed I couldn't remember whether or not I'd locked the door to my holy of holies.'

'I was hoping love would triumph over insanity,' Echo retorted when he eventually found his voice. 'But that was naive of me.' He now noticed a new smell in the laboratory. It was unpleasantly cloying and penetrating.

'I'm proof against boiling fat and water,' Ghoolion cried above a distant peal of thunder. He went over to the cauldron. 'So why shouldn't I be equally proof against love? One's heart can develop calluses, it's only a question of practice and I developed mine during all the nights I spent beside this cauldron, rendering down the animals whose essences I intend to compound tonight. Don't imagine that they didn't affect me at first, all those anguished screams and death rattles! But one thin layer superimposed itself on another until my heart

321

acquired the armour plate that now protects it from all the nonsense known as love and compassion, grief and pity. You picked on the wrong heart, the two of you!'

Ghoolion opened one valve and closed another, releasing a cloud of blue vapour. He tapped the sides of several jars containing Leyden Manikins, then turned back to Echo.

'But you must admit how skilfully I joined in your little game. It gave me great pleasure to put my acting skills to the test. I have to confess that the potion and the perfume had a certain effect on me – one I found hard to resist. I developed a genuine affection for the Uggly, but it only made my play-acting easier. Up on the roof, when the perfume was at its strongest, I found it a positive effort to push her off. Believe it or not, I would sooner have taken her in my arms – her, an Uggly! That's really saying something, so to that extent I pay tribute to her. A toast to Izanuela!'

He picked up a glass of his black slime and drained it at a gulp. The windows were illuminated by a first flash of lightning, closely followed by a peal of thunder. He raised the glass on high.

'This was my antidote, a concentrate of Leathermouse blood. I draw it off when they're in the midst of their digestive slumbers. It awakens the vampire in you! Reinforces your dark side! Numbs your emotions! A Leathermouse out hunting can't afford to feel love or pity. It's also the finest aid to staying awake all night long. The taste is nauseating and it has certain side effects, but if you overcome them, Cratmint loses its effect on you.' He put the glass down and proceeded to heat the cauldron.

'On a normal person the potion would undoubtedly have worked,' he went on, 'but I'm not a normal person. The perfume I might have withstood even without an antidote. I inhale toxic substances day in, day out. Ether, acids, solvents, spirits, hypnotic oils, chloroform, putrescent gases. If they could affect me, I'd have been dead long ago, but they seem to have an exactly opposite effect. A hundred sword thrusts in the Gloomberg Mountains failed to kill me. None of the diseases I spread has ever made me ill. I scarcely eat, I sleep little, I squander my energies, I drink alcohol and smoke the strongest tobacco, but I'm as strong and healthy as a dray horse. I'm not immortal, but I'm far less vulnerable and prone to infection than the average person. And today I shall take the final step that still separates me from total invulnerability: from immortality!'

Ghoolion went over to a table on which lay something covered with a black cloth, possibly a new alchemical gadget or machine. A brilliant flash of lightning momentarily outshone the Anguish Candles, followed instantly by thunder. The Alchemaster struck a pose and declaimed:

'Let my magic brew revive
that which used to be alive!'

Then he whipped off the cloth and looked down, grinning, at what he had revealed. It wasn't an alchemical gadget, as Echo had surmised, but a half-decayed corpse. The face was no longer recognisable and bare bones were showing through in places, but he knew at once who it was from her favourite gown: Floria of Ingotville, his late mistress. Hence the cloying smell of decay that filled the laboratory.

Ghoolion threw up his arms and cried:

'Let my bubbling cauldron seethe
till the creature starts to breathe.
Brought to life it then shall be
by the power of alchemy!'

He lowered his arms and looked at Echo. 'As you're doubtless horrified to note, I've long ceased to shrink from anything. I've even joined the ranks of the grave robbers! Yes, I went to the Toadwoods armed with spade and pickaxe. Many thanks for your tip about the giant toad, by the way. While I was at the cemetery, I took the opportunity to capture the creature. The smell of Toadmoss made it easy enough to find. What a whopper! It took me a whole night to render it down.'

'You're totally insane,' said Echo.

Ghoolion smiled. 'You're repeating yourself,' he said. 'I know you think I'm crazy but it doesn't offend me, it makes me proud. It merely demonstrates your inability to think in my terms. My thought processes are several sizes too big for your feline brain. You can only store facts, not rearrange them and create something wholly different. Only I can do that. It's an essential requirement if one is to take on the toughest of all opponents. Death, in other words.'

He caressed the corpse with his bony fingers.

'I'm sure you thought I was claiming immortality for myself alone, but I want it for Floria as well. I want to extricate her from Death's chill embrace this very night, and for that I need your help.'

Taking a pair of scissors, he cut off a strand of Floria's white hair and dropped it into the cauldron.

> *'Hearken, ghost, to what I say,*
> *and my potent spell obey!*
> *Quit your home in Death's domain,*
> *realm of sorrow and of pain,*
> *hasten through the nameless portals*
> *that divide the dead from mortals.'*

The wind was blowing ever harder through the windows and the light was steadily fading. Ghoolion was getting the thunderstorm he had predicted. Sheets of parchment went flying, chemical powders and clouds of vapour mingled to form miniature tornados, but the Alchemaster seemed to relish the elements' presumptuous invasion of his laboratory. He adjusted the controls of his Ghoolionic Preserver. In so doing he turned his back on Echo, who took the opportunity to tug at his chain. It was no use, though. Only Ghoolion could have released him.

The Alchemaster's voice was quite calm now. 'We've lived together for a whole month,' he said. 'I trust you can't claim to have had an uninteresting time.'

'No, I can't,' Echo said truthfully. The glass pistons in the Preserver began to rise and fall with a faint clanking sound, churning up the liquids in the cylinders.

'I myself have learnt certain things from you,' Ghoolion went on. 'Serenity. Composure. Innate poise.'

Echo suppressed a bitter laugh. The old madman and murderer spoke of innate poise while preparing to awaken a corpse to everlasting life and extract the fat from a Crat. Insanity really did seem to be a disease whose victims remained unaware of it.

'And those', said Ghoolion, 'are the qualities that must govern our parting. Serenity, composure, mutual harmony.' He left the Preserver and went over to a workbench, where he picked up a scalpel and held it in the air.

'I shall make this as quick and painless as I promised,' he said.

If Ghoolion had been holding a carving knife or a bloodstained executioner's axe, Echo might not have been as scared as he was of that surgical precision instrument. Just a diminutive blade little longer than one of Ghoolion's fingernails, it was sharper than any other form of cutting tool. Sharper than an executioner's axe, sharper than a cut-throat razor. Such a little piece of steel, yet capable of sending him to his death.

'I think you now know me well enough to rest assured that I won't cut off your head or mutilate you in any way. I shall simply make a tiny little incision in your throat, but at just the right spot. The blood will leave your body so fast, you'll fall asleep for ever before the wound begins to hurt.'

'Fall asleep for ever ...' thought Echo. What terrible finality there was in that phrase! He had never felt such an overpowering desire to live as he did at that moment.

'We both want you to bequeath posterity a good-looking corpse, don't we?' Ghoolion said, drawing slowly nearer. 'You see that sack over there? It contains the wood shavings I'm going to stuff you with. They come from the Nurn Forest, which means that they're particularly durable and costly. I've spared no expense, you see. It'll be centuries before anyone needs to restuff you, which they undoubtedly will. The way I'm going to embalm you, your fur will still be glossy long after the shavings have crumbled away to dust. That, by the way, is thanks to the fat I extracted from a thousand-year-old tortoise. So you see, you're going to benefit from my research.'

There wasn't a trace of sarcasm in his tone. 'He's being absolutely serious,' Echo reflected. 'He actually thought I'd be interested in knowing what he's going to embalm me with.' In his mind's eye, Ghoolion was already disembowelling him and stuffing him with wood shavings.

Echo instinctively did what all Crats do when threatened. He arched his back, fluffed out his tail and uttered a furious hiss – not that this made any impression on Ghoolion.

325

'Yes,' he said, 'by all means hiss if it makes you feel better. You can scratch and bite as well, but it won't make things any easier for you. The most you'll do is turn this into a painful and unattractive proceeding. My hand may slip. I may miss the artery and have to start again. Make another incision. Ruin your fur. Cause you needless suffering. We wouldn't want that, either of us, would we?'

Echo stopped hissing, straightened his back and lowered his tail. True, it was utterly futile. Why make everything worse? In his own peculiar way, Ghoolion actually meant well by him.

'Simply lie down and shut your eyes, that's your best plan,' the Alchemaster said smoothly. He was holding the scalpel where Echo couldn't see it and take fright. 'It'll all be over in an instant. We ought to say goodbye now. Let's get this over in a dignified manner.'

'He's right,' thought Echo. 'Why make a gory, painful and undignified scene? Better to simply shut my eyes and go to sleep.'

'No!' cried another voice inside him. 'Certainly not! Struggle! Hiss! Bite! Scratch! Resist to the last!'

Just then, something white and transparent interposed itself between him and Ghoolion like a curtain being slowly raised on invisible threads. For a moment Echo thought that he was losing consciousness – that his eyesight was failing and he would pass out any minute. Then he realised that the Cooked Ghost was slowly seeping up through the cracks between the floorboards like a luminous mist from the world hereafter.

Revolution

The Alchemaster was looking dumbfounded. Echo could see his astonished face through the Cooked Ghost's transparent, wavering form. Ghoolion involuntarily recoiled a few steps but retained his hold on the scalpel.

Echo's heart leapt for joy. The Cooked Ghost had come to his rescue! Or had it? Whatever the truth, he was filled with new hope by the realisation that he was no longer facing the Alchemaster all on his own. But what could this insubstantial being achieve in a world where physical intervention was denied it?

'What's the Cooked Ghost doing here?' Ghoolion demanded irritably. 'I thought it had disappeared long ago.'

Malaisea was being stabbed from the clouds by dazzling shafts of lightning, thunder was rumbling around the laboratory and rain lashing in through the windows. Unimpressed by all this, the uninvited guest was hovering a hand's breadth above the floor with wavelets of light rippling through it. The Cooked Ghost reminded Echo of a flag fluttering in a breeze.

Ghoolion quickly recovered from his shock. 'Well,' he said loudly, 'whatever you're doing here, you've chosen the wrong time and place. We're busy, so push off!'

Then he laughed and smote his brow with the flat of his hand. 'What am I doing, talking to a thing that can neither hear nor speak?'

He took a step towards the ghost and flapped his hands.

'Shoo!' he cried. 'Be off with you!'

But the ghost didn't budge. It continued to hover protectively in front of Echo.

Ghoolion hesitated. Then he put his hands on his hips and turned to Echo with a broad grin.

'So you've forged yet another friendship behind my back, have you? First Izanuela, now a Cooked Ghost? A lovesick Uggly and a hoary old alchemistic conjuring trick? What powerful allies you've chosen!'

Echo deemed it wiser not to reply. Ghoolion took another vigorous step forwards – and the ghost moved too. However, instead of retreating as the Alchemaster had intended, it came straight for him and expanded to twice its original size. Simultaneously, it displayed the fearsome countenance Echo had glimpsed more than once, except that this time it was so big and awe-inspiring that it occupied almost all of the ghost's expanse. Its effect was not lost on Ghoolion, who staggered backwards with his hands in front of his face. The sight was almost unendurable, even for an Alchemaster.

For several seconds they both stood their ground like actors in some theatre of the absurd. The thunderstorm had receded, but rain was still hissing down outside the windows. At length the ghost's face gradually faded and it shrank to its original dimensions.

Echo's heart sank once more. Was that the most this harmless ghost could do in the world of the living, give someone a fright? That would never be enough to deter the Alchemaster from putting his plans into effect.

'Well, I'm damned!' Ghoolion said, chuckling. 'That was impressive. Congratulations, you really put the wind up me!' He clutched his chest. 'Phew, you belong in a chamber of horrors.'

Echo was surprised to see a flickering glow appear behind Ghoolion's back. Faint at first, it grew steadily brighter until Ghoolion himself became aware of it. He uttered a sharp cry, dropped the scalpel and leapt in the air. His cloak was ablaze! He cursed and yelled and tried to tear it off, but he became entangled in it and his frantic contortions only fanned the flames.

Echo now saw how it had happened. The Cooked Ghost had manoeuvred Ghoolion to a spot in the laboratory where half a dozen Anguish Candles had crawled on top of one another, waiting to set his cloak on fire.

Suddenly, more fires flared up all over the laboratory. The Anguish Candles ignited bundles of parchments and tinder-dry books, a birchwood besom and a stack of old firewood. They clustered around a glass retort filled with alcohol until their combined heat cracked it. The spirit escaped and caught fire. A wide, blazing stream of it flowed across the workbench and engulfed several jars containing Leyden Manikins, which promptly exploded.

One exceptionally heroic Anguish Candle leapt off a shelf into a tub of powdered sulphur, which sent up a tall jet of flame and ignited the taxidermal specimen of a twin-tailed Crocodiddle mounted on the ceiling.

Echo skipped excitedly to and fro on the end of his chain. Chaos, panic – a palace revolution! Great! Some of the smallest of Ghoolion's victims were rising in revolt, spurred on by the Cooked Ghost, which fluttered overhead like a rebel flag in a gale. The Alchemaster hadn't expected this for a moment. Scores were being settled here. He was paying for all his cruelty to the Anguish Candles, and they were showing their gratitude to Echo for having put some of them out of their misery. Hadn't Ghoolion himself said that the greatest solutions should be sought in the smallest of objects?

The liberated Leyden Manikins also joined in. They knocked over jars and retorts whose liquid and powdered contents ignited or exploded. They opened valves and released gases that turned into hissing jets of flame as soon as they came into contact with the general conflagration. Splinters of glass went flying through the air, which was thick with coloured fumes and stank of sulphur. The hisses and bangs were reminiscent of a firework display. This was a *coup d'état*, an insurrection! And in the midst of it all, on fire, dancing around and crying blue murder, was the Alchemaster. He eventually dashed out of the room like a living torch.

Echo couldn't help coughing and sneezing all at once. Smouldering immediately beside the alchemical furnace was some red powder whose fumes were almost asphyxiating him. He tugged vainly at his chain, realising only now how dangerous his own predicament was. The entire laboratory was likely to go up in flames and turn into a blazing inferno. It would be only a matter of a few seconds before some even more dangerous substances ignited: phosphorus, petroleum and gunpowder, a mixture capable of sending the whole castle sky-high. Resin from the smouldering Crocodiddle on the ceiling was dripping on Echo's head.

And then Ghoolion returned, smoking like an extinguished bonfire. His face was black with soot. He had divested himself of the remains of his cloak and armed himself instead with a sodden blanket. Eyes glinting murderously, he used this to belabour any object that was burning or smouldering.

'Take that! And that!' he yelled as he brought the blanket whistling down on the smaller fires. 'And that! And that!' He worked his way methodically across the laboratory, extinguishing one after another. Then he flung the coal-black blanket aside, seized a shovel, and smothered the bigger flames with sand from a fire bucket. The blazing sulphur barrel he simply hurled out of the window, the Crocodiddle he knocked off the ceiling and disposed of likewise.

'Now for you lot,' he said, meaning the Anguish Candles and the Leyden Manikins. He proceeded to hunt them down, mercilessly smashing one little creature after another with his shovel or trampling them beneath his iron-soled boots. 'There, take that, you confounded rabble!' He dispatched every last one. All that remained of them were motionless splodges of wax or little mounds of peat from the Graveyard Marshes of Dullsgard, the Leyden Manikins' principal ingredient.

In the end he stood panting in the midst of a battlefield of debris and splintered glass from which plumes of grey, black and poisonous yellow smoke were rising. He looked around. The laboratory was badly damaged but not completely wrecked. The Alchemaster had quelled the rebellion with a sodden blanket and a shovel.

'You!' he bellowed, his voice shaking with anger. He aimed his forefinger at the Cooked Ghost, which was still fluttering overhead. 'Now it's your turn!'

He flung the shovel at it like a spear, but it darted aside and the shovel crashed into a shelf laden with test tubes.

'You!' Ghoolion yelled again, and he went for the Cooked Ghost with his bare hands. To Echo, the Alchemaster's malign energy, boundless fury and thirst for revenge were almost physically palpable. The Cooked Ghost flinched away as if Ghoolion had struck it with a whip. Then it flew round him in a wide arc and soared up to the ceiling, where it hovered for a moment, trembling. Finally, it swooped down and dived into the bubbling cauldron of fat from which it had once arisen. It did not reappear.

A Temporary Reprieve

Echo's execution was temporarily postponed. Ghoolion proceeded to restore order in the laboratory, substitute more instruments and chemicals for the ones that had been destroyed, repair the damaged tubes and piping, and remix the spilt liquids. His victim's reprieve lasted for some hours. Meanwhile, the thunderstorm had moved on, to be replaced by a cheerless, continuous downpour.

The Alchemaster did not address a single word to Echo. All that needed to be said between them had been said. The ceremonial atmosphere Ghoolion had conjured up was no more; that, at least, rebellion had dispelled. The old man was in a black mood. He grumbled and swore as he carried out his laborious repairs. Echo refrained from making any remarks that might darken his mood still more. He crouched beside the alchemical furnace and awaited developments. What else *could* he do?

Ghoolion eventually rekindled the stove, which had gone out, and reheated the cauldron. It was growing steadily darker, so he lit some candles – ordinary ones this time. His pathological delight in tormenting Anguish Candles was a thing of the past.

'There,' he said when he had completed his running repairs. 'Order has been restored. Those little brutes almost robbed me of the fruits of all my labours. One should never turn one's back on anyone!' So saying, he left the room.

Echo was feeling really frightened now. His temporary reprieve was over and the laboratory back in action. The full moon was shining brightly in the sky, which had cleared. The irrevocable moment had come. All his trumps had been played and none had proved effective. All his friends and allies had either fled or bitten the dust. He could expect no more help from any quarter.

Ghoolion returned. Every inch the Prince of Darkness, he had washed off the soot and put on his ceremonial red velvet robe and hat of ravens' feathers. He gave the coals beneath the cauldron a poke and went over to Floria's corpse.

'This time it will work, my beloved.' He whispered the words as if speaking to a living person. 'By shedding Echo's blood I shall renew your own. Until now I was just a puppet on life's stage like any other, but from this night onward I shall help to rewrite the book of destiny. I and the universe will meet on equal terms, and Death will be no more than a cur that comes to heel when I whistle.'

He hurried over to the Ghoolionic Preserver and opened all the valves. 'Combine, you juices and acids, fats and lyes!' he cried. 'Let the dance of the elements begin! Before long, my spirit will flow into you and reign supreme!'

The liquids in the piston chambers and glass retorts began to seethe once more, and the more violently the chemicals boiled and bubbled, the more intoxicated Ghoolion became. He went over to a table, took a ball of fat from a receptacle and tossed it into the cauldron.

'Toad fat!' he cried in triumph as it melted. 'The penultimate ingredient. All that's missing now is the fat of a Crat.'

The laboratory was pervaded by the giant toad's unmistakable odour. Echo gagged despite himself.

'It would be nice to see you again,' the old amphibian had called after him.

'So *this* is the form our reunion has taken,' thought Echo. The toad was just a smell, an invisible effluvium. He felt guilty for having drawn Ghoolion's attention to the unfortunate creature. He could still see it in his mind's eye, wedged tightly into its grave below ground.

> *Quit your home in Death's domain,*
> *realm of sorrow and of pain,*
> *hasten through the nameless portals*
> *that divide the dead from mortals …*

Why had those lines occurred to him at this particular moment? The nameless portals … Were they the toad's grave? A still unoccupied, *anonymous* grave … What better division between the dead and the living than a grave? There was some element in the smell of the toad, something emanating from the cauldron of fat, that was prompting him to recite those lines.

'*Quit your home in Death's domain …*' Echo declaimed loudly.

'What?' said Ghoolion.

'*… realm of sorrow and of pain …*' Echo went on.

'Why are you reciting those lines?' The Alchemaster looked mystified. The cauldron's contents had suddenly begun to seethe more fiercely than before. Bubbles of fat were rising to the surface and bursting with a series of explosive pops. The smell of the toad grew stronger and stronger.

'*… hasten through the nameless portals,*' cried Echo, '*that divide the dead from mortals!*'

There was a loud rumbling sound from inside the cauldron. The brew bubbled up and boiled over the lip. It streamed down the vessel's blackened sides and into the flames below, hissing loudly. Echo had never seen this happen before. Neither had Ghoolion, it seemed, because he dashed over to the cauldron and circled it with a look of alarm.

'What's going on here?' he yelled. 'Substances are going to waste! Precious substances!'

'*Zamonium and Spiderfat, oil of toad and graveyard peat!*' Echo improvised.

'Hold your tongue!' snarled Ghoolion. He tore off his hat and hurled it at the floor. 'You'll spoil everything!'

'*Quit the cauldron and arise,*' Echo declaimed at the top of his voice. '*Don once more your former guise!*'

'Stop it at once!' Ghoolion bellowed. 'Not another word or I'll slit your throat!' He retrieved the scalpel but hovered irresolutely between Echo and the cauldron, too alarmed by what was going on inside it to act on his threat right away.

'*Leave your world and enter mine!*' cried Echo, undaunted. '*It henceforward shall be thine!*'

More and more of the brew was flowing over the rim of the cauldron. It changed colour several times, giving off iridescent bubbles that drifted across the laboratory as they had when the Cooked Ghost materialised.

'It'll all be ruined!' Ghoolion screamed, dancing desperately round the cauldron. 'All of it!'

The brew bubbled up more fiercely still. There was a rumble like the eruption of a submarine volcano and every glass vessel in the laboratory started to rattle. The whole room vibrated, small objects danced across the workbenches in time to the tremors and a book fell off a shelf. The air was rent by a shrill, high-pitched note that hurt Echo's ears. Somewhere in the room, he realised suddenly, a channel connecting the laboratory to another world was opening up. Visitors from the hereafter were announcing their presence.

And then the Cooked Ghost arose from the foaming brew, brighter than ever before. It did not have to detach itself from the surface with an effort, as it had the first time, but simply turned into a wisp of luminous vapour and floated across the laboratory. Following it just as effortlessly came another equally luminous ghost. And another. And another. And another.

Ghoolion shrank away from the cauldron, which continued to disgorge a succession of shimmering forms. They congregated on the ceiling and encircled the laboratory like a dome of ghostly light.

'What have you done?' the Alchemaster demanded in a trembling voice.

'I've no idea,' Echo replied.

The Demons

The contents of the cauldron had subsided. The variety of smells that filled the laboratory was exceptional, even for surroundings like these. Although Echo was completely unacquainted with them, he could identify every one.

'I smell Cralamander,' he said in a low voice. 'And Snowswallow. And Voltigork. Ubufant and Zamingo, too.'

'You're right,' Ghoolion whispered. He was gazing gravely up at the strange aerial procession circling below the ceiling. 'I can also smell the many other creatures I've rendered down. They've returned as ghosts the same way they left: via the cauldron.'

'What are they doing here?'

'I don't know. I only know they can't hurt me.'

'Then why are you trembling?'

Ghoolion didn't answer. Echo continued to enumerate the smells in the air: 'A Platinum-Tongued Adder. An Ursine Muskrat. A Ferric Eagle. A Bicephalous Hukkan. A Zinoceros. A Yagg.'

'Be quiet!' Ghoolion hissed. Echo fell silent.

One of the Cooked Ghosts detached itself from the rest. It went spinning down like a sycamore leaf and did a sudden nosedive into the stuffed Nanofox that had scared Echo so much on his first visit to the laboratory. The fox glowed brightly and crackled like an alchemical battery. Then the ghost emerged from the stuffed animal and rejoined its circling companions.

'What was that?' Echo whispered. 'Why did it do that?'

Ghoolion's gaze was riveted on the ceiling. 'No idea. Stop asking silly questions.'

The ghosts began to circle so fast that it made Echo dizzy just to watch their gyrations. At length they peeled off, one after another, and flew out into the passage. The Crat and the Alchemaster were alone together once more.

Ghoolion rubbed his eyes. 'I'm going to find out what's up,' he said. 'I trust they don't intend to move in. My castle isn't a dovecot for Cooked Ghosts.' He gathered his cloak around him and hurried after the luminous apparitions.

What struck Echo as almost more astonishing than the recent course of events was the fact that he was all alone in the laboratory once more. He should really have been dead by now – rendered down into a ball of fat. He tugged at his chain, but it was as immovable as ever. What now? He pricked his ears and listened. Ghoolion's clattering footsteps had died away. Nothing could be heard but the monotonous hiss of the rain.

No, wait, there was something else! Echo cocked his head and listened more intently. It wasn't outside in the passage, it was here in the laboratory. Where had he heard that crackling sound before? When the Cooked Ghost nosedived into the stuffed fox. He looked over at it – and the fur on the back of his neck stood on end!

The creature was stirring. Slowly at first, it turned its head with a sound like gravel crunching beneath someone's feet. The glow in its eyes intensified, then faded, but its brush was waving gently. It closed its gaping jaws and lifted its left forefoot from the base on which it had been mounted. An electrical crackle ran through its fur, which gave off sparks. Then it leapt down and landed in the middle of the laboratory.

'This is too much,' thought Echo. 'Any more of it and I'll pass out.'

The creature took three or four steps and came to a halt, sniffing the air. Having conducted an appraisal of all the strange scents in the room and homed in on the most interesting, it turned its head in Echo's direction, bared its teeth and emitted a low growl.

'Steady!' Echo said involuntarily. 'I won't hurt you.'

But the fox displayed no interest in conversation. It slunk slowly closer, eyes aglow with a ghostly light and saliva dripping from its chops. Whatever had brought it to life had also filled it with murderous intent.

Echo strained in all directions, but the chain brought him up short every time. 'I haven't survived until now, only to be torn to pieces by a canine of the lowest order,' it flashed through his head. 'Not here! Not at this stage!'

Now only a few feet away, the fox was getting ready to pounce. It flexed its hind legs and bared its teeth still more. Its eyes had narrowed to slits.

Echo arched his back, lifted his tail and fluffed it out. He bared his teeth likewise and contorted his features into a mask of grim determination, looking twice his actual size. Then he hissed as loudly as he could.

Deterred by this sight, the fox uttered a terrified yelp and shot out of the door like a streak of red lightning. Echo relaxed, but only for a moment.

There, Ghoolion's metallic footsteps were approaching once more! Echo could also hear other, unidentifiable sounds. Strange and alarming noises that might have been made by dangerous wild beasts.

Ghoolion burst in. 'Quick!' he said, more to himself than his prisoner. 'We must hurry!'

'What's happened?' asked Echo, skipping excitedly to and fro. 'That fox the ghost dived into came to life.'

'Only the fox?' Ghoolion said breathlessly as he hurried across the room. 'You've no idea what a can of worms you've opened!'

The Alchemaster darted over to the only wall in the laboratory not lined with shelves. He pressed some of the black stones and the masonry began to move as it had in the case of his golden treasure chamber.

'The ghosts can't achieve anything in the world of the living,' said Ghoolion, who was now hurrying over to Echo, 'but they evidently can in the world of the dead. They're roaming all over the castle, awakening one mummy after another.'

'You mean they're bringing all your stuffed demons to life?' Echo became more agitated still.

'Yes, it's enough if one ghost enters them. Sometimes two or three do, but they all wake up, and each of the creatures I stuffed has designs on my life!'

Echo didn't know what to make of the situation. Ghoolion was frightened. That was good. Woodwolves and Hazelwitches were roaming around the castle. That wasn't so good.

The Alchemaster opened the door of the alchemical furnace.

'Hey, what are you doing?' Echo demanded.

'You may not believe me,' said Ghoolion, picking him up, 'but I'm not running away, I'm saving your life – temporarily. I refuse to be beaten so easily.' And he thrust Echo into the cold furnace. 'Hide in there and keep as quiet as you can.' He closed the furnace door as tightly as the chain permitted.

'Why not unchain me and take me with you?' Echo asked anxiously through the bars. 'Where are you going?'

'I alone can do what I have in mind,' Ghoolion said. 'Just keep still and nothing may happen to you. And pray that I succeed.'

He went back to the wall, which had opened to reveal a small chamber.

'What's that little room,' Echo asked, 'a hiding place?'

'It isn't a room,' Ghoolion replied, 'it's a lift. Wish me luck!'

The stones began to close up again. It looked as if the Alchemaster were being walled up alive by some unseen agency. Then he disappeared from view.

Echo crouched down on the floor of the alchemical furnace, which stank of cold ashes, sulphur and phosphorus. He dreaded to think of all the creatures Ghoolion had burnt alive in there. Tensely, he peered into the laboratory through the bars.

The room was suddenly bathed in light. A whole flock of ghosts had come flying in, casting a silvery glow over everything in sight. Having

made a few circuits of the ceiling, they proceeded to dive into the cauldron one by one.

'Snowswallow,' thought Echo. 'Voltigork. Ubufant. Zamingo. Cralamander …' There they went, back to their 'home in Death's domain'.

In the end only one was left: his taciturn friend the Cooked Ghost. It slowly revolved in the air as if looking for someone. Then, with a final flash of light, it dived into the cauldron and disappeared.

'Good luck,' Echo said under his breath and strained his ears again. He wished he had bidden the Cooked Ghost a less cursory farewell, but the menacing noises – the panting and growling, hissing and whispering – had now become so loud that he had other concerns. He listened with bated breath.

Then in they came. In the lead was a hunchbacked Hazelwitch with limbs of gnarled timber and a costume of green leaves. Her long wooden fingers were clasped together and her yellowish tongue kept darting in and out of her mouth like a snake's.

The Corn Demon that glided in after her seemed to consist of nothing but a mouldering shroud. A dark hole yawned in its cowl where a face should have been and it made a sound reminiscent of the gusts of wind that sometimes moaned in the castle chimneys.

The next figure to appear was entirely swathed in a winding sheet. A Cyclopean Mummy, it smelt so abominable that Echo shrank away from the bars. Its movements were slow, like those of a sleepwalker, but Cyclopean Mummies were said to possess immense physical strength. They were further reputed to break every bone in their victims' bodies and watch them as they slowly expired.

A Grim Reaper entered the laboratory. The bald head protruding from its grey robe gleamed in the candlelight, and Echo couldn't have said whether the horrific visage beneath it was a mask or its actual face.

Accompanying it was a Woodwolf, one of the most dangerous creatures to be found in the Zamonian outback. It walked beside the Reaper on all fours with resin dripping from its jaws. The Woodwolf was the source of the intimidating growls Echo had heard.

Last of all came a Golden Gondrag. An amphibious creature from the Graveyard Marshes, with golden scales and ice-green, saurian eyes, it left a long trail of slime behind it.

These creatures had terrified Echo even when dead. Now his fears were truly justified. Having come to tear the Alchemaster to pieces with their claws and fangs, throttle him with their tentacles, poison him with their lethal breath and send him to his death in every conceivable manner, they now found the laboratory deserted. Furiously, they proceeded to look for their quarry. They overturned tables and workbenches, hurled bookshelves to the floor and rummaged in cupboards, but all to no avail. The longer they searched, the more enraged they became.

Crawling on his belly and taking care not to rattle his chain, Echo retreated as far as he could. The floor at the back of the alchemical furnace was littered with charred bones and teeth, but he didn't care. It would be only a matter of time before they opened the furnace door and discovered him.

At least he didn't have to see the frightful creatures any more, but he could still hear them only too distinctly. The sounds they made were not of this world – they were the stuff of nightmares. Snarls alternated with hoarse giggles and menacing grunts. When two of them bumped into each other, as they did from time to time, they exchanged indignant hisses and growls. Echo couldn't imagine what they would sound like if they really came to blows.

He wondered how Ghoolion proposed to deal with half a dozen of the most vicious creatures in Zamonia, not to mention all the others that must still be roaming the castle. Impossible! The Alchemaster had probably lied to him and made good his escape long ago, leaving him as bait for these brutes. He was duplicitous enough to have played such a rotten trick.

Something was scratching the metal side of the alchemical furnace. The twiglike fingers of the Hazelwitch? The Woodwolf's claws? There, something was tugging at his chain! They had discovered him!

Echo braced all four paws against the unknown force that was dragging him towards the door of the furnace by the chain round his neck, but it was no use, he kept sliding further forward. The grille was opened, candlelight flooded in, and he found himself looking into the Corn Demon's empty cowl: a gaping black hole. The creature breathed on him and the putrid but icy gust of air almost robbed him of his senses.

'It's all over,' he thought.

The Corn Demon exhaled a second time, enveloping him in a smell of ether as cold as the grave. Echo's legs buckled.

He felt not only dizzy but as weary as he had after his wild fandango and drinking bout with Ghoolion.

'I want to go to sleep,' he thought. 'Just to go to sleep at last.'

The Corn Demon drew a deep breath and prepared to expel its third, and final, death-dealing blast of air.

Suddenly, pandemonium broke out. High-pitched screams in the passage outside mingled with growls and snarls from the creatures in the laboratory itself. The Corn Demon turned away, restoring Echo's view of the room. Hazelwitch, Woodwolf, Grim Reaper and Golden Gondrag – all were staring in the direction of the door.

More despairing cries rang out. Cries of mortal agony? If so, whose?

Who was dying, who was doing the killing? Echo ventured to poke his head out of the furnace. The demons had lost interest in him in any case.

Their attention was no longer focused on him or the absent Ghoolion, but on the being that had suddenly, as if by magic, come drifting across the threshold. It was the Snow-White Widow.

The Dance of Death

Echo flattened himself on the floor of the furnace. Ghoolion had unleashed the Snow-White Widow and she was now, at his behest, hunting the demons down. Having slaughtered one after another, she had come here to complete her work. But where was the Alchemaster?

Eager to see what would happen, Echo plucked up the courage to peer cautiously through the bars. Had as many dangerous creatures ever been assembled in one room before? He doubted it. It must be a record and he was in their midst!

The Snow-White Widow seemed to be enjoying the attention she was attracting. She performed a coquettish pirouette that sent her white hair flying. She danced up and down in the doorway, first to the left, then to the right, then back again. Pulsating like a jellyfish, she rose into the air and drifted, light as a cloud of vapour, to the middle of the laboratory.

'How sure of herself she must be, to venture into the midst of these demons,' Echo thought. What had Ghoolion said of her?

'If she stings you, you're done for. There's no antidote to her venom because she changes it daily. As for its effects on your body, they're unique in the annals of toxicology. Death at the hands of the Snow-White Widow is the loveliest and most terrible, most pleasurable and painful death of all. She's the Queen of Fear.'

The Queen of Fear ... Even the demons seemed to sense her majestic self-assurance, because they preserved a respectful distance from her. Like Echo, they were mesmerised by the sinister beauty of her dancing – by the motions of a unique creature that appeared to be exempt from the laws of nature. It was as if the laboratory were filled with some invisible fluid in which she floated up and down. Her white tresses bunched together or dispersed, formed a dense curtain or separated into thousands of individual strands that rippled in all directions.

It was the Woodwolf that broke the spell. Wanting to know what a Snow-White Widow tasted like, the savage but stupid beast leapt at her. Its progress through the air was abruptly halted. The Snow-White Widow got to the Woodwolf before the Woodwolf could get to her. Before it knew what was happening, she had encircled its throat and jaws with her hair and perforated its body with hundreds of stings. That done, she floated majestically back to the middle of the room. The whole thing had taken only a heartbeat or two.

The Woodwolf rose on its hind legs as if to prove that it was master of the situation, apparently believing that it had withstood the attack. But its movements were clumsy and it tripped over its own feet. It clung to the edge of a table, fighting for breath. The other demons watched it spellbound.

The creature doubled up in agony, uttering howls that would have melted a heart of stone. The howls changed to groans of pleasure and its eyes filled with tears. Again it doubled up, with green froth oozing from its jaws. It gazed around with a bewildered, helpless expression, trembling all over. The leaves that clothed it from head to foot turned slate-grey and some fell off. It doubled up and groaned yet again, shaken by violent convulsions and howling like a whipped cur. Its leaves lost their last vestiges of colour and turned white. They fell off one by one, covering the floor of the laboratory like snowflakes. All that now remained of the huge predator was a bare skeleton with grey organs pumping and pulsating away inside it. Then it subsided on to its knees with a faint sound like ice splintering in the distance. Its bones and organs disintegrated into white flakes until nothing was left of it but a mound of what looked like freshly fallen snow.

The Golden Gondrag, which was nearest the door, was the first to attempt to escape, but the Snow-White Widow was seated on its back almost before it had taken a step. Wrapping her strands of hair round its limbs like an octopus capturing its prey, she bore it up to just below the ceiling. There she constricted the creature to such an extent that its body bent like a bow and its spine snapped with a horrific sound. The Gondrag screamed at the top of its voice, whereupon the Snow-White

Widow simply released her grip and let it fall to the floor in a twitching heap. Then she floated slowly down and performed a graceful dance on her victim's body, whirling on the spot and impaling it at every step with the venom-laden tips of her hair. Finally, light as thistledown, she resumed her place in the middle of the laboratory.

The Gondrag could now move nothing but its arms. It waved them convulsively and uttered falsetto screams. Its scaly skin dulled, becoming pale yellow, then grey and white. Before long nothing was left of it, too, but a skeleton that swiftly disintegrated into flakes.

The Corn Demon was next in line. The Snow-White Widow cut off its retreat in a flash, dived through the hole in its cowl – and disappeared. This was the Snow-White Widow's most astonishing feat to date, and the remaining demons made noises expressive of consternation.

Now it was the Corn Demon's turn to perform a dance. It heaved several of its terrible sighs, which were this time so fraught with pain that they conveyed some idea of the havoc the Snow-White Widow was wreaking inside it. Its whole body twitched and the mouldering grey cloth that enshrouded it became ever paler and more threadbare. The material split open in many places and each rent emitted a hissing jet of green vapour. Eventually, what was left of the shroud also disintegrated into white flakes. All that remained on the spot where the Corn Demon had been standing moments earlier was the deadly Snow-White Widow. She swayed gently to and fro, doubtless debating who her next victim should be.

Echo, who had seen more than enough by now, withdrew his head and crawled to the back of the furnace. He shut his eyes, but that didn't prevent him from hearing the gruesome sounds that accompanied the rest of the Snow-White Widow's settlement of accounts: the snapping, crunching noises as she broke every bone in the Cyclopean Mummy's body and the Grim Reaper's demented screams.

Silence fell at last.

Echo opened his eyes but lay absolutely still. Dissected by the bars over the furnace door, the flickering candlelight danced across the floor of his iron prison. That was all he could see.

Where in the world had Ghoolion got to?

Echo listened for his clattering footsteps, but there was nothing to be heard. No wind, and even the rain had stopped. Utter silence. What was the Snow-White Widow doing? Was she still in the laboratory, or had she moved on in search of other victims? She might be perched on top of the furnace itself or floating along the castle's labyrinthine passages. She might be lying in wait for him just outside, or she might be quite uninterested in him. Whatever the truth, he had better remain as quiet as a mouse for the time being.

Where was Ghoolion?

It wasn't fair of a creature not to make a sound. It wasn't fair that he couldn't detect the Snow-White Widow's scent. No sound, no smell. Zamonian fauna of that kind should be prohibited.

Where *was* the Alchemaster?

'What makes me think the old man is still alive?' he wondered suddenly. Perhaps he'd been the first to be killed by the Snow-White Widow after her release. It was highly probable, in fact, for how could such a creature be tamed? She was subject to no laws, natural or otherwise. Ghoolion himself had thought his plan dangerous. He was probably down in the cellar, right beside the Snow-White Widow's glass cage, reduced to a little mound of white flakes. Or perhaps he was floating along the passages to the castle's sinister music, in company with the dust to which the demons had also been reduced. He might be a tough old bird, but not even he was immune to the Snow-White Widow's venom.

Something was wriggling up the furnace bars like a tendril of ivy. No, it wasn't ivy, nor was it a snake. It was a strand of the Snow-White Widow's hair!

Echo tried to retreat, but he was already up against the rear wall of the cast-iron chamber. The silvery strand insinuated itself between the bars and groped its way inside, then writhed across the floor, making straight for him. A second strand came snaking through the bars. And a third.

'She knew I was in here all the time,' thought Echo. 'She's just been toying with me.'

The third strand wound itself round one of the bars and pulled. The door creaked open and candlelight came flooding in. Then the Snow-White Widow herself rose slowly into view. Her veil of silvery hair looked as soft and fragile as the finest silk, but Echo wasn't deceived; he now knew what she was capable of. He stood up, legs trembling. Even if an attempt to escape had had any prospect of success, his fear was so intense that he would probably have remained rooted to the spot.

The curtain of silver hair abruptly parted and Echo found himself looking once more at that one, terrible eye. Although it didn't scare him quite as much the second time because he knew what to expect, he found it hard to withstand its gaze.

'I know you,' the Snow-White Widow said, addressing him telepathically.

'Yes,' he replied, 'I know you too.'

'I'm glad we've met again,' she said. *'It's nice that we can talk at last. The prison Ghoolion built me was made of antitelepathic glass. Not a single thought could penetrate it.'*

'You want to talk to me?' Echo asked in a quavering voice.

'No, not really, I want to kill you. That's my most pressing desire, but whenever I get an opportunity for some civilised conversation I try to control my murderous impulses. I try to exchange a few words with most of my victims.'

'Really?'

'Yes, when time permits. But they all say more or less the same things, like "No, please don't! I don't want to die! Ooh, you're hurting me! Ooh, I'm in agony!" And so on. Nothing of real interest.'

'I've got a wide range of conversational topics,' Echo said quickly. 'What would you like to talk about?'

'That's nice for you,' said the Snow-White Widow, *'but I'm too impatient for long conversations. I generally allow my victims to ask one question and try to answer it to the best of my ability. Then I get down to business.'*

'Only one question?' Echo would have gulped, but his throat was too dry.

'Yes, just one. You can ask yours now.' The Snow-White Widow closed her curtain of hair. Echo registered this with relief because it spared him the sight of her terrible orb. He didn't take long to think of his question.

'Where's the Alchemaster?' he asked. He might have abandoned all hope, but he wanted some definite information on that point at least.

'I've no idea,' said the Snow-White Widow. 'He was outside my cage the last time I saw him. After he'd opened it.'

'You didn't kill him?'

'That's your second question. Still, I think it's important enough to answer. You mustn't imagine I was merciful to Ghoolion in any way. I'm absolutely merciless, but I'm under contract to him.'

'Really?' said Echo. 'I'm also under contract to him.'

'You don't say! That's interesting. What's the contract about?'

'Well, to cut a long story short ...' Echo hesitated. He still found it hard to utter the words. 'It entitles him to kill me before the night is out.'

'How nice for him,' said the Snow-White Widow. 'However, it won't come to that. Why not? Because I'll kill you first.'

Echo tried to steer her away from this ticklish subject. 'What's *your* contract with him about?'

'That's three questions you've asked me,' she said coldly. 'It's getting to be too much of a good thing. I'll have to kill you now, and I'm sorry to say it, but yours will be an extremely painful death.' She broke off. 'Pah! Of course I'm not sorry, I couldn't care less.'

Echo had another try. 'But only Ghoolion has the right to kill me,' he said. 'He's kept his part of the bargain.'

'There's nothing about that in my contract with him. First come, first served. He should have acted sooner. I don't suppose he thought I'd be so quick off the mark.'

'You really are quick,' Echo said. 'I've never seen anything or anyone quicker.'

'Good of you to say so,' she said, flattered. 'There are times when I wish I could hold myself in check a little. I'd get more pleasure out of it.'

'Then do so!' Echo urged her.

'Do what?'

'Slow down, of course.'

The Snow-White Widow seemed to be considering this. 'Slow down? When? Now, you mean?'

'Exactly. You've got to start some time.'

'You really are a cunning little fellow. I've never spent so long chatting with any of my victims. But you're wrong if you think your gift *of the gab can dissuade me from doing what I do best. Listen carefully: I'm addicted to death. I can't help it, I enjoy seeing other creatures die. It makes me feel alive. That's why I'm now going to say what all addicts say when someone urges them to kick the habit.'*

'Which is?' Echo asked anxiously.

'They say: Yes, I will. Definitely! Tomorrow without fail! But today I'm going to make a real pig of myself for the last time.'

Echo had run out of ideas.

'Well, it's been nice chatting with you,' she said. *'But watching you die will be even nicer.'* Several strands of her hair descended on him. *'I'm sure white will suit you,'* she added.

The strands of hair penetrated his fur. They reached the skin and felt around for some throbbing veins that would help her venom to permeate his body in the shortest possible time.

'I can't make up my mind which vein to choose,' she mused. *'Your heart is beating so fast, they're all throbbing away like mad.'*

'Stop!' A thunderous voice shook the laboratory. 'He's mine!'

At lightning speed, the Snow-White Widow withdrew her hair from the furnace and spun round.

'Phew!' Echo expelled the air from his lungs in a rush. How long had he been holding his breath? The sound of Ghoolion's harsh voice was music to his ears.

'What do you want?' hissed the Snow-White Widow.

Echo tottered to the mouth of the furnace and craned his neck to see what was happening outside.

The Alchemaster was standing in the doorway to the lift, which was open again. The Snow-White Widow, who was hovering in front of the alchemical furnace, had transferred all her attention to him. Ghoolion gathered his cloak around him and strode briskly across the laboratory.

'With all due respect, Queen of Fear,' he said, 'you've had plenty of chances to assuage your hunger. You've exterminated a whole host of demons. Their powdered remains are floating all over the castle – it looks like a blizzard. At least leave me this little Crat.'

The Snow-White Widow turned slowly on the spot. Ghoolion halted a few paces from her. He, too, thought it best to preserve a respectful distance.

'Very well,' said the Snow-White Widow, *'I'll spare the little creature. He's hardly worth killing in any case. I'll let him live, then you can have your fun with him.'*

'Many thanks,' said Ghoolion.

'On one condition,' she added.

'What's that?' Ghoolion demanded. 'Name it!'

'I know I can run as far away from you as I like, but I also know I'll always return to my prison because you whispered it to me in my sleep.'

'So she's also under a spell!' it flashed through Echo's mind.

'And I also realise I can't kill you for the same reason,' the Snow-White Widow went on.

'My life insurance policy,' Ghoolion said with a grin.

'That's just the point. I want you to annul our contract and release me.'

Ghoolion was taken aback. 'But that's impossible,' he protested. 'If I annul the contract you'll not only be free, you'll be free to kill me. I can't take that risk.'

'All right, then I'll kill the Crat. Our contract doesn't preclude me from doing that.'

The Snow-White Widow whirled round. A strand of her hair darted into the furnace and encircled Echo's neck like a hangman's noose.

'Urgh!' was all Echo could get out.

'Stop that!' snapped Ghoolion.

'If you're as worried about the little fellow as that, he must be worth a lot to you. Well, he won't be worth a thing in a minute; he'll be dead.'

She tightened the noose. White sparks danced before Echo's eyes.

'All right,' said Ghoolion, 'it's a deal. I'll annul the contract. Let go of him.'

'You agree? Very well.'

She released the noose and withdrew the strand of hair. Echo could breathe again. Panting hard, he subsided on to the floor of the furnace.

'I'll annul the contract,' Ghoolion repeated, 'but on one condition.'

'So you've got a condition too?' The Snow-White Widow laughed. *'When it comes to negotiating contracts, you really do drive a hard bargain. Well, go on, what do you want?'*

'If I tear up the contract and lift the spell, you'll be free to kill anything or anyone that crosses your path,' said Ghoolion.

She uttered a groan of delight.

'With three exceptions,' he said. 'Me, for one.'

'Agreed.'

'Secondly, the Crat.'

'Yes, yes, who else?'

'The inhabitants of Malaisea – all of them. In this town I do the killing.'

The Snow-White Widow groaned again, but not with delight this time. She sounded dismayed.

'That's a tough one,' she said. *'I'm absolutely famished after all this time. But all right, I'll restrain myself until I'm on the other side of the Blue Mountains.'*

Ghoolion looked out of the window and up at the milk-white moon.

'I don't know if you've got such a thing as a sense of honour,' he said gravely, 'but I'm assuming there's at least a glimmer of one in every living creature, even a Snow-White Widow.'

He tore the contract into little pieces and threw them into the fire beneath the cauldron of fat. They hissed and gave off blue sparks as the flames reduced them to ashes.

'Now lift the spell,' she demanded.

Ghoolion clapped his hands three times.

'Is that it?'

'That's it,' he replied. His voice was shaking, his forehead beaded with sweat. The Snow-White Widow didn't move.

'Now it's your turn to fulfil your obligations,' Ghoolion said impatiently. 'Just go!'

She didn't budge an inch.

'My obligations?' she said in a scornful tone after a long, tense silence. *'What obligations do you mean? I don't have any to fulfil. Promises at most.'*

It resembled an illusionist's trick. One moment she was hovering in front of the alchemical furnace, the next she had wound a thick strand of hair round Ghoolion's neck and pulled it tight. That done, she rose slowly into the air, taking the gasping, struggling Alchemaster with her.

'There's nothing, absolutely nothing to prevent me from killing you this instant,' she said. 'You and your little friend here, followed by every accursed inhabitant of your accursed, disease-ridden town. Because believe me, I'm totally unacquainted with what you call a sense of honour. What's it supposed to be? Fear of admitting that one has told a lie? Self-respect? Those are sentiments worthy of children or lunatics.'

Ghoolion's face had turned blue. His legs were kicking vainly in mid-air.

'You must remember I've a reputation to uphold. What's your name for me? Queen of Fear? Well, noblesse oblige, my friend. Only the merciless merit a reputation for mercilessness.'

Ghoolion's eyes were protruding and blood was trickling from his nose. He had almost stopped kicking, his strength was giving out. The Snow-White Widow carried him a little higher.

'I could hang you now, but I could also inject you with my venom like all the rest. I could simply throw you out of a window like rubbish. Smash you against the walls of your laboratory like a wet rag. Tear you into little strips or render you down in that cauldron. The choice is yours. Which would you prefer?'

Ghoolion's body went limp. He had ceased to struggle. His spindly hands were quivering a little, but that was all.

'Yes, I could kill you in any number of ways – torture and torment you to my heart's content. Instead, I'm going to put you down.'

The Snow-White Widow deposited Ghoolion on the floor like a child discarding a doll it was tired of. His legs gave way. He went down on all fours, gasping for breath. Echo had never seen him so humiliated.

'I'm going to let you live,' said the Snow-White Widow. 'What do you say to that?'

Ghoolion said nothing at all, just sucked in great, greedy gulps of air.

'You needn't thank me. I'm not doing it out of pity, I'm doing it out of love.'

'What?!' croaked the Alchemaster. He gripped the edge of a workbench and hauled himself erect, seized a cloth and wiped the blood from his nose, striving to regain his composure.

'I've developed something of a crush on you, that's why. After all, you saved my life, shamelessly exploited my hopeless predicament and used me for your own ends. *You're the first and only person capable of emulating my capacity for evil. Emulating it, mark you, not matching it, still less surpassing it. I'm the Queen of Fear! As for you, you could be my prince consort.'*

The Snow-White Widow floated over Ghoolion's head to one of the windows and landed on the sill. She was trembling almost imperceptibly, as if chilled by the warm summer night.

'But we're too dissimilar, alas, and our objectives are diametrically opposed. You want to create new life; I want to destroy all life. That would only lead to arguments, so we must go our separate ways.'

The Alchemaster had been standing there in silence the whole time. Echo continued to lie low. They were both thinking the same thing: was this another trick on her part? Would she fly at their throats again at any moment? What was to stop her?

'You owe your life to love,' she whispered, *'love, not mercy. Never forget that and never again put your faith in someone else's honesty. Goodbye!'*

She performed a graceful leap out of the window and allowed herself to be borne away by the gentle evening breeze, as weightless and aimless as an innocent seed head detaching itself from a dandelion clock.

Night Music

'I've boiled Throttlesnakes the length of tree trunks in this cauldron,' Ghoolion said as he reheated the big copper vessel. 'I've disposed of a Red Gorilla that awoke from its anaesthetic and an octopus that tried to drag me into the cauldron with it, but no creature has ever given me as much trouble as you have today. You, a harmless little Crat.'

'Many thanks,' said Echo. He was once more sitting on the floor beside the alchemical furnace. The Alchemaster had removed him from it and put him there, but without unchaining him.

'That wasn't intended as a compliment,' Ghoolion said, shooting an angry glance at his prisoner. 'I simply meant that the fun's over as far as you're concerned. I've never been as close to death as I was just now.'

He took a pair of bellows and pumped fresh oxygen into the flames, which blazed up brightly.

'What was that deal you made with the Snow-White Widow?' Echo asked. 'How did you manage to gain control of such a powerful creature?'

'I found her down below the castle,' said Ghoolion, adding some more logs to the flames. 'In the catacombs beneath the cellars. She was very ill, terminally ill, but I knew of a remedy for her condition. In return she had to sign a contract that made her my prisoner for ten years. She was weak at first, but when she gradually regained her strength I took the precaution of putting her under a spell while she was asleep. I also built her an escape-proof prison.'

'You like doing deals,' Echo remarked. 'Even with the most dangerous creatures.'

'One never knows when a Snow-White Widow will come in handy,' Ghoolion said with a laugh. 'It paid off, too. You benefited from the deal yourself and for that you should be duly grateful to me. What I have in mind for you will be a picnic compared to what those demons would have done to you.'

He turned away from the cauldron, took a scalpel from the table and advanced on Echo.

'We've wasted enough time,' he said.

Echo's instinctive reaction was to run for it, but the chain brought him up short. He tugged at it desperately but only succeeded in choking himself. It was useless.

'Make it quick,' he said.

'That I promise you,' said Ghoolion.

All of a sudden, music could be heard – the strangest music. Loud, intrusive and disconcerting, it came drifting in through the windows from one moment to the next.

Ghoolion stopped in his tracks and listened.

'What's that?' he said.

Echo knew the music. It was familiar to him, but not played at this tempo. There had been something tranquil about it – something almost danceable – the first time he heard it. What had Izanuela called it?

Of course: **Twitchstik**, the Song of the Ugglian Oaks …

It now had a rather menacing ring, like the music with which armies impress their grim determination on the enemy. Campaigns were conducted to the strains of such music. It was music for marching to – for killing to.

'I know what it is,' Echo said.

'You do?'

'You need only look out of the window.' Echo's heart was beating wildly again. He fervently hoped he had drawn the right conclusion from the music; his life might well depend on it. He listened closely. There was something in addition to determination in that music. It was the saddest sound he had ever heard: a funeral march.

Ghoolion had dashed to the window and was looking out.

'Damnation!' he exclaimed, clutching his chest. 'I don't believe it!'

'It's Izanuela's house, isn't it?' said Echo. 'It's Izanuela's house from Uggly Lane. Its music is unmistakable.'

'It's *all* the houses from Uggly Lane!' Ghoolion yelled. 'There must be over a hundred of them. They're all round the castle.'

All of them? Echo was surprised. Still, why not? Izanuela had mentioned that all the houses in the street were alive, but she hadn't said anything about their being so alive they could move from the spot. They must have come to avenge her.

'All the houses, of course,' Echo amended. 'I know. I simply meant Izanuela's house would be there too. It's their leader, isn't it?'

Once again, he could only hazard a guess and hope he was right. He cursed his confounded chain.

As if unable to believe his eyes, Ghoolion snatched up a telescope.

'How should I know?' he said. 'They all look alike.'

'Izanuela's house is bigger than the others.'

'What?' Ghoolion squinted through the telescope again. 'Yes, one of them is bigger than the rest. What sort of creatures are they? Are they plants? I've seen plants that can move, but none as big as these.'

'They're Ugglian Oaks,' Echo said, as if it were the most natural thing in the world. 'The oldest plants in Zamonia.'

How desperately he yearned to look out of the window at that moment! What did the oaks look like when they were in motion? Did their roots act as legs and their branches as arms? Were they rolling those mournful eyes in their knotholes? No matter, he must take advantage of Ghoolion's discomfiture.

'So the Uggly fulfilled our agreement,' he said coolly.

'What agreement?' Ghoolion asked without averting his gaze from the astonishing scene.

'Izanuela was also fond of striking bargains with natural phenomena,' Echo said slowly, 'with animals and plants.' He had to choose his words carefully. 'But not with a view to skinning them and extracting their fat.'

'What are you getting at?' Ghoolion demanded. He put the telescope down on the windowsill and gave Echo a piercing stare,

'What you can see down there is Izanuela's curse!' Echo cried. 'Your duel with her isn't over, Alchemaster, it has only just begun. Her power extends beyond the grave. That's something *you'll* never achieve!'

'What are you blathering about?' Ghoolion snapped. 'What curse?'

'His hands are trembling,' thought Echo. 'I've unsettled him, but I mustn't rush things.'

'Those trees down there have come to fetch me,' he lied boldly. 'Izanuela told them what to do if something happened to her. That was what we agreed. The houses in Uggly Lane heard her scream as she fell. That was the signal. They've come to fulfil her last wish.'

Ghoolion didn't answer. He stared out of the window, listening to the mournful music, then turned back to Echo.

'Fine,' he said. 'Ugglian Oaks, singing plants. I dealt with far worse things today. Let them sing! They're too big to get past the door and they're welcome to besiege the building, I don't intend to leave it. I've enough stores in here to last till doomsday. Besides, if I want to leave the castle I know of other ways out than the front door. Let's get on.'

Ghoolion went over to the cauldron and inspected the contents. Judging by the contented way he clicked his tongue, he seemed pleased with what he saw. He took a big spoon and gave the brew a leisurely stir, even though the music was growing steadily louder. Then he laid the spoon aside and picked up the scalpel.

'The soup is ready,' he called. 'So are you.'

The music continued to swell as he crossed the room, becoming so loud and piercing that every glass vessel in the laboratory began to rattle.

'That's right, sing!' he shouted. 'Sing away! Yours is just the music to skin a Crat by.'

Boom! The whole building shuddered. Plaster trickled from the ceiling and the laboratory floor gave a lurch. Taken aback, Ghoolion stopped short. It was all he could do to keep his feet.

'Hey!' he cried.

Echo was also thrown off balance. What was this, an earthquake?

Boom! Another impact! A glass retort wobbled, fell to the floor and smashed.

Boom! And another! Books toppled off shelves, dust went swirling into the air.

Boom! A lunar globe fell from the ceiling and went rolling across the laboratory.

'Hell's bells!' Ghoolion bellowed. 'What's going on?'

The floor and walls shuddered again and again. Timbers creaked and cracks appeared in the masonry. Ghoolion reeled around like a drunk.

Boom! The fireplace belched a dense cloud of soot.

Boom! The alchemical furnace rocked precariously.

Ghoolion spun round and tossed the scalpel on to a workbench. He ran to a window and leant out as far as he could.

'It's those infernal great trees!' he fumed. 'They're pounding the castle walls with their huge wooden fists and using uprooted tree trunks as battering rams!' He took a closer look through the telescope. 'They're wrenching rocks out of the ground and hurling them! They're going berserk!' His voice broke with fury.

Echo was also feeling uneasy now. No one was safe in this crumbling old pile. He simply had to get rid of this confounded chain.

'You must show me to them!' he shouted above the din. 'That's all they're after. That'll calm them down.'

Ghoolion didn't react. He stood silently at the window, clinging to the sill and staring out.

Boom! A whole bookcase toppled over, spilling hundreds of ancient volumes across the floor.

Boom! The Ghoolionic Preserver clinked and rattled. Gas came hissing out of a fractured valve.

Boom! Fist-sized stones fell out of the walls and landed on

alchemical vessels, shattering them.

Ghoolion tore himself away from the window at last. Having lurched across the laboratory to Echo, he bent down and removed his collar.

'But I warn you!' he growled. 'One false move and I'll throttle you!'

He gripped Echo by the scruff of the neck and carried him over to the window, where he held him up and shouted, 'Here he is! Here's what you're after! Now stop that!'

Echo got his first sight of the Ugglian Oaks clustered around the castle. What a spectacle they presented! Izanuela had told him they never lost their temper. They had certainly lost it now! Some were stomping around on their big black roots, massive trunks swaying to and fro as they pummelled the ancient building with their gnarled wooden fists. Others were prising huge boulders out of the ground and hurling them at the castle like trebuchets. The old eyes in their knotholes were blazing with anger. Their mournful music was almost drowned by the ear-splitting creaks and groans they made in their frenzy. They were so engrossed in their display of brute force that none of them paid any attention to Ghoolion or what he had shouted.

'Pure pandemonium,' Echo whispered to himself. He didn't know whether to be delighted or horrified. The giant trees hadn't come to liberate him; they were bent on sheer destruction.

'They aren't calming down!' Ghoolion exclaimed. 'They're getting wilder and wilder!' He tightened his grip on Echo.

Instead of replying, Echo twisted his head round and bit Ghoolion's hand – bit it harder than he'd ever bitten anything or anyone before. The skin split open like paper and his teeth sank in up to the bone. Even the Alchemaster couldn't ignore pain of such intensity. He uttered a yell and relaxed his grip. Echo promptly took advantage of this to squirm and struggle, hiss and scratch. He raked Ghoolion's face with his claws and inflicted four deep scratches on his cheek. One claw on his other paw caught the Alchemaster's long nose and laid it open from bridge to tip. And still Echo raged on, biting and lashing out in a fury. Ghoolion suddenly found himself holding a wildcat armed with a hundred teeth and a thousand claws. He dropped Echo, who landed on the windowsill, and retreated a few steps.

'Never touch me again!' hissed Echo. He arched his back in a way that made him look twice as big. His eyes gleamed belligerently. 'Never again, you hear?'

There was a massive jolt and a long crack appeared in the laboratory floor. Ghoolion went staggering backwards, caught his foot in it and fell headlong.

'You little devil!' he yelled as he scrambled to his feet. 'You said they'd stop this if you showed yourself.'

'I lied!' Echo shouted back above the din. 'I learnt that from you! You should have listened to the Snow-White Widow! Never put your faith in someone else's honesty!'

This remark seemed to hurt the Alchemaster more than all the bites and scratches he'd sustained. The anger in his face gave way to a look of bewilderment.

'You mean they haven't come to set you free?' he said. 'Why, then?'

'To avenge Izanuela!' Echo shouted. 'And to send you to perdition. She's too powerful for you. She's defeating you after her death.'

Another violent jolt brought down a beam that grazed the Alchemaster's head. He swayed and clutched his bleeding ear but stayed on his feet. A second beam came crashing down on the Ghoolionic Preserver, smashing numerous glass vessels and spattering the room with chemical fluids. The stone lintel above the door became dislodged and fell with another crash. Within moments, a heap of collapsing rubble had precluded any chance of escape.

'Then you'll go to perdition with me!' Ghoolion yelled, pointing to the blocked exit. 'Those Ugglian Oaks don't seem too eager to save your life.'

Echo was prepared to fight if the Alchemaster went for him again, but Ghoolion displayed no sign of aggression. Bereft of all his authority, he simply stood there, swaying under the impact of the blows his castle was receiving. It was as if he himself were being struck.

Yet another violent jolt upset the cauldron. The alchemical soup flowed out across the floor and disappeared down the cracks.

Ghoolion staggered over to Floria's corpse. Taking it by the shoulders, he hoisted it into a sitting position. 'Floria!' he sobbed. 'What am I to do?'

The Alchemaster was begging a cadaver for help! Echo would have liked to revel in his triumph, but this wasn't the moment. The castle was disintegrating around them. If the building was done for, so were they. Ghoolion's question to a dead woman wasn't unjustified. What *could* they do?

There were three possible routes out of the laboratory. One was the doorway, which was hopelessly obstructed. The second was the cauldron, the gateway to another world, but that held little appeal. The third was a window, through which anyone so minded could leap to his death in the town below.

Izanuela's route …

Echo opted for the last-named exit. He looked over at the Alchemaster. Floria's skeleton rattled as he shook it, but that was her sole response: a shake of the skull.

'Floria!' he cried again. 'What am I to do?'

Ghoolion's alchemical universe was going up in smoke. The whole laboratory was a mass of crackling flames fed by volatile liquids escaping from shattered retorts. Stones were falling from the ceiling, powdered chemicals swirling into the air, glass vessels exploding, gases hissing. More and more cracks were appearing in the walls. The castle was doomed. It would soon collapse with an almighty crash.

Echo exchanged a final glance with the Alchemaster. Ghoolion's expression conveyed none of his former majestic malevolence, just fear and consternation. That was how Echo wanted to remember him: as a pathetic madman.

Then he turned and leapt off the windowsill.

'No!' Ghoolion called after him.

But he was already in free fall.

Izanuela's Route

It was over very quickly – far more quickly than Echo had expected. Wind whistling in his ears, the world rotating around him, four or five aerial somersaults and that was it: the roofs of Malaisea were already gleaming in the moonlight just below him. Izanuela's route ... He shut his eyes.

Then came the impact and a terrible pain in his neck.

Strangely enough, though, the pain not only persisted but grew worse. How could it, if he was dead? Would this final pain accompany him to the grave?

He opened his eyes. Fluttering overhead were Vlad the Seven Hundred and Seventy-Fourth and Vlad the Twelfth – he knew this even though the Leathermice hadn't introduced themselves. They were gripping him by the scruff of the neck and carrying him ever higher.

'Ouch!' he said. 'Many thanks. This is the second time you've saved my life. Where are you taking me?'

'This you must see!' said Vlad the Twelfth. 'It's not a sight one sees every day of the week!'

'Our lovely home is going up in smoke,' sighed Vlad the Seven Hundred and Seventy-Fourth.

They carried Echo even higher – higher than he'd ever been before. He gazed down at Ghoolion's castle, which now looked as toylike as the town that lay at its foot. Hundreds of Leathermice were fluttering up here in the night air, many of them silhouetted against the full moon.

Some of the castle's windows were belching soot and its walls were wreathed in long plumes of dark dust. It was collapsing, subsiding into the ground like a sinking ship. Lit by intermittent flashes, dense clouds of powdered stone were billowing into the air. The building seemed to be howling with pain as its ancient timbers burst asunder and its subterranean tunnels and chambers filled up with rubble. Chemicals exploded, demolishing walls, and stones rained down on Malaisea. Flames spurted from open windows and mushroom clouds of brown smoke blossomed on all sides.

'I told you it was a sight worth seeing,' croaked Vlad the Twelfth.

'Our lovely home …' Vlad the Seven Hundred and Seventy-Fourth said again.

The castle now turned into a many-armed kraken and its turrets into flexible tentacles that flailed around helplessly before being sucked into the depths. For a moment Echo thought he glimpsed the Alchemaster's face in the midst of the collapsing ruins, a mask of black tiles contorted with stark terror. Then it folded in on itself and was swallowed up. Storey after storey came crashing down: the mother of all roofs; the Leathermousoleum; the laboratory; the wonderful kitchen; the secret treasure chamber; the galleries containing Ghoolion's pictures; the lunatic asylum's deserted wards; the libraries; the labyrinthine cellars; the Alchemaster's fat collection; the Snow-White Widow's prison. All these disappeared within the space of a few seconds. It was as if one of Ghoolion's disaster paintings had come to life, a masterpiece that had devoured its own creator. All that remained was a smoking crater with the town of Malaisea clinging to its lip, miraculously unscathed.

'We'll never find another loft like that,' Vlad the Seven Hundred and Seventy-Fourth said sadly. 'We'll have to vegetate in barns and caves.'

Echo couldn't make out where the Ugglian Oaks had got to, the smoke was too thick, but their music had ceased. Had they withdrawn in good time, or had they shared the castle's fate?

'We must say goodbye now,' said Vlad the Twelfth.

'Yes,' said his companion, 'we must find ourselves a new abode.'

'Of course,' said Echo. 'Just put me down in the town. Anywhere will do.' The pain in his neck was becoming unbearable.

'No,' said Vlad the Twelfth, 'we must say goodbye here and now. Right away.'

He let go of Echo's neck. Only one of the Leathermice was supporting him now.

'Hey!' cried Echo. 'What are you doing?'

'We don't know,' said Vlad the Twelfth, 'not exactly.'

'You've saved my life twice and now you're going to let me fall to my death?' Echo protested. 'You're joking, aren't you?'

'No, we aren't,' the Leathermice replied in unison.

'But this is crazy!' Echo cried. 'I don't understand.'

'Nobody understands the Leathermice,' Vlad the Seven Hundred and Seventy-Fourth said darkly, and let go.

'Not even the Leathermice!' added Vlad the Twelfth.

'Nobody!'

'Nobody!'

And the vampires flew off giggling as Echo plummeted earthwards.

This time his fall really did take a long time. They had carried him high, high into the sky to a point just short of the clouds. He somersaulted again and again. The full moon and the night sky gyrated around him until he couldn't stand it any more and shut his eyes.

But instead of the darkness he was expecting, he saw a golden glow brighter than the interior of Ghoolion's treasure chamber and, in its midst, regarding him with an amiable smile, was the Golden Squirrel. He could also hear the soothing hum that had accompanied their previous encounter.

'This time we're really in a fix,' said the squirrel. 'I'm here to bring you your third and last insight.'

'I'd forgotten all about you in the excitement,' Echo replied. He had suddenly become quite calm, nor had he any sensation of falling. *Was* he still falling? He didn't care.

'The Cogitating Eggs have developed a special interest in your fate,' the squirrel went on. 'They're hard at work on a plan to make things turn out all right.'

'Really?' said Echo. The soothing hum was more audible than the last time, he noticed. 'Why are they so interested?'

'Because you've recently become a valuable Crat – the most valuable Crat in Zamonia. The knowledge you've gained could prove useful some day.'

'Then the Cogitating Eggs had better be quick,' said Echo. 'I shall soon be landing splat on that town down there.'

'I'll worry about that in due course. Time is standing still while you're absorbing your last insight. The Cogitating Eggs achieve this by holding their mental breath, or something of the kind. Can you feel the wind in your fur or the irresistible pull of gravity?'

'No.'

'You see? Relax and enjoy your third insight.'

Echo really did feel relaxed. With the reassuring hum of the Cogitating Eggs in his ears, he was happy to put his fate in their hands. The golden glow and the squirrel's friendly voice enhanced the pleasant atmosphere. He was on the point of purring.

'Well, what exactly is this insight?' he asked serenely.

'This one isn't like that. It can't be summarised in a single sentence. It's a vision.'

'A vision? What of?'

'Ah, to know that you must see it. Visions have to be seen, that's why they're called visions. The Cogitating Eggs are currently at work on a way of redirecting your destiny. But I can make no promises! All their work is a mixture of the accurate and the accidental, of precision and pure chance. One can never tell what the end result will be.'

'So how do I get to see this vision?' Echo asked.

'The way one sees any vision: by opening your eyes.'

Echo did so and was dazzled. It was broad daylight suddenly. He was still falling, but something strange had happened: the castle was below him once more. Added to that, he was completely enveloped in the scent of Cratmint and surrounded on every side by flowers: red and black roses, marguerites and poppies, flame-red orchids and blue violets, daisies and plum blossom, snowdrops and orange lilies. A long trail of them was streaming out behind him and marking the course of his descent. At last he understood: he was seeing what the Uggly had seen in those last few seconds. This was Izanuela's downward route!

The roofs of the town were getting close; soon she would crash into them. That shabby little street down there behind the crematorium: that would be her point of impact. Izanuela drew one more breath, filling her lungs as full as possible with the scent of Cratmint. She held it for a moment, then breathed out – and left her body in its company. Her mortal remains hit the ground somewhere below her, whereas she herself went soaring over the rooftops as light and free as air. Ahead of her lay Uggly Lane, her true destination! Cheerful, contented and intoxicated by her own scent, she swooped down and dived into the lane's muddy surface, sank through it and mingled with the soil beneath. The countless roots of the Ugglian Oaks absorbed her scent at once. They sucked it in and sent it flowing through their veins.

A crack appeared in the roadway. It extended from the mouth of Uggly Lane to Izanuela Anazazi's house. Only an inconspicuous crack, barely a thumb's breadth wide, but soon more cracks were running off it. Dozens of them at first, then hundreds, they zigzagged in all directions. With a subterranean rumble the ground began to quake and its creeping, crawling inhabitants, alarmed by this phenomenon, fled for their lives.

Izanuela's house was the first to arise. It creaked and groaned as its mighty roots freed themselves from the moist earth with a sucking sound. All the houses in Uggly Lane followed suit. One after another, they detached themselves from the places where they had stood for so many years. It was a long time – night had already fallen – before the last of them was free of the ground. Then they struck up their mournful song and set off.

To avenge Izanuela …

And then Echo was high in the air again. His vision was at an end. Reality had reclaimed him. No Uggly, no Golden Squirrel. No more sympathetic vibrations or golden glow to lull him into a sense of security.

It was night-time once more. Echo could feel the rush of air and the pull of gravity. He was very near the rooftops now – as near as Izanuela had been when she left her body – but there was no chance he would cheat death by dissolving into a scent. He would crash into that roof down there, the roof of a nondescript house with a small garden where he had once … Echo suddenly realised that it was the house in which he'd spent his early days: the house that had belonged to Floria of Ingotville. Fate might be cruel, he reflected, but it did have a sense of humour.

'Ouch!' Something had gripped him painfully by the scruff of the neck. Falling no longer, he was being borne aloft into the night air.

'The Leathermice are back!' he thought. 'It was just a joke in poor taste.'

He turned his head. Sure enough, some powerful talons were gripping him by the neck, but they didn't belong to a Leathermouse. Their owner was Theodore T. Theodore.

'You simply aren't safe on your own,' the Tuwituwu said as he skimmed the rooftops with Echo dangling beneath him. 'I burn my tack for a couple of days and what happens? You're up the peek again without a craddle.'

Love at First Sight

'Where have you been all this time?' Echo asked as they flew over Malaisea's municipal park. Instead of putting him down at once, Theodore had headed straight for that part of town.

'You'll see soon enough,' Theodore said breathlessly. 'Phew, you may have shed a few pounds, my friend, but you're still no wightleight.'

Just beside the pond in the middle of the park was a big weeping willow. With Echo still dangling beneath him like a sack of potatoes, Theodore flew into its overhanging branches and released him. Echo landed heavily on a large, well-upholstered nest.

'This is my nest,' Theodore explained as he touched down beside him, panting hard. He spread his wings. 'My new adobe.'

Echo sat up and looked around. 'I say,' he said, 'what a big place. Far bigger than the chimney. You live here all by yourself?'

'Er, not exactly,' said Theodore. 'You'll see soon enough.'

'You'll see soon enough, you'll see soon enough,' Echo parroted. 'What will I see soon enough? Why so secretive? What have you been up to all this time?'

'Well, for one thing I built this nest,' Theodore said sheepishly. 'Then came the billing and cooing and brooding. The miracle of love, et cetera. You'll see soon enough.'

He gave Echo a piercing stare. 'What's more to the point, tell me what's been going on here. I fly off to the Blue Mountains for a few hours' hunting, I come back and the castle has vanished. Then you appear out of the blue – or the clouds, to be more precise. Come on, out with it! Where's Ghoolion?'

'Ghoolion's dead. He and his castle have gone to perdition. The Uggly ... the Snow-White Widow ... It's a long story. Let me get my breath back first.'

'You went to see the Uggly? Did she help you?'

'Yes. No. Well, in a way ...' Echo tried to marshal his facts in the right order. So much had happened.

There was a whirring sound overhead. He looked up. Two Tuwituwus were coming in to land, a big one and a very small one.

Catching sight of Echo, they applied their air brakes and hovered.

'Don't worry,' Theodore called to them, 'he's a friend. Come down here!'

The two birds landed on the edge of the nest. The smaller Tuwituwu nestled against the bigger one's leg.

'Allow me to indrotuce my friend Echo,' said Theodore. 'Echo, meet my wife Theodora.' He indicated the bigger of the two Tuwituwus, whom he treated to a look of adoration.

'So she's a female,' thought Echo.

'And this is my son, Theodore T. Theodore the Second.' His breast swelling with pride, Theodore pointed to the little bird, which inclined its head politely.

Echo bowed likewise. 'A pleasure and privilege to make your acquaintance,' he said.

The little bird turned to its mother. 'He can hold a conservation,' it whispered.

Theodore T. Theodore put a wing round Echo's shoulder and drew him aside. 'Pretend not to notice,' he said in a low voice. 'Junior has a broplem with long words – can't think who he gets it from.'

'So you've founded a family,' said Echo. 'That explains everything.'

'Yes,' said Theodore, 'the call of nature. You have to obey it when it comes. In my case it came late, but it came. My gioboolical clock was reading five to twelve. We met in the Toadwoods. It was love at first sight.'

He gazed ardently at Theodora, who was climbing down into the nest with her son. 'Well,' he said, 'that's put you in the picture. Now it's your turn.'

Echo complied. He told of his meeting and friendship with the last Uggly in Malaisea, of his adventures as a Leathermouse and a Demonic Bee, of the brewing of the love potion and distillation of the Cratmint. Of the Cooked Ghosts and the demons' awakening. Of how he believed he'd eaten Theodore. Of the Snow-White Widow's lethal dance. Of Izanuela's death and her resurrection in the Ugglian Oaks. Of the castle's destruction and the terrible end of Succubius Ghoolion, Malaisea's erstwhile Alchemaster-in-Chief. It wasn't until he'd finished that he realised how much he'd been through in the last few weeks.

'Good heavens!' Theodore exclaimed. 'What a tanfastic story – well worthy of a place in Zamonian lorefolk. So you weren't just a Meatherlouse, you were a Bemonic Dee as well. By a curious coincidence, I nearly swallowed a Bemonic Dee the other day.'

'Really?' said Echo.

'Yes, it was while I was hunting for mice in a lovely, lush summer meadow. By the time I noticed it was a Bemonic Dee it was almost too late – I already had it in my beak. I managed to spit it out just in time. Do you know what a Bemonic Dee's sting in the gullet can do to you?'

Echo grinned. 'I do indeed.'

Meanwhile, Theodora had fed the little Tuwituwu. She was now rocking it to sleep beneath her wing and humming softly. The tension was gradually draining from Echo's limbs. He was among friends in a safe, warm nest. The Alchemaster was dead, the spell lifted at last. He felt very tired suddenly.

'Tell me,' he said, resting his head on a soft pillow of grass, 'how do you account for the fact that you were there to catch me?'

'Pure chance,' said Theodore. 'I was returning from a hunting trip in the Blue Mountains, as I told you. I had a dead mouse in my talons, a prize specimen. I was on course for Lamaisea when something suddenly came over me …'

'Something came over you?' Echo raised his head again.

'Yes, a strange feeling of … of confidence, I can't describe it any other way. And I heard, well, a humming sound … a kind of, er …'

'Sympathetic vibration?'

'Exactly, a sempathytic bivration! I seemed to be flying along a beam of golden light that guided me to my nestidation through all the chimneypots in Lamaisea. At the same time I was puzzled that the castle has disappeared during my absence and worried about my family – a strange state of mind. And then you came falling out of the sky. I just managed to drop the mouse and grab you. It was a combination of chance and precision.'

'Exactly,' Echo said with a smile. 'Chance. Chance and precision.' His head subsided on to the grassy pillow and he fell into a deep, dreamless sleep.

Malaisea's Awakening

Echo was thoroughly rested when he awoke the next morning. Theodore T. Theodore and his family had been considerate enough not to wake him and flown off, possibly on a hunting trip. Echo, who wanted to spare himself and them a sentimental farewell, seized the opportunity to depart without more ado. He climbed down the tree, left the municipal park and set off on a last stroll through the streets of the town that had hitherto been his world.

Malaisea had just begun to stir. The full moon was still visible in the paling sky. The town and its inhabitants were waking the way people wake after a long illness, when a last night of fever has sweated their remaining symptoms out of them: still unsteady on their trembling legs, with dark rings round their eyes and chalk-white cheeks, but filled with renewed hope and certain that the worst is over.

They emerged from their homes and stared in disbelief at the place where Ghoolion's sinister castle used to stand. All that marked the spot was a heap of rubble and a thin haze of grey dust. An ancient and unloved building had collapsed with a crash in the middle of the night. A row of deserted houses had vanished. The shattered remains of an Uggly had been found in a side street. Who cared? Before long, it would all seem no more than a bad dream.

Bandages and handkerchiefs were tossed into gutters to be washed away by the next shower of rain. Pharmacists stood helplessly outside their shops, waiting for non-existent customers. The usual smells of ether and antiseptic, pus and iodine, sickness and death were overlaid by new scents of all kinds: thyme and garlic, pan-fried bacon and chicken soup, chips and tomato ketchup, roast pork and bouillabaisse, pancakes and toast, sage and lemon, coriander and curry, saffron and vanilla. The Malaiseans were busy cooking, for what was the first thing people did after recovering from a long illness? They cooked themselves their favourite meal. That was why all the pedestrians in the streets, far from being on their way to the doctor or pharmacy, hospital or dentist, were off to the butcher or baker, grocer or greengrocer. No more camomile tea, sticking plasters or cough syrup for them; they were after fresh pasta, ripe cheese and olive oil.

They paid scant attention to the little Crat threading his way between their legs. The townsfolk of Malaisea knew nothing about a contract, about Crat fat and Cooked Ghosts, Prima Zateria and the biggest treasure chamber in Zamonia. They hadn't sampled any nuts from the Tree of Nutledge and were ignorant of Anguish Candles and Demonic Mummies, Shadow Ink and metamorphotic meals.

Echo didn't care. He was wholly indifferent to the town and all who lived there. His connection with Malaisea was at an end. Every step took him a little further from the sickest town in Zamonia. Malaisea was now on the road to recovery, but without him. Echo was the only creature there that wasn't hungry. He didn't intend to eat again until the next full moon. Till then he would go without – he still had enough fat on his ribs to last him.

He didn't pause until he reached the outskirts of town. Ahead of him lay the unpredictable wilds of Zamonia. Strangleroots by the roadside, wild dogs in the fields, poisonous snakes and scorpions in the long grass. Rabid foxes, Woodwolves and Corn Demons. Raging torrents and treacherous bogs. Mistwitches, Voltigorks and Snow-White Widows. All those dangers were said to be out there.

But so was that other kind of Crat, the one of which Theodore had told him. Echo set off in the direction of the Blue Mountains. Awaiting him somewhere beyond them must be the miracle of love.

The End

Optimus Yarnspinner

Epilogue

Anyone even vaguely familiar with my writings will know that I have never disguised my profound respect for the works of Gofid Letterkerl. For me, his novel *Zanilla and the Murch* is still one of Zamonian literature's outstanding achievements, and most of his other books also rank high in my estimation.

My godfather Dancelot Wordwright read me Letterkerl's *Echo the Crat* again and again when I was a youngster, and I have cherished a special liking for that slim novella ever since. I shall not attempt to explain or justify my predilection here; instead, I shall simply leave the story, which can now be read by anyone so inclined, to speak for itself. My sole concern is that Letterkerl's tale of the Crat and the Alchemaster be accessible to as many readers as possible.

Echo the Crat is the first of seven so-called *Culinary Tales*, all of them written by Letterkerl and set in the Zamonian town of Malaisea. The 'culinary tale', a literary genre originated by Letterkerl himself, has inspired countless imitators. One has only to think of Glorian Gekko's *Princess in Pea Soup*, Rimbo Demoniac's *Incorrigible Liver Pâté* or Knulf Krockenkrampf's *The Potato Tycoon*. But Letterkerl not only founded this genre; he brought it to a pitch of perfection. None of his imitators has ever succeeded in producing such a close-knit fusion of literature and the culinary arts. Even today, many physicians advise their overweight patients to avoid reading his Malaisea stories on the grounds that they promote obesity.

But let us face facts: Gofid Letterkerl is perhaps the supreme exponent of classical Zamonian literature. He attained his greatest popularity hundreds of years ago and his style – I say this with all due respect and circumspection – was considered, even during his lifetime, to be as ponderous as a wardrobe and as much an acquired taste as a trombophone concerto. I myself have always been enraptured by his style because it conveys Orm* in its purest form. However, I can well

---

*According to Dancelot Wordwright in Optimus Yarnspinner's *City of Dreaming Books*, p. 20: 'A kind of mysterious force reputed to flow through many authors at moments of supreme inspiration.' [Tr.]

imagine that Letterkerl's linguistic idiosyncrasies are more likely to drive modern readers, especially those of the younger generation, into the arms of certain authors of light fiction whose names I shall refrain from citing here. (The *Prince Sangfroid* novels are a case in point. Need I say more?)

I have, therefore, taken the liberty of transposing *Echo the Crat* into a somewhat more up-to-date New Zamonian idiom so as to reacquaint the public with the novella and, I hope, assure it of renewed popularity.

I have also ventured to rework the story a trifle and provide it with a new title. I have called it *The Alchemaster's Apprentice* for commercial reasons, I freely admit, because how many modern readers would buy a book about a harmless little Crat named Echo? The word 'Alchemaster', on the other hand, immediately conjures up mysterious happenings and hair-raising alchemistic horrors. And so, if you picked up this book purely because of its title, be honest and admit it. Don't be ashamed of never having previously read such an Orm-infused story because you found its original title insufficiently sensational.

Furthermore, I have been presumptuous enough to amplify Gofid Letterkerl's story with a few improvisations of my own, for without them the creative element would be lacking.

I can already hear critics accusing me of robbing the dead – of spiritual theft. Suffice it to say that Letterkerl's oeuvre is out of copyright, and how can anyone steal something that belongs to all?

So go ahead and sue me!

Optimus Yarnspinner